SMACK GODDESS

SMACK GODDESS

A NOVEL

Richard Stratton

A Birch Lane Press Book
Published by Carol Publishing Group

A Birch Lane Press Book
Published by Carol Publishing Group

Editorial Offices
600 Madison Avenue
New York, NY 10022

Sales & Distribution Offices
120 Enterprise Avenue
Secaucus, NJ 07094

In Canada: Musson Book Company
A division of General Publishing Co. Limited
Don Mills, Ontario

Manufactured in the United States of America

10 9 8 7 6 5 4 3 2 1

Library of Congress Cataloging-in-Publication Data

Stratton, Richard
    Smack goddess : a novel / by Richard Stratton
        p.   cm.
    "A Birch Lane Press book."
    ISBN 1-55972-045-X : $18.95
    I. Title
    PS3569.T691337S6   1990
    813'.54--dc20   90-39987
                                               CIP

Carol Publishing Group books are available at special discounts
for bulk purchases, for sales promotions, fund raising, or
educational purposes. Special editions can also be created to
specifications. For details contact: Special Sales Department,
Carol Publishing Group, 120 Enterprise Ave., Secaucus, NJ 07094

For Gabriella . . .
    and to Frin X—
        Wherever she may be . . .

Contents

It is only the just whose eyes never light up. It is the just who have never known the secret of human fellowship. It is the just who are committing the crimes against man, and it is the just who are the real monsters. It is the just who demand our fingerprints, who prove to us that we have died even when we stand before them in the flesh. It is the just who impose upon us arbitrary names, false names, who put false dates in the register and bury us alive. I prefer the thieves, the rogues, the murderers, unless I can find a man of my own stature, my own quality.

—Henry Miller, *Tropic of Capricorn*

Don't question why she needs to be so free
she'll tell you it's the only way to be.

—The Rolling Stones, "Ruby Tuesday"

PART ONE

Busted

Chapter One

The bust made front page news in all the New York dailies. Early editions pictured a wan, chic-looking freak around thirty with large dark eyes full of foreboding. She was in handcuffs, her arms gripped by federal agents as she peered out from her headlines like:

DEALER TO THE STARS FALLS

and:

DRUG QUEEN BEE'S NEST SWARMED

Agents had captured her at an Upper West Side brownstone supposedly owned by punk rock star Rickie Rude. Seized in the apartment, according to reports, were two kilos of pure China White heroin, half a pound of equal quality cocaine, three hundred and eighty thousand dollars in cash, and other assorted drugs and drug paraphernalia. Hardly a big bust by New York standards. Also confiscated in the raid was an address book the feds claimed contained many well-known names and unlisted phone numbers. As usual in major conspiracy roundups, more arrests were expected. Rickie Rude himself was being sought.

Grimm watched as she was pushed from the inmate elevator and herded along with several male prisoners into the attorney visiting room at the jail. The investigator had come to the Metropolitan Correctional Center to see her on this Sunday morning because of a call he received in the middle of the night from Aaron Held, the famed New

4 SMACK GODDESS

York criminal trial lawyer who represented both Rickie Rude and his manager, Saul Diamond.

Held was a close friend and business associate. His firm used Grimm's investigative services exclusively. Before the call from Held, Grimm had planned to drive up to his farm in Millbrook for the weekend. "Sorry, babe," the attorney had said, "but this one is important. This is a lady with well-connected friends. I need you to go down there and see her right away. Hold her hand."

The woman looked vulnerable and tender as a bruise. She had white, moist skin like milk. Her big somber eyes, ringed with circles, made him think of a startled raccoon; her eyes had a wily feral look. She had large features, a long oval face with an upturned nose and a wide mouth with nicely curved, full lips. Her tall body was statuesque; she had good, sturdy looking hips and legs—though she looked too thin.

The papers said she was British, from an upper class family; Grimm imagined her playing field hockey with rosy cheeks and a glowing smile, but that would have been years ago. Now the transplanted London "Junk Queen," as the *Post* was calling her, looked slightly worn after her night in jail, and harried from the rigors of catering to a transcontinental clientele purportedly comprised of the rich, the hip and the famous. Her name was Sonia Byrne-Downes. The papers said everyone knew her as "Downtown Sonny."

The attorney visiting room at the federal jail in lower Manhattan has a thick plate glass front wall that always made Grimm think of an aquarium. It was filling with male prisoners arrayed in blaze orange jumpsuits. They looked like bright tropical goldfish, and lawyers swam among them like sharks, vying for the big fees from the latest drug busts. Grimm had secured one of the private conference booths at the rear of the room and claimed it with his briefcase.

He was a big man, just over six feet, with a good build he kept in shape through daily exercise. He had a full beard, black and close-cropped, shoulder-length hair and blue eyes. He had that comfortable-in-his-body look of a professional athlete or a tough undercover cop. On the chance that he might still get out of town for the weekend, he had come to MCC wearing jeans, cowboy boots and a tweed sports jacket with leather patches at the elbows. He managed to look both Ivy League and Western Conference at the same time. Grimm nodded to

Sonia Byrne-Downes as she entered the room and looked around. He then introduced himself as he led her into the conference room.

"Are you my lawyer?" she asked tentatively.

"No. Not exactly," he told her as they sat down.

"Would you like a soda?" he said. They were alone, staring at each other across a table in the small, cell-like room. Wide oblong steel bars covered the windows. The air smelled of stale tobacco smoke and nervous sweat. Grimm had always imagined the cells in the units on the floors above to be like these cubicles: spartan, lonely.

"No, thank you. But I'd love a cigarette." Her voice was deep, her accent British with a New York inflection.

"Oh, here." He took a pack of cigarettes from his pocket and handed them to her. "Aaron told me you smoke *Galois*."

"Mmmm, lovely. And he smokes English Ovals," she said with a smile.

"Yes, but only five a day," Grimm said and returned her smile with the thought that so far she had not missed a beat.

She wore the institutional outfit for female prisoners: powder blue nylon slacks and a dark blue smock. The smock hung open over a pale pink T-shirt. Grimm found her attractive in an English way, slightly forbidding, with her beautiful complexion and wavy, chestnut colored hair. But he felt she was too thin, almost bony, unhealthy and punk looking, like a genteel delinquent child. Her hair was bleached platinum at the ends and gathered into a pony tail that stuck straight out from one side of her head. On the inside of her right wrist she had a marijuana leaf tattoo with some Arabic lettering which Grimm could not decipher.

Looking closer at her eyes, he noticed that one was brown, almost hazel, while the other appeared tri-colored. He thought it might be a contact lens, but then he saw that she had a faint birthmark streaked across half the eye, a sort of crimson stain that started just above the eyebrow and contributed to her bruised look. Her movements had a nervous edge that seemed to come not so much from being ill at ease as from physical pain.

"Here, these you better stash. They're loaded," Grimm said as he passed her a few loose cigarettes that he had emptied out and repacked with fine Thai marijuana.

Sonia looked at him and her whole body seemed to go slack. "God, you're a lifesaver,'' she said and gave him a smile like the one he'd imagined, only without the rosy cheeks. She had nice teeth, her thick lips curled back, and when she smiled, her face lost the wary look. ''Now that's what I call service.''

She's got a Jones, he thought, a habit, though he wondered just how sick she was. There were no tracks on her arms; he decided she probably didn't care for needles. Still, he knew, a junk habit is a junk habit and sick people troubled him. At least she didn't reach across the table and beg him: ''You've got to get me out of this place,'' as so many others did. No, he would say Sonny was holding up, though it was still early. From Held's terse instructions, Grimm had been expecting an emotional wreck shattered by the trauma of the bust. This woman struck him as a veteran, a survivor despite her habits. Experience reminded him never to trust a junkie.

''How're you feeling?'' he asked her.

She sighed. Her fingers trembled slightly as she unwrapped the pack of cigarettes. ''Actually, it's just beginning to get rough.'' Grimm lit her cigarette. ''I haven't slept a wink all night.''

She removed all the cigarettes from the pack, stuffed the pot-laced ones in, then replaced the others. ''But this will help,'' she said, looking up at his eyes with her probing gaze. ''You're a darling.''

''How're they treating you? Any problems?''

''No. This place is an absolute madhouse.'' She exhaled a cloud of blue smoke, sat back and crossed her long legs. ''Everyone's so caught up in their own problems, no one has time to hassle anyone else. And the people who work here all seem to be mad.''

Grimm laughed. Sonny had summed the place up. MCC was brutally over-crowded and often brimming with noise and confusion even on the lower floors where some members of the public were allowed. Grimm could only imagine what it was like upstairs in the units. The prisoners usually described it as a zoo.

''Anyway,'' Grimm said, ''I have some friends here. Good friends. Just let me know if you have any problems. Also, if there's anything you need—books, magazines, underwear—call my office and my secretary will make sure you get whatever you want. I put a couple of hundred in your commissary account this morning.''

''Why, thank you. That's very thoughtful of you, Mr. Grimm.''

She's got a great smile, he was thinking, watching her eyes as he reached into his pocket and took out a business card. ''Hopefully you'll make bail soon. Until then—'' He handed her the card. ''My secretary's name is Miki. Call anytime. If I'm not around, just tell her what you need.''

Grimm watched her as she looked at the business card. Sonny looked up with amusement flashing in her tired eyes.

''Grimm Investigations,'' she said. ''Jesus, not too grim, I hope.''

He took a yellow legal pad out from his briefcase. ''I'd say that depends a lot on you.''

''Really? How so?''

He spoke carefully, picking his words as he wrote the date, time and her name at the top of a clean sheet of paper.

''This case is just beginning. You've been busted. Now you're in jail. The U.S. Government has just ripped open your life.'' He put the pen down and looked at her. ''Maybe you think the life you led was pretty exciting, but believe me, now is when things start to get intense.'' Grimm paused, nodding his head.

''The final outcome will depend a lot on how you handle yourself over the next few months,'' he went on. ''So listen to me. You've got to be very careful. Talk to no one about the case, and don't get involved with anyone else's trip. Stay off the phones. They're all monitored. Don't let anyone you care about come here to visit you, unless they're straight. If you need to get a message to someone, call me and I'll come down. That's what I'm for. This place is like a sieve, and the U.S. Attorney's office is right next door. There are informants and sometimes agents planted on every floor. Trust no one.'' He hesitated to let his words sink in.

Sonny exhaled. ''I see.''

''You're in enough trouble already. Another thing, I don't work with liars or informants. If I'm going to help you, you've got to be honest with me. Should you decide it's in your best interest to cooperate with the government, we part company. I'm not advising you, just telling you.''

''Fair enough, Mr. Grimm,'' said Sonia. She got up, crushed out her cigarette, then laced her fingers on the table in front of her like an attentive schoolgirl. ''I appreciate your candor—and the advice. Now what shall we do?''

''Suppose we dispense with the Mr. Grimm routine and you start calling me Arthur.''

''Sounds good, Arthur. I'm Sonny.''

"Do you want to talk about it?"

She shrugged, blinked her huge eyes. "There's not a whole lot to say, really. I'm guilty. Whatever they say I did, I did—and probably a hell of a lot more."

They both laughed. Now that was refreshing, thought Grimm. Usually in the beginning they all cry innocent.

"I was afraid of that," he said. "So why don't we talk about bail. Monday morning they'll take you in front of a magistrate over at the federal courthouse"—he waved toward the barred window—"just across the alleyway. Someone will be there to represent you, either Aaron or another lawyer from the office. What I need is a little background information. Okay? First of all, you're not an American citizen, right?"

"Right. I'm British."

"Green card? Resident alien?"

She frowned. " 'Fraid not. I'm here on a tourist visa." Her eyes widened. "And it's expired."

Grimm put down his pen and shook his head. "Well, so much for the bail discussion. Looks like you'll be here awhile."

Sonny made a face. "Not to worry," she said. "I spent over a year in prison in India. This place is relatively mild. I'm really only worried about my little girl, Carmen. I have an eleven-year-old daughter. Last night, when they arrested me, I left her with neighbors in the flat below ours. I've spoken to her, she wants to go stay with some friends over on the East Side. If someone could just see that she's looked after—"

"I'll take care of that," Grimm said decisively.

"Thank you. As long as I know Carmen is all right, I'll manage. Has anyone heard from Rickie?"

"Not yet. Apparently the cops are looking for him. They're going to arrest him if he turns up."

"Why? Rickie has nothing to do with any of this."

"Do you know where he is?"

"Actually, no, I don't. I suppose he's in California, L.A. At least that's where he was when I last spoke with him. He hasn't called for several days. Doesn't what's-his-face know?"

"Saul?" Grimm shook his head.

"He'll be in touch," Sonny said and gave him a weak smile.

"What can I say, Arthur? I told everyone my phone was bugged. I mean, it was so obvious. You could hear this constant clicking sound on the line. And I warned them agents were watching the flat. But no one would believe me. Or they just didn't care. People kept ringing me up and coming 'round.''

"Yes, but Sonny, drugs, money and books all in the same place. What were you thinking about?"

"That's exactly what I'm talking about." She hesitated, as though wondering whether to go into it. "I never . . . hold like that. That was an accident, a last minute sort of thing." Her eyes opened wide again and she leaned forward staring at him. "They missed the stash."

Grimm raised his heavy dark eyebrows. "Really," he said, putting aside the legal pad and his pen. "Okay, I'm going to be meeting with Aaron Held later. If there's anything that can be done as far as getting you out of here, Aaron will figure it out. Let's you and I concentrate on what we do from here. You can't afford any more accidents."

"I know that. Can you help me?"

"Sonny, I told you, that's what I'm here for. Just tell me what you want me to do, who you want me to contact."

I guess I might as well forget about going to the farm for the weekend, thought Grimm. Again. My dogs are going to forget what I smell like.

He spent the rest of the day taking care of odds and ends for Sonny Byrne-Downes. She had given him numbers for some of her friends, but no one was home. Everyone seemed to know about the bust. All day as arrests continued, the media played heavily on the celebrity dope sweep. Toilets were flushing all over Manhattan. Besides Sonny, eight others were already in custody, including an English earl, an actor, the owner of a Lower East Side rock 'n' roll club, the former bass player with Rickie Rude's group, Brain Damage, and an infamous doper and music critic known as Moon Landing who had written an article about Rickie that was adapted into a feature film. Sonny, billed as the ringleader, was portrayed as a spider woman controlling a vast web of illicit drug activities. Rickie was provoking headlines like:

"RUDE" DISAPPEARANCE

Grimm made arrangements for Sonny's daughter, Carmen, to stay with her friend until Sonny's sister could come over from London. He called England and spoke with both Edward Byrne-Downes, Sonny's father, and her sister, Prudence. They already knew of Sonny's arrest—Fleet Street was hot on the scent of British blue blood—neither seemed particularly disturbed by the news. Then he went to the brownstone on 77th Street and Central Park West to pick up Carmen.

The building allegedly owned by punk rocker Rickie Rude was just a few blocks from Grimm's place and notorious in the neighborhood for the number of limos that lined up in front blocking traffic on any given New York night. It was a well maintained, large townhouse that had been divided into spacious apartments overlooking the park. Grimm was surprised to learn that Rickie supposedly owned the place through a company, because the musician was renowned for his quixotic ways and bohemian lifestyle. Rude actually lived in a suite of rooms at the Chelsea Hotel when in New York, or camped at his manager's mansion in Southampton. It just didn't seem at all like Rickie to be a landlord.

The Drug Enforcement Agency had Sonny's top floor apartment sealed. She had asked Grimm to go in and remove some of her more valuable paintings and carpets, but that would have to wait until Aaron Held could get a court order.

Carmen was expecting him; Sonny had called her from the jail. He found her alone waiting for him in the apartment beneath her mother's. She had a small suitcase with her and a black-and-white cat called Merlin.

Carmen seemed like a well-adjusted little girl. She was bright, composed, articulate and pretty, with exquisite English manners. She had a curly mop of rich auburn hair, her mother's fair skin and turned-up nose, and a sense of calm Grimm found almost disconcerting; he felt as though he were in the presence of a much older person. During the ride across town, she remarked that she thought it was stupid for the agents to have broken down the door and burst in with guns drawn.

"They should know Mummy doesn't allow guns in the house," she told him.

Grimm gave her some money and both his home and office phone numbers. With her suitcase in one hand, and clutching Merlin with the other, Carmen thanked Grimm as he delivered her to the doorman at her friend's building in the East 80s.

Early that evening, the investigator met with Aaron Held at the Oyster Bar in the Plaza Hotel. Since both their offices were nearby, the Oyster Bar was a regular watering hole. The lanky, six-foot-four attorney put his arm around Grimm's shoulders and steered him to a table.

"Arthur," Held told him soberly, "I need your noodle on this one."

Held and Grimm had met when both were undergraduates at Columbia back in the 60's. In those days, the famous dope lawyer had been a campus radical, member of the Students for a Democratic Society, and an active and vociferous leader in the civil rights and anti-war movements. Now firmly entrenched in the criminal justice system, he was delivered to courthouses and jails in a chauffeur-driven limousine, and his clients were among the elite in the international criminal subculture.

"Wait a minute," Grimm said when they were seated. "First of all I need to know who I'm working for."

"Me, of course." Held frowned.

"Yes, but who's paying me?"

"Ah ha, good point," said Held, holding up a long index finger. Everything about the man was long: he had a long angular face, long, thin brown hair he wore slicked back and tucked behind his long ears, and a long and photographically accurate memory. "I have a retainer on account for Rickie, but Saul still owes us for that last fiasco of his. He wouldn't burn us on this, would he?"

Grimm held out his hand.

"Arthur, you insult me." Held chortled as he reached into his inside breast pocket and withdrew a checkbook. He hunched over the table, his hair falling forward from behind his ears as he scribbled a check to Grimm for twenty-five thousand dollars.

"Just to make it official," Held said, handing Grimm the check with a look of glee. "Right, pal?"

"Absolutely." Grimm folded the check and tucked it into his pocket. "Everything on the up-and-up."

They both laughed.

"Listen to me," Held said after they had ordered drinks. "The big thing is, we've got to find Rickie and bring him in before the cops do. I don't want him arrested. I want to surrender him. That way I can get him bail. If they hunt him down, they'll say he ran away and call him a flight risk."

"Is he hiding?"

"Well, I don't know. Let's put it this way, he seems to have disappeared, but then Rickie's always disappearing. What did Sonny say?''

"She says he's not involved.''

"Of course he's not involved. Arthur, you know Rickie, he's no drug dealer. A consumer, yes, but—the man doesn't give a fuck about money! They know that. They put him in this case for publicity. Okay, so he knows Sonny and she lives in a building he owns. That's no crime—yet.''

"Rickie really owns that place?''

"Some company of his, Saul was rather vague. Rickie probably doesn't even know he owns it. Personally I suspect they fronted it for Sonny, but I'm not sure.''

"Sonny, from what I can gather, is a goner.''

"She's dead. Not a prayer,'' said the lawyer emphatically. "It's a defense counsel's nightmare. They have hundreds, maybe thousands of hours of tapes. Money, drugs, books. Surveillance. The search was no doubt legal. No, unless there's something I don't know about, we'll be looking to plead her out as quickly and quietly as possible. I'm afraid they might bring an 848 against her.'' Held combed his hair back behind his ears with his fingers. "Are you reading me?''

"Yes,'' Grimm said. "Who's prosecuting?''

"Also bad news. Vaggi, the Dragon Lady herself, your friend and mine. She'll take a perverse delight in putting the screws to Sonny.''

"No shit. That is bad,'' Grimm said, thinking of Vita Vaggi, the Assistant U.S. Attorney in charge of narcotics and major crimes for the Southern District. She was a tough, methodical prosecutor who rarely lost a case. She also disliked both Held and Grimm, particularly Grimm. "Let's hope we get a decent judge.''

"That's vital,'' Held agreed. He made a gesture like hanging himself. "Otherwise she's fucked.''

"Who's going to represent Sonny?''

Held took a deep breath. "I don't know yet. I've got to think that one over very carefully. I don't want Vaggi screaming conflict of interest, yet we've got to control Sonny. We may end up having to go with someone from another firm.''

"That can get touchy.'' Grimm shrugged.

"True. Listen, is she going to be all right?''

"Well, you know how that goes. She's in jail. You never know how people are going to react to being locked up. Still, I get the impression there's a tough chick under that soft shell.''

"Oh, no question," said Held, waving a hand at Grimm. "You don't get to where she is in the business unless you're tough." He sat forward and leaned across the table.

"Anyway, pal, I want you to stay close to her. Baby-sit her. You know, comfort her in her hour of need. Look out for her. The woman has some very important friends who are concerned about her welfare. Okay, babe? The government will be mounting intense pressure to try to get her to roll over. I don't see them giving her bail.''

"No, we've discussed that. She's not hollering to get out, yet."

"She's still in shock," said Held. "Let's see what kind of shape she's in after about a week in that place." He sat back and crossed his legs, gazing at Grimm with an abstracted look.

"You know she's got a drug habit," Grimm said.

"Occupational hazard," said Held with a shrug. He bounced his leg and looked around for the waiter. Grimm could see Held was getting impatient to move on. "I believe she'll stand up—especially with you around to give her continued moral support." The attorney winked. "Know what I mean, babe? As only A.G. knows how to do." Held sat up and leaned toward Grimm. His eyes narrowed conspiratorially.

"See if you can guess who was the first person to call and wish Sonny well.''

Grimm thought about it. The goods, the so-called China White heroin, were the clue. Though the investigator was not as steeped in the junk milieu as he had once been, his intuition told him that Held was probably referring to Jack Moriarty, a semi-legendary figure of the New York drug underworld both Held and Grimm knew well.

"I think I could guess," he said.

Held nodded his long head vigorously, rolling his eyeballs. "Lights going on all over the place, hey babe?" He sat back. "Depending on who you're talking to—her or him—they either were or still are lovers.''

Grimm was mildly surprised. "Yeah? Jack and Sonny? That's interesting. She doesn't strike me as his type.''

Held glanced at his watch. He reached across the table and patted Grimm's bearded cheek. "Just find Rickie for me, Arthur, before the DEA gets their hands on him. Please, give it your undivided attention.''

They stood up and shook hands.

"We're going to have a good time with this one," said Held, putting his arm around Grimm and giving him a hug.

"Sounds like drugs, sex and rock 'n' roll to me," said the investigator.

"And money," added Held. "Never forget money."

On his way home that cool September evening, ever mindful of security, Grimm stationed himself at an outdoor pay phone in Columbus Circle. He made calls to the Coast and waited for people to call him back. He then booked himself on a flight for L.A. in the morning.

Before going to his place, Grimm took a walk along the edge of the park and past the building where the bust had gone down. He stopped in the shadows and looked around. Across 77th Street from the brownstone there was a beat-up sedan with a small but telltale antenna stuck to the trunk. A pair of bearded, hard-looking types were slouched down in the front seat of the car. Grimm would have bet the retainer in his pocket they were agents of the Drug Enforcement Administration.

Chapter Two

Grimm felt as if he was suffering from a case of chronic jet-lag as he stepped from the terminal at Los Angeles International Airport into the glaring noon sun. He put on his sunglasses to survey the sea of parked cars, muting the harsh light shimmering off the expanse of chrome and multi-colored metal, then walked off toward the rental car lot. The air seethed and seemed to glitter as though lit up with iridescent metallic particles suspended in the atmosphere. Grimm blasted the overheated interior of his rental car with air conditioning as he headed out on the freeway to Beverly Hills.

Never a good sleeper, lately it seemed that the only time he slept was while slumped in the First Class cabin jetting between New York and California. He never woke feeling rested but instead felt wearier at some profound level—bone weary. Then when he would crawl into his bed, usually after smoking a joint of the strongest reefer on hand, he'd doze for a few hours fitfully and start up as though expecting to arrive in another city. Often he awoke in pitch dark hotel rooms and spent the first few moments remembering where he was.

Because so much of his business came from the illicit drug trade, and because dope lawyers and their clients demanded and paid well for his services, his company maintained a branch in Los Angeles in addition to the main office in New York. He shared space with a prominent California law firm in a suite of offices in Century City. At least twice a month, he traveled to the Coast for a few days. Also there were quick, unexpected—unofficial—trips like this one. He wouldn't check in at the office but would instead remain incognito, go about his

business, and immediately return to New York. With the kind of
money they were making, it would soon be time for the company to
spring for a private jet.

This case, Grimm recognized, had the potential to become one of
the three or four heavy earners it took to make a highly successful year.
If Rickie Rude was indicted and ended up going to trial, Held's fee
would be at least half a million. There was no telling how much
Grimm would make since his work was not clearly defined. Grimm
found it quite ironic that he and Held profited from the trouble people
found themselves in, and the deeper the trouble, the higher the fee. It
did not take an astute observer to see that Sonia Byrne-Downes, with
her alluring agate eyes, was a woman in deep trouble.

Grimm checked into a bungalow at the Beverly Hills Hotel. He
made calls from the pay phone in the lobby, left messages, then went
to his bungalow to shower and smoke his first joint of the day. High,
he immediately felt better. The pot energized him and he was inspired
to put on his bathing suit and go to the pool to swim a few laps.

Grimm had been staying high, smoking three or four strong joints a
day since he first got turned on to high quality Southeast Asian pot
while working with the Montagnard tribesmen in the Central Highlands of Vietnam. Marijuana, Grimm would own, was one of the
genuine loves of his life, along with his dogs.

Like his friend and sometime partner, Aaron Held, Grimm was also
trained as a lawyer. After Columbia, he had gone to Harvard Law
School where he graduated cum laude. From law school he went into
the military, Army, his father's branch, and served with Special Forces
during the final years of the debacle in Vietnam. Once the war ended,
he remained in Southeast Asia working for Defense Intelligence before
returning to the States to settle in New York. A member of the New
York and California Bars, he tried practicing law for about a year
before the long office hours made him restless and he conceived the
idea of founding his own investigative agency. He still made the
occasional courtroom appearance, usually before magistrates or at pretrial hearings when Held or some other attorney he was working for
couldn't make it.

For the most part, though, he preferred investigative work. He felt
his nature was better suited to the solitary, stubborn backstage legwork
of gathering information and making the right connections; the endless
abstractions and contradictions of legal argument frustrated him.

Now, with Uncle Sam's domestic war, the shadowy war on drugs, Grimm's business was prospering. His company had become one of the top agencies in New York. The office in L.A. recently hired a new secretary/receptionist and three more full-time investigators to meet with the increased assignments, and contract investigators were employed in Miami, Houston and Dallas. A good seventy percent of his business was drug-related.

On the American crime scene, drugs were what was happening, as the agents, prosecutors and lawyers knew only too well. Drugs paid the bills, drugs got out the vote, drugs were the action. So long as there were large numbers of Americans who wanted to consume illegal drugs, and so long as the government chose to keep those drugs illegal and prosecute the traffickers, anyone whose livelihood was connected to the trade could only grow wealthy, or go to prison. Grimm could see no end to it.

Grimm thought about the rest of his life. At times like these, lying stranded with a headful of THC beside the pool in the blazing Southern California sun, he would console himself by thinking of it as on hold. He was thirty-eight years old and still single. He had never married. He had no hopes for a family which troubled him because lately he'd discovered how much he enjoyed being around kids. Like the day before when he was with Sonny's little girl, Carmen, he was cheered by her fresh, clear outlook. Of course the agents were stupid to burst in with guns. Of course it was important to hold on to your cat in times of crisis. Kids, when they were happy, could be so centered. Whatever else Sonny Byrne-Downes may have done with her life, Grimm was ready to credit her for having raised a delightful daughter.

Part of him regretted that he was not good at long-term relationships with women. His former live-in girlfriend, Danielle, had decamped and moved to London to pursue her career as a dancer with the Royal Ballet. That was nearly three years ago. They still saw each other once in a while, when he visited her in Europe or she came to New York, though this coming together seemed to be happening less and less frequently and there was no doubt in either of their minds that they were drifting apart. Danielle hated Grimm's work; it always came down to that. She wasn't impressed with the money. The people scared her. She said there was no lasting worth to anything he did. And she believed his need for action was a dangerous addiction. Grimm still ached at the thought of her.

But loneliness has its bleak rewards. Grimm was able to feel both depressed and satisfied by the thought that he had no one to answer to, no loved one waiting for him to come home or call. He did pretty much what he wanted when he wanted.

The truth was, he thought as he returned to the bungalow, he was used to being alone. He was an only child, and had learned early to trust himself. He liked dogs and animals so much because they offered companionship without the demands, complaints and risks involved in getting close to another person. His mother had taken her life when Grimm was four years old, leaving him to grow up in boarding schools and military academy. He loved women, he was fascinated by them, but, though always anxious to take chances in any other aspect of his life, he was leery of depending on them for emotional solace.

His father was a real oddball. A career Army man, he was aloof and self-absorbed, a military intelligence analyst whom Grimm had only come to know in the last ten years. He noticed his father began taking a cautious interest in him about the time he started making serious money.

Like so many of his generation, Grimm's life seemed divided into two stages: pre- and post-Vietnam. The war undid the person he was before he got there. The war and the mysterious action of cannabis in his consciousness radically altered the way he perceived life. He was at once the contemplator and the man of action, living in a meditative state, as though always observing himself in the third person.

Now, while he pondered the thoughts triggered in his mind by Sonny Byrne-Downes, seeing in his inner vision her unique variegated eyes and the raw taint of the birthmark, he realized it was the disintegration of her life that had caused him to wonder at the course his own life was taking. She intrigued him. Who could say what kind of money the woman had stashed? Drugs were the catalyst, drugs had brought them both to where they were.

Sonny had spent a year in prison in India. What sort of harrowing experience must that have been? Held had said she was Jack Moriarty's lover, and Jack was one of the true heavyweights in the world's most dangerous business. Grimm had mixed feelings about his ilk. Then too, he might have found Sonny less interesting had he not met Carmen. Who could have fathered that precious entity? Now years of imprisonment yawned before Sonny like the abyss. Here she would discover what psychic material she was made of. Everything in the case would hinge on whether or not she held up. Grimm had seen more than a few durable characters crushed by the ponderous weight of the United States Justice Department.

Grimm's thoughts gradually shifted to the reason he was in California: to locate Sonny's unlikely landlord, the Prince of Punk, Rickie Rude. This technique, he thought with a sense of contentment, is known as Zen Investigation: sitting quietly doing nothing, waiting for the mystery to reveal itself. Thought has its own inner powers of revelation.

Rickie Rude was no stranger to Grimm. They had met on a number of occasions: at Held's office, at parties, at Rickie's manager's mansion in Southampton. Both Rickie and his manager, the rock 'n' roll impresario Saul Diamond, had previous run-ins with the law, mostly for possession of small amounts of controlled substances.

Rickie had been a cult hero with a moderate but devoted following in New York, L.A. and London. Then the rock music critic known as Moon Landing, who was also busted on the case, wrote a feature article about Rickie and his group that appeared in *Rolling Stone* magazine. The article was adapted into a film script called *White Noise* and shot by an innovative young director. Rickie starred, playing himself. The film became a box office phenomenon. The public either loved Rickie or they hated him. His albums had been going platinum ever since.

Rickie remained the *enfant terrible* of rock. Said to be a "white Jimi Hendrix on guitar," he and his group Brain Damage sent chills up the spines of the middle-class parents who heard the primitive beat and anarchistic overtones of his songs. His lyrics were complex, poetic and political. The interesting thing about him, as far as Grimm was concerned, was that Rickie seemed to be sincere; he actually believed in and lived by the ideas expressed in his songs.

As Aaron Held had commented, the punk didn't care about money. In New York, at his place in the Chelsea Hotel, he could fit his personal belongings into a couple of suitcases. He was known for giving away large amounts of money, to the entourage of followers and groupies who clung to him wherever he went, and to a variety of causes he supported. Grimm was still not comfortable with the thought that Rickie owned property in New York.

On a personal level, Grimm found Rude friendly and unpretentious. A small man with large, startling blue eyes, Rude had an ornate pattern of lavishly colored tattoo work covering his arms and much of his torso. Though closely associated with the nihilistic drug subculture, Rickie was no spaced-out drug degenerate. Grimm knew him to be intelligent, well-read and fascinated by politics and philosophical ideas. He was one of those acid visionaries who never came back from the Sixties. His associations ran the gamut of nonconformity and deviance; they ranged from revolutionaries and underground poets to bikers and organized crime junk merchants. The investigator suspected more behind the government's motivation in seeking to rope Rickie into this drug distribution network than simple star-fucking.

Grimm worked with these thoughts as he dressed to go out for the evening. At the cocktail hour, he went to the bar in the Polo Lounge and ordered a drink. The place was resplendent with Hollywood glitterati. Grimm looked around and soon found himself returning the vaguely familiar smile of a young woman with long, wavy, strawberry blond hair and a freckled nose.

Where do I know her from? he wondered as she walked toward him with an athletic, boyish stride. She looked strong, even muscular, and she had a mouth full of big white teeth. A real Southern California girl, he thought, still trying to place her. She didn't look much older than twenty, and Grimm knew few girls that age. Dressed in sheer, billowy white pants and a lacy blouse, she came straight for him.

"Hi, Arthur," she said, offering her hand like an eager young pledge.

Her grip was firm and callused. With a look of real surprise, Grimm pulled her into his arms and hugged her.

"Cassy!" he said and then gave her a kiss on the cheek. He held her at arm's length and looked her over with a wide, admiring smile. "You look great."

"You didn't recognize me at first, did ya'? You smile like that at all the girls." She gave him a wink and a nod.

"How was I supposed to?"

"Hey, guy, we all grow up, ya' know."

She smiled brightly and hugged him again. Her fragrance of crushed flowers clung to him as together they moved up to the bar. She wore very little makeup, her eyes were light blue, almost gray, and her big teeth were slightly bucked.

"Tell me the truth, you called Max and he told you I was comin', yeah?"

"No, really, I remember you. How could I forget that face? It's the body that threw me. The last time I saw you you were playing forward in a high school basketball game—remember? Max and I went to watch the playoffs."

"Sure I remember. I was sixteen. I used to think you were some kind of freak. My brother and his hippie friends."

"You're staying at Max s?" he asked her.

"Yeah. He didn't tell you? I'm going to film school at U.C.L.A. and playing on the tennis team. This year I'm gonna live at the house in Malibu 'cause Max wants someone there when he's up at the ranch. Anyway I like it much better, livin' at Max's, I mean. I go runnin' on the beach with Max's dog every morning. You've never been to the house in Malibu, right?"

Grimm shook his head and smiled at her. Cassy looked down at his drink. "Well?" she said. "Ready? C'mon, let's blow this popsicle stand."

She put her arm in his as they walked from the lounge out to the porte-cochere in front of the hotel. Cassy gave the parking attendant her stub, and he ran off with his sneakers squeaking on the pavement. A few minutes later, he pulled up in front of them in a shiny new pale yellow Rolls-Royce Corniche.

"I see you traded in the VW," said Grimm.

"Big Bro's. Class, huh?"

They drove north on the Pacific Coast Highway. Cassy gripped the wheel with both hands and stared at the road in front of her.

"Drive much?" Grimm teased.

"Man, I'm so scared some asshole's gonna smash into me. I never should'a taken this thing, but I wanted to impress you."

"I'm impressed," he said, "but not with the car."

"Yeah?" She smiled. "Hey, so listen. What's this about Rickie being hot? Max said you came out lookin' for him."

"That's right. You know Rickie?"

"Yeah, sure. I was with him all last week. We're shootin' a video for Suzi Sapphire. Max 'n' Rickie're in it, too."

"Where's Rickie now?"

"That I don't know, but Max probably does. I haven't seen him since Thursday night. Me 'n' Max 'n' Rickie 'n' Suzi all had dinner. When I crashed, they were still up talkin'. You know Suzi?"

"Not personally. I like her music."

"Me too. She's hot. Man, you'll love Suzi, she's such a trip. Max says she's gonna be really big. His company's producin' her new album. Anyway, I got the impression Rickie 'n' Suzi split together. Don't quote me on this, but—man, it was love at first bite. Then we heard the news, you know, about the heat in New York lookin' for Rickie. You can imagine it was panic stations. I guess last night after you called, Suzi called."

"And what did she say?"

"Dude, I don't know." She glanced at him. "You'll have to ask Max about that. I been out playin' tennis all day. Next thing I heard when I got home Max told me you were comin' out to find Rickie. So what's the deal? Is he in deep shit?"

"He might be," Grimm said.

Cassy drove the Rolls carefully down a narrow oceanfront lane that ended in a cul-de-sac. She parked next to a few other expensive looking automobiles.

"Whew," she sighed. "Well, guy, we made it." She switched off the ignition and smiled at Grimm.

The sprawling beach house stood behind a tall weathered gray wooden fence. Grimm followed Cassy through a gate out onto a wide deck built above the beach. The sun was setting in a viscous blood-red haze along the horizon. Grimm looked out at the vast spread of the Pacific.

"Nice," he said. "I should kick back and stay out here for a few days."

"Yeah. Do it. We got plenty'a room."

Muted rock music sounded from somewhere inside. They stood at the deck railing looking out at the even swells of the surf. Behind them the glass front of the house looked as though it were ablaze with the reflected sunset.

"I'd love to, but I've got to get Rickie back to New York right away."

"Maybe some other time," Cassy said, looking up at him. She walked to the front of the house and slid open a door in the glass. Unconsciously, Grimm turned and checked out her ass as she walked away from him. Not bad at all, he thought. The music grew louder as Cassy went inside calling for her brother.

A few moments later, a friendly golden retriever came padding up to Grimm and stuck its wet nose in his hand. "Hey, Goldilocks," he said, squatting down to pat the dog. "How do you like your new home?"

Then Max Steiger came out onto the deck with open arms. Grimm stood and the two men embraced each other. In Grimm's arms, Max looked like a frail woman. His dark red hair hung to the middle of his back, and he was thin and pale in contrast to his kid sister who exuded health and strength. There was a strong resemblance between Max and Cassy. They both had rounded noses, freckled cheeks and pale eyes with light, almost white eyebrows. But Max's face was bony and seemed cast in a perpetual scowl while Cassy's was smooth and seemed to glow. Grimm and Max stepped back and clapped their hands together in the hooked-thumb Brotherhood of Eternal Love handshake.

"A.G.," Max said. "Welcome, bro."

The dog whimpered excitedly, wagged her tail and rubbed up against the two men. Max, barefoot, was dwarfed by Grimm. He wore faded jeans and an oversized Willie Nelson T-shirt. Grimm put one arm around Max's shoulders, the other around his sister's waist, and the three of them walked inside.

Grimm and Max Steiger had known each other for ten years. When they first met, Max was a singer, composer and guitarist with one of the Sixties' most popular rock groups. Bouts of heavy cocaine use and drinking nearly ruined his career, but, in the late Seventies, he released three solo albums that re-established him as one of the most influential voices in rock music. He was also a powerful force in the production end of the music business and had begun branching out into producing music videos and films.

For a rock superstar, Max kept a low profile. He rarely gave interviews, toured infrequently, and, though a millionaire many times over, dressed casually, wore no jewelry and generally shunned the ostentatious trappings of rock 'n' roll wealth. He did have a large ranch near Big Sur, complete with its own herd of buffalo and state-of-the-art recording studio. He also had the Malibu home, a fleet of new and classic cars, and a Greyhound Scenic Cruiser bus which he had converted into a motorhome.

Both Max and Rickie were known for organizing concerts to benefit specific causes. The two rock 'n' rollers were drawn together as much by their mutual interest in alternative politics as by music.

But from the earliest days of Max's career there were rumors that he was involved in the financing and organizing of large-scale marijuana smuggling ventures. Two of his younger brothers had been busted and served time as active members of major pot conspiracies. Federal authorities alleged that Max was the moneyman and brains behind one of the biggest international cannabis smuggling groups in the world. Variously known as the Brotherhood of Eternal Love, the Hippie Mafia, the California Connection and Cosa Nueva, the group had been decimated through a series of busts during the Seventies. Max had been arrested on a number of occasions, though only minor possession charges ever stuck. No witness would take the stand and name Max Steiger, no agent could produce hard evidence against him. Still he remained a target of federal police agencies, local cops and government prosecutors looking to make a name for themselves.

The rock star led Grimm through the house and into what he called his sound room. As soon as Grimm sat down, Max handed him an elaborately carved wooden rolling tray with a handful of fat, lime green sinsemilla buds and said, "Do the honors, bro."

He adjusted some dials in a bank of electronic amplifiers built into the wall. Grimm was crushing the spongy buds with his fingers, and soon the room was pulsating with sound and permeated with the smell of high-grade marijuana.

"How'd you like those sticks I sent?"

"Excellent." Grimm had to shout over the music. "I'm still smoking them."

"I'll give you some more. Hey, listen to this. It's a demo tape of Suzi Sapphire's new album. It's dynamite."

The music was so loud they were forced to sit next to each other and yell to be heard above the wail of Suzi Sapphire's voice.

"I just got off the phone with Aaron," Max told Grimm. "He wants you to call him right away. He's out in the Hamptons."

"Now what's happening?"

"I don't know, bro. I didn't want to get into it over this phone. I'm paranoid they're gonna try to tie me in on this thing."

"You? Why? Do you know Sonny?"

Max nodded. "Sure. Everybody knows Sonny. All my numbers are in her little black book."

"Did you do business with her?"

"A.G., you know better. I don't do business with anyone. Since when does that matter?"

"Where's Rickie?"

"Safe. I got him stashed at the ranch."

"Shit, Max, that's not too bright. If they grab him up there, they'll definitely pull you in. At the least they'll charge you with harboring."

"Bro, ain't nobody gonna find him up there." Max cracked a bony smile and took the joint. "What's going on, anyway? He been indicted yet?"

"No, but there's a warrant. Aaron wants me to bring him back so he can surrender him. That way he figures they'll give him bail."

"He's already on probation. They might just lock his ass up."

"That's just some bullshit State possession beef. If he surrenders, he'll get bail, even if it's a couple million."

"Hey, I don't get it. What do they want Rickie for? He's not involved in Sonny's trip."

Grimm shrugged. "Publicity. All the more reason he should give himself up. Aaron thinks it's a bullshit move. We'll find out. The point is, he can't hide. Where the fuck's a guy like Rickie going?"

"True," Max agreed. He took a drag on the reefer and handed it back to Grimm. "But there are other complications."

"Aren't there always?"

"It seems Rickie and his pal Sonny have got a serious problem."

Grimm scowled. "What kind of problem?"

"From what Rickie tells me, it's not the heat he's worried about. There're other people looking for him. You know the people I mean. Sonny was holding heavy when the bust came down."

"I know that," said Grimm. "She had two packages and three hundred and eighty—"

"No, no, that's not what I'm talkin' about, A.G." Max interrupted. "I mean *holding heavy.*"

A short while later, Grimm was walking along the beach back to Max's after having gone to a pay phone where he called Aaron Held. He stopped and threw a piece of driftwood into the surf for Max's dog to fetch. Then he heard someone approaching, like a breeze stirring, and when he looked up he saw a small, wild-looking leather-clad blonde woman running toward him through the sand.

"Arthur Grimm?" she panted.

He recognized Suzi Sapphire in the rich twilight. He nodded and she came close to him, actually pressed herself up against him. The top of her white gold head came to his lower chest. Head averted, she hissed, "Rickie wants to talk to you." Then she turned and ran off toward a house set back from the beach. Grimm followed to the sounds of electric guitars.

There was music but no people. Suzi seemed to have disappeared. Grimm walked into the open front room of the house and looked around. Noticing a phone off the hook, he walked over and picked up the receiver. "Rickie?" he asked into the phone.

"Hey, big guy. What's happening?" said the punk rocker.

"Where are you?"

"Some one-horse town up the Coast. Hold on. . . . Hey, John, where are we?" Rickie yelled to someone. "I'm in a place called Half Moon Bay, A.G."

"Good. Stay where you are. Whatever you do, don't go back to the ranch. There's no sense drawing heat to Max. I'm coming up. Give me the number where you are, stay there and I'll call you back in an hour when I'm on my way."

"So what're we gonna do? You takin' me back?"

"Rickie, you've got to go back. There's no reason for you to run."

"A.G., I'm not sweatin' the bust, I mean, as far as I'm concerned. Fuck those people. What about the other situation? You hip to that?"

"Not everything. You'll have to fill me in. But don't worry, I'll handle it."

"You gonna talk to those people, A.G.?"

"I'll talk to them," Grimm assured him.

" 'Cause they gotta understand, I have no idea where that thing is. I mean, believe me, I never even got close to it."

"We'll get it straightened out."

There was a pause. "How's Sonny?" asked Rickie.

"She's all right. I was with her yesterday."

"Everybody's all flipped out, A.G. But I know her, she's hard as nails. I just don't want these dildos comin' down on me when I don't know shit from shineola—you hear what I'm sayin'?"

"Rickie, I hear you. I promise I won't let anyone fuck with you. I know those people. Let's just get you back there before things get any worse."

"I could always get plastic surgery," Rickie said. "Go live in Borneo or someplace. I'm kind 'a sick of this life, anyway."

"Maybe," Grimm said. "But you can't run out on Sonny."

"Yeah, you're right. Fuck it, it's all experience, right, A.G.? All we get to keep is the experience. Suzi, you there?"

"Yeah, I'm here." She was listening on an extension.

"He's right, you know. I gotta go back."

"Okay, but I'm goin' with you."

"Why get mixed up in this mess?"

" 'Cause I love you, asshole."

Cassy drove them to the Beverly Hills Hotel. There they picked up Grimm's luggage and rental car. Grimm chartered a plane and he and Suzi flew up the Coast to Palo Alto where they met Rickie. Early the next morning, the three of them were on a red-eye special headed from San Francisco to New York.

Chapter Three

RUDE TO SURRENDER

read the headlines in the *New York Post*. Grimm, Suzi Sapphire and the punk fugitive appeared in New York in a blaze of flash devices. At Kennedy Airport, wading through reporters and their proffered microphones, Grimm transferred Rickie and Suzi to Aaron Held's waiting limousine. They made plans to meet at a news conference scheduled for later that evening. Meanwhile, reporters seized on Rickie's facetious claim that his manager, Saul Diamond, had hatched the drug bust as a promotion stunt. The limo slid away carrying Rickie to the federal courthouse in lower Manhattan where he was to be arraigned.

Grimm was relieved to get into his own car and fade back into relative obscurity. Traveling with Rickie and Suzi had shown him what it was like to be a celebrity: the public acted as if they owned you. This case, he thought, already had a hectic life of its own. He wanted to avoid the limelight and do his part in the dark.

His part, for now, was to try to locate a large sum of money Sonny was supposedly holding when the bust came down. Just how much money no one seemed to know. "Millions," Rickie had said, gazing at Grimm with his huge blue eyes. "Those guys think I know where it is." Those guys were Jack Moriarty's people, organized crime people, in particular a man called Guy Stash who was Moriarty's partner.

Sonny, when Grimm spoke to her at the prison early Saturday, had been under the impression that a man who worked for her had delivered the money to Guy Stash as planned on the night of the bust. But

Rickie told Grimm that Sonny's man had never arrived for the appointed money drop, the money was missing, and Guy Stash was on a
rampage trying to find it. Grimm assured Rickie that he would reach
out for Guy Stash to let him know Rickie had no idea what had
happened to the money.

It was a mild September day in New York, just a hint of approaching
fall in the air. Grimm drove into Manhattan and crosstown to his
apartment. He was exhausted, having slept only a couple of hours on
the flight from California. Once inside, he called the office and picked
up his messages. He told the answering service to direct all calls to his
secretary. Then he took a hot bath to relax and went to bed.

On his way downtown after his nap, Grimm heard on the radio that
Rickie was free on a million dollar bond secured by the deed to the
Southampton mansion owned by his manager. Sonny was still in
custody in lieu of a $2.5 million cash bail. There was a short statement
from Vita Vaggi, the Assistant United States Attorney in charge of the
case.

Vaggi denied Rickie's allegation that his manager engineered the
bust as a publicity stunt. She said it was ludicrous to suppose federal
authorities could be manipulated in such a manner. Rude, Vaggi
declared, had been arrested because there was evidence linking him to
a large-scale drug distribution network. The prosecutor said the arrests
came as the result of an eighteen-month undercover investigation code-
named "Operation Dope Star" mounted by a joint FBI and Drug
Enforcement Administration task force. Vaggi went on to say the
government believed that this ring, headed by Sonia Byrne-Downes,
was responsible for at least thirty percent of the heroin distributed in
New York City. It was a "highly organized group of dealers who
employed couriers and other means to smuggle the drugs from abroad,
then distributed the illegal substances in major American cities,"
Vaggi stated.

"We'll see about that," said Grimm to the radio. He parked in a lot
across from the high-rise federal jail just off Foley Square. From a pay
phone in the jail lobby, he called Aaron Held at his office.

"Hey, babe, where are you?" the lawyer asked.

"At MCC. I'm on my way in to see her now. Any messages?"

"Tell her Carmen's fine. I just spoke to her a minute ago. And her
sister called to say she'll be in town tomorrow," Held replied. "You

know the rest. Oh, and listen, call your office. Miki's got a message for you."

In fact, she had several, but the only one that struck Grimm as cryptic enough to be related to this case was from a Dr. Bruce McMenimen asking that Grimm call to confirm their appointment. Since Grimm knew no Dr. McMenimen, he figured it could only be one person; the Irish alias was a Moriarty cue.

The lobby of the jail had the drab atmosphere of a third-rate Mexico City hotel. Grimm filled out the attorney visiting forms and checked his gun with the cop at the front desk. Once inside the elevator, any illusions of being anywhere but in jail were quickly dispelled. A pale, pimply faced guard sat on a plastic milk crate and barked orders at the prisoners.

"Move back! Touch your buddy! Make someone smile!"

He kept up a continuous barrage of insults, referring to the prisoners as "patos" or "motherfuckers." When Grimm stepped in, he ignored the guard, who was a rookie, and who looked up at him and demanded, "Who're you?"

Grimm said nothing. He looked down at the guard disdainfully and pointed to a tag hanging from his jacket lapel that identified him as a visiting attorney.

"I didn't say what're you. I said who're you. What's your name?"

The guard made it clear he wasn't going to move the packed elevator until he got an answer.

"Abraham Lincoln," Grimm said. "Who're you?" But Grimm paid for the wisecrack. It took over an hour for the guards to bring Sonny down from the women's unit on the fifth floor. The attorney visiting room was crowded; all the small conference rooms were occupied. Grimm took a spot at a table in one corner of the outer glass-walled room and sat reading about the case in the *Times* while he waited. Three more arrests had been made during the time he was in California; he recognized two of the names as mid-level drug dealers. Still others thought to be fugitives were being sought. Grimm wondered if that list included the name of the man who worked for Sonny and who failed to show for his meeting with Jack Moriarty's partner, Guy Stash.

On the front page of the Metropolitan Section of the paper, Vita Vaggi was pictured standing beside her boss, Ralph Vallone, the United States Attorney for the Southern District of New York, and Gus

Schumann, the head of New York's DEA office. They stood behind a table laden with seized contraband, now evidence: plastic bags full of money, bags of dope; scales and paraphernalia, and weapons that had been confiscated at various residences. Below this picture there was an insert photo of the West Side brownstone allegedly owned by Rickie Rude.

When Grimm looked up and saw Sonny through the glass wall as she emerged from the elevator, she smiled and waved to him like an old friend. He had a flash of recognition that went far beyond their brief acquaintance, an eerie sense of having known her before, almost as though he had always known her. Yet with the feeling of familiarity there was the mystery that is at the bottom of all intimacy. Who was she really? What did their lives have to do with each other?

As she came in, he was impressed by how much better she looked after only two days; she seemed rested, calmer, and the raw redness and dark rings around her eyes were not so noticeable. She looked sharper and more at ease with herself. She even appeared to have gained a few pounds. Amazing what a few days off drugs can do, he thought. He guessed they had her on methadone.

"You look upset," she said when he stood and she pressed his hand in greeting. "Is everything all right?"

"There're a few problems," he said, "but I'm just pissed off because these assholes have kept me waiting for over an hour. Here, sit down." Grimm pulled up another chair. "How do you feel? You look a lot better."

"All I've been doing is sleeping and eating and watching TV. It's a pretty soft life," she said with her charming smile. "Now tell me what's going on."

Sonny brushed back her hair with her hand and Grimm caught a glimpse of the birthmark over the corner of her eye. She was sitting up straight with her back arched and leaning toward him. He couldn't help but notice the outline of her breasts as they pressed against her pink T-shirt. She was braless and had full tits with protruding nipples like buttons. Grimm's eyes went back to her face.

"You know I found Rickie in California."

"Yes. It's been all over the news."

"Rickie was . . . in hiding," Grimm said. Sonny stared at him but said nothing. "Guy Stash has been hounding him."

"Guy Stash?" Sonny scowled. "What on earth for?"

"You have no idea?" He tested her.

"Arthur, I'm in here. All I know is what I hear on the news, or what you tell me. I've been following your advice, I'm not making any calls. Please, tell me what's happening."

"It seems your man never made it to the meeting the other night."

A little shriek escaped from Sonny's throat. Panic widened her eyes. She glanced around the room anxiously as though to see if anyone had noticed her loss of composure. "Just a minute. What are you telling me? Jack didn't get the money?"

He nodded. "That's the way it looks."

Sonny reached across the table and gripped his arm with both her hands. "Oh, God. Jesus, where's Karl? Was he busted? Tell me exactly what Rickie said."

"He didn't say much, believe me. He said Guy Stash came looking for him in L.A. I guess Guy was out there—"

"Yes, yes he was."

"And Jack was around somewhere. They were expecting to make a large collection, from you. It never happened. I imagine because you got busted, Guy went looking for Rickie to try to find out what went wrong. Rickie panicked and went into hiding. That's all I know."

"But for God's sake, where's Karl?" Sonny gasped. "What the fuck happened to Karl?"

Grimm shook his head. "I don't know. I don't even know who Karl is."

"Karl, for Christ's sake, the guy who works for me. Didn't Rickie tell you?" Her face was set in a look of fierce concentration. She kept kneading Grimm's forearm with her hands.

"All Rickie said was that according to Guy Stash, your man never showed. At this point, that's all anyone seems to know."

Sonny looked stunned. She was staring at him, but her eyes weren't focused. Abruptly she let go of Grimm's arm and got up. She shoved her hand in the pocket of her smock and fished out a crumpled pack of cigarettes. Her hands shook as she pulled one out and stuck it in her mouth. "This is a bloody disaster," she said to herself. Then, looking at him again, she asked, "Do you suppose he's been busted?"

Grimm got out of his chair and lit her cigarette. "If so, they're keeping a tight lid on it."

"What does that mean?" She touched his arm again. "Are you saying . . . you mean he might be—I don't understand, Arthur."

Grimm put his arm around her shoulders. He couldn't resist the urge he felt to touch her, to comfort her. "Relax, Sonny," he said, thinking what a big woman she was; she had to be at least five-ten, and she had broad shoulders. He was used to feeling himself huge next to most women, but holding Sonny he felt almost normal. "Just take it easy. It's not going to do any good getting yourself all worked up."

"Arthur, this is terrible. This is . . ."

She didn't finish. She let her head rest on his chest and he gently stroked her hair.

"You'd better explain," he said.

Karl, Sonny told Grimm, was a photographer and graphic artist who sometimes designed record album jackets for Rickie's company, Rude Productions. His full name was Karl Lundgren, but most everyone knew him by his street name, "Loose Karl," because he was a tall, gangly sort of fellow with a loose-jointed walk and odd sprawling movements. He was also Sonny's right-hand man. Even before it had become obvious to her that she was under tight surveillance, she hired Karl to sit on her stash and run errands. At the time, Karl was broke, crashing at Rickie's rooms in the Chelsea Hotel, living off Rickie's generosity and waiting for something to happen. Karl lived with his constant companion, an English bulldog named Myrtle who was being tormented by Rickie's two Siamese cats.

Sonny began looking around for a place to rent for Karl where he could live and stash large amounts of drugs and cash. Around this time, Rickie's company acquired a building in SoHo. Karl, who was a carpenter and handyman, began remodeling the lofts into studios. Soon, he and his dog were staying in one of the lofts. Rickie never objected, but Sonny was concerned about Rickie's exposure, and so a rental contract was drawn up between Karl and Rude Productions to protect Rickie.

The SoHo loft gradually became Sonny's main city stash location. For security reasons, she barely went there, and no phone was installed. Instead she rented Karl an electronic pager. Typically, she would call his beeper number from a pay phone, leave a number where she could be reached, and wait for him to call her back. At the time of the bust, Karl was handling close to ninety percent of Sonny's local business. He made deliveries and picked up money. Myrtle stayed at the loft to guard the stash. To minimize contact, Sonny gave Karl most of his instructions pay phone-to-pay phone. Only when it became absolutely necessary did they meet to go over the books or to discuss complicated delivery procedures. With the rising heat on Sonny, Karl began to handle the large money drops to her main people, Jack Moriarty and Guy Stash.

"So Karl was supposed to meet with Guy Stash. When?" Grimm asked.

"Friday evening, the day of the bust. Jack and Guy were in California. There had been some problems out there. In any case, I wanted to unload the money because it was becoming too big. We were expecting Guy for a couple of weeks. Finally, I reached Jack and told him he had to send someone to pick up the money. That was last week sometime. On Wednesday, he got in touch, through Rickie, and told me to expect Guy Friday. I told Karl to rent a car so he could take all the money and go to the airport to meet Guy. That was how we usually did it. Karl would meet Guy—or whoever they sent to pick up the money, but usually Guy—he'd give him the keys to the rental car, with the money packed in suitcases in the trunk. Guy would do whatever he did with the money, then either return the car to Karl or drop it at the rental agency."

"But what I still don't understand," Grimm said, "is what you were doing with three hundred and eighty grand and two k's of junk if you had Karl to handle things for you."

Sonny closed her eyes and shook her head. "Everything was so fucked up that day. Karl was out running around collecting money. I wanted to get together as much as I could. And then this asshole, Donnie Randazzo—he's upstairs now, the jerk—he wanted to go out of town. He insisted on clearing the books before he left. I was so pissed off at him, he knew how hot I was. Actually, it was four hundred and fifty thousand he gave me, plus the two kilos he returned."

"So the agents stole seventy thousand?"

Sonny sighed. "That's the least of my problems. What on earth could have happened to Karl? God, do you realize how serious this is?"

"How much did Karl have?"

Sonny stared at him. She ran her fingers through her bangs, then tugged at her pony tail. "Too fucking much," she said absently. "I might as well go up and hang myself."

Grimm waited a few moments, then he said, "I'm going to be getting together with Jack, so you might as well tell me."

"Arthur," she said, opening her eyes wide and looking at him, "are you ready for this? Would you believe me if I told you I honestly don't know? We were incredibly busy, it was crazy, the money was coming in so fast, Karl was out picking up from people all day. We never had a chance to go over our records. We hardly had time to count it. I told him to give it all to Guy, whatever was there, just so I wouldn't have to worry about it anymore. I don't know, but it had to be . . . as of last Thursday I know it was already over six million."

Grimm made a soft whistling sound. Six million, he thought. A serious payday. No wonder Jack and Guy Stash are freaked out.

The news conference was already under way by the time Grimm arrived at the Algonquin Hotel. Rickie, flanked by Aaron Held and Judy Roth, who was Saul Diamond's executive assistant, sat at a long table near one end of a narrow, densely packed conference room. Cameramen and soundmen crouched on the floor in front of the table, and others seemed to hang from the walls.

Grimm worked his way through the crowd to the opposite end of the room where his height afforded him a view over the heads of the newsmen. The music and entertainment press were present in full force, as were reporters for all the dailies and the major radio and TV stations. Even the national networks had people occupying positions. Grimm could see Suzi Sapphire along with Rickie's friend, the writer Moon Landing, squeezed off in a corner behind Rickie. He assumed the other freaky-looking characters he saw in the crowd were part of the Rude entourage, here to gather at the feet of their demigod, and doubtless a few were undercover federal agents.

Rickie was in rare form. His hair, which was cut short, had been bleached and dyed black and blond in spots like a leopard's skin. On his upper body he wore only a black leather vest covered with pins, studs, and SAVE THE WHALES buttons. In the bright arc lights, his skin was like alabaster, with his intricate and vividly inked tatoos, he looked like a hand-painted porcelain statue. To Grimm, Rickie looked unreal in the intense light, like an apparition, some captive wraith from another dimension.

Held was seated on Rickie's left. The attorney's long, fine hair was straight but swept up in curls at the ends. It had dried in the hot lamps and come unglued from his head. He was dressed in a conservative blue suit and light blue shirt with white collar and cuffs. His long hands were gesturing in the air as he made an emphatic point.

"All we have thus far are allegations," Held was saying, "and not very concrete allegations at that. My client has not yet been indicted. This is all Vaggi's grandstanding, Vaggi and Vallone, and I find it irresponsible of members of the United States Attorney's Office to go around making public statements about Rickie at this sensitive stage in the proceedings. We've called you here in an effort to balance things out. All we ask is that Rickie get a fair trial."

"Yeah! What he said," said Rickie with a grin.

"What kind of evidence does the government have?" a reporter asked.

"That's a good question. You'll have to ask Vita Vaggi about that."

"But Rickie does own the townhouse where Sonia Byrne-Downes was living at the time of her arrest, correct?" someone else asked.

"Rickie's company, Rude Productions, owns it, yes. We're not denying that," Held replied. "But let's be realistic. If they arrested the owners of every apartment in New York where illegal drugs are found, you wouldn't have many landlords left."

"What is this, Russia?" Rickie called out and the reporters laughed.

"How 'bout it, Rickie—are you innocent?" one of them asked.

Rickie smiled benignly, sat forward and shook his head, arms outspread. "As a new born babe," he sang.

Judy Roth, a dark haired woman with severe, sharp features who virtually ran Diamond Star Enterprises, Saul Diamond's parent company, ruffled Rickie's spotted head as though he were a pet ocelot. "Of course he's innocent," she said, and Rickie nuzzled up to her. "Rickie's an artist. He's a poet. He's no junk dealer."

"What's the story with the new hairdo?" someone called out.

"Ah ha!" Rickie exclaimed. He sat up and recited: "Glory be to God for dappled things— / All things counter, original, spare, strange; / Whatever is fickle, freckled (who knows how?)"

The reporters scribbled furiously.

"Do you advocate drug use?" a woman reporter near the front asked. An impatient rustle went through the room as though the answer to that question was obvious. But Rickie, ever polite despite his name, considered carefully before answering.

"Let me put it this way," he said. "What I advocate is freedom of choice. If someone wants to use drugs, as long as they're not hurting anyone else, that's their business. That's their right in a free country."

"Are you saying you don't believe drugs like heroin and cocaine are harmful?"

"No, that's not what I said, and don't you dare write that. Listen to me carefully. Read my lips. Drugs can be harmful, too much of anything is harmful. But that's not the point."

"What is the point?" asked a woman standing just in front of Grimm.

"The point is freedom," Rickie replied. "Personal liberty. This is America, the great experiment. What this country is about is freedom. That includes the freedom to alter your consciousness."

"Rickie, maybe you should run for President," said the same woman, who was dressed a bit punkishly and looked like a true believer in the Rude philosophy.

"Yeah! If that's a nomination, I accept! Put a real punk in the White House!" Rickie shouted with a laugh. "Here we go, here's my platform: First, I repeal the 55-mile-an-hour speed limit. I legalize anything that doesn't hurt other people, no victim, no crime. And finally, I'm sure you'll all go for this one, I abolish the IRS!"

There were cheers and exclamations of agreement. Rickie shot his hands up with fingers spread in the V sign and wagged his head in imitation of Nixon.

"That's right, my fellow Americans—I am the funky President!"

Everyone laughed at his impersonation of the former President.

"Keep America free!" he shouted as he stood and took a bow.

Grimm was mesmerized by him, and fascinated by the control he exercised over the crowd—and these were newspeople. Rickie was a consummate performer; he had a kind of élan that was magnetic. The punk looked around for Suzi, spotted her, and called her up to the table. Suzi, petite, her hair a white blizzard, was wearing a tight swath of red material around her hips and black fishnet stockings. They beamed at each other and kissed for the cameras.

"And now I'm gonna tell you about the heaviest drug known to man," said Rickie. "Love. Love is the drug. Yeah. We're gonna get married and have some little baby punks complete with mutant chromosomes. Yeah!"

With Suzi perched on his knee like a sexy little elf, Rickie went on to announce the soon-to-be-released Suzi Sapphire album, *Figure of*

Sound, and told the press that they had just finished shooting the most erotic rock video ever made.

"It may be too rude," he said, "if you get my drift."

"What will you do if you get convicted and have to go to prison?" said a woman Grimm recognized as a writer for a well-known magazine.

Again Rickie was thoughtful. "Flow with it," he answered with emotion. "Life is all experience. When we die, that's all we take with us. If I have to go to prison, then I become that experience, whatever that makes me."

Some of the reporters dashed out to write stories. Held, Judy Roth and Rickie were still hemmed in by the crowd. Grimm caught Suzi's attention and beckoned to her.

"Hi ya' Grimm guy," she said in her pert manner. "What's up?"

"Suzi, do me a favor. Tell them I'll see them downstairs in the Oak Bar. I need to make a phone call."

Grimm was standing at the bar having a drink when they all trooped in, still flushed with excitement from the news conference.

"Hey, A.G., how's Sonny?" was Rickie's first question. "Does she need anything?"

Grimm put an arm around Rickie and took him aside. "Have you heard anything from Karl?" he asked.

"Not a word. Was he busted?"

"I don't know. His name hasn't come up anywhere, but that doesn't mean they haven't got him. I don't suppose you have a spare key to the loft?"

Rickie shook his head. "I never went there. I don't even know where it is. But listen, A.G., you're gonna talk to those other dudes for me, right? Guy Stash and those guys. Tell 'em I don't know where their package is."

"I'm seeing Jack tonight. Don't worry. I told you I'd take care of it."

Aaron Held walked over to them. "Well," he said, "how're we doing so far?"

Rickie excused himself and joined Suzi, Moon Landing, Judy Roth and the others at the bar. Held and Grimm walked into the lobby.

"We need to find out if they arrested a guy named Karl Lundgren," Grimm told the attorney.

"Who's Karl Lundgren and why do we care about him?"

"He works for Sonny, her gopher. He also knows Rickie, used to stay at Rickie's suite at the Chelsea. He was sitting on the stash in a SoHo loft owned by Rickie."

"Oh, shit. I see," Held said. "Could be a bad one."

"Could be very bad."

"Well, my son, that's where Arthur Grimm comes in. You better find out what happened to this Karl Lundgren character. Now, what about Jack, the man calling himself McMenimen?"

"I'm supposed to meet with him late tonight. Out at Saul's."

"Is that wise?"

"Probably not, but that's the way they want it."

"Hmmmm," said Held, stroking his chin thoughtfully. "What's his problem? Is he concerned that Sonny might roll over?"

"I'm sure he's thought about that possibility, but at this point I think he's worried about the same thing we are," Grimm said.

Held frowned. "You mean the whereabouts of Karl Lundgren."

"Right. Karl Lundgren and the—"

Held held up his hand. "I don't think I want to know about this. Just tell me, are you going to discuss money with them?"

Grimm chuckled. "I'm sure the subject will come up."

He drove from the Algonquin to the SoHo address Sonny had given him. The building owned by Rickie was on a side street off West Broadway. It was a medium-size block of lofts typical for the neighborhood. Grimm parked his car across the street.

Above the buzzer and a mailbox stuffed with junk mail, he saw the typed name: RUDE PRODUCTIONS. But Grimm did not ring the bell. He took out a pocket burglar's latch and lock pick and sprung the front door. He then climbed up the stairs to the second floor hallway.

A large bloodshot eye was painted around the peephole in the metal door. Grimm pressed his face against the door and listened for noise from within. He heard the sounds of a dog's nails scratching on wooden floors, then a throaty growl. No music or other sounds of human occupation.

"Myrtle, is that you?" Grimm called through the door. The dog's growl became a whine. He felt the bulldog shove against the door. "Good girl," he said, trying to soothe the dog as he went to work picking the locks.

The investigator had experience handling dogs. He bred and trained working dogs at his farm in Millbrook. Grimm loved dogs and ordinarily they took to him. He knew he should not let the animal sense any fear. When at last he got the door open, he quickly knelt down and confronted the half-starved, parched and weakened bulldog.

The poor animal was so glad to see someone that she nearly knocked him over. Grimm immediately found the kitchen and gave Myrtle a bowl of water. She lapped it up thirstily. There were piles of dog shit and piss stains on the hardwood floors. Myrtle had upset the trash can and spilled out the garbage in her search for food. She had also practically chewed a hole in the bathroom door trying to get to the water in the commode. Another couple of days and she would have been dead. He found tins of dog food in one of the cupboards, and filled Myrtle's matching red plastic bowls with meat and more water.

"See, girl, I'm your pal. I'm here to help you," he said, and knew he'd made a friend for life.

It was obvious no one had been in the loft for days. While Myrtle ate and drank noisily, Grimm took a look around. The rear of the loft was sectioned off into a bedroom, a darkroom and a storage area; a bathroom and kitchen were mid-floor; and the entire front half was one large, open room.

Grimm walked into the bedroom. He stood for a moment transfixed by a huge poster mounted on the wall. It was Suzi Sapphire, naked from the waist down. She was crouched on her knees and elbows with her bare ass stuck up at an angle to the camera like a pale moon with a dark cavern in the middle. On her head she wore wrap-around sun glasses, and her hair was matted and stuck together in wads. She wore chrome belts with sharp studs around her neck and waist, a short black leather jacket, and black lace gloves on her hands that looked like spider webs. Her head was turned and she was looking back over her shoulder at the camera with a vague animal snarl on her face, lips parted.

But what caught Grimm and held him rooted to the floor was the girlish charm of Suzi's upended ass. The labia were slightly parted like her red mouth, and a fringe of ginger pubescence showed through from the mons venus. "Whew," Grimm whistled aloud, "Old Rickie'll never get enough of that."

SUZI SAPPHIRE'S ALL NEW FIGURE OF SOUND the poster read.

Back in the front room, Grimm looked through some photographs, negatives, and other assorted papers. Myrtle, who had finished eating, came scratching out from the kitchen and regarded him with an air of suspicion mixed with gratitude. "Don't worry, old girl. I'm your friend," he told her as he rummaged through the trash on the floor. "Where's your boss? What'd he do, take the money and run? Leave his old girl behind to starve?"

The dog looked at him and made yawning sounds. Grimm wasn't sure exactly what he was looking for. Sonny had told him that Karl built a stash into the walls somewhere in the loft. He talked to the dog and she followed him while he made his rapid and thorough search.

Back in the bedroom he found some of Karl's personal belongings: clothes, a .38 caliber revolver, pictures and papers identifying the missing man as Karl Lundgren, born in 1950, originally from Darien, Connecticut. Grimm pocketed a snapshot of the tall, raw-boned aging hippie.

Searching the closet, he noticed faint grime smudges on the small end wall. He began poking around and found that the baseboard pulled off. He was then able to slide the wall aside to reveal the stash, a long, narrow crawl space behind the false wall. Excited, Grimm went back into the bedroom to get a flashlight, then crawled into the stash with the hope that he would find the six million.

There were shelves against the inside wall. He found a triple-beam balance scale, jars containing small amounts of drugs, an envelope with five thousand in hundreds in it, and a stack of receipts stuck inside a spiral notebook filled with figures, initials and dates. The stash had been cleaned out of all large amounts of cash and drugs. Grimm noticed white powder residue on his knees when he crawled out. "Shit," he muttered. "I thought I had it."

Taking the five thousand, the notebook and the stack of receipts, he replaced the false wall and sat on the bed to study the records. Myrtle squatted at his feet watching his every move. The receipts were mostly for gasoline purchases, meals, hotel rooms and airline tickets. All of them were paid for by a credit card bearing the imprint of Rude Productions, Inc., and all were signed by Karl Lundgren.

From the entries in the notebook he was able to determine that the organization generated huge cash flow. Next to the notation "GS" was a date, 6/30, and the figure 1.75. This was followed by daily entries of numbers in the hundreds of thousands. The last notation, made the day before the bust, showed a balance on hand of 6.325 million.

"Big business," he said aloud and looked down at the bulldog. She pushed off her haunches and rubbed against his leg. Grimm put his arm around her thick neck and scratched the loose skin under her collar. He knew the dog was staying close to him because she was afraid of being left alone again.

"Don't worry, old girl. I won't abandon you."

His fingers felt a button attached to the dog's collar. He pulled up on Myrtle's head to take a look at the button. WE TRY HARDER read the white print on a green button. Grimm smiled to himself.

"Yeah, you sure do," he said. And then an idea took hold: Avis.

Myrtle looked so miserable, he decided to take her with him. Out on the street, he let her run around for a few minutes, then he opened the door to his Jaguar XJ-6, and she leapt into the backseat and sat up as though she belonged there. Driving away, he took the spiral notebook, receipts and envelope full of cash and shoved all of it up under the seat.

He would need to find a place to leave the dog until her master was found. If he was found. It was beginning to look like Karl had taken the money and split. Still, the departure struck Grimm as too abrupt. The man loved his dog, so why not take her with him? And why leave the five thousand, his gun and all his belongings behind? Because with six mil plus he could buy brand new everything. Maybe it was a spur of the moment decision. Karl felt the heat coming down, and fled.

"Then too," Grimm said to the dog as he drove around looking for a telephone booth with a directory, "he could have been busted. Right, Myrtle? Maybe he didn't take off on you after all." Vaggi and the DEA could have him in deep security while they debriefed him, trying to get as much information out of him as they could before they alerted people and gave them an opportunity to run. Vaggi kept alluding to nameless others being sought. But then, if Karl had been busted, surely the DEA would have secured the stash and cleaned out all the evidence. And they would never have been able to hush up a seizure of that much cash. They would have had to go for the glory. Unless . . .

Lost in thought, still trying to find a phone book, Grimm failed to notice the pair of beat-up, stripped-down sedans that were switching back and forth expertly as they followed him.

He found a phone booth with an intact Yellow Pages and turned to the automobile rental agency listings. The closest Avis office was on East 11th Street. When he got there, Grimm asked to see the shift manager. He showed his New York investigator's license to the friendly, middle-aged woman and asked her if she had rented a car within the past week to a man named Karl Lundgren who would have been using a credit card in the name of Rude Productions, Inc. He also showed her a photo of Karl, which she didn't recognize. The manager looked through the active file under L and under R, but could find no contract.

"Would you do me a favor and check your computer to see if perhaps he rented from one of your other offices?" Grimm asked.

The woman keyed the information into the computer. "Okay, here it is," she said with a look of triumph. "Rude Productions. The vehicle was rented on 9/12 from our West Side office on 76th Street."

"Has it been returned?"

"No. We show an expected date of return of 9/13 with a JFK drop-off. The vehicle is three days overdue."

"What kind of car is it?"

She tapped at the keyboard. "It's a full-size Lincoln Town Car, new, tan, with New Jersey registration KJL-437." She gave Grimm a concerned look. "Is there some problem? Should I call the West Side office and notify them?"

"Give it another day or so. I'll let you know if I find out anything."

"Well, Myrtle, what now?" he said to the bulldog as he got back into the car. "It looks like wherever that boss of yours is, he's still got the car. What d'you say, girl? We might as well take a look around the airport."

Sonny had told him that she knew for certain Karl made a money pick-up the day of the bust from a Colombian named Micky Hoyos who lived in Queens. Hoyos had also been pinched on the case and was now in MCC. From Queens, Karl was supposed to have gone to the airport to meet Guy Stash. Somewhere between his meeting with Hoyos and the scheduled rendezvous with Guy, Karl disappeared. Guy Stash had flown into New York from L.A. on an American Airlines flight. He was to meet Karl, who was to give him the keys and the parking ticket for the rental car. Guy was then to return it after he removed the suitcases full of money. According to Guy, Karl never showed up.

At Kennedy Airport Grimm drove to the long-term parking area near the American terminal. It was a long shot.

Dusk had fallen and Grimm was confronted with acres of parked cars. "This calls for a joint," he said, glancing over his shoulder at Myrtle, who sat patiently looking out the window of the Jaguar. Grimm smoked the joint as he drove up one row of cars and down the next. He finished the joint, rolled down the window and dropped the roach. A wave of hot air smelling of burnt jet fuel wafted into his face. He was stoned, and suddenly felt a vague sense of paranoia as though the heated air and the hard, glittering surfaces of the parked cars were charged with hostility. The high-pitched whistling of heavy jets landing and taking off sounded continuously. Grimm stared out the window, his eyes scanning the cars and license plates as he cruised the rows. Everything seemed to slow down and the sounds grew louder. He had a mounting sense of another presence around him.

And then he saw the car. He had covered a little more than half the lot when he came upon the Lincoln. Grimm's pulse quickened; he had that uncanny sense of knowing this would happen.

The big car looked oddly bereft. Grimm stopped the Jag and re-checked the numbers on the Jersey tags. KJL-437. No question about it, he had found the rental car.

"Shit," he said under his breath as he got out of his car and approached the tan four-door sedan. He could feel the heat closing in around him. He didn't know if he should go on with what he was doing or get back in his car and try to leave. He walked around the Lincoln, looked in the windows and wondered if he were imagining things. He looked up to see men moving toward him from all directions as quickly and quietly as shadows.

"Freeze, asshole!" someone shouted.

A man appeared in front of him. He was in a half-squat position and held a gun with both hands leveled at Grimm's solar plexus. Slowly, Grimm lifted his arms. At that instant, he caught a putrid whiff in the air that he knew was not his fear.

He had known who the men were even before he saw them. As soon as he stopped the Jaguar and got out, he had sensed their tension in the air. Now he was surrounded by hairy, scruffy looking thugs all aiming guns at him. The men were as hyped-up as hounds bringing their prey to ground.

"Move away from the car," said one of the men as he waved a

pistol. He was Hispanic, with a thin moustache and a nose that looked as though it had been flattened with a fist. He nodded and two men patted Grimm down, removing his Browning Hi-Power 9mm automatic from under his left arm. Grimm could feel drops of cold sweat rolling down his sides. Myrtle uttered a few confused barks, but the men ignored her. Their attention was focused on Grimm and the trunk of the Lincoln.

Grimm knew the Hispanic as Julio "Julie Zoo" Zuluaga, a Special Agent with the Drug Enforcement Administration. And he knew Zuluaga knew him. A couple of the other agents' faces looked familiar under the hair, hats and sunglasses. After disarming Grimm, they seemed unsure what to do next. Zuluaga, a well-built middleweight with medium brown skin and curly hair, looked from Grimm to the Lincoln, then back again.

Then Zuluaga made up his mind. With his pistol, he pointed to the trunk and waved the gun up and down. When the lid of the trunk was popped, the stench was overwhelming. It was not the smell of six-and-a-half million.

The man known as "Loose Karl" lay curled on his side in a fetal position. His shirt had been ripped from his upper body and lay in shreds around his waist. His flesh had already begun to turn livid and swell. His hands were clasped between his knees. Grimm saw that his gray-streaked pony tail was caked with dried blood and there was a black hole behind his ear. His face was stuck to the floor of the trunk as though he'd been looking for his reflection in the pool of congealed blood.

Chapter Four

"Who you workin' for, Grimm?" Julio Zuluaga wanted to know. "Tell me that, an' I forget about everything else."

They were sitting in an office at the Drug Enforcement Administration headquarters on West 57th Street. Grimm, escorted by two of Zuluaga's men, had driven his car back to Manhattan from the airport, "for questioning."

Grimm had had previous run-ins with Julie Zoo, both as an agent in the field and in the courtroom testifying at drug trials. Originally from Miami, Zuluaga had been assigned to the New York office for about two years. In the circles in which the two men traveled, Zuluaga was known to have the scruples of a hyena and the subtlety of a knife in the back. Just knowing Zuluaga was on a case was enough to cause defense attorneys to shudder and begin plea negotiations.

He and the men in the Special Operations Group he commanded were suspected of stealing money and drugs, shaking down dealers, accepting bribes, and manufacturing evidence against agency targets. When the cases came to trial, they would sit in the witness box like choirboys and tell bold-faced lies.

Once during recess in a long trial where Aaron Held had represented the lead defendant, in the corridor outside the courtroom, Zuluaga, in a voice loud enough for all to hear, had asked a fellow agent, "What's the difference between a dead dog lying in the street and a dead lawyer lying in the street?" The other agent said he didn't know. "The dead dog has skid marks in front of it."

Such was the affection between Aaron Held and Julie Zuluaga. The agent's feelings for Grimm may have been tempered by the understanding that they both operated in the same sphere of activity.

"Am I pinched, Julie, or what?" Grimm asked. "Because I really don't feel like answering questions."

"You wanna be pinched? No problem."

"Get me in front of a magistrate."

"I'm gonna get you in front of a grand jury, that's where I'm gonna get your smart ass. Listen, motherfucker, I got you with a picture a' this guy in your pocket. I got you with a weapon next to a stiff with a bullet in the head." Zuluaga laughed. "I even got you with this dead cocksucker's dog in your car. How you gonna explain that one?"

"Do I look worried?"

"Grimm, you look stupid." The agent's flat, murky river-bottom eyes blinked. "You wanna see me give you that body, asshole? You wanna see me come up with a ballistics report that proves your gun killed that scumbag?"

"Fuck you, Zuluaga," Grimm said, looking straight at the man's battered face. "You're so full of shit, your breath smells. You think I'm some punk who just rolled into this town last night?" Grimm sat forward in his seat. "I've been working in this city a lot longer than you have. Why don't we just give Bernie Wolfshein a call and tell him you're holding me in violation of every Constitutional—"

"Oh, Jesus," Zuluaga said, slapping himself on the forehead. "Spare me the Constitution, will ya' Grimm? I wipe my ass with the Constitution. Fuck Wolfshein, fuck Held, fuck you an' all the other smartass New York Jews. We ain't in the courtroom now." He leaned on his elbows and lolled his head on his shoulder. He had to breathe through his mouth because of his smashed nose. Grimm had heard he had once been a professional fighter. "You're workin' for Jack Moriarty, aren't you?"

Grimm shrugged and reached for the phone on the desk. Zuluaga's hand shot out and slammed down on top of his.

"You're a fool, Zuluaga," Grimm said. "They're gonna hang you by the balls for this one."

Zuluaga glared at him. "Who? What're you talkin' about?"

"Operation Dope Star. You blew it. Eighteen months you had this trip under surveillance, now all of a sudden large amounts of money are disappearing. A major player gets clipped right under your nose."

"Who whacked this kid, Grimm? Where's that motherfuckin' money?"

Grimm stood. "Use your head, Zuluaga. If I knew where the money was, what was I doing at the airport?"

The agent seemed impressed with Grimm's reasoning. "So who're you workin' for?" he asked almost gently.

"I'm working for Held. Who else?"

"Sure." Zuluaga sneered. "That fag cocksucker's always got his nose in somewhere. Grimm, lissen'a me. We're talkin' serious papers ova' here. Large," he whispered.

"So I understand."

"What's that cunt got to say?"

"Who?"

"You know who. Jack's English bitch you been in to see twice already."

Grimm shook his head. "You really fucked this one up. Wait'll Vaggi hears about this."

"Grimm, I'm tellin' ya', you better play ball with me or I'm gonna bury these people. You can tell Held I'll make sure that little freak client 'a his takes it up the ass for the next twenty years. I'm not fuckin' around, Grimm. I'm gonna—"

At that moment the door opened and Bernard Wolfshein walked into the office. Wolfshein was Regional Agent in Charge of Intelligence for DEA's Northeast Division. Though Zuluaga was a Group Supervisor, Wolfshein was at least a couple of Government Service levels above him and clearly his superior. He was also a good friend of Arthur Grimm's.

"Sorry. I didn't mean to interrupt," Wolfshein said, glancing first at Zuluaga then at Grimm. He was a wiry man, of average height, with thick salt and pepper curls he wore brushed straight back from his high forehead. "I heard you were around," he said to Grimm, "so I thought I'd stop by and say hello." Now he looked at Zuluaga. "Everything all right, Julie?"

Zuluaga leaned back in his chair and stuck his hands in the waistband of his trousers. "Nothin' I can't handle," he said, scratching his groin.

Wolfshein reached up and touched his horn-rimmed glasses, sliding them back on his nose. He was wearing a plain brown suit and scuffed loafers. He looked more like a legal-aide attorney than a high level drug cop.

"Julie got himself a ripe one at the airport," Grimm said.

"Yeah? Anyone I know?" Wolfshein looked to Zuluaga for an answer.

Zuluaga nodded slowly. "Lundgren," he said, getting to his feet. "The missing gopher."

Grimm and Wolfshein left Zuluaga's office together. The agent took Grimm to retrieve his gun from the property clerk, then gripped him by the elbow and led him from the DEA building. "We need to talk," he told Grimm.

"How did you know I was in there?" Grimm asked as they stepped onto the sidewalk. He looked at his watch. "And what're you doing in town at this hour?"

"Let's have a drink," Wolfshein answered.

Grimm's friendship with Bernie Wolfshein was an old one, and deep with roots that went all the way back to the vibrant green and waterlogged landscape of Vietnam.

Wolfshein was from a middle-class Jewish family out of Boro Park in Brooklyn. He was a few years older than Grimm, and was reasonably happily married with three young children. A gifted pianist from a musically inclined family, he had attended Juilliard and aspired to a career on the concert stage before he was drafted into the Army. In Vietnam, he and Grimm served for a time with the same unit of Special Forces.

The war changed them both. Grimm, though groomed for Service life, fell out of love with Uncle Sam over the war. Wolfshein went the other way and became a government man. After the war, he worked for the Customs Service, later transferring to the federal drug agency. Grimm, who reached the rank of lieutenant colonel while attached to Military Intelligence, finally quit the Army when an investigation he was supervising for the Pentagon was quashed by the CIA.

Even now, though working for opposing interests, the two Army buddies remained close. Wolfshien had recently been reassigned to the New York Regional Office after having spent a number of years in Washington with DEA's CENTAC, an ultra-elite strikeforce. For a time, he also served as the drug agency's liaison with Congress, "trying to explain drug trafficking to politicians," as he once put it. There had always been a strong element of competition to their friendship; they still got together regularly to play racquetball, or tennis, or to work out at the New York Athletic Club.

"Who tipped you I was in there with Zuluaga?" asked Grimm over a drink in a bar around the corner from the DEA building.

"I got a call," Wolfshein answered. "I still have a few friends left."

"But Julie Zoo's not one of them."

Wolfshein looked up with a thin smile. "Yes, that's true. I guess you could say Julie and I have a different view as to what constitutes good police work."

In the late Seventies, Wolfshein, with considerable help from Grimm, had spearheaded an investigation that arose out of the Internal Affairs Division of DEA. As a result, several rogue agents had been dismissed, transferred or prosecuted for illegal activities. These events and the fact that Wolfshein was a Jew who fought his way into the upper echelons of a notoriously anti-Semitic agency made for a lot of departmental resentment.

"Well, by the looks of it, I'd have to say he's fucked this one up real bad," Grimm said.

Wolfshein gazed at him and nodded his head. "Do you know how bad?"

"There's the money, for one thing." Grimm hesitated, watching Wolfshein closely. "And now this body. The guy gets taken out right under Zuluaga's nose. That's curious. I get the distinct impression this case is out of control."

Wolfshein pushed his glasses up his nose and looked down at his drink. "It's in the U.S. Attorney's hands now," he said with a resigned sigh. "Whatever happens, Sonny Byrne-Downes has got herself a major headache."

"So it would seem," Grimm said, still probing, "unless whoever represents her can come up with a crucial flaw in the way the government accumulated its evidence."

"I wouldn't bank on things being that fucked up," the agent said. "Who's representing her, anyway?"

Grimm shrugged. "I don't know. I don't think she's decided on a lawyer yet."

Wolfshein looked at him with a skeptical frown. "C'mon, Arthur, don't gimme that crap. You and Held have been all over her from the moment she got pinched.''

"Aaron represents Rickie Rude. You know that. Rickie's only connection with this case is through Sonny. So naturally we're interested in how she's doing.''

"How is she doing?''

"She seems to be doing all right.''

"Yeah? How's she like jail so far?''

Grimm laughed. "Damn, Wolf, you've got Sonny on the brain. I've never known you to take such an interest in a defendant before. What is it you like most about her?''

"Her friends,'' said Wolfshein without a trace of humor. "All her heavyweight friends.'' He took a sip of his drink, then put it down. "Obviously, we'd be real interested in having a little chat with Sonny Byrne-Downes. When you find out who her lawyer is, you might just relay that information. I don't need to tell you, Arthur, this is a big case. Lots of media attention. The U.S. Attorney is going to make sure someone ends up with a shitload of time.''

"They bringing a CCE?'' Grimm asked, referring to the Continuing Criminal Enterprise statute, also known as 848, which carries a penalty of up to life with no parole.

Wolfshein shrugged his lean shoulders. "Somebody's gotta be boss. Your girl's got all the right stuff. Unless she's willing to turn us on to Moriarty and his crew, it looks like the buck stops with her.''

"What about Rickie?''

"Held may have himself a winner.''

"You mean, if Sonny's willing to cooperate?''

Wolfshein adjusted his glasses and took another sip of his drink. "His tie-in is tenuous, at best. But you know how it goes in these big conspiracy cases. There's a lot of spillover. Once the jury gets a look at piles of drugs and stacks of money, they have a tendency to convict everyone. Rickie's a freak. His life-style was bound to get him into trouble sooner or later.''

"Interesting,'' Grimm said, smiling at his friend. "I'm to assume this comes straight from Vaggi?''

"C'mon, pal, don't bust my balls. I'm talking to you as one friend to another, strictly off the record. All I'm saying is, there's a lot at stake here. There's no indictment yet. If Byrne-Downes is willing to help us, maybe Rude walks.''

"I'll keep that in mind. Can I mention it to Aaron?"

Finally, Wolfshein gave him a full smile. "You know you will anyway. Just don't tell him it came from me."

They went on to talk about Wolfshein's family. For a cop, Wolfshein devoted a lot of time to his family, and he never lost an opportunity to urge Grimm to find himself a good woman and settle down.

"And how's your mother?" Grimm asked him.

Wolfshein chuckled. "I just came from seeing her," he said. "She's amazing, Arthur. She doesn't get older, she gets tougher. Always asks for you. Whenever I tell her how well you're doing, she says to me, 'See, I told you you should've been a lawyer.' "

When Grimm got to his car, he immediately reached beneath the driver's seat. The spiral notebook, five thousand in cash, and the bundle of receipts were still there.

"See, Myrtle," he said to the dog as he stared the engine, "that's the trouble with these people. They've lost the basic skills of investigation. Without their rats, they're nothing."

His next order of business, to get the bulldog bedded down for the night before he headed for Southampton and his meeting with Rickie's manager, Saul Diamond, and the fugitive junk lord, Jack Moriarty, also known as "Black Luigi," who was lately calling himself Dr. Bruce McMenimen. Grimm contacted one of his dog trainers who lived just a few blocks from him in the West Eighties. She agreed to take Myrtle until the dog could be moved to the kennels in Millbrook. He dropped off the dog, then stopped by his own place to shower and change his clothes. The confrontation with Zuluaga and the corpse of Karl Lundgren at the airport had brought on a nervous sweat.

Saul Diamond lived in and operated his company, Diamond Star Enterprises, from a sixty-four-room oceanfront mansion known as Dune Castle located in the exclusive Long Island resort community of Southampton. Before leaving the city, Grimm took steps to make sure he was not being followed. First, he swept the car with an electronic scanner to make sure Zuluaga's men had not attached a bumper-beeper so they could track his movements. He felt the discovery of Lundgren's body—and the disappearance of the 6.5 million—would keep Zuluaga and his men occupied temporarily. Still, when meeting someone as hot as Moriarty, there was no room for carelessness.

Twice he exited the Long Island Expressway and doubled-back to check for tails. Not until he was well out on the Island, and positive that he was clean, did he feel comfortable enough to slow down and light a joint of the Thai weed his friend Max Steiger had given him. He let his mind ponder the events of the long day. The sight of Karl Lundgren's hideous, bloated body and the smell of rotting flesh still had not left him. Grimm let the strong, spicy smoke stream from his mouth and up into his nose to try to kill the smell.

Strange, he thought, all the dead bodies he'd encountered in his life, not a few of them killed by his hand. He always felt the same sense of guilty embarrassment at his reflex reaction: Better you than me, pal. Better Karl Lundgren, aging hippie photographer, than old A.G. Better the incredibly small and doll-like Vietnamese. Better his best friend, the redheaded captain from Hot Springs, Arkansas, whose last words gurgled from a hole in his neck as he tried to tell Grimm his death wish.

So much death in his life, so many bodies, and each brought back memories of the first he'd ever come upon, that of his mother. His dark, lonely mother, just an obscure memory. He had discovered her body buried in a heap of empty luggage on the floor of the closet, dead, he learned later, of an overdose of barbiturates. A suicide. A self-murder. Grimm had been four years old when he found his mother's body. His father was away at the time and there was no one else in the house. Many years later, his father confessed that she had killed herself to punish him for his infidelity. About all Grimm knew of her, besides vague memories, was that she was Jewish, and she had defied her own father's wishes when she married Grimm's WASP father.

He traced much of what his closest friends recognized as an emotional numbness to that discovery, which was reinforced by a lonely childhood, and later enhanced by the surreal horrors he experienced in Vietnam. So much death; he couldn't help but wonder what harsh karmic debt he owed. Much of it, he knew, had to do with his need to live on the edge, the thin line where nothing but survival mattered.

Like everything else in this life, such experience came at a cost. He had difficulty sleeping. He had all the classic symptoms of Post Traumatic Stress Disorder: nightmares and flashbacks, restless energy and survivor guilt. It was hard for him to get close to people, much as he might care for them; it was hard for him to give himself up to an intimate relationship, particularly with women. He realized he was afraid of that kind of submission, afraid that a woman could do what his mother had done.

Before he had gone to Vietnam, he had been too caught up with achieving to question what it was he cared about in life. Up to that point his energy had been channeled into impressing his distant father with his grades and athletic prowess. The war changed all that. His inner life became hypnotic. Marijuana set off a revolution in his consciousness. He would never forget the first time he smoked a joint of the potent pot grown by Montagnard tribesmen in the Central Highlands. He looked around and knew nothing would ever be the same. From that time on he had questioned everything.

Grimm left the expressway and continued along the old Montauk Highway until he reached Southampton. Once there he drove through the village and down to the beach where he turned right onto Dune Road. Soon, he came to the entrance to Dune Castle, Saul Diamond's lavish estate.

The Tudor mansion glowed like a cruise ship in the misty night. Security was unusually tight. At the end of the long, winding driveway, four of Saul's men were positioned beside a jeep and a dune buggy equipped with two-way radios. They stopped Grimm's car and flashed a spotlight in his face. He recognized one of them as an ex-Marine called Gene Machine who had recently been released from federal prison after serving four years on drug smuggling charges. Machine nodded to Grimm and he was allowed to pass.

It was past midnight by the time Grimm parked near the mansion, and yet the place was still humming with activity. Dune Castle, sometimes referred to in the gossip columns as "Playboy Mansion East," had been in the news from the day Rickie Rude's manager bought it and squandered a fortune turning it into one of the most garish eyesores on the Long Island shore. Even before the legendary boy wonder of the rock 'n' roll business relocated the control center of his empire from Manhattan to Southampton, the estate made headlines when state police and federal agents, acting on an anonymous tip, interrupted an off-loading operation conducted from the Diamond property. Men in Zodiac boats and Boston Whalers ferried sacks of high-grade black hashish from the "Final Analysis," a sixty-foot yacht lying off shore, to a beachhead near the mansion. Saul was on tour with Rickie in Japan at the time; when they returned, Saul was questioned, but no charges were brought against him.

The mansion was a constant source of stories and scandals after Saul and his entourage took up residence there. Wild weekend drug and sex orgies were disrupted by local cops who invariably turned up small amounts of controlled substances and famous people in compromising situations. A Fourth of July bash at the "sin palace," as it was dubbed by the *Post*, resulted in the hospitalization of a daytime soap opera star who was picked up wandering around Southampton dazed and disheveled, suffering from multiple bruises and lacerations and from acute cocaine toxicity. Saul was currently embroiled in a lawsuit which charged him with gross negligence for allowing the woman to be beaten and whipped by her date on his premises. He also faced State charges for third-degree assault and possession of drugs and weapons. What Bernie Wolfshein had said about Rickie Rude was equally true of his extravagant manager: Saul Diamond's life-style invited trouble. And trouble was Arthur Grimm's business.

Saul's Chinese houseboy, Dr. Wu, opened the door. Wu ushered Grimm into Saul's office. At just about any time of the day, at least thirty people roamed around the vast interior of the house. In addition to the staff of company employees and servants, many of whom lived at the mansion, there were friends, relatives, actresses, models, groupies, and a motley crew of extras known as "Saul's Men": bodyguards, drivers, glorified gophers, bagmen, drug suppliers, roadies and soundmen.

The entrepreneur's inner sanctum looked like the lounge in a yacht club. It had a nautical decor somewhere between New England Yankee Whaler and South Florida Feedship. When Grimm was admitted to the office, the impresario was alone, seated behind his desk with all the bulk of a beached whale. Grimm, who hadn't seen Saul for a couple of weeks, would swear Diamond was growing by the day. In the past few years, he packed on a good fifty pounds and was now breaking the three-hundred-and-fifty-pound mark. At thirty-two, he had a boyish face stuffed with fat. He had a sparse, reddish-brown beard, short dark hair and bulging, cloudy brown eyes. In his red and gold Chinese silk dressing gown, his body glistening with scented oil, he reminded Grimm of a Buddha reigning over his domain.

Saul was talking on one of the telephones on his desk. His voice, his most attractive feature, was a melodious bass rumble full of self-assurance and money. A smile rippled through the wads of fat in his cheeks and he winked at Grimm as he intoned into the receiver, "Okay, baby. Just get into the limo and haul that cute little ass 'a yours out here. We'll all be waiting." He slammed down the phone and heaved out of his chair.

"A.G. My main man!" Saul bellowed, moving from behind the desk with surprising agility as he grabbed Grimm and hugged him. He was barefoot and nude under the robe. Saul took Grimm's head in his hands and gave him a big kiss.

"You hairy fuck. What, somebody's gotta get pinched so I can see you?" He let go of Grimm's head and reached down to stab a button on the intercom. "Judy, honey, Arthur's here. Sit. What can I get you? A drink? Something for the head?"

"No thanks, Saul. I'm all set."

"Fuck you. You're having a drink. I hate guys that say that. 'I'm all set,' " Saul whined. "Not in this house."

Judy Roth, Saul's executive assistant, came in from an adjoining room. She had changed her clothes since the news conference and was now wearing white jeans and a mauve pullover top. A small woman with short black hair and shrewd dark eyes, she kissed Grimm in greeting.

"Hello, Arthur," she said. "How's Sonny?"

"Better," Grimm replied. "She's getting rested."

"Jesus, that's what we all need," Saul said, as he poured Grimm a drink from a pitcher full of lime green liquid. "That's the only way anyone can get any rest around here. You gotta go to the slammer."

Judy sat on a leather sofa and stared at Grimm. "Tell us what you think, Arthur," she said.

"As far as Rickie's concerned, we don't even know what they have." Grimm looked from Judy to Saul. "Sonny hasn't got a hope. All we know for sure is that the government will try everything in its power to force Sonny into rolling over."

"Of course," Saul agreed. "That's their move. Without Sonny, they got nothin'."

"For Christ's sake, Rickie's innocent," Judy snapped. "Surely they must realize that."

Saul waved at her. "Honey, with these people, everybody's guilty. Tell her, Arthur. I've been trying to explain how they work—"

"Anyway," Judy cut him off, "Sonny's not going to go against Rickie. I know her. She loves Rickie."

"You never know what—" Saul began.

"No, Saul. I know. Believe me, you don't have to worry about Sonny."

"Let's hope you're right," Grimm said, "because this thing has just begun to turn ugly."

Dr. Wu entered the room carrying a tray with a pitcher full of margaritas. He also carried plates of fresh boiled shrimp and lobster tails.

"Give the man a refill, Wu," Saul said, pointing at Grimm.

"Man, the last time I got started on these things I couldn't drive home," Grimm said as Wu handed him a new glass rimmed with salt.

"That's the whole idea. Why do you think I got a house with thirty bedrooms? So no one has to go home. I hate guys who go home."

Wu put the plates of shrimp and lobster tails on Saul's desk.

"That's Saul's sea food diet," Judy said. "Everything he sees he eats."

"C'mon, honey, get some new jokes, will ya'?" Saul said as he munched on a lobster tail.

"He's the only man I know who can snort two grams of coke, then sit down to a full meal." Judy shook her head in amazement.

"Oh, hey, A.G., listen," Saul went on between mouthfuls. "Suzi an' Rickie're around here somewhere. Rickie wants to talk to you before you take off. Max's kid sister, Cassy, is on her way from the airport. She's bringing the rough cut of Suzi's new video we just shot in L.A. You should check it out. There's no telling when that other guy will show up. C'mon, you guys, eat," he ordered, pointing to the plates.

"What do you mean, begun to turn ugly?" Judy asked when Wu left the room. She stood and took one of the plates from Saul's desk, offering it to Grimm.

"Do you know this guy Karl Lundgren who worked for Sonny?" he asked them both.

Saul looked up at him. "Yeah, we know him. What about him?"

"Somebody shot him in the head," Grimm said as he selected a plump shrimp. "His body was found in the trunk of a car rented to Rude Productions."

Saul blanched. "Whaaaat?" His face seemed to melt and his eyes went blurry. "You mean Karl the—?" He made a gesture like a photographer snapping a picture.

Grimm, his mouth full, nodded.

"Oh, my God," Judy said. "When did this happen?"

"I found the body early this evening. It was in the trunk of a car he rented using Rickie's credit card. The car was parked in a lot at Kennedy. The bad part is that the DEA was right behind me. They must have followed me from the news conference."

Judy looked at Saul. "Wait'll the newspapers get a hold of this."

Saul was visibly shaken. His jaw hung slack and he was gaping at Grimm with a stupid look on his face.

"Ah, Judy, honey," he managed after a moment, "leave us a minute, will ya', babe? Call L.A. Tell 'em the shit's about to hit the fan."

Judy got up and left the room.

"A.G., what about the stamp collection? The money?" Saul asked desperately as Judy closed the door behind her. "Jesus, where's the fuckin' papers, bo?"

"Gone," Grimm said.

For a while, Saul looked as though he would pass out. His breath came in gasps and his head broke out in sweat. He covered his face with his hands and began to sob aloud.

"I'm totally fucked," Saul moaned. He struggled to his feet and began pacing beside his desk. His stomach was so big it looked as though he had to steer it when he walked.

"What am I gonna do, Arthur?" he blurted out. "Who could'a done this? What're we gonna tell Jack?" He stopped short and stared at Grimm as though he'd been struck with an idea.

"Listen. It had to be the heat. The fuckin' agents must'a whacked Karl and took the money."

Grimm said he thought that was unlikely as Julie Zuluaga had been there with his men when the body was discovered, and the agent had been most anxious to find out what was in the trunk.

But Saul was not convinced. "That could'a been a setup, like to throw off suspicion," he said and went to his desk where he took out a vial of cocaine. They talked a while longer, Saul pacing and ranting between snorts of coke. Buttons blinked on and off and glowed along the console of his telephone. But the promoter's main concern seemed to be how to break the news to Jack Moriarty, who was expected at

Dune Castle at any time. Saul never asked how much money Karl was supposed to have had with him, and Grimm did not offer the information. Saul, he knew, was hinting around trying to get Grimm to agree to talk to Jack, which they both knew would happen anyway.

So, with a tacit understanding that Grimm would be called upon to report to Jack, he left Saul to his phone calls and went to look for Rickie and Suzi. Judy Roth intercepted him as he walked away from Saul's office and led him into her work area. Grimm was surprised to see another huge Suzi Sapphire *Figure of Sound* poster on the wall of Judy's office. The poster looked like the one he had seen in the loft bedroom in every detail except that Suzi wore a pair of skin-tight black leather hot-pants.

"Karl took that picture," Grimm said.

"Yes," Judy said. She stood beside him looking up at the poster. Then she put her hand on Grimm's arm and turned him to face her. "What's going on, Arthur? What's he got us into now?"

"Saul?"

"Saul and his greedy gangster friends. They're going to ruin this thing, you know. Everything. Rickie's career. Does this mean Rickie and Sonny are going to be charged with murder?"

They moved to a small sofa and sat down.

"I don't know," Grimm said. "It's possible they may try to allege the murder happened as part of the conspiracy, but I don't see any evidence linking Rickie or Sonny. Tell me what you know about Karl."

"Not a whole lot," Judy said. "He had talent." She nodded toward the poster. "His stuff is striking. And he was easy to work with, laid-back yet dependable. I never had any problems with him. He came up with good ideas. He did the covers for Rickie's last two albums and he did all the *Figure of Sound* stills."

"Where did he come from? I mean, who brought him in?"

"He was a Rudie, you know, one of Rickie's groupies. Rickie put him to work with the road crew moving equipment around. He was always taking pictures, doing drawings and paste-ups. He showed his stuff to Rickie, eventually we started using some of it. But he was also, you know, involved." Judy waved her small hand toward the outdoors to signify peripheral activities.

"In what way? You mean, with Sonny?"

"Arthur, I stay out of that. I don't want to know about it. But, certainly he was involved with Sonny, also with Saul. You know, when they go off and whisper in the corner, when they ask me to leave the room. That shit. The other business. I suppose it's all going to come out. Karl was Sonny's man.''

"Was he involved in the 'Final Analysis' trip?"

Judy turned her palms up and shrugged. "I don't know, Arthur. Probably. He was around then."

Grimm looked again at the poster. "Was he hung up on Suzi?" She gave him a quizzical look. "What makes you ask that?"

"I don't know. The picture, I guess. Did he know Suzi?"

Judy laughed. "Know her in the Biblical sense? You're sweet, Arthur. These days we say, were they fucking each other?"

"That's not exactly what I mean. A lot of times people fuck each other without really knowing each other. I'm trying to get an idea of what kind of relationship they had."

"They did know each other from before. They both came from the same hometown in Connecticut. It was Karl who turned Rickie on to Suzi. Then Rickie made Saul go see her. They went to Max to produce *Figure of Sound*. Why?"

"I'm trying to get an idea of how Karl fit in."

"He was inner circle, close to Rickie. He made himself useful. I don't know if he was fucking Suzi. I can't keep up with who's fucking who around here."

"And then Sonny put him to work. Tell me about Sonny."

"Sonny." Judy shook her head. "We're good friends, I'm very fond of her, although I think she's out of her mind. She's an amazing woman, and she's devoted to Rickie. She's been trying to help him out. Rickie's whole trip is such a mess."

"In what way?"

"Financially." Judy jerked her thumb toward Saul's office in the next room. "That lunatic in there. I'm only telling you this because I trust you, Arthur, but Saul's got everything so completely fucked up I don't know if this company is going to survive. He's gambling all the time. He stays coked-up constantly. He's involved with all these weirdos and shady characters."

"Have you spoken to his mother?"

Judy sighed. "She won't listen to me. In Fanny's eyes, Saul can do no wrong. She won't even see how fat he is. I'm the only one who knows how much trouble he's got himself in."

"What about Sonny and Jack? I understand they're lovers."

"No, not anymore."

"How long's that been over?"

"At least a year. They still see each other, but it's purely a business thing now. I don't think Sonny still loves him, if she ever did. It was a peculiar relationship from the beginning."

"Tell me about it. I'm interested in these peculiar relationships."

"I noticed that. You're a pretty nosy character, Mr. Grimm."

"What can I say? It's my job."

"Well, lemme see if I can explain. Sonny's so much more, I don't know, classy? Jack comes on as this big shot mafioso, or whatever. He can be charming at times, but when you come right down to it, he's just a tough Irish hoodlum from Queens. Sonny blew his mind. He'd never met a woman like her before. She puts him down without really trying, and that got to him. I think Jack was out of his depth with her, but it's hard to tell what's going on with them because the business plays such a big part in their relationship."

They were interrupted when a buzzer sounded and a light flashed from the console on Judy's desk. She got up and pressed the button on the intercom.

"Okay, Wu. Send her in." Then to Grimm she said, "Cassy Steiger's here. Max's sister. Do you know her?"

Grimm caught himself feeling excited by the prospect of seeing Cassy. Relax, he told himself, she's the kid sister of one of your best friends.

Cassy Steiger and Jack Moriarty arrived at Dune Castle within minutes of each other, Cassy in a limousine from the airport, Jack in a plain dark sedan driven by one of his men and accompanied by Guy Stash. Their arrival was not announced over the intercom.

Chapter Five

Grimm was still in Judy Roth's office talking with Judy and Cassy when Saul opened the door, stuck his head in and said, "A.G., Luigi's here."

"I'll be right in," Grimm said. He would have preferred to stay where he was. Cassy was bubbling with enthusiasm over the *Figure of Sound* demo tape, and Grimm was charmed by her energy. Reluctantly, he excused himself and followed Saul.

Saul's spacious office now felt cramped and dense with male presence. In addition to Saul, there were Guy Stash, Jack, Jack's driver and Saul's man Gene Machine. When Grimm walked in, they were all seated except Saul. He moved around dispensing cocaine as though it were the Eucharist.

Jack did a small hit in each nostril, then looked up and grinned at Grimm. "A.G.," he said, getting up to shake hands. "Good to see you, bo."

The man's once black hair had turned almost completely gray in the two years since Grimm had last seen him, the two years that Jack had been on the lam. His eyebrows, though, were still jet-black and bushy with a raffish sweep. He had a young looking face for fifty, and smooth skin mottled with freckles and sun spots. It was a pug Irish face, round, snub-nosed, a little puffy around the eyes and jowly from too much drink. There was a deep cleft in his chin with a nobby mole in it like a rock in a crevice. When he smiled, his whole face seemed to break apart and reform: the eyes crinkled, the cleft parted, and his thin-lipped mouth drew back over expensively capped teeth.

They hugged each other. "You know my good friend, Guy," Jack said, half turning to the man seated next to him.

"Sure," Grimm said. "Hello, Guy."

Guy Stash glanced up at him. "Hey, what's up?" he said without standing or offering his hand. He was younger than Jack, closer to Grimm's age. Both men had spent a number of years in prison and looked young for their ages. Except for the eyes. The same was true of Gene Machine. He had a well-preserved appearance, though his eyes had an added blazed-out craziness, what Grimm thought of as the Vietnam look. Guy Stash was a slim man, around six feet tall, with rounded shoulders and a hunched-up posture. He was intense and sullen, chain smoked, and had a way of making everyone around him feel ill at ease.

These guys are masters at creating atmosphere, thought Grimm as he moved through the tension in the air. Jack was his usual affable self. Nothing was stated, but it was clear something was very wrong. Gene Machine had not been asked to sit in for the pleasure of his company. Machine was hardcore. Nobody to fuck with no matter who you were.

At Jack's request, Grimm explained how he had come upon Karl Lundgren's body and been surprised by Zuluaga's DEA team. Guy then recounted how he had arrived at Kennedy on time at 9:40 P.M. on the scheduled day. When he could not find Karl at the American Airlines terminal, he went to Brooklyn and made some phone calls. He tried to reach Sonny but grew suspicious and hung up when a man answered her phone and claimed to be her friend while pumping him for information.

"Agents," Saul growled. "Listen to me. It hadda be those rat cocksuckers. They clipped Karl, they took the money, then they went over and pinched Sonny."

"Wait a minute, why didn't they pinch Guy?" Jack asked. He was seated in a leather armchair with his legs crossed, looking like the most relaxed person in the room.

"Maybe they didn't know Guy was comin' in. Or maybe they wanted to get the fuck outta there once they took the money."

"It don't make sense, A.G." Jack's blue eyes sparkled. "What d'you think, bo?"

"It's possible. From everything I know of Julie Zuluaga, he's capable of pulling a move like this."

"But?"

"Like you say, it doesn't add up. Why leave the Lincoln at the airport? And why follow me out there if they already know what I'm going to find?"

"Yeah." Jack let out a deep breath and stood. "The whole thing stinks if you ask me."

Jack was about five-ten, maybe twenty pounds overweight. His clothes were expensive and well-cut, though a bit too flashy for Grimm's rather reserved taste. With his gaudy jewelry, he looked like a Las Vegas high-roller decked out to make an appearance at the gaming tables. It was hard for Grimm to picture him with Sonny.

But his power was undeniable. His face was pleasant and animated, and he exuded an Irish charm mixed with New York street smarts. He was not overbearing, and yet he was the boss, the center of attention in the room. Power flowed from him. Everything about him spoke of the unique and hard-won position he had attained in organized crime circles and the junk world hierarchy.

"C'mon, bo, let's you an' me take a walk on the beach," Jack said, speaking in his tight-lipped manner and putting his arm around Grimm's shoulders.

Strictly speaking, Jack Moriarty was not in fact a "wiseguy." He was not a made member of one of the five New York crime families. But he was one of them. He grew up in a large, poor family in the Corona section of Queens. Most of his childhood friends were Italian kids who became members or affiliates of one organized crime family or another. Jack, because he was Irish, was never "made" or "straightened out," the gangsters' terms for official induction into one of the families. Jack never got his badge, but over the years he got what he wanted, which was their fear and respect. He also had close ties with the violent West Side gang or "crew" of Irish criminals known as the "Westies." While still in his teens, Jack was running errands and providing muscle for a particularly ruthless Brooklyn crew said to be under the auspices of the Colombo family.

At twenty-two, he did six years in Attica for second-degree homicide. This was his rite of passage into the criminal establishment. Jack came home from Attica with a reputation for keeping his mouth shut and using his head. Later he did another four years mostly at the federal penitentiary in Lewisburg, Pennsylvania, a sort of graduate school for criminals, on an extortion, loan-sharking and gambling beef. It was while at Lewisburg that Jack met and took the young Guy Stash under his wing. When he got out the second time he was a "knock-around guy," trying his hand at the various rackets, living by his wits and by the gun. Then he discovered the junk business.

From the terrace of the mansion, Grimm and Moriarty descended a long stone stairway through the dunes to the beach. Jack's jewelry twinkled in the hazy moonlight. His hair was a satiny silver gray. Low clouds scudded before the moon. The surf rolled in and then breathed on the sand.

Grimm first met Jack in Bangkok at a bar known as Lucy's Tiger Den not long after the fall of Saigon. Both New Yorkers, they got drunk together. Jack claimed he was with an American construction company, and he may have been. But from the start Grimm made him for a junk merchant. They ended that night in Bangkok's largest disco and brothel which was owned by an Australian friend of Grimm's who was also in the milieu.

In the months that followed their first meeting, Grimm and Jack got together whenever Grimm returned to Thailand from trips he was making for the Pentagon into the Shan States and Burma. Later, after Grimm resigned his commission and was living in Bangkok, he learned from his Aussie friend that Jack was shipping large amounts of morphine base to Sicily where it was refined into heroin and smuggled into the United States.

"So, how's my girl doin'?" Jack asked as they started across the beach.

Grimm pretended he didn't understand. "Your girl?"

"Sonny. How's she handlin' bein' locked up?"

"She's doing all right."

Jack stopped walking and smiled at Grimm, nodding his head. "You better believe it, bo. Sonny's the best there is. I should know. I want you to take real good care of her."

Grimm felt like asking him what Sonny was best at, but instead he said, "She seemed a little shaky at first, but she's better now."

"That's the shit. Kid likes to get her nose into it. Used to piss me off, but there's nothin' you can do. Sonny does what Sonny feels like doin'."

"They're going to squeeze her, Jack," Grimm told him. "They

know she's connected with you, and they're going to threaten her with big time. They're going to look to hurt Rickie, to try to force her to give them you.''

Jack was still smiling. "So what else is new?"

Grimm shrugged. "As long as you're not worried."

"Bo, I told you, that's my girl. She loves me. No way she's gonna give me up."

Jack turned and walked along the beach. Even in the Southeast Asian days Jack had been something of a legend. He earned his nickname, Black Luigi, in Vientiane, Laos, when he tricked two Corsican hit men who had been sent to murder him into killing each other. Grimm had always had mixed feelings about the junk business and the people who worked in it, but he had to admit he liked Jack.

Their friendship had began in the East where there is no distinction between drugs except in their cost. The Chinese middleman who arranged for a load of Thai sticks also dealt opium, morphine base and heroin. The opium traders had been among Grimm's most trusted contacts. In the East it was all business, whereas in the States there were rigid divisions between smugglers, depending on the product involved. Marijuana purists like Grimm insisted that heroin and cocaine—almost all drugs other than cannabis—brought negative energy that ultimately came back to those who profited from their use.

"So who's gonna represent her?" Jack asked after they had walked for a few minutes without speaking.

"We don't know yet. Maybe Jerry Zuckerman. Aaron had him there for the bail hearing."

"Who the fuck is he?"

"An associate of Aaron's."

"Yeah, but is he any good?"

"He's good. Anyway Aaron will be right there keeping an eye on everything he does."

Jack turned and gave Grimm a sharp look. "See, 'cause you tell Aaron, I don't want no two-bit shyster. I want the best for her, the best next to him. I want somebody who knows how to talk." He kept touching Grimm's arm as he spoke. "And bo, I want you right there beside her all the way. Not that I'm worried, understand, just that whatever she needs, whatever she wants, you take care of it for her. You listenin' to me?"

"Jack, relax. We've already established that. I'll take good care of Sonny."

Again Jack stopped walking and flashed him a grin. "Yeah, bo, I know you will. Now, tell me the damage."

"Looks like somewhere around six-and-a-half million," Grimm said, enjoying the opportunity to rattle Jack's hard facade.

Jack's expression remained unchanged but it was as though all of a sudden his brain seized and the blood drained from his head. For a moment, Grimm thought he might faint. "Holy Jesus," he whispered, still gazing at Grimm. "Six-and-a-half mil?"

Grimm nodded.

"You sure?"

"It may be more. It could be seven."

"Get the fuck outta here. Bo, how could it be so much?" Jack's knees seemed to give way and he collapsed on the beach without waiting for an answer. "You gotta be pullin' my chain, A.G. I mean, how'm I suppose ta cover that kind'a money? What'm I gonna tell people?" he murmured, talking mostly to himself.

Grimm sat down beside him. He reached in his pocket and took out a joint. "People," he knew, meant mob partners and associates. Grimm had always been interested in Jack's longstanding relationship with the major crime families. It was based on business, as everything they did was, but beyond being a good earner Jack was well liked, trusted, and even feared by most of the top bosses. He had groomed Guy Stash to be his inside man with the Italians, and Guy, who became a made member of the Colombo group, rose quickly as a result of Jack's tutelage and the power that came with narcotics money.

Jack had also intimated to Grimm that he had a *campare*, a highly-placed old man whom he tithed and who watched out for his interests. It was said the Irishman could call a sit-down with anyone. Over the years he built his own organization into a rich and formidable entity and he was recognized as an independent, semiautonomous boss in his own right and as a major force in the world of international narcotics trafficking.

Jack's career in the junk business began when an old Navy buddy began smuggling heroin from Marseilles to New York. Through Guy Stash, Jack middled the packages of French goods to various connected wholesalers. After Turkey temporarily shut down as an opium

source, Jack went to Saigon behind the construction company front.
There he got caught up in a power struggle with the Unione Corse, the
Corsican gangsters who controlled exportation of morphine base.
Jack's eventual supremacy came from the fact that he not only arranged for the purchase of raw goods in the East, but through his Mafia
relations, he was able to act as a conduit for the refined junk to reach
American distributors through a complex international air-freight
smuggling system that brought the finished product home right in his
backyard at Kennedy Airport.

Once the Communists forced the Corsican and American junk dealers from Vientiane and Saigon, Jack turned up in Thailand looking for
new sources. When he met Grimm's Australian friend, his operation
resumed and expanded. Morphine base and pure heroin went west to
Sicily and into the hands of Mafia smugglers, and it went east to Hong
Kong where new air-freight routes and smuggling methods—through
Australia, Japan and the Hawaiian Islands—gave Jack's organization
direct access to huge West Coast distribution systems.

Now he was in shock from the biggest loss he'd ever faced. "No,
no," Jack said, grimacing and waving his hands at Grimm. "How can
you smoke that shit at a time like this?"

Jack's lips were so drawn the blood left them and in the pale
moonlight it looked as though he had on white lipgloss. Abruptly he
looked his age, older, crumpled and beaten.

"I gotta think this thing through," he said. "You gotta help me,
A.G."

Grimm said nothing. He smoked the joint and watched Jack fret.
Once, some years ago, Jack had tried to pay Grimm half-a-million
dollars for the Bangkok introduction that enabled him to become one
of the largest bulk importers of heroin in the country. Grimm refused
the money. The favor, he said, had been repaid many times over in the
form of referrals and acceptance by Jack's colleagues who became
some of Grimm's best clients and gave him respectability in the
criminal community. Jack and Grimm remained close friends.

For the last couple of years Jack had been on the lam from a federal
racketeering indictment, traveling under a host of aliases and passports, living in Europe and the Bahamas, moving around continually.

"Listen, A.G., what about this fat fuck?" Jack asked after a few
minutes. "Could he 'a done this?"

"Saul?" Grimm said with genuine disbelief.

"Hey, I put nothin' past this slippery prick. To begin with, he's nuts. Okay? An' between you an' me, he's in shit up to here." He made a salute, then he gripped Grimm's arm. "He knew this kid, right? Karl, the kid that got whacked. Fuckin' kid worked for him."

"Wait a minute. Karl worked for Saul? I thought he worked for Sonny."

Grimm was aware that some sort of business relationship existed between Jack and Saul, though he never understood how it all fit together. Saul's father had been a professional gambler, onetime speakeasy owner and loan shark before his death. He was said to have had close ties with Jewish organized crime figures like Longy Zwillman from New Jersey and even Meyer Lansky, and there was speculation that Saul's career had been helped along by friends of his father. For his part, Jack was fascinated by the whole L.A. scene, and the music and entertainment business that was Saul's world. Jack liked to party with hip young women, and one of Saul's specialities was cultivating groupies, what Judy Roth referred to as "the bimbo brigade."

"Yeah, yeah. I mean before. That's what I heard, he did things for Saul. Wasn't he part'a that boat trip that went down out here?"

The yacht bust, thought Grimm. Grimm remembered that Judy Roth said Karl was probably involved, then waved her hand toward the sea.

Jack got up and brushed the sand from the seat of his pants. "Fuckin' piles're killin' me. I can't sit no more, bo. Lissen, if I find out this fat motherfucker robbed that money, I'm gonna cut him up in little pieces an' feed him to the sharks."

Grimm was smoking, looking up at him. "Jack, I really don't think Saul would—"

"Bo, you don't know him. You don't know how devious this prick is, an' you don't understand the trouble he's got. The way he's been throwin' other people's money around, investin' in every half-assed, coked-up scam that comes down the pike. Lissenna me, A.G. Help me, pal. Do this for me. I wanna hire you, bo. You gotta find out who robbed this money. There's gonna be a serious beef over this, an' I need to know what happened."

Grimm stood. He knew there was a pitch coming and he didn't feel comfortable negotiating with Jack looming over him. Beneath his outward good humor and amiability, Jack was known as a ruthless business man and a savvy trader.

"Wait a minute, Jack. Slow down," Grimm said. "I'm working for Aaron, helping with the defense. I can't get mixed up in this."

"Why not? Who d'you think's payin' Aaron? Who d'you think's pickin' up Sonny's lawyer bill? Huh? Yours truly. I'm the head sucker. I'll give you ten percent of whatever you get back."

"Ten percent. You cheap prick. You people wouldn't do it for less than half."

Jack managed a half-hearted smile. "Fuckin' Jew. Okay, make it twenny. I got a hunnert grand out in the car. I'll give you that up front. I want you to put everything else aside and give all your attention to this."

"Hold it," Grimm said. "I haven't even agreed to do it yet. Let me talk it over with Aaron first. If we can work it out, I don't want anything up front. I'll do it on spec. But only if it can be done so I'm hired as an investigator on the drug case and not working for you. I've got to cover my ass."

"Hey, bo, I don't give a fuck how you work it out, jus' find the cocksucker who robbed that money."

"What about Sonny?"

"You take care'a her, too. You can handle it, bo."

"Okay, here's what I'll do. I'll give the hundred grand to Aaron as a retainer towards Sonny's fee. That way I can draw my expenses. And I get my usual fee, two grand a day."

"Two grand. Man, you're an expensive old whore."

"This is dangerous work," Grimm said with a smile. "Also, I want twenty-five percent of whatever I get back."

Jack's eyes narrowed. He shook his head and squinted at Grimm. "I see that shit don't bother your business head," he said as Grimm took a last hit on the joint and flipped it into the surf. "All right, you fuckin' hippie. Twenty-five percent." Jack stuck out his hand. "Agreed. And you vouch for everything with the Chinese."

"What?" Grimm said, drawing his hand back. "Hold it, what Chinese? I'm not vouching for anything. All I'm doing is trying to find out who killed Lundgren and took the six mil."

"Yeah, yeah, but that's what I mean. I might have to call you in to explain a few things to people. No big deal."

"Jack—"

"Bo, lissen, I'm in a bind here. These people know you, they'll listen to you—both of us—if we gotta explain things. You know what I mean. I got people uptown, people downtown. They'll be glad to know you're workin' on this. All you gotta do is back me up.''

"I'm working for Aaron, period. Jack, we've got to watch ourselves on this one. The feds are going to be all over me, especially after what happened at the airport. Zuluaga's already threatening me with grand juries.''

"Zuluaga can suck my dick.''

"I'm telling you, this is a big one for them. We've got to be real careful.''

Jack stood smiling at Grimm. Again he offered his hand, his gold jewelry glinting in the moonlight. ''That goes without sayin', A.G. In this business, all the time we gotta be careful.''

Grimm was not able to locate Rickie and Suzi in the extended household at Dune Castle. They were presumed to be asleep somewhere, though no one was sure what room they were in. He did, however, see the punks' images on giant-screen video.

Saul had a screening room like a small movie theater. Cassy Steiger had brought the rough cut of Suzi's music video to New York to show to Saul, Judy, and some of the other Diamond Star people before she did the final editing. The video, *Figure of Sound*, was a To the Max Production; it was produced and directed by Cassy's brother Max, and videotaped by Cassy. By the time Grimm and Jack returned from their walk on the beach, Saul had everyone gathered in the screening room to watch the video.

As a rock performer, Suzi Sapphire was a little bundle of talent. She danced like a whirligig, a spinning top of musical energy charged on the raw power of rock 'n' roll. Her voice had tremendous range and versatility, and a gripping tonality that was at times like a caterwaul, a yowl, then a scream, a throaty purr, a lusty moan. It was almost as though she sang in a new language of sounds. With her white halo of hair and muscular little dancer's body, she made Grimm think of a punked-out version of Tinkerbell. Everyone was convinced that Diamond Star Enterprises had another big success story in the making.

The video was clearly stamped with Max Steiger's artistic imprint. Max was not one to be content with run-of-the-mill videos made up of cuts from performances interspersed with camera gimmicks and shots of pretty girls. His videos were like short stories on film based around the lyrics or action of the song and, more often than not, the story had a message, like one of Max's own songs.

The *Figure of Sound* tape—which featured both Max and Rickie on guitar—played with an illusory nymph theme, a dreamy story of a supernatural female, Suzi, who seemed to be created from the clashing sounds of two electric guitars. As Rickie and Max played, Suzi seemed to materialize from the chords of the guitars to dance, sing and drive the men mad with longing. Max and Rickie, looking like futuristic minstrels wandering through a bombed-out ecological wasteland, are tormented with desire for what may be the last female in existence. Meanwhile, shots of L.A. and its environs appear like hallucinations, or like the aftermath of nuclear war. Suzi flirts, she entices, but is finally unattainable; she dematerializes each time Rickie or Max stops playing. In one extraordinary sequence, Rickie is about to fuck her but ends up humping his guitar. Suzi, as she fizzles into thin air, as she bursts into sound, taunts them that she is, ". . . new dimensional . . . body and mind creational . . . like from the soul sounds sensational . . ."

Grimm found the symbolism in the video vague but haunting. It was nearly dawn by the time he closed his eyes and tried to get a few hours' sleep in one of the guest rooms, and the image of Suzi dancing entered his dreams.

Cassy wanted to get a ride into New York with him in the morning; she asked him to wake her before he left. Jack and Guy Stash gave Grimm a briefcase containing a hundred thousand in cash, then drove off before daylight. Saul, who had downed margaritas and snorted coke non-stop all night, tried to get Grimm to tell him what he and Jack had talked about on the beach, but Grimm begged off, saying they had discussed payment of Sonny's legal fees.

At eight, Grimm was up and in the adjoining room to wake Cassy. Bright sunlight streamed in the windows. Grimm stood beside the bed looking down at his friend's sister as she slept. The sun shone off her thick, reddish gold hair spread over the pillow and across her tan shoulder. She looked so much like a pretty, healthy version of Max, it was unnerving. Grimm was attracted to her but he was doing everything he could not to admit it to himself. He reached down and brushed the hair from the side of her face.

"Cassy, my beautiful one, wake up," he said.

Her eyes opened. She saw him and smiled. "Good morning."

Grimm still had not removed his hand. He sat down on the edge of the bed, let the back of his hand caress her cheek, then he ran his fingers through her hair. They were both looking at each other's eyes.

"Your hair is so beautiful," he told her. "It's like . . . shiny strands of copper."

For a moment he thought he was going to lean down and kiss her. Cassy seemed to expect it, too, and a tension grew between them. But for Grimm it was too strange, even though Cassy was a beautiful young woman he still thought of her as a sweaty-palmed kid running around a basketball court. Amazing how they change, he thought. And then there was Max. He and his sister seemed almost unnaturally close. Grimm wasn't at all sure how his friend would take to the idea of his trying to seduce his kid sister. He smiled at her, chucked her under the chin and stood up. Then he walked over to the window.

Cassy jumped out of bed and dressed quickly. Grimm stood looking out the window at Gene Machine who was down by the side of the mansion working on what looked like various parts of a sailboat. He had a long mast set up on blocks and he was refinishing it.

"Arthur," Cassy said, and Grimm turned to see her wriggling into a pair of jeans, "Max said to ask you if it's okay for me to stay at your place in the city. I gotta be in the studio a lot, and this place is, you know, too far out. Know what I mean?"

"Sure, sweetheart. You don't even have to ask." But in a sense he felt it was her way of saying, Look, I trust you.

Cassy turned to him and Grimm caught a glimpse of her breasts under her hair as she lifted her arms to pull on a T-shirt.

He helped her carry her suitcases and equipment out to the car. No one was around, not even Dr. Wu. The huge house seemed eerily quiet. Outside it was brilliant. The humidity had lifted and left a dazzling late summer sun. While Grimm put the bags in the Jaguar—including the briefcase from Jack—Cassy ran back inside to leave a message for Judy Roth.

Grimm took a stroll down the sandy, unpaved road that led from a large turnaround and parking area in front of the mansion down to the side of the house where Gene Machine had the mast laid out. A double garage under the house had been converted into a workshop. Through the open door, Grimm could see more sections of the wooden yacht in various stages of repair. Machine was seated on a stool hunched over a workbench.

"Morning, Gene," Grimm said as he walked into the workshop.

Machine jerked up from what he was doing as though Grimm had caught him stealing something. "Hey, all right, how you doin', Grimm?" Machine got up and moved toward him. "Man, you're up early."

"Yeah, I've got to go into the city. What're you working on?"

"Ah, friend'a mine's boat. Just screwin' around, kind of a hobby."

There was a layer of fine sawdust over everything in the shop. Even Gene's dark hair and eyebrows looked frosted.

"Listen, do me a favor," Grimm said to him. "When you see Rickie, tell him he should give me or his lawyer a call as soon as possible."

"RUDE" ROADIE RUBBED OUT

glared the headlines of the *Post*. The front page picture showed Karl Lundgren as Grimm had found him curled in the trunk of the Lincoln. Grimm scanned the article, saw no mention of his name, and threw the paper in the trash can. The newspaper story said Karl's body had been discovered by airport security cops. Good, Grimm said to himself, they're covering it up.

Aaron Held's sleek black Caddy limousine slid up to the curb in Foley Square outside the United States courthouse. Grimm opened a rear door and got in beside the long-legged attorney. He had with him his own briefcase as well as the cheap Samsonite Jack had given him.

Held was stretched out in the rear of the limo, surrounded by briefs. "Where in hell have you been?" he asked without looking up from his paperwork.

"I told you, I had to go out to Saul's."

"I suppose you've seen the papers."

"I saw them."

"I got a call from a man named Doug Whelan this morning," Held said and finally looked up at him. "Does that name ring any bells?"

"No. Who's he?"

"FBI. Organized Crime Strikeforce, or some such nonsense. Just up from Washington. Interestingly enough, and contrary to popular belief, he tells me that my very own investigator, namely you, discovered this dead person at the airport.'' Held was peering at Grimm with an arch expression. ''Of course I pretended I knew all about it, since you supposedly work for me. Now, Arthur, do you mind telling me what the fuck is going on?''

''Well,'' said Grimm, ''how much time have you got?''

Held looked at his watch. ''Exactly thirty-two seconds. I'm due to argue an appeal upstairs at half past two.''

''I can't possibly explain everything in thirty-two seconds. It is true, I found the body, but Julie Zuluaga was right behind me.''

''Oh, him,'' Held said in a disgusted tone.

''Yes, your friend. He sends his regards. Later I got together with Jack, who gave me this.'' Grimm kicked the Samsonite briefcase with the toe of his cowboy boot.

Held's eyebrows shot up. ''I'd been meaning to ask you why you're carrying two briefcases,'' the lawyer inquired.

''This one is for you. It's got a hundred grand in cash in it, to be credited towards Sonny's account. Jack says to make sure you get her somebody who knows how to talk.''

Held laughed. ''Wonderful,'' he said. ''But just so I don't feel left out, tell me, if you don't mind, who is this dead person?''

''The guy I was looking for, Karl Lundgren.''

''Arthur, I know that. I mean, what's his role?''

''Good question. He worked for Sonny. He was a photographer, among other things. The car he was found in—well, you know that, that was in the papers. Aaron, there's a lot more. I had a fascinating discussion with Bernie Wolfshein last night. This case is blowing up in their faces.''

''Really? I'll have to hear all about it. Call me at the office later and we'll get together,'' Held said and he began gathering up his papers and stacking them into an oversize briefcase.

''What are you going to do with that?'' asked the lawyer, pointing a long finger at the Samsonite briefcase.

''Give it to you, of course.''

The two men climbed out of the limousine. Held left the money in the care of his driver.

''Arthur, you've made my day,'' Held said. ''If we weren't standing at the portals of justice right now, I'd give you a big kiss.'' Then he turned and began climbing the wide granite steps into the courthouse.

Grimm went next door to the prison and checked in to see Sonny. It was mid-afternoon on a court day so the attorney visiting room was not crowded. Grimm was able to occupy one of the small private conference rooms and hold it until Sonny arrived. Again, they kept him waiting for over an hour.

"They've put me in the hole," Sonny protested as she strode into the room. Her cheeks were flushed and she looked hot with anger.

"What for?" Grimm asked.

"That's what I'd like to know." She sat down in a huff. "Some sort of investigation, the lieutenant said. How many investigations are there? It sucks. They keep me locked up all day."

"Must be because of what happened," he said.

Sonny's eyes held his. "You mean Karl? Surely they don't believe I had anything to do with that."

"Of course they do. He worked for you."

"Yes, but Arthur—" Sonny stared at him. Grimm was lost in her eyes. "—they had me under surveillance. They know bloody well where I was."

"Obviously they don't think you pulled the trigger. But they might think you ordered it."

Sonny's eyes widened. "Really, Arthur, the man was a friend. Why would I want him murdered?"

"I'm not saying that's what I think. I'm saying that is probably the theory the government is working with—or one of their theories—that, for whatever reason, you or someone close to you decided to get rid of Karl. These things happen, especially when there's millions of dollars involved."

The lids closed over her kaleidoscopic eyes. She was looking rested, stronger every day. And as she got healthier, her energy seemed to intensify. "The money," she said, slowly opening her eyes, "which is gone I suppose."

She reached across the table and clutched Grimm's hands. "Jack is going to kill me."

"No," he said, "I don't think so. As a matter of fact, he sends his love. He also gave me some money toward your legal fees."

"Jack did that? Goodness, what's got into him?" She drew her hands back and folded them in front of her. "He must be worried."

"Not about you. He's very worried about the money, but he's really only concerned with your welfare."

Sonny gave a little laugh. "How sweet," she said facetiously.

Grimm decided not to pursue it. "I'll see if I can find out what's going on around here and try to get them to let you back into population."

"Yes, please do. People may get the wrong idea."

"I wouldn't be surprised if Vaggi was the one who ordered this."

Just then, outside the large anteroom, a guard began pulling curtains closed over the plate glass partitions, shutting in the attorney conference room. Sonny turned and looked through the small window in the door to the cubicle.

"What's that all about?" she asked. "Why are they drawing those curtains?"

"They're moving one of the protected witnesses," Grimm explained.

"Moving what?" she asked, turning to face him.

"The Witness Protection Program. Unit Three is right around the corner. That's where they keep the protected government witnesses. No one is allowed to see their faces, so they put bags over their heads and close the curtains. They shut the whole joint down whenever they move them back and forth to court to testify."

"Really? You mean snitches?"

He nodded. "Big time snitches."

"Good Lord, how can anyone live like that?" Sonny said. "Surely they must still look in the mirror."

Grimm stayed at MCC and talked with Sonny through the 4:00 P.M. prisoner count. He told her how he'd located the loft, searched it, and rescued Karl's dog, Myrtle. "Thank God for that," Sonny said. "Carmen will be relieved. She adores Myrtle."

She was stunned to learn it had been Grimm who discovered Karl's body. He explained that Julie Zuluaga's interests probably dictated that he keep both his and Grimm's name out of it while the investigation into Karl's murder proceeded.

"I'm not sure I follow," she said.

"The money. Zuluaga has his own agenda. If he doesn't know where the money is, then he wants to find out. And he doesn't want a lot of people knowing he's looking. On the other hand, if he does know where it is, then he definitely wants to keep the others from knowing."

Grimm did not tell her that Jack Moriarty had retained him to try to find the money. Nor did he tell her about the spiral notebook he found in Karl's stash. They talked about the arrangements being made for Carmen, about Rickie and Suzi, Suzi's new album and the *Figure of Sound* video. He told her everyone had asked for her and sent their fond regards.

"That's nice," Sonny said. "Please give Rickie my very special love."

"Now, is there anything you need? Reading material?"

"No, thank you. I got a big parcel of books and magazines from your secretary. She even brought me some new undies. You've been so good to me."

"Do you need cigarettes?"

"No more. I've decided to give up that filthy habit. Actually, I thought as long as I'm here I may as well make good use of this time and try to mend this sadly abused body of mine."

"Excellent idea," Grimm said. "So there's nothing I can do for you?"

Grimm looked at her and smiled. Sonny gazed back at him, tilted her head and pouted. "Well," she let on, playing the demure little girl, "I am feeling a bit . . . wistful."

It was her eyes that compelled him. They were like a whole new world he tripped into where other forces held sway. Grimm felt himself drawn toward her across the small table. It was the second time that day he thought he was on his way to a kiss, but this time was different. Nothing held him back. He kept moving toward her and saw her face come up to meet his. Then his eyes closed and he seemed to fall into the incredible softness of her slightly opened mouth.

Chapter Six

The federal courthouse for the Southern District of New York is an imposing structure that commands Foley Square in lower Manhattan. Fronted by an expanse of granite steps which climb between mighty stone columns and into marble-lined foyers and hallways connecting somber, wood-paneled courtrooms, the building announces to the accused that they stand opposed to the awesome authority of the United States Government.

Few would recognize the obscure, monolithic building behind the courthouse as an ultra-high security prison which houses some of the world's most notorious criminals. The Metropolitan Correctional Center, MCC, opened in the mid-Seventies to accommodate the rapid increase in the numbers of federal prisoners, is attached to the courthouse by an enclosed, suspended foot ramp, an umbilical cord which feeds jailed defendants into the womb of justice. The prisoners are brought down from their cells in the high-rise jail, handcuffed, and escorted by deputy U.S. Marshals through the tube into holding pens in the bowels of the courthouse. Usually after hours of waiting in the dirty, smoke-choked pens, they are brought before the court without ever stepping outside.

Arriving in Foley Square early one morning a few days after the discovery of Karl Lundgren's body, Grimm was not prepared for the scene that confronted him on the courthouse steps. He had just learned of the indictment handed down by the grand jury late the previous evening. Yet legions of Rickie's fans waited at the courthouse for the arrival of their idol. The crowd was filled with hardcore kids, skinheads and outrageous punks sporting psychedelic dyed Mohawks and spiked hairdos. Many were outfitted with so much chain and hardware, they'd never make it through the metal detectors inside the courthouse. They camped on the stone steps and drank beer in brown paper bags. They looked like an occupying army of freaks that had usurped the seat of justice from the judges and lawyers in some kind of cultural coup d'etat.

And there were plenty of cops, uniformed and plainclothes, deputy marshals and federal agents. Then there were representatives of the media and the usual courtroom buffs milling around and eyeing the punks apprehensively as though they were a different species. Grimm, dressed like a lawyer in a dark blue three-piece suit, started into the crowd just as a shout was raised from a group stationed alongside the building. Suddenly there was a mass migration toward a rear entrance.

It turned out to be a false alarm, someone impersonating Rickie. Minutes later, as Grimm stood at the top of the courthouse steps talking with Sonny's sister, Prudence, and Sonny's daughter, Carmen, Aaron Held's limousine appeared in front of the courthouse.

Rickie, his girlfriend Suzi Sapphire, Aaron Held and two briefcase-toting assistants got out of the stretch Cadillac. They were immediately surrounded by fans and newspeople. The cops attempted to clear a path up the steps. Rickie, dressed in a sleeveless, studded black leather motorcycle jacket, black jeans, and wearing wraparound dark glasses, waved to his fans and blew kisses with one arm while he held on to Suzi with the other. Suzi wore silver lamé boots over black fishnet stockings, a leather micro-skirt and a richly embroidered matador's jacket. Her white-gold hair stuck out in all directions as though electrified. She wore pink, heart-shaped sunglasses and a cigarette dangled from her cherry-red lips.

"This looks like a good time for us to sneak inside and try to get seats," Grimm said. He took Carmen's hand and they walked into the building.

Sonny's sister Prudence, called Pru, had arrived from London the day before. She was younger than Sonny and smaller, with short-cropped hair and a long elegant nose. Sonny's accent had been moderated through years of living abroad, but Pru spoke with an undiluted upper-class British drawl. She appeared mildly amused by the goings-on and lacked her sister's uninhibited charm. Carmen called her "Auntie Pru," and the child seemed to sense her aunt's uneasiness.

Exercising her subtle control, she explained to Pru who everyone was, and somehow filled in for her mother.

The arraignment on the indictment was docketed for half past nine in the cavernous first floor courtroom reserved for jury selections and celebrated or major multi-defendant trials. There were other proceedings in progress before the magistrate when Grimm, Carmen and Pru walked in and maneuvered to the front of the spectator benches.

"Where's Mummy?" Carmen wanted to know once they were seated and watching the repetitious proceedings.

"She's downstairs," Grimm answered. "Watch that door. She'll come in through there as soon as the judge calls her case."

"Is her lawyer here?" Pru asked. "Or will Aaron Held be representing her as well?"

"No. Sonny has another lawyer. I haven't seen him come in yet, but I'm sure he'll be here."

A procession of mostly black and Hispanic men and a few women entered from the side door and pled to charges of sales of small amounts of drugs. Most were assigned court-appointed lawyers and, as they had no funds or assets to meet the bails set, were remanded and sent back to MCC. There seemed to be an endless supply of hapless, poverty-stricken drug dealers waiting in the wings. All bullshit cases, Grimm thought, nickel-and-dime stuff the feds wouldn't have touched before the war on drugs spilled out onto the sidewalks with the advent of cheap cocaine.

One of Aaron Held's assistants, a bright young law student named Andrew Devlin, came in, looked around for Grimm, then hurried up to him. "Aaron wants to see you outside," he said.

But just as Grimm got up and excused himself, the bailiff announced: "United States of America versus Sonia Byrne-Downes, et al."

There was a commotion in the courtroom as lawyers, defendants, journalists and punks began swarming into the room. The side door opened and those defendants who remained in custody were brought in one at a time by the marshals. Rickie and his entourage were making their way along the aisle between the spectator benches to the row of defense tables set in a wide semicircle in the arena before the bench. Still Grimm had seen no sign of the government prosecutor, Vita Vaggi.

"Is the government ready?" asked the magistrate as though he too had noticed Vaggi's absence. He was an elderly, benign looking man who peered out at the gathering crowds through wire-rimmed spectacles.

Then the side door opened again and Sonny was led into the room by two deputy marshals. Rickie, Aaron Held and his two assistants seated themselves at the defense table while Suzi Sapphire squeezed in next to Grimm and Carmen in the front row of the spectator benches. Other defendants and their lawyers assembled at the defense table. In all, including Sonny, there were twelve defendants and at least as many lawyers.

Newspeople stood at Rickie's elbows ready to record any tidbits of irreverence he might toss off in passing. When he saw Sonny being brought in, Rickie got up and left the defense table. He and Sonny embraced and kissed like long lost lovers. Held turned to Grimm and rolled his eyeballs as if to say: Be ready for anything. Then he beckoned to him.

It was a free-for-all. "Mummy!" cried Carmen when she saw her mother. The little girl jumped from her seat and rushed to hug Sonny.

"Is Ms. Vaggi present?" asked the magistrate, who had been observing the action and now seemed obliged to assert his authority.

"Your Honor," piped an Assistant U.S. Attorney Grimm recognized as one of Vaggi's underlings. He was just entering the court.

No one had settled down. Grimm stood and approached Held.

"The word is Vaggi's not ready," Held whispered to Grimm while everything continued around them. Grimm kept his eyes on Sonny as she, Rickie and Carmen moved toward them.

"Listen, babe," Held continued. "Jerry's not going to be able to make it. He's tied up on a murder trial in Queens. I need you to stand in for him today and appear for Sonny."

Grimm turned to look at him.

"Ms. Vaggi asked me to beg the Court's indulgence," said the assistant prosecutor as he arrived at the front of the courtroom and addressed the bench. "The grand jury handed down the indictment in this case late yesterday afternoon. As your Honor is aware, there are a number of defendants. At this moment, the indictment is being prepared and copies are being made for each of the defendants and counsel. Ms. Vaggi asked that the hearing of this matter be adjourned until eleven-thirty to give the government ample time to complete the preparation of the documents."

"You think you can get someone else by then?" Grimm murmured to Held.

"Arthur, for God's sake. Just for today. It won't kill you."

"That's not the point. Look at all the reporters. My name's going to be mixed up in this thing. You know how much harder that makes it for me to work. And you were the one who said you didn't want Vaggi to start screaming conflict of interest."

"Let me worry about Vaggi. I'll—"

Held was interrupted by the magistrate who asked, "Are all the defendants and their counsel present?"

A dozen lawyers stood up.

"Good morning, your Honor," Held said, turning away from Grimm and immediately taking charge in his position as lead counsel. "Aaron Held for the defendant Rickie Rude." Held then stepped aside and left Grimm exposed to the bench.

"Arthur Grimm, your Honor, appearing for the defendant Sonia Byrne-Downes," he said, realizing he'd been sandbagged.

While the other lawyers entered their appearances, Grimm turned back to Sonny. This was the first time he had seen her in anything other than the institutional outfit, and he wondered if that accounted for how lovely he thought she looked—beautiful, he was tempted to say, though not in any conventional way, and he guessed half the men in the room would not agree.

In the first place, she was too big; seeing her next to Rickie, Grimm could appreciate just how large a woman she really was. Not only was her bone structure big, but she had a big face, one of those horsey British faces that is saved from being lantern-jawed by high cheek-bones and a wide, voluptuous mouth. Just recalling the feel of that moist, yielding mouth on his caused his cock to stir in his crotch. And more: she was intimidating.

She wore an olive-green, one-piece jumpsuit which was pegged at the ankles, snug at the hips and waist, open at the neck down to her cleavage. The long sleeves were pushed up over her forearms. On one shoulder there was a peace symbol patch, a white dove with an olive branch in its mouth, and on the other, bright fuchsia lieutenant's stripes. She wore what looked like a black karate belt tied like a sash around her slim waist, accenting her full, strong hips and thighs. She was made up a bit punkishly, glossy red lipstick and rouged cheeks, and her hair was frizzy as though it had been teased. She looked like some sexy mock commando, a masochist's fantasy from the cover of a pulp magazine. A wild getup for court, thought Grimm, though compared to Rickie, his fans and Suzi Sapphire, Sonny looked almost tame.

This was also the first time Grimm had seen her since the attorney visiting room kiss. He'd been trying to get down to the jail to visit her over the last couple of days, but he'd been unable to break away from the demands of his business. Sonny moved toward the defense table, stopping to brush cheeks with her sister and kiss Suzi. Then she turned and smiled at Grimm. He noticed she'd made no attempt to cover the birthmark over her eye, and again it struck him as strangely attractive, giving her eyes a fascinating look of both passion and vulnerability. Her little group was flanked by two deputy marshals: a black woman deputy and an older, barrel-chested man Grimm knew. Grimm moved toward her.

Both of Sonny's arms went out to him and she seemed to ease herself into his embrace until her body pressed against his.

"Grrrr," she growled into his neck. "Where have you been, you mean man?"

Grimm gave her what he intended to look like a friendly kiss, but they lingered. Meanwhile, the attorneys had finished entering their appearances and the magistrate was conferring with his clerk.

"Are my ears deceiving me, or are you my lawyer now?" Sonny asked and she stepped back to look up at him.

"Just for today. Your real lawyer's on trial."

"We'll see about that."

In a colloquy with the magistrate, Aaron Held said that although he felt it would have been preferable for Ms. Vaggi to notify the parties earlier in the day and advise them of the delay, he guessed there was nothing anyone could do about it. The magistrate agreed and adjourned the arraignment until half past eleven, recommending that everyone remain close at hand.

"Shit. I hope they don't take me back to the bullpen," Sonny said. "My poor bottom's killing me. I've been sitting on those hard benches since six this morning."

"Did they let you out of the hole yet?" Grimm asked.

"Yes. The next day. How did you manage that?"

Grimm gave her a wink. "Connections," he said and nodded at Aaron Held, who was just coming over to them.

"Hello, Sonny," Held said as he took both her hands and they kissed cheeks.

"I'm her attorney," Grimm said to the two deputies. "Frank, do us a favor and see if you can arrange to allow Sonia to stay in the courtroom and visit with her daughter while we're in recess."

The barrel-chested man raised his eyebrows but said nothing.

"Good morning, marshals," Held butted in. "What Mr. Grimm really means is that he needs this opportunity to confer with his client. Right, Arthur?"

"I'll have to check with my supervisor," the deputy said, indicating another marshal standing near the jury box.

"No, no. Let me." Held said, and he strode away.

As it turned out, there were several more delays. Vaggi herself finally appeared at around one o'clock only to ask for more time due to some last minute revisions that had to be made to the indictment. The magistrate, though clearly perturbed, gave her until 3 P.M.

Once again the crowds marched out of the courtroom to the foyer where attorneys and newspeople vied for pay phones while the defendants who were free on bail stood around smoking cigarettes and drinking coffee. Sonny was allowed to remain in the courtroom guarded by the two deputies. She sat with Pru and Carmen. The other defendants all came by and paid their respects.

"Not like dear Vita to get caught with her panties down," Aaron Held remarked to Grimm after Vaggi made her appearance. "She seems a bit out of sorts. What do you make of it?"

"I told you, they're all fucked up. She has no case against Rickie. I think I know what her problem is, but I'll let you know later. I'm getting together with Bernie Wolfshein for a drink this evening. We're still on for dinner?"

"By all means," Held said. "Julia will be there. You're bringing Max Steiger's sister, correct?"

Because of the fans and journalists, Rickie and Suzi—along with Rickie's friend, rock critic Moon Landing, also a co-defendant—had been whisked away in Aaron Held's limousine after the first adjournment. Held had one of his assistants stationed near a pay phone so he could call the car and summon them once it looked as though the proceedings were set to begin.

Held fidgeted. He was in and out of the courtroom every ten minutes making telephone calls, conferring with the other attorneys. He obviously resented this sacrifice of his valuable time. Grimm too used the pay phone to rearrange his schedule and make some business calls, but then he was content to be near Sonny and observe how she behaved.

What she has, Grimm decided, is a fine-tuned self-awareness. She seems to know exactly who she is and what she's doing, strange as that may seem under the circumstances. Even with the journalists who tried to interview her, she was civil and witty, but oblique and offbeat in her answers. Was she once Rickie's lover? one asked. More like his wayward soul sister, Sonny replied. How was she finding prison life? asked another. Sonny said she just woke up in the morning and there it was. But seriously, it was soft compared to life in a British boarding school. Did she think she had a chance of winning this case? Anything is possible if you can just keep your confidence and sense of humor.

At last it looked as though the government was ready. Vaggi's assistant preceded her into the courtroom and distributed copies of the twenty-eight-page indictment. Then, the Dragon Lady of the Southern District appeared, still looking a shade disconcerted. The incarcerated male defendants, Miguel Hoyos, the Colombian, Dominic "Donnie Boy," "Little Dom" Randazzo, from the East Harlem neighborhood, and Brad Caine, owner of a Lower East Side rock 'n' roll club called "Little Babylon," were returned to the courtroom from the bullpen. Soon everyone was present except Rickie and Moon.

"Your Honor," Held explained, "due to my client's renown, it is difficult for him to have to linger in public. He has been waiting in my car nearby. I've just been informed he will be with us momentarily."

Vaggi could hardly protest. She set about arranging her files, sorting her papers, getting ready, Grimm knew, to counter any application for reduced bail he might make on Sonny's behalf.

In her early thirties, a divorced woman of Lithuanian descent, Vita Vaggi was known as perhaps the most ambitious and hardworking of the Assistant United States Attorneys in the Manhattan office. She was the first woman to be named chief of the Narcotics and Dangerous Drugs Task Force, and in the first year she had held that position, she won a record number of important convictions including two life-without-parole sentences imposed on the ringleaders of large-scale New York junk syndicates. She was tireless, known to work sixteen- and eighteen-hour days for weeks on end. She was also painstaking in attending to the small details of a prosecution, a trait which made up for her rather stiff, uninspired courtroom style. Held said he liked working with Vaggi because he claimed she was the most honest prosecutor in the New York office; she would not stoop to manufacturing evidence or to subornation to win a conviction. Held maintained Vaggi had scruples. She was a fierce fighter, he said, but not a dirty fighter.

She stood about five-six, had perfectly erect posture with a slim, attractive figure and very long, thick black hair. She had an oval-shaped face with prominent cheekbones, cool brown eyes and a big, hawklike nose. This day she was dressed in a blue suit and white blouse with ruffled cuffs and bosom. She wore a red hair band, matching high heels and stockings that made her legs look white like a nurse.

Grimm had never been able to break through her stony manner. He'd met her a few times socially, and when he tried to talk to her she cut him dead. She had cross-examined him twice when he testified at drug trials and had done her utmost to impeach his character. He knew she regarded him as something less than legitimate, one step removed from the criminals he worked for.

Vaggi, like her boss, the United States Attorney Ralph Vallone, was messianic in her zeal to clean up the streets of New York. She was quick to let Grimm know she saw him as a renegade who acted as though he were immune from the rules because he wasn't a member of the club.

A murmur at the rear of the packed courtroom signaled the arrival of Rickie, Suzi and Moon. Here was a trio for Vaggi to contend with, thought Grimm. No amount of experience with the underworld could prepare her for this.

Rickie still had his hair done in the leopard skin mode he'd first appeared in at the Algonquin news conference. Arriving at the defense table, he removed his motorcycle jacket with an exaggerated flourish. Beneath it he was wearing a T-shirt, dyed purple, and on the back, written in a fancy script of sequined letters, was the word: PUNKTUAL-ITY! Rickie turned around so that Vaggi and even the magistrate could see the back of his shirt. Then, as Vaggi began to speak, Rickie interrupted her.

"I'm sorry I'm late, Judge," he said. "I always try to be *punk-tual*."

Most of the room broke up with laughter. Even the magistrate smiled. After waiting most of the day for the government, Rickie had turned everyone's anger and frustration into a joke at Vaggi's expense. The impudent little punk sat down, whipped off his dark glasses, and beamed at Vaggi, whose reaction was stone-faced. She was all business.

The prosecutor began with a summary of the indictment. There were, she said, a total of seven separate counts:

Count One, the overall conspiracy count, charged all twelve defendants with conspiring together to possess with intent to distribute various Schedule One and Schedule Two controlled substances, to wit: heroin, cocaine, marijuana, hashish, LSD and psilocybin mushrooms.

Count Two was a substantive count charging Sonny, Moon and other defendants—not including Rickie—with actual possession of illegal drugs: the heroin, coke and miscellaneous drugs found in Sonny's apartment as well as quantities of drugs recovered in raids conducted at different dwellings.

Count Three charged an importation conspiracy naming Sonny, Miguel Hoyos, a/k/a Micky, and two others: Jason Trowbridge, a/k/a "Jay" and "Drawbridge," an Englishman who was said to be an earl; and Peter Dickinson, a/k/a "Sneaky Pete" and "Sneakers," a boat captain from Fort Lauderdale, as well as others "known and unknown to the grand jury" with conspiring to import marijuana, hash, coke and heroin into the United States from abroad.

Counts Four, Five and Six were substantive importation counts. The overt acts listed in furtherance of these counts charged trips made to Hong Kong, Bangkok, Mexico City, Delhi and Bombay, Beirut, Medellin and Cali, Colombia, and half a dozen other cities that read like an itinerary for a world tour of dope producing nations.

Finally, Count Seven, naming only the defendant Sonia Byrne-Downes, a/k/a "Sonny," "Downtown Sonny," Vaggi read aloud.

"The Grand Jury further charges: From in or about January 1979 and continuously thereafter up to and including the date of the filing of this Indictment, in the Southern District of New York and elsewhere, the defendant Sonia Byrne-Downes, also known as Sonny, unlawfully, intentionally and knowingly did engage in a continuing criminal enterprise in that the defendant Sonia Byrne-Downes, a/k/a Sonny, did violate Title 21, United States Code, Sections 812, 841, 841(a)(1), 841(b), 846, 952, 960 and 963 as alleged in this indictment and which allegations are incorporated by reference herein, and did commit other violations of said statutes, which violations were part of a continuing series of violations of said statutes undertaken by the defendant Sonia Byrne-Downes, a/k/a Sonny, in concert with at least five other persons with respect to whom Sonia Byrne-Downes, a/k/a Sonny, occupied positions of organizer, supervisor and manager and from which continuing series of violations Sonia Byrne-Downes, a/k/a Sonny, derived substantial income and resources.''

Here was the ominous 848 Count, known as the "kingpin statute" or "CCE," for continuing criminal enterprise. If convicted on Count Seven, Sonny could be sentenced to anywhere from a minimum of ten years up to life in prison with no possibility of parole. There was a forfeiture clause annexed to this count which directed that upon conviction the defendant "would forfeit to the United States all profits and proceeds of profits obtained by her in such enterprise, and shall forfeit her interest in, claim against, any and all property and contractual rights of any kind affording a source of influence over such enterprise.''

As Vaggi finished reading, Sonny looked up from her copy of the indictment and whispered to Grimm, "I did all that?"

"Sonia Byrne-Downes," the magistrate intoned.

Grimm touched her beneath the table. "Stand," he said, also rising.

"Arthur Grimm, your Honor, appearing for the defendant Sonia Byrne-Downes."

Vaggi was on her feet. "If the Court please, the government is concerned that the representation of Ms. Byrne-Downes by Mr. Grimm may pose a conflict of interest. Mr. Grimm, though a member of the New York Bar, is more regularly employed as a private investigator for the firm of Held and Associates, representing the defendant Richard Rudinowski."

"Excuse me, judge. That is not quite accurate," Grimm rejoined. "I have my own company and do contract work for Mr. Held's firm. Furthermore, I am representing Ms. Byrne-Downes solely for the purpose of this proceeding as her attorney of record, Mr. Zuckerman, has been kept absent due to a trial in Queens."

"Yes, yes," said the magistrate with a vexed tone. "This can be taken up with the trial court. We're here this morning—or I should say, this afternoon—simply to arraign the defendants on the charges and to discuss bail. Now, Mr. Grimm, has your client read the indictment? Does she waive formal reading of all the counts at this time?''

"Yes, your Honor. My client has heard enough."

The magistrate scowled and looked at Sonny. "Sonia Byrne-Downes, do you understand the charges against you contained in this indictment?''

Sonny hesitated before she answered. She tilted her head to one side and said, "Actually, your Honor, no, I don't."

The magistrate gave her a bewildered look. "Exactly what is it you don't understand, Ms. Byrne-Downes?''

From the corner of his eye, Grimm could see Aaron Held squirming in his seat. The defendants were placed at the table in order of their appearance on the indictment with Sonny at the right side and Rickie somewhere in the center. A restive moment passed.

"Well," said Sonny, "I've read it. But what does it all mean?''

A few of the other defendants tittered. Rickie was grinning.

"What it means, young lady," the magistrate said, "is that you stand accused by the United States Government with a number of serious violations of the laws regulating the importation, possession and distribution of dangerous drugs and narcotic substances. If convicted of these crimes, you may be sentenced to a substantial period of incarceration. Now do you understand?''

Sonny hunched her broad shoulders. "I understand it on that level, of course. But what I mean is: isn't it all rather silly?''

Grimm couldn't believe his ears. There were guffaws in the courtroom. The magistrate, too, seemed dumbstruck by this remark.

"Silly?'' said the magistrate, looking to Grimm. "Mr. Grimm, I suggest you explain to your client the severity of these charges. Count Seven, particularly. There is nothing silly about the possibility of life imprisonment with no parole.''

"This is a philosophical question, your Honor, and not something that need be discussed here. As to the charges in the indictment, Ms. Byrne-Downes pleads not guilty.''

The magistrate turned his gaze back to Sonny. "Is that your plea, Sonia Byrne-Downes?''

"Certainly, your Honor,'' she said with a smile. "Not guilty.''

Each of the other defendants stood and pled not guilty—except for Rickie.

"Richard Rudinowski," said the magistrate.

Held stood and addressed the court. "I would like to make an application to have the indictment amended, your Honor. The whole world knows my client as Rickie Rude. This is his professional name. He has not used Rudinowski since he was eighteen years old. And we can show that Rude is his legal name and not an alias, as the indictment purports."

"Mr. Held, again, this is a matter to be taken up with the trial judge. And I hope to get around to selecting someone to try this case before the afternoon is over. Perhaps Ms. Vaggi will agree to change the indictment. What I want to do is get on with these proceedings. Now, Mr. Rudinowski—or Rude, if you prefer—have you read the indictment? And if so, how do you plead to the charges?"

Rickie looked like a little boy as he stood beside his towering attorney. Pinned to the front of his dyed undershirt he had a button that read: MARIJUANA PLANTS—NOT NUCLEAR POWER PLANTS. He was also wearing a necklace made to look as though a large bolt had been screwed through his neck.

"Insanity," he responded with a gleeful ring in his voice.

Then, as the first burst of laughter was dying down, Rickie pulled a device from his pocket. It looked like a radio and made electronic beeping sounds as he fiddled with the dials. He spoke into the device.

"Spock. This is Captain Kirk. *Beam me up immediately.*"

Even Vaggi seemed to lose her composure. Nearly everyone laughed and for a moment there was an unmistakable atmosphere of absurdity loose in the room.

The magistrate, however, was quick to regain control of the mood. "You may indeed be insane, Mr. Rude," he said, "but we need not decide that at this stage in the proceedings. Mr. Held may apply to the Court for a competency hearing on your behalf. I take it that you plead not guilty."

"Yes—" Aaron Held opened his mouth.

"Innocent would be more like it," Rickie interrupted.

"Fine," the magistrate said. "Not guilty."

The Court heard from the remaining defendants, who all pled not guilty. Once all the pleas had been entered, the magistrate was ready to discuss bail. He ordered that the bonds posted for those defendants who had been released on bail should be continued. Vaggi asked for an increase in defendant Jason Trowbridge's bail based on what she saw as a flight risk. The magistrate said that he was satisfied Trowbridge had "roots in the community" (an American wife, two kids, a job as an actor's agent, and assets in the form of New York real estate) that argued against his being tempted to flee.

Grimm tried to make the same argument on Sonny's behalf. She was the mother of a young daughter; Carmen was pointed out to the Court. Carmen attended the Ethel Burnham School for Girls in Manhattan where she was an honor student. Grimm assured the magistrate Sonia was a devoted mother who would not put her child's future in jeopardy by fleeing. The two-and-a-half million dollar cash bail set for her was "unattainable" and therefore, Grimm maintained, in violation of the Bail Reform Act, which requires bail to be set within a defendant's means. He moved the Court to reduce Sonny's bail to five hundred thousand dollar surety bond to be posted as deeds to Manhattan properties.

"Does the government wish to respond?"

"Most assuredly, your Honor," Vaggi said, her dark eyes smoldering as she stood to the challenge. "The government strenuously opposes any reduction in this defendant's bail. Ms. Byrne-Downes is not an American citizen, and in fact she is in this country illegally as her visitor's visa expired over six months ago. She had nearly four hundred thousand dollars cash in her possession at the time of her arrest, evidence that she is in a position to obtain large amounts of money. The government has information that Byrne-Downes has a number of passports in different names, only two of which were recovered during the search of the premises where she was staying. She has no roots in the community. She is an international criminal with no permanent home, no family ties—as we know them—who has lived with her daughter in several foreign countries and, the government is convinced, would not hesitate to do so again."

Vaggi stepped back from the prosecution table. She turned and cast a quick glance at Sonny and Grimm as though for emphasis. Momentarily, Grimm's eyes met hers. The mood in the room was solemn.

"Furthermore, your Honor," she continued, looking back at the bench, "the government is in possession of information that Byrne-Downes once escaped from detention in a foreign country by means of bribery and trickery. The government therefore maintains that the defendant Byrne-Downes poses a substantial risk for flight."

The prosecutor placed both her hands on the table and leaned forward. Everyone in the room hung on her words. Grimm was struck by her serene efficiency. Vaggi summed up: "The nature of the conspiracy charged in this case, the importation and distribution of massive amounts of deadly drugs, the seriousness of these charges—which your Honor heard the defendant admit she finds 'silly'—and the position the government believes Byrne-Downes occupies in this conspiracy, that is, organizer, supervisor, the brains, if you will, behind this highly sophisticated criminal enterprise, as well as other facts known to the government concerning the illegal activities of this woman and her role in international drug trafficking, based on this, your Honor, the government would submit that the defendant Sonia Byrne-Downes represents a threat to society. For all these reasons, the government opposes any reduction in Byrne-Downes' bail, and would further move this Court to order that the defendant be held without bond as a flight risk and a danger to the community. Thank you, your Honor."

There seemed to be no question about it. Grimm suddenly felt foolish, there was no way he could argue for reduced bail. He felt sweat breaking out along his spine.

Sonny turned to him and her eyes widened. "Goodness," she whispered. "Perhaps we ought to quit while we're ahead."

"Your Honor," Grimm said, getting to his feet with no idea what he would say. He just opened his mouth and hoped the words would come out, "The prosecutor is talking as though my client had already been tried and convicted. We must not lose sight of the fact that at this stage these charges are merely allegations. One of the primary principles of the American justice system is the presumption of innocence. A defendant is entitled to reasonable bail because in this country we believe everyone must be considered innocent until proven guilty. Ms. Vaggi alludes to information possessed by the government concerning Ms. Byrne-Downes, but she does not tell us the source of her information. Where is the proof? I submit the ends of justice are better served by reducing Ms. Byrne-Downes' bond to a reasonable amount and allowing her to post bail so that she may be released to help in the preparation of her defense against these charges."

Grimm surprised even himself. Sonny gave him a winning smile as he sat back down, but he knew how weak his argument was. Vaggi had all the ammunition.

"Thank you, Mr. Grimm. As ordered, the bonds previously set

shall be continued at their present amounts,'' the magistrate said and dismissed the subject. ''Now, if there is nothing further, the clerk will draw the name of the judge who will preside over this case.''

All eyes went to the clerk as he revolved a wooden drum, which looked like a small beer keg, then stuck his hand in and withdrew a slip of paper. He handed the paper to the magistrate, who glanced at it, whispered in conference with the clerk while they consulted a calendar, then made the announcement, ''Honorable Dudley H. Gass, United States District Court Judge. Court is adjourned.''

''All rise!'' the bailiff called out as the magistrate rose and descended from the bench.

Grimm turned and looked at Aaron Held. The lawyer shrugged and rolled his eyes toward the ceiling. It could have been worse. Judge Dudley H. Gass was a crusty old Brahmin appointed to the bench by Eisenhower in 1958. Gass was intelligent, an exacting jurist, though known for his pro-prosecution bias in criminal cases, his imperious courtroom manner, and the stiff sentences he handed out, particularly in drug cases. One thing they had going for them was that Gass was a notorious male chauvinist who delighted in humiliating female prosecutors and defense attorneys. He and Vaggi were hardly congenial.

Still, Grimm thought as he stood and his glance settled on Rickie, just wait 'til the pompous old goat gets a load of the Prince of Punk.

Chapter Seven

C*ui bono?* Grimm posed the basic question of detective work. Who benefits from having Karl Lundgren murdered? For obvious reasons the person—or persons—who stole the six-and-a-half million benefit considerably. But was the rip-off the only motive for killing Lundgren? Grimm did not think so. Someone had gone to unnecessary lengths to send a message with that corpse.

He was sitting at one of the outside tables at Tavern-on-the-Green, nursing a drink and waiting for his friend Bernie Wolfshein. He'd spoken to the drug agent that morning to ask for a favor, and Wolfshein suggested they meet for a drink. Grimm's apartment was only a few blocks from the restaurant; after the hearing he'd gone home to change and leave a note for Cassy. Later they had a dinner date with Aaron Held and his wife, Julia.

Though Cassy had been staying at Grimm's since the night at Saul Diamond's Dune Castle, he'd scarcely seen her. It reminded him of the time he lived with Danielle, they had been on different schedules, although once in a while they rolled into each other in bed. The only signs he found of Cassy's presence were half-eaten health food items in the refrigerator, an occasional note, and an agreeable female scent lingering in the bathroom. She was gone before he came out of his room in the morning, and usually she was asleep in her room by the time he came in from his last meeting of the day. Cassy was doing the final editing and mixing on Suzi Sapphire's *Figure of Sound* video, and she was hard at her work. Big brother Max was due in town any day to collaborate on the finished product. Tonight, this dinner with the Helds, was to be Grimm and Cassy's first date.

But for Grimm, the evening would be a mixed social and business engagement. He and Aaron Held had a lot to talk about. In his effort to devote as much time as possible to Rude/Byrne-Downes, he had used the past several days to tie up loose ends and to shift ongoing investigations to other people in the office. Rude/Byrne-Downes now occupied all his concentration and energy on both levels; he had more than enough to do to help Held fight the case while attending to Sonny's needs and fulfilling his obligations to Jack Moriarty.

"Counselor. Good evening."

Bernie Wolfshein appeared beside the table. He put his hand on Grimm's shoulder and sat down.

"Don't be a wiseguy, Wolfie," Grimm said, and he waved to the waiter.

Wolfshein adjusted his glasses and gave him a long, penetrating look. "Must be one hell of a fee to get you to pull your three-piece suit out of mothballs."

"Never happen. That was just for today. I had to fill in. Jerry Zuckerman is her lawyer."

"Well, be that as it may. You're obviously in tight, so to speak." Wolfshein's smile became a modest leer. "I hear they hit her with an 848. You weren't surprised, were you, pal? She's a perfect candidate."

Grimm shook his head. "Nothing surprises me."

"So, what's she want to do? Did you talk to her?"

"Wolf, how'm I supposed to talk to her? In the first place, I have nothing specific, nothing official, from Vaggi. From what I saw today, I'd say she's on the warpath. I can't imagine her offering Sonny a deal. Besides, I told you, I'm not her lawyer."

"Arthur, you're fucking with me."

"No, I'm not. I just don't understand why Vaggi doesn't contact Zuckerman and lay her cards on the table. Unless, of course, she's got a problem. Or unless Vaggi's not really part of this. Is that what you're telling me?"

"Look, for Christ's sake, you know how these things work as well as I do. Better. Vaggi takes orders like the rest of us. She'll do whatever she's told to do."

"Oh, man, you don't mean this is coming from the boss himself?"

Grimm said. "Not Vallone. Vallone doesn't make deals." Grimm let a note of sarcasm into his voice.

Wolfshein shrugged his shoulders. "You know what kind of deal we're talking about."

Grimm made no response. The waiter arrived with Wolfshein's drink, and the agent took a swallow before continuing. "She's going to go to prison for a long time. Does she understand that? Do you? I hear no one's taking this very seriously. What is she"—he twirled his finger next to his temple "—a nut job? I mean, we know her lawyer is."

Grimm laughed. "Wolfie, I keep telling you: I'm not her lawyer. She may be a little eccentric. But then, this is not your typical drug conspiracy. These people, some of them, anyway, are different."

"Oh, Arthur, cut the shit. I don't give a damn how different they are. We've seen a lot of weirdos come and go in our time. One thing they all have in common, they all end up going to prison."

"Unless they're willing to make a deal."

"Right." Wolfshein sighed. "Arthur, face it, she's dead. Surely you must realize that. Held knows the score. There's no way she can beat this thing. If she goes to trial, Gass will give her at least forty years with no parole. Count on it. Vaggi will see to it that she gets buried alive, believe me. She'll be an old lady by the time she gets out, if she gets out."

"So what do you want me to tell her?"

"Tell her—for Christ's sake—tell her she should talk to us. Tell her not to be a fool."

"Us?"

"Vaggi, all right? I'll see that Vaggi calls you personally."

"Bernie, I don't want Vaggi calling me. She should call Jerry Zuckerman. Or Aaron. By the way, who's this guy Whelan? How does he fit in?"

"Whelan? You mean Doug Whelan? He's FBI. Why? Has he been in touch?"

"You people better get your signals straight. Look, I'm going to be honest with you. Sonny's not my client. I'm working for Aaron. But even if she were, you know I'm not going to counsel her to cooperate. That's not the way I operate. Aaron and I don't work for rats. You know that." Grimm paused and took a sip of his drink.

"Now, going beyond all that," he said, gazing at Wolfshein, "I'm looking at this case, and I'm saying to myself, something is very wrong here. I've seen Vita Vaggi in court many times, and I've never seen her as fucked-up as she was today. I think this case is blowing up in her face. Now I see lines out from top level DEA—you—purporting to come straight from Vallone himself, and I have no reason to doubt that. Finally, some mysterious FBI big shot's snooping around. What am I to infer from all this?''

Grimm studied his friend as he spoke. Wolfshein sipped his drink, he slid his glasses up his nose and said, ''I don't know what you're talking about.''

''Okay, Wolfie, if that's the way you want to play it. It really doesn't matter to me. I'm going to find out anyway. Meanwhile''—he smiled—''you're the worst liar I ever met.''

''Look, even if you're right, you know I'm not at liberty to discuss that. We're talking about Byrne-Downes, and none of that makes any difference, not as far as she's concerned, not with all the shit they got on her. Forget about it. The tapes alone, plus they got some diplomat, some Swede they pinched at Kennedy six months ago, and he's been running his mouth ever since. You think some of these other assholes won't flip? C'mon, you know how these people are. I'm just saying, right now, she's the one who's in position to make the best deal, both for her, and for the other weirdo, the singer.''

''Wolfie, she's got a wonderful little girl. She loves her kid. And, I get the impression she enjoys being alive, even in jail. Jack Moriarty and his crew are not exactly hippie peace-love-and-brotherhood types. Look what happened to Karl Lundgren.'' Again Grimm watched his friend's reaction. ''These are serious people.''

''You're damn right they are. That's why I'm coming to you. No one else needs to know about this.''

''You mean like Julie Zuluaga?''

Wolfshein shook his head. ''Zuluaga is out of it.''

''I doubt that,'' Grimm said. ''Not with all that energy floating around.''

There was a pause. Wolfshein adjusted his glasses and squinted. ''Arthur, let me ask you this: are you sure it's floating around?''

''I don't follow.''

''Think about it. And in the meantime, you should make an exception in this case. You should talk to Byrne-Downes for me. Okay? You owe it to the punk rock guy, Aaron's client. I'm going to have Vaggi contact you and give you the whole rundown on their offer as soon as they get it together. Maybe this goes against your code of ethics, or whatever, but like you said, in this case there's a different element involved and there's a lot going on here I don't think you know about. Byrne-Downes should realize, these people play for keeps. When it comes to a guy like Jack Moriarty, even she's out of her league."

"I really think you should have Vaggi contact Jerry Zuckerman."

"C'mon, pal, who the fuck is Jerry Zuckerman? You I know. What do I know from Jerry Zuckerman? If I wanted this thing all over town, I'd put an ad in the fuckin' newspaper."

"Take it easy. Have Vaggi contact me. And tell her she better be nice."

Wolfshein chuckled. "What's the matter, you don't like Vita?"

"Vita would prosecute her own mother. You people're all weird. Why do you do this? At least I get paid." Grimm stuck his hand out and made a grasping motion. "Now gimme. I don't have all night."

"You know you're out of your mind," Wolfshein said. "I just hope you realize that."

"It's been said before."

"One of these days all this shit is going to backfire," Wolfshein said as he reached in his jacket pocket and took out an envelope. He handed it to Grimm.

"All what shit? I'm just doing my job. Like you."

Grimm opened the envelope and looked at the piece of paper inside. It was a note, on Wolfshein's DEA stationery, authorizing Grimm to inspect the impounded Lincoln Town Car found at Kennedy Airport.

"Arthur, you can't spend the rest of your life walking a tightrope. Sooner or later you're going to slip up."

"Maybe so, Wolfie." Grimm folded the paper and put it back in the envelope. "But that's what keeps it interesting. Better than sitting on my ass in some government pigeonhole." He put the envelope in his pocket and winked at his friend. "Thanks, buddy."

"That's what you wanted?"

"Perfect. Now, where is it?"

"At the Agency garage on West 56th. Show that to whoever's on and tell them to call me if there's any questions."

"You're a pal."

"Talk to Byrne-Downes. Don't fuck me, Arthur," Wolfshein said as he got to his feet. "This is strictly a *quid pro quo* deal."

"Hey, Wolf, aren't they all?"

Cassy was in the bathroom dressing when Grimm returned to the apartment. "Hey, guy," she called to him. "They just mentioned you on the news."

"Great," said Grimm. "Exactly what I don't need."

"I'll be ready in ten minutes."

"Take your time."

He went to a closet and removed a carrying case. The case contained a hand-held, battery operated vacuum cleaner. Grimm switched it on to make sure the batteries still had plenty of power; he checked his supply of filters, plastic bags and swabs. Satisfied, he left the carrying case beside the door and poured himself a drink he carried into his study.

Off and on for the past few days, he had been perusing the spiral notebook he'd found in the stash at the SoHo loft, trying to get some insight into what Karl Lundgren was doing just prior to his murder. Grimm kept the notebook hidden in a safe behind a false panel in his study. Wolfshein's comment about the dubious nature of the money rankled; Grimm had no wish to waste his time searching for cash that didn't exist. He took the record book from the safe and sat down with it at his desk.

From his reading of the figures—and the fact that he found the notebook in the stash—Grimm decided this was Lundgren's private ledger from which he would compile accounts to be presented to Sonny. The figures seemed to be broken down into at least four separate categories. One was clearly the cash flow section, which showed a dramatic increase in the amounts collected over the past two-and-a-half months. The figures jumped from receipts in the tens of thousands in late April and May to $110,000, $223,000, and $266,000 in one day beginning around the end of May. Obviously something heavy had come down, and as Grimm rechecked the figures, there was no mistake about it: in excess of six million had been on hand when Lundgren was murdered. So what was Wolfshein talking about? The money had to be real.

Another section listed individual accounts, with pages for each customer detailing product they received, payments they made, and running balances. There were at least three different products being moved: "st," "doog," and "nose." Grimm recognized some of the initials or nicknames used on these pages as belonging to co-defendants. A quick summation of the outstanding balances showed Sonny's organization had accounts receivable of another $1.5 million. "Little Dom" alone owed $754,000, mostly for "doog," which Grimm knew meant junk. Even Micky Hoyos, who Grimm figured for a supplier, owed $330,000. It seemed everyone owed Sonny money.

Next there was a paid-out section listing dates and amounts of payments to "Stash," which probably meant Guy Stash, totaling $3.62 million as of the last payment made in July. Grimm noted a $150,000 payment to "machine." Here Karl recorded deductions for his expenses (car rentals, plane tickets, hotel bills, even gas slips and his beeper fees), and his salary, two grand a week, as well as what appeared to be bonuses for special trips like "Aspen run." Annexed to this section were Karl's own accounts showing the five thousand he'd left in the stash as personal money. Here Grimm noted several payments to "ss" amounting to about eight thousand. Karl had also been running an ounce business of his own on the side, bringing in another two or three grand a week.

Finally there was a section of coded phone numbers beside initials or nicknames. Grimm fired up a joint and turned his attention to this section. He'd been trying to break the code. One number particularly interested Grimm. It was next to the name "zoo" and had no area code.

Cassy knocked on the door to the study. "Ready when you are."

"C'mon in," Grimm answered.

"All right," she said, smelling the reefer. "That's what I'm talkin' about."

Grimm handed her the joint. Cassy stood beside the desk with her hand on her hip and took a couple of deep tokes. "I haven't smoked a doob since I left L.A."

"You look absolutely stunning," he told her, and she did. She was wearing a simple, low cut black dress, and her hair was done up in a twist at the nape of her long neck with the odd wisp looking casually astray. Her California tan and the rosy hue of her hair were heightened by the dark material of the dress. She was lightly made up, with silver toning above the eyes and pale lipstick. She wore diamond stud earrings and a pearl necklace.

"Yeah? Thanks. You like the dress?" she asked, turning around. "I just bought it today. Max said to go wild, spend some bread. Sheesh! I blew five grand."

They left the apartment and drove across town to a small French restaurant on 82nd Street near the Helds' townhouse. Grimm introduced Cassy to Aaron Held and his third wife, Julia, a small, attractive dark blonde who had given up a promising career as a trial lawyer when she married Held. She had been with the United States Attorney's Office for three years before going into private practice. Once when Grimm asked her why she had quit, she told him, "Probably for the same reason you did. I hate the profession. It's full of liars and phonies."

"Now, Arthur. What's this I hear about you practicing law again?" Julia said to Grimm once they were seated at a table and had given the waiter their drink orders.

Held, who ordinarily dominated most conversations, liked to sit back and let Julia direct the talk in social settings. She was an inquisitive woman who always seemed to have prepared a number of direct questions she wanted answered, residue, Grimm suspected, of her days as a prosecutor.

"Aaron finessed me," said Grimm. "He tricked me into that just to rile Vaggi. He knows how she loves me. But that's it. Today I made my one and only appearance."

"Really?" Julia asked with a quizzical look. She glanced at her husband, who just smiled. "But Aaron tells me you're representing this drug pusher now."

Held sat forward and cleared his throat. He couldn't suppress the wry smile shaping his mouth. "Please, darling. Not drug pusher. Our clients don't push drugs. That term went out with reefer madness." To Grimm he said, "Ah, that's the way Sonny wants it, babe," and he laughed.

"What're you talking about?"

"She called me at the office this afternoon, right after I got back from court. I tried to talk her out of it, but she's got her mind made up. And my feeling is once Sonny's made up her mind, that's it."

"No. That's not it," Grimm said. "This is your idea."

"My dear man, I'm telling you what the lady said. She wants you to represent her. She likes you. She likes the way you handled Vaggi this afternoon. And Sonny's used to getting what she wants.''

"Aaron, I don't believe this. This is something you cooked up so you won't have to cut Jerry Zuckerman in.''

"Oh, Arthur." Julia Held laughed. "That's mean.''

"How can you say such a thing?" Held objected. "Ask Sonny. It's her idea.''

"You're trying to tell me it was Sonny's idea for me to fill in for Zuckerman today?''

"No. That was a legitimate necessity. Jerry couldn't be there. But now she says she likes you, she feels comfortable with you, she trusts you, and that's important. She's going to plead, Arthur. You're not going to have to try this case. Personally, I think it's a good idea. It would be best for all concerned if you represented Sonny.''

"Aaron, what about Vaggi? You think she's going to go for this?''

"I don't think it matters. Vaggi will have to go for it. Anyway, since when do we give a shit about Vaggi?''

"We'll discuss it later," Grimm said as the waiter arrived with their drinks.

"What's she like, Arthur?" Julia Held asked after they had ordered. "This drug empress. Aaron tells me she's bright and quite charming. Of course, I don't put much faith in Aaron's judgment of women.''

"What an extraordinary thing to say!" Held remarked. "I picked you, didn't I?''

"No, darling. I picked you.''

"I'd agree she's charming," Grimm said. "I'd even go so far as to say she's captivating. A very unusual woman.''

"Really? How so?" Julia asked.

Grimm looked at Held. "She's—Aaron, what would you say? Is she going to make it?''

"Well, this is the six million dollar question," Held said, and Grimm was struck that he should choose that amount. "If she stands up, she's going to go to prison for a long time.''

"Yes, and how do you think Sonia Byrne-Downes will handle that?" Julia raised her pale eyebrows and looked from her husband back to Grimm. "I would have to bet she'll become a government witness.''

"And the odds are you'd be right," Grimm said.

"What would you do?" Aaron Held asked no one in particular. "What would any of us do faced with Sonny's options? She's got Vaggi poised at her jugular, just waiting to turn her into a government zombie. Meanwhile, they're using the case against Rickie, which is pure bullshit, to add more pressure. The Honorable Dudley H. Gass is standing by like Father Time. He is capable of giving her forty, fifty, maybe sixty years, a virtual life sentence, even on a plea. She's still a young, attractive woman, and she's got a daughter she loves. That's an awful lot to think about." He turned to his wife. "What would you do?"

"Cooperate, of course," Julia said. "So would just about anyone else."

"But what if they wanted you to testify against Aaron?" Grimm asked.

"I'd give him up in a heartbeat," Julia said and they all laughed.

"No. It's a serious question," she went on. "And I have seen them pit wife against husband, brother against brother, son against father. I honestly don't think anyone can say how they would handle it until they're faced with the decision. It's a terrible choice they give us: inform on your friends and loved ones, or go to prison."

"There's an old adage," Held said, "and it happens to be true: Don't do the crime if you can't do the time. People who're afraid to go to prison should not break the law. It's that simple. Why do you think I'm scared shitless to do anything wrong? I don't want to go to prison, and I'm happy to admit it. I hate having to go to MCC to visit clients. As far as Sonny is concerned, she may not have bargained for what she's got herself into. I doubt if she understands just how serious this government is." Held held up his forefinger.

"This is why, my dear boy, I'm convinced it's an excellent idea for you to represent the young lady. She needs your strong support, she needs your heartfelt compassion and deep commitment to truth, justice and the American way. And besides, we need her money."

Again everyone laughed.

"Is she filthy rich?" asked Julia.

"You know, she's never mentioned money," Grimm said.

"The rich ones never do," Held put in. "Of course she's rich. She's partners with Saul Diamond and Jack Moriarty, two of the richest drug dealers on the East Coast, if not the whole country. Saul once confided to me that his end alone on a deal he did with Sonny was over three million. One deal! Imagine what she must've made. And she was doing several such trips a year. I'll bet she's got tens of millions stashed away.''

"Then she's a fool," Julia said. "She should've quit while she was ahead and gone off to live in Madagascar, or some such place.''

"Well, she may be rich, but then again she may not be," Grimm said. "Lawyers think all drug dealers are rich. And drug dealers think all lawyers are rich. Look at Aaron. No matter how much money he makes, it's never enough.''

"Yes, but think of my overhead.''

"What, drug dealers don't have overhead? What about lawyer's fees?''

During the meal, the waiter came to the table and said there was a phone call for Cassy Steiger. As soon as Cassy left the table, Julia Held asked, "Is this a romantic interest, Arthur? Or just friends?''

"Friends," Grimm replied without hesitation. "Max is a special friend of mine.''

"It's Max," Cassy said when she returned to the table. "He wants to speak to you.''

Grimm went to the alcove behind the bar and picked up the phone. "Hey, bro. How did you find us?" he asked.

"I'm connected to a light bulb," Max said.

"More like a crystal ball.''

"Everything all right? You takin' good care 'a my kid sister?''

"Everything's fine.''

"No it ain't, bro.''

Grimm felt a sinking sensation in the pit of his stomach. "What's wrong?''

"I hear heavy duty rumblings. You better be careful.''

"What kind of rumblings?''

"Rumblings of war, A.G. Watch out you don't get caught in the crossfire. You know how small this world is.''

"Where are you?''

"Out. It's cool." There was a long pause, then Max said, "You know that fat dude? I hear his stock is dropping fast.''

"Tell me what you hear." Grimm could feel Max was way out in the land of prolonged synapses.

"People love to tell me things. It's my karma. Everybody wants to tell me their trip. Truth is, I don't want to know. Some people are very upset.''

"What people?"

"You know, the Bros. Those people.''

"What have they got to do with this?"

"More than you might think. It's a complicated setup, nothing to get into over the air. I'll tell you about it when I see you. I'm getting together with them tonight. It all relates to that big stick thing that happened up North, those sticks I gave you. I just found this out today. The Brothers are hot 'cause someone tried to pull a fast one. Even that other dude, what's-his-face, Jack. His own people're pissed at him. Your name has come up.''

"In what context?"

"Only that you're looking into this thing back there, you know, who offed that dude and took the heavy stamp collection everyone's lookin' for. Some people're sayin' that was a setup. I'm just tellin' you, please be careful, bro. You know, I'm only interested 'cause Rickie's involved. And whatever you do, don't let anything happen to the kid. I love her mucho.''

After they were finished eating, Held and Grimm left the table and moved to the bar. "So as not to bore you ladies with business talk," Held told them.

"I'm shocked and amazed," the lawyer said. They were both drinking cognac from snifters.

"At what?"

"You, dear boy. What is going on between you and the infamous Ms. Byrne-Downes?"

Grimm sighed. "I'm not sure," he said. "Maybe nothing. Maybe some sort of infatuation.''

Held chortled. "Why, how *un*like you, Arthur. How *un*professional. And how *un*realistic. She's a doomed woman.''

"Maybe that's the attraction," Grimm said with a thin smile.

"In any case, she's apparently quite smitten herself. You should have heard her on the telephone. 'I want him,' she said, and with what intimations of unbridled lust.''

"Well, you can rest assured, I won't let it interfere with business.''

"Oh, I know you won't," Held said with a leer. "That's one of the things I like about you, babe. You don't let your priorities get muddled. We must always remember, this is a business." He took a contemplative sip of his brandy.

"Now, as to the subject of business, with regard to money, I've thought that through, and here's what I've come up with. Since you're busy with whatever else you're needed for on this case, my office will generate all the necessary paperwork: briefs, motions, memoranda, letters, what have you. You make the appearances, argue, and handle Sonny's plea negotiations. We split her fee down the middle. Naturally, you continue to draw your fee for the investigative work." Held raised one of his question mark eyebrows. "How does that sound so far?"

"Well, if you're sure you want me to do it, I have no problem with that. You write the briefs and I submit them. What Vaggi doesn't know won't hurt her."

"Exactly. I think you and Vaggi can work this thing out. Now, how much do you think we should charge Sonny?"

"We've got a hundred grand already. That's a lot for a plea."

"Is that her money or Jack's?"

"I don't know, but whichever, at this point it doesn't make any difference. We're not going to ask for more."

"No?" Held looked disappointed.

"We better leave it for now and see what happens."

"All right. The thing is to concentrate on getting Saul to cough up Rickie's fee."

"How do you stand there?"

"Well, you know Saul, that cheap prick. Trying to get money out of him is like trying to get the government to admit they've made a mistake. I have the retainer, of course. He keeps assuring me he'll take care of it. Meanwhile, I've got a defense to prepare. I may need you to lean on the fat bastard." Held took another sip of his drink.

"All right. Enough of that. Now tell me what Bernie Wolfshein said."

"Very interesting," Grimm said. "Remember the 'Final Analysis' bust?"

"The sailboat full of hash off Saul's. Sure I remember."

"That supposedly came down as the result of an anonymous tip, which we always felt was bullshit. There was more to it than that. A leak in the off-load crew, right?"

Held was nodding his long head, and his thin, limp hair fell from behind his ears and hung down beside his eyes. He scowled, his whole body seemed to hunch in concentration.

"My theory is," Grimm went on, "there's a spy in the camp. Actually, I should say, there *was* a spy in the camp."

"Ah ha!" Held exclaimed, suddenly straightening up and fixing Grimm with a wide-eyed stare. "The dead person in the trunk. The perforated photographer. Now I see what all this is about."

"Right. Now listen to the rest. I'd be willing to bet my share of the fee that Karl Lundgren was a Secret Confidential Informant, and that Julie Zuluaga was his control agent."

"Of course." Held gripped Grimm's elbow. "That would certainly explain why Vaggi is so screwed up on this case."

"Yes. Lundgren, who was to have given her Jack, Guy Stash, Saul, and who would have been able to put Rickie firmly in the case, Karl Lundgren is murdered. Suddenly Vaggi's star witness is no longer available."

"Jesus, Arthur, that would explain why she . . . Think of it, she probably had a massive RICO case all prepared. Diamond Star Enterprises. All the mob connections. But without this witness, she had to go back in front of the grand jury and revamp her whole case. Could that be? Would she let it all ride on one witness?"

"One major witness, and don't forget, Zuluaga and the other agents for corroboration. Plus the tapes. Also, they have some Swedish diplomat."

"Wolfshein confirmed this?"

"He wouldn't come right out and say it, but he wouldn't deny it, either. Then when I told him about the other guy from FBI, Whelan, that upset him. He knows DEA blew this case. Zuluaga fucked up in a big way, and it's rebounding on the Agency. So now Wolfshein is all but begging me to help. I've never known Bernie so anxious about a case."

"You mean, he wants you to give him Sonny?"

"As you've already seen, without Sonny they lose Jack, they lose Saul and the wiseguys. It becomes just another drug case. Their big organized crime RICO goes out the window. So they throw Rickie in for bargaining power. Rickie becomes negotiable."

"Wolfshein said they'd cut Rickie loose?"

"Again, in so many words. He wants me to talk to Vaggi."

"Hmmmmmm. And what did you say to that?"

"I told him we don't play that way. He's pressing me, so, reluctantly, I agreed to hear their pitch. I figure it can't hurt to know what kind of offer they're willing to make.''

"You're absolutely right. We need to know how desperate Vaggi is. Undoubtedly they'll go to work on the other defendants and try to get some of them to roll.''

"Yes, but my guess is that only Sonny can do what they need done. There are levels to this conspiracy. Lundgren was the go-between. Only Sonny has access to the upper levels Vaggi is trying to reach.''

"Maybe so, but what I'm worried about is what the others can say to hurt Rickie. Because if what you're telling me is true, without Lundgren their case against my client now hinges entirely on Sonny. If she stands up, they have no case. Otherwise, they would never be willing to cut Rickie loose.''

"There it is,'' Grimm said. "Vaggi has got to make a deal.''

Held's eyes narrowed. "What will Sonny do?''

"Aaron,'' Grimm said and shook his head, "how can I know that? She . . . she seems strong to me. Jack's convinced she'll stand up. I don't see her helping them. Do you?''

"God, Arthur, they'll offer her the Taj Mahal and all the junk she needs for the rest of her life. On the other hand, they'll threaten her with bread and water and no cock for the next forty years. I wouldn't want to be in her shoes.'' The lawyer frowned and sipped his cognac. "Yes, old boy, it all boils down to the fascinating Ms. Sonia Byrne-Downes. You know, my friend, I'm beginning to think this infatuation of yours may not be so crazy after all.''

Held put his arm around Grimm's shoulders and they began moving back toward the table where Julia and Cassy sat chatting. "Let me ask you one more thing, though I know how you hate to tell me anything you think I need not know—''

"To protect you, Aaron,'' Grimm interjected.

"God bless you, my son. Still, I'm Jewish, I want to know everything. Who was it? Who discovered the spy in the camp and decided to air out his brain?''

"Would you believe me if I told you I don't know?''

Held looked at him askance. "Probably not.''

Grimm ordered a magnum of champagne and when it arrived he proposed a toast.

"To Cassy. To her debut in the movie business. And to the success of *Figure of Sound*.''

Cassy glowed. They touched glasses and she smiled at him with her whole being. "You're sweet, Arthur." She leaned over and gave him a kiss on the cheek. "Thank you. What a great celebration I'm having!"

But after a few minutes the conversation turned back to the Rude/Byrne-Downes case. Held, feeling his wine, became expansive. He told the whole story of Rickie's performance at the hearing. Julia Held was aghast.

"He better not try those antics in Dudley Gass's courtroom," she said. "Gass will crucify him."

"Let's face it," Held said, "whatever Rickie does, if he's convicted, even if we show he had next to nothing to do with this case, Gass will hang him. Thank God there's only one count. At least he won't be able to give him any more than fifteen."

"Fifteen years?" Cassy was astonished. "You mean Rickie could get sentenced to fifteen years in prison?"

" 'Fraid so, my dear," Held said.

"And you're right," Julia agreed, "Gass will give it all to him, even if he doesn't believe he's guilty. Gass is going to loathe Rickie. Sonny, as a woman, is probably better off with Gass. He's such a snob, he'll like the fact that she's hoity toity. And he's such a sexist, he'll never accept that she's the ringleader. He'll think she's taking the weight for some man out of a misplaced sense of loyalty. All she has to do is look sexy, bat her eyelashes at him, then break down and cry."

"But Rickie is innocent, isn't he?" Cassy asked, looking from the Helds to Grimm. "How can they send him to prison for fifteen years for something he didn't do?"

"Ah, but that's precisely the point, my dear. It's called conspiracy. He may not have done anything, but he was involved," Held told her. "In a conspiracy case, that is the problem. Guilt can be hard to define. Involvement with guilty people can be made to look like guilt."

"The one thing we have going for us is that Gass despises Vaggi," Grimm said.

"Yes, that's true," Aaron Held agreed. "He can't understand why she's not at home making babies and cooking. Vita will be nervous in front of Gass. Still, she's the government. He'll abuse the shit out of her and still end up screwing Rickie."

"Poor Rickie," Cassy said. "And Suzi. She'll die. They love each other so much. They think there's no way Rickie can go to jail, 'cause he didn't do anything. I don't even think Rickie's taking this seriously."

"Obviously not," Julia said.

"Serious for Rickie means something different than what it might mean for any of us," Held said. "I think Rickie sees this as political theater."

"Yes, but darling," Julia Held said, putting down her glass of champagne, "in the theater if the audience doesn't like your act, they boo you or they walk out. In court, they find you guilty and you go to prison."

"Let's not count him out just yet, dear. We have been known to win a few from time to time, haven't we, Arthur?"

"Fewer all the time," Grimm said.

"God. Now I'm depressed," Cassy said.

On the sidewalk outside the restaurant, the two couples parted. The Helds needed to walk only a few blocks to get to their townhouse. Grimm declined Aaron Held's invitation to go back to their place for a nightcap; it was still early, but he said he had something he wanted to take care of. As they walked to the garage where they'd left the Jaguar, he casually put his arm around Cassy.

"You know, wow, I was so loaded, I couldn't even talk," Cassy told him. "That joint we smoked, I got fucked up. I felt like such a dummy. Was it obvious?"

Grimm looked down at her. "No, not at all. I thought you talked very well. I don't think anyone even noticed. I didn't."

"Man, did you see how much I ate? A real piglet. It all tasted so fantastic. I'm still tripped out."

"Relax. You're perfect."

"Yeah?" Cassy turned and hugged him. "And you lie a lot."

Grimm had his arms around her. He put his hand on the back of her neck and Cassy looked up at him. Again he felt a strong urge to kiss her. Cassy reached up and touched his beard.

"Handsome," she said.

Grimm brushed his fingers across her cheek. "Beautiful," he said. "But so young."

She gave him a playful punch in the stomach. "C'mon, you old fart. If you're not going to kiss me, let's get outta here."

Grimm drove back toward the West Side. Cassy kicked off her

shoes and tucked her legs up beneath her, turning in the bucket seat to look at him. Grimm lit a joint.

"No," Cassy said when he offered it to her. "Forget it. I'm still wrecked. And all that wine I drank. Hey, you know, you smoke it as much as Max. Rickie, too. You guys stay high."

"We're from the old school," Grimm said. "I behave myself better."

"Yeah, huh? Tames the savage beast." She laughed. "Makes you think twice. Right?"

"Sometimes three or four times."

"You smoke it in the morning, too?"

"Only if I have something important to do."

"Max too. Blows my mind. First thing he does when he gets up is roll a fat doobie of some Thai stick. It never seems to affect him, though. Just keeps him mellowed out. Not like when he was doin' coke. Man, I hated him when he was doin' coke. I couldn't even be around him, he was such a fuckin' tyrant."

"You love him a lot, don't you?"

"Hey, you know it. It was such a trip growing up with Max Steiger as your older brother, I can tell ya'. All the other kids wanna hang out so maybe they can meet him."

"I'm sure there were other reasons," he told her.

"But you know what I mean. The fame trip is so heavy. It's been real hard on my other brothers, like havin' to live in Max's shadow. But now, since I been livin' with him in Malibu and up at the ranch, I've come to love him as a person, nothing to do with who he is."

Cassy put her hand on Grimm's shoulder. "And I'll tell ya', he's a great guy, Arthur. He's so supportive. He really cares about me and what I'm doing. Without his help I don't think I ever would'a had the nerve to break out of the old hometown scene and try something different."

"So now you live in Malibu and drive around in a Rolls."

Cassy laughed. "Big fuckin' deal, huh? Hey, you know what I'm tryin' to say. I wanna do something interesting with my life, something different, something besides gettin' married to some lame and havin' a bunch of kids."

"I know exactly what you mean," Grimm said. "I'm just teasing you. I admire you for what you're doing, and I think you're good at it.

All I'm trying to say is don't let yourself be fooled by the superficial stuff. They're a lot of unhappy people driving around nice neighborhoods in fancy cars."

"Tell me about it. I've met a lot of them."

"Max told me you saved his life," Cassy said after they had driven in silence for a few blocks.

"Well, I helped him get off coke, and coke was killing him. Coke and booze."

"He really loves you, Arthur."

"And I love him. Max is a genius. And he's one of the kindest, most generous men I've ever known. But he's . . . fragile."

"Where're we goin', anyway?" Cassy asked.

"I've got to make a quick stop at a garage to check something out. Shouldn't take but a few minutes."

Grimm found the place he was looking for, a private parking garage around the corner from the Drug Enforcement Administration headquarters on West 57th Street. He squeezed his car into a tight spot across the street and down the block. Cassy was sitting with her eyes closed and her head back on the headrest.

"Will you be all right?" he asked.

"Yeah, I'm fine. High as a coot, but fine."

He reached in the back and took out the carrying case with the portable vacuum in it. "Take a little nap. Stay in the car and keep the doors locked. I'll be out in ten minutes."

Grimm crossed the street and entered the office of the garage. He had purposely chosen to come here in the evening when only a few agents would be on duty. A large, dark haired man with a full beard and acne scars on his forehead was seated at a desk behind a glass partition. He was watching a small portable TV, but looked up as Grimm walked in.

"Help you?" the man asked, standing.

Grimm, who was armed, opened his jacket and removed the letter Bernie Wolfshein had given him. He saw the DEA man take notice of his weapon as he took out the letter and handed it to him.

"Lemme see some I.D.," the man said after a quick scan of the authorization note.

Grimm showed him his private investigator's license. The man took a green log book from the desk.

"Sign there. What's in the bag?"

Grimm placed the carrying case on the counter and opened it. "A vacuum for sweepings. Swabs. And plastic bags."

"Okay. Don't remove anything from the vehicle, except samples. That's the Lincoln Town Car." He wrote in the log book beside Grimm's signature, then referred to a locator. "Level three, section M. Right through there to the elevator."

"Keys?"

The DEA man removed a set of keys from a drawer under the counter and tossed them at him. A real sweetheart, thought Grimm. As he walked toward the door leading into the garage, the man activated an electric release unlocking the door.

He found the Lincoln, which still stunk of Karl Lundgren's dead body, and went to work conducting a thorough examination of the car. First, he took out the hand vacuum and made sweepings of residue from the interior, including the trunk. After each sweeping he changed the small, round cotton filter in the vacuum, sealing the different filters in separate plastic bags which he labeled.

Once the sweepings were completed, he took swab samples. He wiped different areas of the outside of the car, such as the headlights, front bumper, and rear tire well, again bagging and labeling the swabs. He then checked the glove compartment and was amused to find the rental contract there. These people amaze me, he thought as he recorded the mileage entered on the contract when the car was rented to Karl. He had seen no evidence of fingerprint dusting. They hadn't even got around to shaking the vehicle down yet, probably all balled up in dispute over who had jurisdiction over the investigation. At a glance, he could see Lundgren had put close to two hundred miles on the car in twenty-four hours.

The whole process took him under a quarter of an hour. Grimm packed away the vacuum cleaner and the bags of samples, took a final look around to see if he'd missed anything, then locked the doors and headed for the elevator.

Outside in the Jaguar, Cassy didn't know how to feel. She had grown fond of Rickie and Suzi these past few weeks while working on Suzi's video. She was deeply troubled by the thought of Rickie going to prison for something she was certain he had nothing to do with. Fifteen years. It was crazy. It was scary. Though she knew nothing concrete, Cassy was aware that her brother Max probably had a lot more to do with drug scams than Rickie did. Two of her brothers were deeply into it, and Max was like a guru to the whole family of freaks and hippies who did nothing but hang out and smuggle big loads of pot. These guys and their old ladies were always showing up at the ranch in Big Sur. Max promised he wasn't involved, but she would have to be a space cadet not to know something was happening.

But Rickie was different. Rickie was all music; music was his way of trying to change things. Life is such an intense experience, she thought, still in the profound headspace brought on by the reefer, specially when you're stoned. How can these guys go around like this all the time? Everything seems so heavy, I'd be burnt to a crisp in a week. She opened her eyes and looked around, trying to quell the dizziness she was feeling.

C'mon, Grimm, she said to herself and she started to shiver, let's go. Take me home.

As she sat in the car shivering, now feeling queasy in her stomach and still dizzy, Cassy noticed a car stop at the end of the block. She thought nothing of it until a man got out of the rear door, the car pulled over to the curb and the man started walking down the sidewalk toward her. Now who's this creep, she wondered, and what's he up to?

Cassy was instantly alert, no longer stoned. She thought of all the horror stories she'd heard of muggings, rapes and murders in New York. She reached over and made sure the driver's door was locked, then slid down in the seat until she could see just above the dashboard. There was something fishy about this guy, the way he was taking his time, like looking around checking things out. The car that let him off hadn't driven away. It was still sitting down there at the end of the block with some other guys in it. Too weird.

Shit, she thought, maybe these assholes drove by before and saw me sitting here alone in the car. She was pissed at Grimm for leaving her out here, but at the same instant she turned and saw Grimm emerge from the garage. Whew, she thought. But then she realized in a kind of vivid flash that the man was after Arthur. She reached for the door handle, yanked it. Locked. Her fingers fumbled for the lock button and pulled it up.

Grimm had walked out of the office of the DEA garage and was nearing the curb on his way to crossing the street. Cassy flung open the passenger's side door, scrambled out, looking from Grimm to the figure moving along the sidewalk. She clearly saw the man reach behind his hip and pull a gun. She screamed.

"Arthur! Watch out!"

Cassy's scream jolted him. He turned, saw the man, dropped the carrying case and came out with his own automatic all within a split second. But even as he crouched, cocked his gun and began to take aim at the figure on the sidewalk, he felt a bullet slamming into him. His body spun from the force of the slug.

Then the pavement was in his face, close up like a magnification. He saw the texture of the concrete, the sheen of accumulated oil and filth. Everything seemed to be slowing down. Grimm heard his assailant's gun go off again and he rolled reflexively, pleased that he cared so much about staying alive. He could hear Cassy yelling his name, but from what seemed like a long way off. There was no pain, but he felt a warm soaking and odd looseness on his left side.

Grimm lay motionless in the gutter. In his right hand he still gripped the Browning Hi-Power. The figure, the gunman, hesitated, taking aim.

"Get down," Grimm shouted at Cassy as she came toward him. He fired and hit the man with a grazing shot that caused him to drop his weapon. Grimm saw the man turn and start to run toward a car waiting at the end of the block. The headlights flashed on and a rear door opened.

Grimm's ears were ringing with the noise of his gun. Suddenly he felt relaxed. He steadied the heel of his gun hand on the pavement and took aim as though he were at the target range. Nothing but time. This is what I do best, he thought as he squinted along the barrel of the gun. He gently squeezed off another round. Watch the poor fuck take this in his ass.

He saw the gunman thrown at the open door of the car as though he'd been given a swift kick from behind. He was hit. Someone grabbed the man and hauled him into the car as it pulled away. Cassy was up now and on her way to him. Grimm saw her running across the street.

PART TWO

Rude Awakening

Chapter Eight

For the next ten days, Grimm was confined to a hospital bed as he recuperated from the gunshot wound. A bullet had caught him in the left shoulder just below the collar bone, which it snapped, then ripped out through the back of his trapezius muscle. His shoulder had been separated by the impact of the slug and had dislocated in his fall to the pavement. The doctors cut it open and pinned the joint back together. Emerging from the depths of nausea in the recovery room, semiconscious, Grimm woke to find his left arm in a cast suspended in traction like a crustaceous, bone white claw.

He needed no one to tell him that had the bullet entered a few inches lower it would have hit his heart. Cassy's scream saved his life. She was at the hospital to visit him every day, and though he didn't say anything to her about it, a new intimacy existed between them. Grimm was helpless, and Cassy made herself available to do things which enabled him to keep close tabs on developments in the Rude/Byrne-Downes case. She had even kept the presence of mind to retrieve the carrying case with the sweepings and swab samples from the sidewalk where he dropped it. Grimm had her take the samples to a friend who was a technician in the New York City Police Crime Lab.

He had a private room with a telephone, and with drugs to numb the pain and discomfort, he was able to work a good part of the day. News of the attempt on his life received front page coverage. Grimm was getting famous despite himself. Reporters haunted the hospital. He refused to give interviews, so the media people encamped and besieged his numerous visitors. Sonny sent fresh flowers and fruit baskets and get-well cards almost daily. She called from MCC two or three times a day. Even Jack Moriarty sent a box of chocolates filled with liqueur.

But it was Cassy who ministered to him, Cassy whose strong hands massaged him with cream so he wouldn't get bed sores, Cassy who became his arms and legs to run around the city, and Cassy who nursed him with warmth and tenderness. They took to kissing long and lovingly whenever she came into or left the room, and sometimes she would just sit beside the bed stroking his face and hair, looking at him. Grimm was flattered, confused and worried by the affection growing between them.

Meanwhile, life went on outside the hospital. Suzi Sapphire's *Figure of Sound* album was released and began a steady climb up the charts. The video was shown on cable TV music stations around the country. Cassy brought all the music and media magazines to Grimm's room and read him the reviews, which generally praised the album and video. Suzi made the cover of *Rolling Stone, Spin, Musician* and several other rock magazines.

The Rude/Byrne-Downes case moved ahead at its own inexorable pace. Aaron Held's office prepared a Motion for Discovery of Evidence, which Grimm submitted to the Court and U.S. Attorney's Office on Sonny's behalf. A pretrial conference in front of Judge Dudley H. Gass was scheduled for mid-October.

Soon material began to flow from Vaggi's office. The mountainous stacks of cardboard cartons contained warrants, agents' affidavits, surveillance reports and photographs, transcripts of wiretap tapes, reports of ongoing investigations known as "DEA 6s," DEA lab reports, detailed inventory sheets, copies of Sonny's long-distance telephone toll records, receipts for airline tickets and hotel bills. Vaggi had amassed an impressive offering of documentary evidence to prove her case against Sonny.

Grimm read through all this material as it was released by Vaggi and brought to the hospital from his office by Cassy. He gave special attention to the DEA 6s and the affidavits prepared by agents seeking court orders to install taps. Although he assumed Vaggi had scrutinized the documents and removed anything considered too sensitive, Grimm hoped to find some thread of evidence bearing out his spy-in-the-camp theory. A few of the affidavits made reference to a "reliable informant'' who was not named; the DEA 6s mentioned ''information received from sources close to the investigation.''

But the government intended to base its case on investigative work which resulted from the arrest of an attaché with the Swedish Embassy who had been caught at Kennedy Airport trying to smuggle three kilos of cocaine. According to the reports, the Swede immediately agreed to cooperate and tipped agents on the arrival of another courier, a woman, who was allowed to pass through customs and eventually led the agents to Sonia Byrne-Downes. The case was composed to look like a neat example of police diligence and sound investigative technique.

Karl Lundgren was sanitized out. He was not mentioned by name in any of the DEA 6s or the surveillance reports. No reference to the SoHo loft appeared anywhere in the documents. Further, there was no evidence whatsoever of Sonny's ties with Jack Moriarty, Guy Stash, Saul Diamond or any other organized crime figure. The upper orbits of the conspiracy remained inviolate. Either Sonny had been scrupulous in her efforts to conceal her relationship with Moriarty's organization, or the government was covering it up. Undoubtedly the latter, Grimm decided. To anyone familiar with the way cops work, the case Vaggi had constructed for public display, although clearly convincing in its condemnation of Sonny, was a house of cards built on a void. The proof of Lundgren's role was implicit in its very absence.

Grimm pointed this out to Bernie Wolfshein when the drug agent remained behind to talk with him after a perfunctory interrogation by the city cops assigned to investigate the attempted murder. The detectives, well aware of Wolfshein's position in law enforcement, and apprised of the fact that the incident was related to a federal drug case, were merely going through the moves for the sake of form. They took a cursory statement from Grimm, who said he had no idea who might be trying to kill him, and were relieved to defer to Wolfshein.

''You know, Wolf, if I didn't know you better, I'd have to say you set me up,'' Grimm said after the detectives had left them.

''You're sure you weren't followed?''

''Positive. If I'd been followed, they would have known I had someone in the car with me. No, I was expected. You can bet that guy working at the garage made a call. Better call in the plumbers, pal. Your office is a sieve.''

Wolfshein did not disagree with him. The agent looked tired and upset. Grimm could imagine what was going through his mind. Much of Wolfshein's career had been consumed with housekeeping chores, trying to root out corruption within the drug agency. It was a thankless task. Many of his fellow agents feared and despised him. With so much money involved, corruption was endemic, as commonplace in the high stakes business of drug interdiction as black lung is to coal miners.

Grimm waved at the discovery materials with his good arm. "Vaggi's case," he said. "It reads like an episode in a TV series. You can check every piece of paper in those boxes and you won't find Karl Lundgren's name. To me that says Lundgren was working for you guys."

"So what if he was?" Wolfshein was shaking his head. His glasses slid down his nose and in a practiced gesture he pinched his face and pushed them back in place as he began pacing beside Grimm's bed.

"Then it's true?" Grimm wanted to confirm it.

"I'll concede that. The guy was an informant. All right? Now clue me in. What does that tell you?"

"Shit, Bernie, it tells me a lot of things. It gives me the whole tone of this case. Look, for a start it tells me why Lundgren was murdered and why his body was disposed of the way it was. It also tells me that Julie Zuluaga wants me dead because he's afraid I might find out who killed Lundgren before he does."

"Because he's trying to find the money?"

"Yeah, the money you say doesn't exist."

"Well, you may be right. We have it from an informant that the murder and rip-off was a setup, an inside job done by someone within the conspiracy who's looking for an excuse not to pay certain people their end."

"You mean Saul Diamond? And you think no one knew Lundgren was with you?"

Wolfshein shrugged. "Please. Not with me. With Zuluaga."

"If so, it was a pretty neat trick with Zuluaga and his crew buzzing around Lundgren like flies on shit. I can't see it," Grimm said. He lay on the bed trying to get comfortable and watching his friend pace. "The fat man must be a lot swifter than he lets on. Also, that implies Saul's ready to risk war with Moriarty and Stash, and I can't believe that. That's not Saul's style. He's got too much at stake."

Wolfshein stopped pacing and peered down at Grimm. "So who

knew Lundgren was a rat?'' he asked, shrugging his shoulders and holding up his palms.

"It's hard to imagine any of them knowing and continuing to use him in such a sensitive position, unless they were using him *knowing* he was working for Zuluaga."

"You mean, feeding him bogus information."

"It's a possibility. Anyway, my guess is that Julie Zuluaga has a pretty good idea who knew about Lundgren, and he's real anxious to stop me from finding out. You've got to remember, you can't always trust the information you get from these rats, Wolfie. Not only do they lie a lot, but sometimes they're used to tell you what someone else wants you to hear."

Wolfshein sighed and ran his fingers through his curly hair. "Yeah, I know. Listen, like I told you, Zuluaga is officially out of this thing now. We know he's been mixed up in a lot of questionable deals, but he's got big time protection from high up. He's in thick with that whole anti-Castro Cuban crowd in Miami. We got him up here after a shake-up in South Florida. He's the kind of guy who gets away with a lot because he produces. And because he's done heavy things for important people."

"Official or not, he's trying to kill me. Somebody's got to call him off, Wolf. Or I'm going to kill him."

"But who, Arthur? What makes you think I have control over this guy?"

"Who's he take his orders from?"

Wolfshein nodded. "Yeah, right. Come up with the answer to that one and you go to the head of the class. Like I said, South Florida, the Cubans. You take it from there."

"Tampa," Grimm said.

Again Wolfshein gave an exaggerated shrug of his shoulders. "Maybe Moriarty's getting too big, maybe he's stepping on toes. Somebody wants to knock him out of the box. So they sic Zuluaga on him. We know Moriarty's overseas connections go back to the old Corsican mob, and they're definitely out. Sure, he has his goombahs here in New York, and he has his greaseballs back in the old country. The fact remains he's Irish, he's not one of them, and I don't need to tell you how clannish these wops are. They'll make money with him until it comes time to stick a knife in his back. See what I'm saying? Then there's the Chinese. The word we get from the street is that the

Chinese are looking to sidestep the Italians, set up their own distribution networks directly with the blacks and Hispanics. If that happens, Moriarty's no longer indispensable.''

True, all of it, thought Grimm, and none of it. Wolfshein's words helped him tune in the larger picture behind the conspiracy. There was always an overall pattern. Yes, Grimm told himself, in the world of large-scale drug trafficking, patterns exist. There were circles within circles, networks like neural systems, ever-present and ever-changing like a mutating intelligence. Information was old by the time it was comprehended. Change was the only constant. Even as they spoke, forces were at work mixing it up.

Max Steiger was in New York for the release of Suzi's album and video which his company, To The Max Productions, had produced. His appearance at the hospital created an event for the newspeople camped in the corridors. Both the Steigers' names were stirred into the spicy stew of Rude/Byrne-Downes coverage. The *Post* boiled with headlines like:

ROCK STAR VISITS DRUG QUEEN'S ATT'Y?

Max was also a sensation for the hospital staff, many of whom had grown up listening to his music. His fans were a more diverse breed than Rickie's, they included Sixties kids who were now in their thirties and forties and settled into the American mainstream, as well as young rockers and punks. Max—like Bob Dylan, The Rolling Stones and a few others—had managed to survive and had become a rock 'n' roll legend without major changes in his music or his image.

He still dressed exactly as he had twenty years before when he first left his Long Island home and hitchhiked to California. Max was no pretty boy; as he sauntered into the room with his sister, he looked more like an out-of-work ranch hand than a millionaire rock idol. He wore faded blue jeans tucked inside scuffed cowboy boots, an old suede vest over a T-shirt, and a bandana tied around his head which kept his long red hair out of his face. He charmed the newspeople and hospital staff with his friendly, unpretentious manner.

Max came to the hospital three times to visit Grimm. He usually came with Cassy, who would stay behind after Max left. Appearing mildly amused by the obvious bond growing between Grimm and his kid sister, he kept the conversation light until his third visit. He then

announced that he would leave for the Coast the next day, and he asked
Cassy to give him some time to talk with Grimm in private. She
gathered up a stack of discovery materials Grimm had read through,
and told Max she would meet him back at the apartment. Grimm could
feel Max's eyes on them as Cassy kissed him and said she'd be back to
see him later that evening. When she was gone, Grimm felt ill at ease
with Max.

"You don't like to listen when people tell you things, do you, bro?"
Max said with a serious tone. "I told you to watch out."

"I listened. I was being careful, but—"

"Not careful enough." Max stood up, waving his hand to stop
Grimm from speaking. He snapped a tape into the cassette player and
moved close to the bed.

"What's your involvement in this thing, A.G.?" He spoke so that
no one but Grimm could possibly hear. "'Cause whatever it is, you
should cut it and get out."

"Why?"

Max gave him a baffled look. "What the fuck're you, crazy? Next
time they might kill you."

"Who?"

"What does it matter? You'll be dead."

"Listen, Max, why don't you tell me what you know."

"I will. Then you tell me what's happenin' with you and the kid."

"Max—"

"Hold it. Me first. I want you to hear what I got to say, then you tell
me about your interest in this. Yeah?"

Max explained that the heroin in this case had been imported on the
West Coast, through San Francisco, along with several tons of Thai
sticks from Bangkok, via Tokyo, hidden in a multi-container commercial shipment. The people responsible for the stateside end of the
smuggle, the "door," as Max referred to them, were people Grimm
knew, a faction of a loosely knit consortium of Vietnam vets active in
drug smuggling. This sub-group was headed by two brothers, whose
work names were Lance Romance and Weird Roger, also known as
The Brothers, who were known for their rough efficiency and bold
resourcefulness. Max explained that The Brothers had never been told
that a large amount of high quality heroin had been secreted inside
some of the goods used as a cover for the marijuana: "a smuggle
within a smuggle," Max called it.

The Brothers, Max insisted, would have rejected the contract if they'd been told about the heroin. These were marijuana smugglers, some of whom had been strung-out on junk during the war and had sworn off it. They discovered the white powder by accident when they dropped a crate off the forklift while moving part of the load. Naturally, they were angry with the East Coast people who had organized the shipment, claiming they'd been lied to and cheated, and that their whole operation had been jeopardized. The Brothers were now clamoring for a much bigger pay off; they were threatening repercussions all over the country. And to make matters worse, their original end, which was to be taken out in product, was only half top-grade Thai sticks; the rest was garbage, dried out, scraggly leaves wrapped around bamboo slivers.

The Brothers had decided to hold back a large portion of the load, both junk and Thai sticks. They were demanding a huge cash settlement. From what Max had been told, apparently Sonny was caught in the middle of all this. She was able to negotiate for the release of a portion of the junk. The rest of the goods were said to be stored somewhere out West and would not be turned over until someone—presumably Jack Moriarty—came up with a multimillion dollar cash payment. The Hong Kong and New York Chinese who had supplied the goods were also agitating for their pay off.

"The last thing Jack needed was to lose all that paper back here," Max said. "With that, he might have been able to shut everybody up long enough to get more product and hold the trip together. Now the whole thing is comin' apart."

Saul Diamond, Max told Grimm, was said to be in the worst position. It was Saul, through Sonny's introduction, who had negotiated the deal with the West Coast smugglers, so they blamed him for the double cross. Also there was speculation that Saul had orchestrated the rip-off and murder of Karl Lundgren both because he was desperate for cash and to try to weaken Jack's position with the Chinese and the Italians in an effort to usurp his dominance.

Sonny, it was believed, did not know ahead of time about the planned double cross. People who knew her respected her business scruples and felt sure she would not have gone along with the deal if she had been aware of what either Jack or Saul or both of them had been up to.

"Not that she won't handle junk," Max pointed out. "We know she does. But when it comes to business, she's straight. She would have insisted all the cards be put on the table. Lance has been doing things with her a long time. If anything, they figure she got fucked, too."

Finally, there was Guy Stash. When the trouble began he turned up in California to lay a heavy "the Mafia's gonna get you" threat on Lance and Roger to scare them into giving up the junk. "Bro, you know how those red-necks are. You don't get heavy with Lance and Roger. They made their bones killing Vietcong. They don't give a fuck about no Cosa Nostra."

It got ugly, Max told Grimm. Roger slapped Guy Stash, "I mean, he bitch-slapped him, bro. Then he said he was gonna melt him down an' send him back to New York as a bottle of salad dressing."

Grimm laughed. "That must've been good for Guy's ego." He looked at Max. "That fuckin' Jack," Grimm said. "He didn't tell me any of this."

"So you're workin' for Luigi?"

"Yeah. He hired me to try to find out who got that money. Did you know this guy Lundgren?"

"Called him Loose Karl. Sure, I met him. He was one'a Rickie's groupies. Good photographer."

"He was also a stone rat."

"*What?*" Max looked flabbergasted.

Grimm nodded. "The truth, bro. This is between you and me. Lundgren was working for the heat, at least as far back as the 'Final Analysis' bust. Remember that one?"

"Yeah."

"If Karl had lived, you would have seen him on the witness stand."

"Not me, bro. You know I got nothin' to do with any'a this shit, and he couldn't put me in it, or anything else. Still, it blows my mind. He was like Suzi's old man."

"He was?"

"Well, maybe not her old man, but he had it bad for her. He was the one who turned Saul an' me on to Suzi. I always figured he was her old man before she fell in love with Rickie."

Grimm's mind was on Jack Moriarty. He had to have assumed Grimm would learn of the California events. As he lay there, he felt his medication beginning to wear off and experienced sharp twinges of pain. The pin through his shoulder felt as though someone had nailed him to the bed with a spike.

"I can't believe Jack would do this to me," he said after a moment. "How could he let me walk blind into something this fucked-up?"

"Sometimes I wonder about you, bro. Your judgment of character is not always the best. Both 'a these guys, Jack and Saul, they're motivated by nothin' but pure greed. Look, they fucked the energy on this whole scam. Why shouldn't they try to fuck you, too?"

"There's reasons," Grimm said. "I've known Jack a long time."

"People change, A.G. The kind of power Jack has now can warp anybody. Listen, they're both so fucked-up they didn't even take time to have their people check the quality of the sticks over there. All they care about is their precious junk. But look how the energy works. A freak accident, the forklift flips over, and our guys find the junk. Trouble is, you know they had to check it out. Nobody heard from them for three days. Now they're all noddin' an' scratchin' themselves. Cut it loose, A.G. Just tell Jack you want no part of it."

"That's no problem. But what am I supposed to do about Sonny? This thing keeps changing up. Now I'm representing her, and with Rickie caught up in it."

Max thought for a few moments. "You can still be Sonny's lawyer. I'm sure a lot of people will be glad to hear you're with her. Just stay away from the rest of the shit."

Grimm looked at him. "How much junk was in the load?" he asked.

"Are you ready for this? Five hundred kilos, bro. Pure. Number 4."

Grimm felt it was time to bring the conversation around to Cassy.

"Listen, Max, about your sister. I don't want you to start jumping to conclusions."

Max smiled and said, "I know the kid. She's got a bad one. Have you fucked her yet?"

"No," he said, never expecting Max to be so blunt. "She saved my life," he went on, thinking this might have some bearing on Max's question. "I won't tell you the idea never entered my head. I mean, obviously we like each other. But you're my friend and I'm not going to do anything to jeopardize that. Your friendship means a lot to me."

"Thanks, A.G. I love you for that. Cassy's a big girl. It's her life. The thing is, I hate to see the kid get hurt too bad, especially by one'a my best friends."

"Don't worry, Max. I'm not going to hurt her."

He shrugged. "Just be gentle. I'd hate to see her get messed up."

"You make it sound like I'm some kind of creep."

"Just be honest with her. That's all I ask. Don't drive her crazy. You know how sensitive us Steigers are."

After Max left, Grimm began to feel more and more uncomfortable. The pain in his shoulder intensified as he waited for the nurse to give him his next injection of pain-killer. Grimm had had a lot of injuries in his day, but the pain from the pin felt as though he'd been shot with an arrow and the arrow was still in his shoulder. He wished he had a couple of lines of that pure Number 4.

Five hundred kilos. The vibrations coming from a scam that size were enormous, and all of them bad. The wealth generated from this one trip could topple empires, new regimes could take control. Grimm had no desire to get caught in the middle of a heroin war. The main thing on his mind was to get out of the hospital and tell Jack Moriarty he was quitting the case, at least as far as investigating who killed Karl Lundgren and ripped-off the six-and-a-half million.

But he would continue to represent Sonny. Yes, his conscience would allow him to do that. After all, the woman was entitled to representation no matter what she had done. And Grimm could think of no one better qualified than himself to act in her stead.

Chapter Nine

Grimm fired a joint of some Afghani skunk weed Max had left for him. He inhaled deeply, feeling a twinge in his lungs, then he eased back in the seat and let the fragrant smoke pour from his nostrils. Almost immediately he was high.

No one took any notice of him. Cassy, who was driving Grimm's car, sang quietly along with the John Lennon/Yoko Ono *Double Fantasy* tape playing in the cassette machine. Sonny's daughter Carmen was in the back seat with her arm around Myrtle, the English bulldog, who was curled on the seat beside her. Quite a trio of ladies, thought Grimm, and to think a month ago I hardly knew any of them. But they all seemed happy, and they were not surprised by people lighting joints first thing in the morning.

They were on the Taconic Parkway heading to Grimm's farm in Millbrook, New York. The first day he'd met Carmen, she told him of her love for animals, especially horses, and Grimm made a promise to take her to his farm. Whenever he saw or called her, Carmen never let him forget. At last, the weekend following his release from the hospital, he was making good on the promise.

Grimm took another long toke on the joint and let his mind wander. Since he left the hospital, he'd been smoking even more than usual, staying high. He couldn't work out, which made him feel frustrated and lethargic, so he abandoned his straight head and took up residence in the land of cannabis.

For the most part, his thoughts revolved around the Rude/Byrne-Downes case; Grimm recognized he was obsessed with it. He and

Aaron Held had been doggedly preparing the pretrial motions. They were handling Sonny's case like Rickie's, as though they had every intention of taking it to trial. For years, Grimm had been listening to criminals complain about the exorbitant fees charged by lawyers, and he had to agree that too many attorneys did not begin to earn their money. Like vampires they sucked their clients dry. Then bled their families and strung them along with false hopes. When the money was gone, clients were left in the lurch as the lawyers went off in search of fresh blood. Grimm knew many who took far more cases than they could handle, then delegated the work to subordinates while they spent their time chasing fees. In the end, they sold out their unsuspecting clients by making shoddy, underhanded deals with prosecutors.

Even Held was guilty of flying after fees and fragmenting his attention in too many directions. But he had a superb support staff, and he delivered a defense that was worth every cent. In a case like Rude/Byrne-Downes, when the government was spending millions, it was nearly impossible to charge too much. For one thing, at least from Rickie's standpoint, the case was winnable. The outcome would depend in large measure on the scope and impact of the defense Held was able to mount. And that meant money. As Held was fond of saying, in America justice is expensive.

The government could call upon dozens of salaried Assistant United States Attorneys to prepare and try their cases. They used an army of agents and investigators to gather evidence, find witnesses, and harry the defense—all fueled with unlimited funds provided by taxpayers. More importantly, the entire might of the system was behind them to awe jurors, to intimidate witnesses, and to grind down defendants and defense counsel until they were ready to surrender. The judiciary, supposedly balancing the scales of justice, openly sided with the government.

It was a lie that the government was losing the war on crime. In fact, as Grimm and Held and anyone who worked in the field knew, there was no war: it was a business. Lawyers, judges, prosecutors, agents, cops, prison guards and administrators, even politicians—all were in the crime business, as were the criminals. Crime in America was a growth industry, and despite all the political rhetoric, no one was really looking to stop it. There was too much money involved.

Most of the criminals who went to jail, for all their angry posturing, knew they were better off in prison than they had been on the streets.

In prison they had no responsibilities, and at least they knew where their next meal was coming from. For every Jack Moriarty, who might go ten years between falls, there were tens of thousands like the kids Grimm had watched file before the magistrate the day Sonny and the others were arraigned: young men, mostly blacks and Hispanics, who led desperate lives, repeat offenders caught up in the relentless machine of the criminal justice system.

Rude/Byrne-Downes, as everyone involved knew, was a special case. On one level it was a media showcase, the courtroom equivalent of a major Broadway or Hollywood production complete with a star-studded cast. Reputations were at stake, important career moves were in the offing.

The United States Attorney's Office for the Southern District of New York was the most politically high-geared office in the nation. The next step was Washington, D.C., then on up the line in the Justice Department, and perhaps even a run for elected office. It was no secret that the chief prosecutor, Ralph Vallone, was warming up to run for something. His assistant, Vita Vaggi, smarting over the loss of her star witness and the prize defendants, had to save face. Rickie Rude, though no criminal, was the perfect government target. He was a celebrity doper, an outrageous iconoclast, and an articulate critic of government policy. A voice. If he beat this case, heads would roll. The fact that he might be innocent was lost. He had been named in a criminal conspiracy, and conspiracy was as nebulous as a state of mind.

An omnibus brief on a variety of motions was in the final draft stage. It would be printed and submitted the next week. The government would then answer the motions and the judge might call for oral argument and hearing on some pretrial issues before he ruled. Once the motions were decided, a trial date would be set. In the federal system, the Speedy Trial Act was supposed to guarantee trial within seventy days of the indictment. In Rickie's interest, the strategy was to push the case to trial as quickly as possible. He had been thrown in the conspiracy almost as an afterthought. The defense did not want to give the government time to strengthen its case.

For Sonny, the strategy was altogether different. Even without Karl Lundgren, the evidence against her was overwhelming. Ultimately, Sonny would plead, though for the time being, Grimm was keeping all options open. He'd had a tentative talk with Vaggi on the phone, but nothing definite had been discussed.

In the Southern District, no set deals were made, no agreements between judges, prosecutors and defendants for a cap on the sentence were negotiated in exchange for guilty pleas. In just about every other federal district in the country, and even across the river in Brooklyn's Eastern District, such deals were commonplace. However, in Manhattan, the best you could hope for was an agreed upon recommendation by the government as to the length of sentence. The judge could either go along with the recommendation or not, according to his whim. So the game plan for Sonny's case consisted of trying to play Vaggi and Judge Gass against each other. Grimm and Held could see no other hope for Sonny. They had come up with a few ideas to accomplish their objectives.

Grimm had not yet met with the FBI agent, Doug Whelan, though such a meeting, being set up by Bernie Wolfshein, was in the works. Whelan's role in Rude/Byrne-Downes was still unclear, Grimm knew only that he operated out of Washington coordinating major criminal investigations with overlapping jurisdictions. With the turf war going on between FBI and DEA over the high-profile drug cases, Grimm suspected Whelan had been designated to salvage the wreck Zuluaga had made of this case. Then there was the feud between the New York and California crime groups, Grimm was sure the FBI had at least some inkling of this imbroglio through their network of informants. He also knew that if he played his cards adroitly with Vaggi and Whelan, he might be able to pick up some valuable intelligence.

So far he'd had no luck contacting Jack Moriarty. He had left messages with the Dr. McMenimen answering service and at a few mob haunts frequented by members of Guy Stash's crew. Earlier in the week, he had gone to dinner at an Italian restaurant uptown in East Harlem where he'd left a message with a friend to reach out for Jack through the upper strata of the underworld. Grimm also stopped by a café in Little Italy, another mob joint, where he left a message for Guy. The owner of the café, nicknamed "Baby Louie," was the son of a Gambino family capo for whom Grimm had once done some investigative work. Grimm asked Baby Louie what the word on the street was about who was trying to kill him. "Agents," he replied.

In the two short visits he'd had with Sonny since his stay in the

hospital, Grimm had been friendly but all business. The private conference booths had been occupied during the times he visited her, so they
were forced to discuss their business amidst other lawyers and prisoners. Grimm focused on Sonny's criminal defense and avoided discussing the shooting or any aspect of the parallel investigation. If Sonny
was aware of Karl Lundgren's status as a DEA confidential informant,
she wasn't letting on. When Grimm mentioned that he would base one
of his pretrial suppression motions on the fact that the government's
chief witness was no longer available, Sonny looked at him and said
nothing. Her eyes, though, said it all.

Fine, he thought, two can play this game of veils. He felt more
comfortable now that his relationship with Sonny was clearly delin-
eated. He was her lawyer. He could concentrate on the task at hand.
No more flirting with witchery, no more walking on the wild side. He
would approach her on a professional level, at arm's length. To win
this case, as he and Held were aware, it was essential to control Sonny.
So Grimm would have to go into the cage with her every so often and
gently crack the whip, always mindful that he didn't stray close
enough to get mauled.

Thinking of Sonny, Grimm turned in the seat to get a look at her
daughter. A miracle, he thought. She was absentmindedly kneading
the folds of flesh on Myrtle's neck and gazing out the window at the
lush, late summer foliage. Dressed in a navy blue T-shirt, tan slacks
and little running shoes, she looked complete and self-contained, a
little cosmos unto herself.

She was a smaller version of her mother, though more symmetrical,
prettier, and as pure as fresh air. Grimm was struck by how much she
reminded him of Sonny.

"What are you thinking about, Carmen?" he asked her.

She blinked, then turned her big, soft brown eyes on him.

"All sorts of things," she answered. "I can't wait to get there and
see the horses."

Cassy downshifted the Jaguar and glanced back over her shoulder as
she changed lanes and headed for the exit ramp. Looking over at
Grimm, she said, "This is the exit—yeah, Dad?"

Grimm's estate, "the farm," as he called it, consisted of a large old main house, two barns, and a caretaker's cottage all on three hundred acres of hills, pastures and woodlot located some eight miles east of the town of Millbrook in Dutchess County.

Next to his business, the farm had become the most important thing in his life. He likened the whole Millbrook project to a vast, multi-dimensional work of art, his magnum opus. He poured money and work into the structures, into the land, and into the livestock. Often when he was off on business somewhere and feeling disgusted with his life and occupation, he was consoled by the thought that at least he had done one thing right. The farm and what he was trying to do there with the animals made sense even if nothing else did, even if the rest of his life was meaningless.

The house stood back from the road at the top of a hill looking down on the barns and kennels, the paddocks and pastures, and beside the pond that had been created by damning a spring-fed brook. A mile-long gravel driveway led from the dirt lane through two huge maple trees standing like sentinels on either side, up past the barns and kennels, ending in a circular turnaround in front of the rambling old Colonial house. The caretaker's cottage, where Grimm's foreman and his family lived, was on the other side of the property.

It was just past mid-morning when Grimm pointed out the driveway between the maple trees. "Here we are," he said, and Cassy made the turn.

The grounds were surrounded by four-rail wooden post fencing painted the same dark green as the external trim on the house. As the car came along the driveway, a half dozen mares and their foals looked up from where they stood grazing in the pasture.

"Look, Carmen," Cassy said and stopped the car.

But the little girl already had her head stuck out the window.

"C'mon," Grimm said, "let's say hello."

They all got out and walked up to the fence. Some of the more adventurous foals and a couple of the brood mares wandered over diffidently. Carmen gripped Grimm's hand, she stared at the horses, then looked up at him as though unwilling to trust her senses.

Life on the farm had a rhythm all its own. There was always plenty to do: animals to feed, stalls and dog pens to clean, the daily round of chores finished just in time to begin again. Carmen spent practically every waking moment either in the stables grooming and feeding horses, cleaning stalls and tack, or she was out in the fields riding. Cassy helped her. They were inseparable, they palled around together and took over like a couple of country sisters. Grimm looked up from the desk in his study Saturday morning and saw them through the window as they stood in the paddock beside the stables. Carmen was explaining something to Cassy, who stood with her hands on her hips and watched Carmen hold one of the horses by a lead line. They looked so serious, so right at home, he caught himself wondering how the place had managed without them.

It was a weekend Grimm would long remember as one of the happier times of his life. Hampered by the injured shoulder, he was forced to relax and enjoy the place. In the mornings, he worked in his study. He proofread the omnibus brief and checked citations. Then in the evenings after supper, Grimm, Cassy and Carmen would take the dogs for a walk to the stables where they would leave Carmen, then continue over the dam and up through the high pasture behind the house. Later, once Carmen had gone to bed, Grimm and Cassy would sit on the patio overlooking the pond and drink wine. Grimm had intimations of what it must be like to have a normal life: a wife, children, an almost sane profession. What scared him was how much he liked it.

By Sunday evening, the phone calls began. Grimm could feel the world of the city, the reality of jobs and careers, drawing them out of the idyllic life on the farm. Max called from the Coast. Aaron Held phoned to set up an appointment with Grimm for Tuesday morning. Even Bernie Wolfshein called to ask Grimm if he would agree to meet with Vita Vaggi and Doug Whelan sometime during the coming week. Finally there was a long-distance call.

"Hey, bo," said the voice Grimm recognized as a friend of his from the East Harlem neighborhood, a wiseguy elder statesman known as Tommy Vegas. They made small talk and Tommy said he had to run. "But call me, bo. I wanna hear from you." He gave Grimm a pay phone number.

Cassy had excused herself and gone to take a bath. Grimm asked his foreman to drive him into Millbrook to a public phone. Someone else answered the number he called in Nevada, but Tommy Vegas soon came on the line.

"What is it, kid? How you doin'? I hear some fool tried to clip you, got himself a new asshole. Don't these scumbags know better? You all right, bo?''

"A little shaken up on the play, much better now, thanks."

"I hear you been reachin' out for that Irish guy."

"That's right. I need to see him."

"So I understand, bo. Consider it done. I'm gonna be in the city in a few days. There's some people wanna talk to you. Just go about your business and I'll be in touch. Figure on hearing from me by the end of the week. That all right by you, bo? You gonna be in town?''

"That's fine," Grimm told him. "I look forward to seeing you."

On the ride back to the farm, Grimm lit a joint and mulled over the phone conversation. The words, "There's some people wanna talk to you," and the tone Tommy gave them replayed in his mind. He knew what that meant. Someone had called for a sit-down. It was probably not serious, at least not as far as he was concerned. These Italians have a flair for the dramatic, he thought. Still he was glad he had left his messages before anyone had come looking for him.

"You're so good with kids," Cassy said to him. "How come you never wanted any of your own?"

They were sitting on a sofa in the living room just inside from the patio. Carmen had gone to bed. Cassy was drinking wine. Grimm had switched to cognac.

"Who says I don't want kids?"

"Well, I mean, you don't have any, do you?"

"Not that I know of."

"How come you never got married? You know, Dad, you ain't gettin' any younger."

"Thanks for reminding me. Aren't we talking about two different things here? Kids aren't the problem. It's the wife part I have trouble with."

"Usually one goes with the other," Cassy said with a smirk.

"Right. And that answers your question."

They had not made love after Grimm's release from the hospital, even though for a time both had anticipated they would. For some reason, it just never happened. Instead, a physical remoteness, mostly of his making, had expanded between them as the days went by. He grew cool and aloof toward Cassy, concentrating on his work. Cassy, if she were disappointed or hurt, never showed it. She too was busy, and she was still anxious to help him. She accepted the change in his feelings, and she never questioned him about it, preferring to remain friendly and helpful.

She sat on the sofa looking at him. She had her legs tucked up under her and her long, reddish blond hair down. They listened to some new albums she'd bought before they left the city.

"You know what I think?" Cassy said after a moment.

"No. Tell me."

"I think that under that hard-ass, Mr. Toughguy exterior you like to show the world there's a really kind, good man."

"Yeah? What makes you think that?"

"Lots 'a things. This place, for one. The way you love animals. The way you are with Carmen. Even the way you treat the people who work for you. You can't fool me, Grimm."

She was leaning back in the corner of the sofa with her head cocked. She wore a long, loose robe like a caftan. Grimm was sprawled out with his feet up on an ottoman and his snifter of cognac resting on his stomach. The cast and pin had been removed from his shoulder, but his left arm was still in a sling, strapped to his side in what felt like half of a straitjacket.

"I'm not trying to fool you," he said and sat up. He began struggling with the sling, taking it off to relax his arm.

"Here, let me help you with that." Cassy got to her knees and lifted the sling over his head. "There. Better?"

"I would never try to fool you, Cassy. You're special. You saved my life. I have a commitment to you."

She sat back down on her haunches. "That was so weird," she said. "I mean, the way it happened, almost like I saw it coming. I didn't know what I was doing, like it was all happening to someone else. Has that ever happened to you before? You see what's happening even before it happens. It was heavy."

Cassy got to her knees again and leaned over him. "Anyway, I owed you, for what you did for Max. Lemme take a look at that thing and see how it's healin'," she said. Grimm could feel her warmth, he could smell her hair and bath oil. "How's it feel, big guy?"

"I feel like a weak, broken down old man."

"Bullshit," Cassy said. "For sure it's gonna feel weak, that's only normal. I mean, what d'ya expect?"

The fresh scar from the bullet wound and operation on his shoulder ran from the tip of his collar bone down across the front of his shoulder. Cassy touched the scar lightly with her fingertips, leaned down and kissed it, then ran her tongue along it.

"There," she said, looking up at him, "make it all better. And strong again."

Grimm couldn't resist her. He put his good arm around the small of her back, his hand on her hip. She let herself ease down across his lap and they kissed, the first long, deep kiss they'd shared since he left the hospital.

"Mmmmmmmmmm, that's more like it," Cassy said, nuzzling her face in his chest. "I just wanna cuddle here with my Dad."

"Why do you call me Dad?"

She looked up at him and smiled. "I don't know. Is that weird? I guess it's because you make me feel all warm an' safe. Strange, huh?"

Grimm kissed her again. She was naked under the robe, and he let his hand move underneath the material to feel the warm contours of her thigh and hips. Her skin was slippery with bath oil. When he let his hand move around onto her ass, she sat up abruptly and pushed away from him.

"Now hold it, pal," she said. "Let's not go startin' things we have no intention of finishing. You're gonna get me all horned up, then leave me to freak-out all night."

Grimm was in a sweat. He wanted so much to make love to her, but for some reason he couldn't bring himself to go through with it, and she knew it. It's this shoulder, he told himself, though he didn't believe it. It's her age. Her brother. What the fuck is it?

"It's not that I don't want to make love with you, Cassy," he told her, not knowing what he would say next. "Believe me, I do." He paused and she turned to look at him. "It's just that—" He sighed. "I don't know. For some reason it doesn't feel right."

"It's okay," she said. "You don't have to explain. I'm Max's little sister an' you got some kind'a hang-up about that. It's cool, don't worry about it. We can still be friends."

"Good," he said, "because I'm very fond of you."

"Trouble is, I really get off on kissing you. Let's just kiss a lot. How's that sound?"

"Listen, baby, the way I feel right now, one more kiss and it's all over."

"Is that a threat or a promise?"

"Listen to me, Cassy. I like you too much, and I'm too close to Max. We're like brothers. You know that. And we both know how he feels. He doesn't want this, and I feel like I'm betraying him."

"He's afraid I'm gonna get all twisted up over you. So what's so bad about that?"

"Can't you tell?"

"No, I really can't. Your age? Big deal. That's not important."

"No, it's not my age. It's my life."

"Okay, maybe you've been involved in some serious shit. And for sure you still are. So? That doesn't make you a bad person, does it?"

Grimm took a sip of his cognac. He didn't have the answer to that question. He was tired, he was sick of the way his life was going. Lately he was unsure about so many things. At times his deepest motivation seemed to be to try to confuse himself, to make life more complicated, more demanding. Cassy might be exactly what he needed, and if she had been anyone other than Max's sister, he might have let it happen.

Sonny sat forward and folded her hands on the table in one of the private conference rooms at the federal jail. Her schoolgirl pose, thought Grimm. It doesn't fool me. She gave him her most delightful smile and said, "In any case, Arthur, it was kind of you to take her. She hasn't stopped talking about your farm and the horses since she got back. I nearly had a row over the phone last night because Carmen wouldn't let me ring off."

"She told you her plan?"

"Told me? Arthur, she's eaten up with this idea to go to work on your farm. She talks of nothing else. She's even enlisted friends of mine to lobby her cause. Judy's bringing her along tomorrow so we can discuss it. I'd love to tell her yes, and it's wonderful of you to agree, but it's impossible, really, I don't see how I can allow it."

"Well, I told her it was up to you."

"She's going to despise me. Dear little child. Actually, I'd love to have her in this country so she could come visit me. But my parents wouldn't hear of it. They're very fond of their granddaughter. And really, I suppose she's better off in England."

They were sitting across the table from one another, Grimm leaning back against the wall. He had arrived at the prison early, as yet there were no other attorneys or prisoners in the conference room. In about an hour he was to meet with the government prosecutor, Vita Vaggi, and Doug Whelan, the FBI man, at Vaggi's office.

Earlier in the week, Grimm had obtained a court order directing that Sonny be permitted to listen to the tapes of her tapped telephone conversations. Boxes of cassette tapes were stacked on the floor, a cassette player with two sets of earphones was set on a chair, and more tapes and transcripts of conversations were spread over the top of a small table against the wall.

"Where will they send me?" Sonny asked him after a moment. "Some of the other women told me I'd probably go to a prison in West Virginia, what's it called, Alderton?"

"Alderson," Grimm said.

"Do you know anything about it?"

"It's the women's penitentiary. No men. The feds used to have a few co-ed joints, but not anymore."

"Oh, that's a drag."

"Alderson has all security levels, everything from maximum lockdown to little cottages for the women who behave themselves. It's prison, but at least you'll be able to get outdoors and have some fresh air and sunshine. The food couldn't possibly be any worse than this joint."

"Careful, mister. You're talking to an MCC kitchen employee. Anyway, I do intend to get fit." She straightened her spine and rolled back her shoulders, thrusting her breasts out. "Did I tell you we've started an exercise group? There are eight of us so far. We work out for forty-five minutes every day. Aerobics and calisthenics. And I haven't had a cigarette in over two weeks. Aren't you proud of me?"

Grimm nodded. "Very proud. It shows already. I can't get over how much better you look."

"Why, thank you, kind sir. Perhaps you should send Ms. Vaggi my thanks for locking me up. The government probably saved my life."

"I'll be sure to tell her how grateful you are."

"By all means."

They smiled at each other. There was an awkward pause, then Sonny asked, "Arthur, what are you going to tell her?"

"I have no idea. I'm going there mainly to hear what she has to say, although really, I know what they're after."

"Which is cooperation, of course. Such a quaint euphemism. You know what you can tell her to do with that."

"Still I think I should pretend we'll take it into consideration." He sat forward. "That may not be altogether honest, but we don't want her to know that we're committed to any set course of action. We let her make her overtures, we flirt with her and play hard to get. Then at the last minute we tell her to go fuck herself."

Sonny laughed. "Ah ha, so that's how you do it. Fine, you're the tactician."

Again there was a silence. Grimm made no effort to take up the slack in the conversation. He watched Sonny closely; he could feel that he was putting her on edge, and he enjoyed it.

"Did I tell you I got the job in the kitchen?" she asked. Grimm nodded his head. "Yes, I started a few days ago and already they want to put me in charge of the Kosher kitchen and special diet meals. I was desperate to get off the unit," she went on, "before all this"— gesturing toward the tape machine. "It gets so bloody tedious hanging around all day with all that noise."

"It must be awful," Grimm said.

"Now I go to work early in the morning, and the day goes by much faster. Thank you for your help. They weren't going to let me work, because I'm not sentenced yet and I have such high bail, but whoever you called arranged everything."

"What about these tapes?" he asked. "How bad are they?"

"Oh, dear," she said and made a groaning sound. "They're terrible." She waved her hand and then brushed her hair back from her eyes. "I never want you to hear them. Not only are they incriminating, they're obscene. They're so embarrassing!" She gave a little laugh. "I was just listening to one that had me in fits of laughter. A friend of mine rings me up. He's so excited because he's finally seduced a wealthy heiress socialite he's been after for months. I say, 'Congratulations. How was it?' sounding not the least bit interested. He insists on going into detailed descriptions about what a great fuck she is, her marvelous titties, which I know are silicone, her lovely firm ass, and he keeps on about what a tight pussy she's got and how happily surprised he was. Finally I say, 'What did you expect, for God's sake. She's had the whole bloody thing reconstructed.' "

They both laughed. "Can you imagine what the jury would think of me if they heard conversations like that?"

Grimm lifted his briefcase up onto the table. He was still wearing the sling and he had his jacket slung over the wounded shoulder. From the case he took a copy of the omnibus brief and a few current magazines and gave them to Sonny. "Some reading material," he said, putting the briefcase away. Then he glanced at his watch.

"Rushing off, Arthur?" she asked.

"No, I've got a few more minutes."

Again silence. Grimm kept looking at her and wondering if he should bring up the subject of Karl Lundgren. Sonny will only stonewall me, he thought, and beyond personal curiosity, I have no stake left in that aspect of this case.

Grimm realized he was staring into Sonny's eyes. The fascinating fusion of passion and vulnerability reflected in those polychromatic eyes drew him to her.

Then, knowing it was risky, he let his gaze wander down from her eyes to the impression her breasts made against the thin material of her T-shirt. Unabashed, he stared at her tits. He tried to imagine what those nipples would look like bare. Better still, what they would feel like. The sensation they would create in his mouth.

Sonny, aware she was being stared at, moved reflexively. Her breasts stirred, nuzzling against the T-shirt.

"Sonny. Show me your tits," he said, looking again at her eyes.

"Arthur!" She gave him a surprised look. "How rude." But she was smiling. Then she glanced over her shoulder.

The door behind her was closed, but there was a narrow, rectangular window in it. Other people had come into the visiting area while they were talking, but had gone into one of the other cubicles. Sonny turned back to him. She arched her back and reached down to pull her T-shirt out from her pants. As she lifted the shirt, she leaned forward and watched his face.

Her bare breasts were every bit as lovely as he had imagined. "Ohhhh, man," Grimm said when he saw them. The nipples were nut brown and concentrated. The pale breasts were full and shaped like pearls, traced with faint blue veins. He reached out and touched one, lightly caressing the nipple with his thumb and fingers. The nipple engorged with blood and became hard. Then Grimm cupped the whole breast in his hand as though holding something precious and bent over to kiss it.

Sonny shuddered as his mouth tugged at her nipple. "Mmmmmm," she gave a little groan. "Arthur," she said, "what's got into you?"

"You," he told her. "You're driving me out of my mind."

Sonny's look deepened. Her eyes seemed to swell. "My darling," she said, stroking his head, "I want you so much. From the first time I saw you, all I've been able to think about is how much I want you."

"C'mon," he said, "let's go for it."

"Here?" Again she looked around. "Do we dare?" But even as she said it, she was getting up and unhitching her slacks.

"What about your shoulder, darling?" Sonny asked. "How will you manage?"

Grimm stood and slipped off his jacket. "I'm not going to fuck you with my shoulder," he said and they both laughed.

"Arthur, you're mad," Sonny said.

He watched her as she pulled the blue institution slacks down over her ass and stepped out of them gracefully. She wore a pair of white panties with lace frill around the edges. They were stretched taut across her wide hips. She still had on her T-shirt and the institution smock. She wore pink sneakers. Looking at him and smiling, she took up a coy pose, lifting one knee and crossing her legs.

"Well," she said, "how do you want to do this?"

Grimm swept aside the tapes and transcripts that were on the small table against the wall. With his uninjured arm, he swooped Sonny up around the waist and sat her on the table. She lifted her buttocks so he could slip off her panties. Then she sat there, facing him, with her long legs spread.

"If anyone comes in, we'll tell them you're my gynecologist," she said and burst out laughing.

They were giddy, full of wild mischief. But there was nothing silly about her cunt. Grimm was awed by the dark, glistening snarl of hair and the puckered lips. He reached down and fingered it.

"Quickly, darling. I'm going to come," Sonny gasped, though he had only just begun to run his fingers through her wet cunt. "Hurry. Fuck me. Fuck me now, please." She was panting.

They were both so primed for each other, so ready, nothing could have stopped them. Grimm had his cock out and inside her to the hilt. Sonny straddled him, wrapping her strong thighs around his waist, mounting his cock and riding it with her hips thrust into him and her arms clasped around his neck. Grimm held her under the small of her back so she could arch over and shimmy up and down with rotations and humps of her pelvis. With one arm strapped to his side, he held on to Sonny with the other as she bucked and rocked furiously. Back in the saddle again, thought Grimm. Then, like a sudden eruption, they both exploded and came all over each other.

"Oh, God! Unnnnnnnnnhhhhhhhhh!" Sonny cried. She moaned so loudly while she was coming Grimm was sure the people in the other cubicle would hear. But he was beyond caring. He could feel Sonny's warm juices sluicing his cock.

"Oh, man. Oh, Arthur. That feels so good." She squeezed him with her legs, riding more slowly now.

Sonny kissed him, her mouth clinging to his as he sat her back down on the table. "No, leave it in just a moment longer," she said as he began to withdraw from her. Then she moaned again.

They gazed at each other like drunks. Sonny let him ease out of her and took hold of his cock.

"Nice," she said. "That was one of the nicest things that's ever happened to me." She squeezed him gently.

Grimm gave her a crooked grin. "Now you can really say you got fucked by your lawyer."

She laughed. "You're so crazy, Arthur. I love you."

Grimm was trying to get his swollen prick back into his pants. He was a mess, wrinkled and covered with come. He looked up at Sonny and again they both broke up with laughter. She extended her arm with an exaggerated limp wrist and said, "Be a darling and hand me my undies," as she squeezed her knees and rubbed her thighs together.

Chapter Ten

You are a sick man, Grimm, he told himself as he stepped from the prison lobby into the bright morning sunshine. He felt he should air himself out, get rid of the smell of sex that clung to him as he staggered across the street toward the U.S. Attorney's Office. Better smoke a joint, he decided, before I face Vita Vaggi and the FBI.

If he and Sonny had been caught fucking in the attorney conference room at the jail, it would have meant the end of his career, certain disbarment and revocation of his investigator's license. What would Aaron Held say? Only a fool or a madman would take such a chance. Oh, well, he thought as he took a last hit on the joint and flipped it into the gutter. Fuck it. It was worth it.

The elevator doors slid apart and Grimm moved into the hallway. To his left were the wide plate glass doors to the United States Attorney's Office for the Southern District of New York. I'm not really up for this meeting, he thought as he reached for the door. I'm too high, I'll never be able to handle it.

"Arthur Grimm," he said to the receptionist, relieved at how calm his voice sounded. He was careful to shield his crotch with his briefcase. "I have an appointment with Ms. Vaggi."

"Please have a seat," she said, indicating a sofa beneath the Great Seal of the Justice Department. "Ms. Vaggi will be with you in a moment."

Grimm's heart was pounding. He sat down feeling a powerful delayed rush from the marijuana. I'm going to pass out, he thought. What's happening to me? I haven't been this buzzed in years.

He looked around the reception room trying to bring himself down with the reality of his surroundings. Shit, don't lose it now, he told himself, not here, not in Vaggi's antechamber.

But then the panic gave way to a feeling of energy surging from the base of his spine in spirals up to his brain. He had the feeling he was growing, diffusing, blasting off into space and leaving below all he had ever been. Grimm sat back and let himself go with the rush until he felt it begin to ebb.

He was doing his best to look like a responsible member of the bar, but in his mind there was lawlessness. At MCC, he'd gone to the men's room and scrubbed the come stains from his suit. He had on a dark striped shirt, wrinkled from Sonny's embrace and still damp with their mingled sweat. He could still smell her sex lifting in wafts from his groin. God, what if Vaggi smells me? he wondered. Would she suspect I just came from fucking my client? Never. Someone else, perhaps.

Grimm stood as he saw the prosecutor come out of a door and walk in his direction. She was wearing a long beige skirt and an ecru silk blouse, her long black hair draped down her erect back. Her wide cheekbones and deep set, dark eyes gave her a melancholy look. Vaggi was always so deadly serious, so stiff in her demeanor. Grimm wondered what it would take to make her loosen up and laugh; he couldn't remember ever having seen her laugh. Her courtroom presentations had about as much style and wit as a government manual on proving federal crimes.

And yet, as he watched her coming toward him, there was something about her he liked. He admired her competence. She was like the student in class who always handed in her papers on time. She had dignity, she took pride in herself and in a job well done.

About all Grimm knew of her personal life was that she had been married once some years back but was now divorced and living alone. Probably her only real weakness as a lawyer was her temper. She had a tendency to take personally the low blows and cutting insults common to the adversarial system. She was overly conscious of the fact that she was a woman near the top in a traditionally male-dominated office. Aaron Held was not above using this sensitivity against her in the courtroom.

She placed a cool, almost waxen hand in his and said, "Good morning, Mr. Grimm. I'm sorry I kept you waiting."

"Think nothing of it," Grimm said with a smile. He stooped to pick up his briefcase. "I put aside the whole morning for you."

"Fine. I believe you were advised that Agent Whelan of the FBI wishes to take part in our discussion. That is agreeable with you, correct?"

Vaggi seemed nervous. She talked as though she were conducting a cross-examination. Grimm caught her glancing at his shoulder, and he wondered what she thought about that. He smiled at her again. She almost smiled back. He felt she was a little less hostile, but then that might be her come-on. She was, after all, hoping to get something from him. Her eyes were grave and inscrutable as stones.

"This way," she said, as she led him along the corridor.

They entered a conference room walled with shelves of law books. In the center of the room stood a long table with chairs placed around it. One of their war rooms, thought Grimm, where the assistants gather for brainstorming sessions with their commander, Ralph Vallone.

The FBI man, Doug Whelan, did not look at all as Grimm had imagined. He had come to expect a certain ordinary appearance, like a government stamp, on FBI agents.

Whelan, though, looked like a senator. He was tall, lean, with graying dark hair and a hard, angular face set in an expression of controlled calm. Whelan could have been a politician who played end on his college football team. He had the bloodless cool of Hoover's finest, bred in the Bureau in the days before they dirtied themselves with the seamy corruption of drug work. Definitely a heavyweight, thought Grimm. The Bureau's first string.

"I'm Doug Whelan," the agent said as he and Grimm shook hands. "Good to meet you, Mr. Grimm." He leveled on Grimm an unwavering stare as they both sat down.

There were files and what looked like discovery materials from the Rude/Byrne-Downes case piled on the table. Grimm spotted a stack of glossy photographs, but Whelan shuffled his papers and made a point of covering them.

"Agent Whelan is with the Organized Crime Strike Force," Vaggi began, also pushing files and papers around on the table in front of her. Grimm noticed she had lovely hands, with long, tapered fingers and fine bones. She wore little jewelry. She seemed about to go on, but hesitated and looked at Whelan.

"Specifically, I'm assigned to the President's Task Force on Organized Crime," Whelan said. He prefaced his pitch by mentioning Grimm's friendship with Bernie Wolfshein, and noting that Grimm had a distinguished career with Military Intelligence during and just after the Vietnam War. By leading off this way, Whelan hoped to show he'd done his homework, and also tried to establish some common ground. Whelan said he'd been a Navy pilot.

"Bernie tells me you became a little disenchanted with the government after the war," Whelan said.

"Really, it was before the war ended," Grimm said. "I couldn't handle the hypocrisy and all the lying. Then I got caught up in a Pentagon investigation of the Southeast Asian opium trade. The CIA and the White House quashed the assignment and nearly got me killed in the process. I learned never to trust the bureaucracy."

Whelan raised his eyebrows and glanced at Vaggi. As if on cue she started speaking with her precise courtroom phrasing, tilting her head forward and looking at Grimm earnestly. She really believes all this shit, Grimm thought.

"Mr. Grimm, as you're no doubt aware, the government would like very much to have your client, Ms. Byrne-Downes, cooperate in this and other cases. Agent Whelan and I have been discussing this possibility, and we're in touch with Washington, going over exactly what the government would be prepared to offer Byrne-Downes in exchange for her full and truthful cooperation."

As she spoke, Grimm could sense her tension. For some reason, she's not at all happy about this case, he realized. She's like a salesman who's trying hard not to doubt the quality of her product.

"Agent Whelan is in charge of a special task force which is investigating organized crime narcotics trafficking," the prosecutor went on. "The government has reason to believe that Byrne-Downes is in a position to provide the task force, and the President's Task Force, with vital information, and perhaps assist them to effectively cripple and even wipe out one of the largest heroin importing and distributing groups operating in the world today."

"Ms. Vaggi is referring to the Moriarty organization," Whelan continued, "headed by an individual I understand you're acquainted with, a man by the name of John Moriarty, who is at this time a fugitive from a federal racketeering indictment." He handed Grimm a few photos across the table.

Grimm looked at the first shot, taken with a telescopic lens, of a couple climbing out of a Learjet at what looked to be an airport somewhere in the tropics. It was Sonny and Jack, and there were black customs and police officials standing near the plane. Grimm's initial impression was that they made a better looking couple than he would have imagined.

Next, he looked at a shot of them poolside. Sonny was in a bikini with her long, pale body stretched out on a chaise longue. Jack squinted in the sun in the direction of the camera as though he were aware they were being observed. Grimm felt a sharp pang of jealousy at the thought of Jack enjoying Sonny's body. The next picture showed them standing beside each other at a craps table in a crowded casino. In another, they were walking along a pristine white beach before a low, flat landscape, with their arms around each other. Grimm felt sick.

"These pictures were taken about two years ago," Whelan told him. "As you can see, your client and Moriarty are close, intimate. They shared the same hotel room on this particular trip."

Whelan gave Grimm more pictures. One showed a restaurant scene, with a large table and about twelve people around a full spread of bottles, glasses, plates and platters of food. Grimm recognized Sonny in an evening dress looking elegant as she smoked a cigarette and spoke to a distinguished white-haired Chinese man Grimm knew as Master Quok, one of the Hong Kong leaders of a heroin trading triad. Jack was also at the table, as was Guy Stash. On Sonny's other side was another Chinaman Grimm knew, a young gang boss named Pang who lived in New York and who had once spent eighteen months at MCC for refusing to testify before a grand jury investigating Asian criminal activities.

In other pictures, Sonny was in New York on the arm of none other than Saul Diamond. One showed them with the two San Francisco smugglers, Lance Romance and his brother Weird Roger. Here too were pictures of Sonny with Karl Lundgren, the murdered informant, pictures that had been edited out of Grimm's discovery package. There was a shot of Sonny, Karl and Guy Stash, and a surprising picture of Rickie, Suzi and Guy together with some Hollywood types at a table in a nightclub. Finally, there was a shot of Rickie and Sonny in what looked like a passionate embrace on a New York street corner.

Grimm's overriding impression as he looked at the pictures was of the illusory nature of privacy, and of Sonny's poise and complex charm. There was something almost anachronistic about her. She looked like a Forties movie star. She dressed tastefully and with an odd originality. She was so photogenic she actually looked better in pictures than she did in real life, or maybe it was just that in the photos she seemed more defined, more knowable. Grimm recalled the first time he'd seen a picture of her on the front page of the *New York Post* the morning after her arrest. His immediate reaction was of how attractive she looked in a wan, dissipated way. He had been enchanted by the picture, though not prepared for the mesmerizing force of her personality.

"Your client is close to a lot of people the government would like to put out of business and behind bars," said Whelan as he took back the photos and returned them to a file folder. "She's right up there with the big boys," he added, "just in case you weren't aware. DEA has known about her for a long time. But nobody knew exactly where she fit in. She's a Class I violator, though she's never been known to be involved in heroin trafficking before this year. DEA had her classified as a large-scale marijuana smuggler, and Interpol has a file on her in connection with hashish source country investigations."

Whelan continued, "We knew she was close to Moriarty, but we thought it was just a sexual, or whatever, kind of thing. We didn't realize how deep the business relationship was. Turns out, we now believe Moriarty and his sidekick Stash teamed up with Saul Diamond, then went through Byrne-Downes to make things happen. So she's a lot heavier than we'd imagined. She's got those important international connections, and everybody trusts her."

Whelan hesitated. He sat back and nodded his head. "She could be an invaluable asset to us," he said and looked over at Vaggi.

The prosecutor sat forward and fixed her dark gaze on Grimm. "What we would like, Mr. Grimm, is for Ms. Byrne-Downes to, first of all, assist the government in an ongoing investigation by making contact with some of the individuals pictured with her, and then helping to secure indictments against them and others the government knows to be involved in drug trafficking. We would then expect her to testify at any and all trials related to these prosecutions. Mr. Whelan and other agents would naturally want an opportunity to debrief Byrne-Downes as to her knowledge of the activities of these individuals and her past experience with them, as well as her understanding of international drug trafficking procedures and the handling of funds generated by these groups. Finally, Ms. Byrne-Downes would be expected to appear before the President's Commission once she had fulfilled her other obligations.''

''That's all?'' Grimm said with a smile. ''You mean you want her to tell you everything she knows about everyone, set up a bunch of people so you can arrest them, then take the stand and testify against these people at trials all over the country.'' He stared at Vaggi and smiled. ''Phew! Then you want her to go before the President's Commission. That's a tall order, Ms. Vaggi. You must have some very enticing bait to offer her to get her to go for all that.''

''Well, I was getting to that,'' Vaggi began, coloring slightly.

''Before we get into this, do you think there's any chance she'd be willing to help us?'' Whelan asked. ''Have you discussed it with her?''

''How could I? I had nothing to discuss with her. Look, Sonny's a clever woman. If she were to agree, it wouldn't be from any sense of civic responsibility. Her first question's going to be, 'What's in it for me?' ''

''In return for Byrne-Downes' assistance,'' Vaggi began haltingly, then looked at Whelan, who nodded, ''the government is prepared to offer the following. The 848 continuing criminal enterprise count would be dropped. The importation conspiracy and distribution charges would also be dropped. Ms. Byrne-Downes would be allowed to plead to a simple possession count, for which the government would recommend she receive a term of probation. This of course would all be contingent upon the number of indictments and convictions the government was able to obtain due to Ms. Byrne-Downes' assistance. She and her daughter would be placed in the Witness Protection Program, given new identities, and, once she fulfilled her obligations to the government, she would be allowed to leave the country and go wherever she likes.''

''What about money?'' Grimm asked. ''How's she going to live? I think she would want the money, all the money, confiscated from her apartment returned.''

Vaggi frowned. Then she glanced at Whelan.

''C'mon, Grimm,'' Whelan sniffed. ''Don't try to tell us Sonny's broke. She's got millions.''

''Really? I don't know that,'' Grimm said. ''All I know is you're asking her to set up people who could make life hard for her. I think she'd need her money back. If she's not going to trial, then you don't need it as evidence, right?''

Now Vaggi and Whelan looked at each other. Grimm could practically hear them thinking: Is this guy for real?

"Well, we can look into that," said the prosecutor after a moment. "I can let you know about that."

"Good. Now what about Rickie?"

"Mr. Rude?"

"Mr. Rude. Something's got to be done for him. And for Gunther Mullen. Those two have no business in this case."

"Well—" Whelan started to say.

"Well nothing," Grimm snapped, sitting up. "Now look, you know, and Vita knows, Rickie and Moon may be occasional users, but these guys had nothing to do with the business end of this operation. They were thrown in for bargaining power. So let's bargain. I know Sonny. She's going to insist that they both get cut loose."

"Look at the evidence, Mr. Grimm. As far as these two individuals are concerned, I don't think you can say—" Vaggi stopped. She was looking at Grimm, who gazed back at her and shook his head.

"Please," he said, "I know all about the evidence. You're creating the conspiracy. All you've got is possession of personal amounts on Moon, and that was illegally obtained. On Rickie you've got nothing but guilt by association."

"That's not true," Vaggi insisted. "Rude was aware of what was taking place. He furthered—"

"It'll never work," Grimm said with a note of finality in his voice. He shifted in his seat as though he were getting ready to leave. "I hope you're not thinking of trying to get Sonny to testify against Rickie. No way. She'll never go for it. I could not counsel her to consider such an offer. I don't even see how you can suggest it. The man is innocent." He pushed back from the table.

"Just a minute, Grimm," Whelan said and he gave Vaggi a nod.

"Let's suppose the government would be willing to dismiss the charges against Rude and Mullen," Vaggi said, looking flustered. "It would have to be a separate agreement."

"Whatever. That can be arranged with Aaron Held and Mullen's attorney," Grimm said, thoroughly enjoying Vaggi's discomfort.

"Maybe something could be worked out during motions, so it looks good for everyone concerned. Now how's Sonny supposed to do all this for you if she's locked up?"

Grimm was staring at Vaggi's dark eyes, trying to see some sparkle there.

"She would be allowed to post bond. You might make a motion for reduction of bond, which the government would not oppose, that is, with the understanding Byrne-Downes will be released into Agent Whelan's custody for the specific purpose of assisting in the apprehension of Jack Moriarty and others. That's the only way we can agree, if she goes to work for us immediately."

Vaggi was trying to make it look as though she would have to bend over backwards to throw out the charges against Rickie and Moon. Grimm knew this was negotiable from the beginning. Once Karl Lundgren turned up dead, Vaggi no longer had her ace in the hole, and Rickie went up for trade. It was apparent Vaggi had no real faith in her case against Rickie, but he was a famous defendant, so she would prosecute vigorously and argue for a lengthy sentence if no deal could be struck. Amazing, he thought. Here we sit trading people's lives as though we own them.

"We're being frank with you, Grimm," Whelan said. "The government is anxious to put an end to the criminal career of Jack Moriarty and his buddies. We've been after this group for a long time. This man and his underlings are responsible for a large percentage of the heroin distributed here in New York and elsewhere. We also know that this group has committed a number of drug-related murders, including the man whose body you found at the airport. And we have information to the effect that he is behind the attempt on your life. I've heard the theory that agents, or men working for agents of DEA—"

"Specifically, Julie Zuluaga," Grimm interrupted.

"Well, let me finish. All right, we're investigating Zuluaga's role in this. Bernie can tell you that the Bureau and DEA's own Internal Inspection Division are actively pursuing any and all leads having to do with the agents assigned to this case. We want to get to the bottom of what happened here, but we can't do this without help from your client. The information we have at this point leads us to conclude that Moriarty discovered Lundgren was acting as an informant, and so had him murdered. He may even have done it himself."

"But why would Moriarty want to kill me?" Grimm asked. He sat forward and leaned on the table. The thought was worth examining. "How does that follow?"

Whelan raised his eyebrows and made a slight shrug. "Of course, I can only speculate. I will tell you, though, that we have information from a reliable source that tells us Moriarty's group is attempting a sort of coup in the narcotics business by the elimination of some major rivals."

"Surely you're not suggesting I'm a rival of Jack's in the junk business," Grimm said with a grin.

"No, but Saul Diamond might be. And you and Mr. Held are at times engaged by Diamond. So . . ." he trailed off.

Whelan was choosing his words carefully. So the heat was aware of the power struggle, Grimm thought. But as usual, they had misinterpreted and misunderstood what was going on. It was an indication, though, of the confidence the Bureau placed in Bernie Wolfshein that Whelan would be so candid with Grimm. What would prevent Grimm from reporting directly to Moriarty? Only his friendship with Wolfshein. Whelan's theory wasn't logical, but then he did not know that Grimm was working for Jack. At least there were some things the FBI didn't know.

"Let me ask you this, Mr. Whelan, while we're on the subject, where is Zuluaga now? Is he still the case agent?"

Whelan stared back at Grimm. "I don't know where he is," he said and glanced at Vaggi. "Vita, do you know of Special Agent Zuluaga's whereabouts?"

"It's my understanding he's been loaned to another region to assist in an unrelated investigation. He is no longer expected to participate in this case."

Grimm laughed. "I should hope not. He's screwed it up enough already. You know," he said, looking from Vaggi to Whelan, "what I can't figure is how someone could've got close enough to kill Karl Lundgren without his case agent knowing who that someone is. You people amaze me. How do you sleep at night? You let a guy like Zuluaga run around with a badge and a gun, and yet you want to send Rickie Rude to prison unless Sonny agrees to sell her soul to you. And you call these people criminals?"

"Just a minute, Mr. Grimm," Vaggi said, "we're not here to discuss government policy or the case against Mr. Rude. A grand jury has returned an indictment against him. There is substantial evidence linking him to this conspiracy. The government does not make a practice of prosecuting innocent people."

"Please, spare me. I've been around long enough to know how the government operates, Ms. Vaggi. Look, I represent Sonny. It's my obligation to discuss your offer with her. And I'll do that. But this case stinks. We all know that. And whisking Zuluaga out of the picture may not be enough. How can you expect me, in good conscience, to advise my client to become a party to what is obviously a cover-up?"

Vaggi started to respond, but Whelan interrupted.

"Because," he said, "you're her lawyer. You have her best interests to consider. Don't concern yourself with Zuluaga. We'll take care of him. Your client is facing life without parole. If she's interested in helping herself, and her friend Rude, then her only hope is to help the government. Moriarty can't do anything for her now. And raising a stink about the case won't help her either if she gets convicted. She's got to start thinking about taking care of number one."

"All right," Grimm sighed, "I'll tell her what you have in mind. Then I'll get back to you and let you know what she wants to do."

"Fine, that's all we ask. If she's interested, we'll bring her over and the four of us will sit down and work out the details. Do you have a pretty good rapport with her, Mr. Grimm?" Whelan asked.

"Yes," he said. "I think so."

Whelan nodded. "Great. That sounds good. I know she's a bright woman, and she knows her way around. I'm sure she'll realize it's in her best interest to accept our offer."

The agent gave Grimm a thin smile and turned to Vaggi. "Vita, anything else you want to discuss with Mr. Grimm?"

"No, I don't think so," Vaggi replied, keeping her eyes on Whelan. "Of course you realize, Mr. Grimm, our discussion is strictly confidential."

"Of course."

"How soon do you think you'll be able to let us know something?" Whelan asked.

"I'll go see her this afternoon." Grimm glanced at his watch. "I'm sure she'll want some time to think about it, but I should be able to give you an answer by the end of next week. Perhaps sooner."

Whelan and Vaggi looked at each other.

"That's fine," the prosecutor said, turning to Grimm. "If there's anything else you need to know in the meantime, don't hesitate to call me."

Grimm stood and shook hands with them both.

"How's the shoulder coming along?" Whelan asked.

"Slowly. It's frustrating."

"I can imagine. Bernie tells me you're a pretty good athlete. Can you beat him at racquetball?"

"Sometimes. When he's got a lot on his mind."

Whelan grinned. "Then you must beat him all the time. We'll have to get together and play some time, when the shoulder's back in shape."

"What did you expect?" Aaron Held asked. "It's all part of the game. My God, Arthur, you know that. You're not supposed to ask people like Vaggi and Whelan how they sleep at night. They probably take sleeping pills, or drink themselves to sleep, like everyone else in this business."

They were standing in the lobby at the Metropolitan Correctional Center waiting to be admitted into the jail to see Sonny and some other clients. The lobby was crowded with lawyers, loved ones and friends who had come to visit prisoners. There was a delay in clearing the afternoon prisoner count, so all the visitors were detained in the lobby. Held, pressed for time, kept looking at his watch.

"What's the matter with these idiots?" Held fussed. "Can't they count? Goddamn, it seems as though every day they get the count fucked up."

At last the attorneys were allowed in. Held shook his head and rolled his eyeballs. "You see, no one escaped. They simply can't count."

On the elevator, he turned to Grimm and said, "Do you realize how extraordinary that deal is? Jesus, Arthur, Vaggi practically gave you the fucking courthouse!" His eyes bulged. "Just play your part and don't deviate from the script. Damnit, we need this case."

There were a number of visitors and prisoners in the visiting room. Aaron Held seemed to know everyone. In this room, Held was a star. Grimm marveled at his friend's ability to discuss one complex case after another with hardly a pause. The other lawyers were laden with heavy briefcases and sheafs of notes. But Held carried nothing, his brain was like a computerized law library. He moved from one conversation to another like a chess master playing a dozen opponents at once.

While Held mingled, Grimm noticed Sonny's Colombian codefendant, Miguel Hoyos. He was a tall, olive-skinned man with hair parted high on his head. He wore tinted glasses which only partially hid an ugly scar over the bridge of his nose and under one eye. Grimm, who had been introduced to Hoyos at the arraignment, walked over to talk to the Colombian.

"Hey, man, how you doin'?" Hoyos said. "Where's Sonny? She comin' down, man?"

Grimm shook Hoyos' limp, clammy hand. "She'll be here. Who called you down, Frank?"

"I don't know, man. I hope so. They tell me lawyer visit, but I don't see him. I gotta talk to Sonny, man. These people been pressin' me. You know what I'm sayin'? About Karl gettin' hit, they wanna put *me* in that. I got nothin' to do with that shit."

"Who's pressing you?"

"The feds, man, who else? They tell me, 'Listen, you don't play ball with us, we gonna give you that body.' They know Karl was at my house the day he got clipped."

"What time was he at your place that day?"

"I don't know, maybe around five, five-thirty, no later. He was with me for half an hour. I know 'cause I left right after him and that was at six."

"Was he alone?"

"Yeah. See, I beeped him, then he come over. I had papers for him, you know, money. I give him three hundred grand. He jus' takes the money, writes it down on a piece of paper, sticks it in his bag, we do a couple 'a lines, an' he splits."

A guard came to the door of the attorney visiting room, unlocked it, and let in another crowd of prisoners and lawyers. Among them was Hoyos' lawyer, Frank Hernandez, a Brooklyn attorney of Spanish descent who represented many Colombian and Cuban drug dealers.

"Hello, Frank." Grimm shook his hand.

"Arthur. Where's Aaron?" Hernandez asked.

"He's around here somewhere."

"What's happening?"

"Aaron wants to discuss the motions and strategy. We've come up with a few thoughts we'd like to share. Did Micky tell you about his visit from the FBI?''

"That was not the FBI, Arthur," Hernandez said. "I had those guys checked out. That was DEA, a couple of Zuluaga's boys. They're out for blood. Listen, hold on a sec, I want to tell you something else I just heard.''

Hernandez took Hoyos aside and spoke to him in Spanish. The inmate elevator door opened and more prisoners surged out into the hall in front of the attorney visiting room. Grimm recognized two more of Sonny's co-defendants, Dominic Randazzo and Brad Caine. Randazzo was yelling at the elevator operator. They all trooped off around the corner. The staff elevator arrived and Sonny, accompanied by a lieutenant and a female guard, was admitted to the attorney visiting room. While the door was open, Randazzo and Caine reappeared and also tried to get in. Grimm moved toward the door to meet Sonny.

"Hold that door!" Randazzo yelled but it was too late. The lieutenant locked the door and walked away, leaving Caine and Randazzo in the hallway.

"Hello, gorgeous," Sonny said, taking hold of Grimm's hand and leaning up to kiss his cheek.

"What's going on out there?" he asked her.

"Oh, Donny's freaking out. I don't know what it's about. They didn't want me to ride on the same lift as Donnie and Brad. They're so silly. What difference does it make?''

Held and a group of lawyers and prisoners emerged from the same cubicle Grimm and Sonny had fucked in that morning.

"Over here, Arthur," Held called.

At that moment, the guard operating the elevator opened the door to admit Caine and Randazzo.

"You take it in the ass," Randazzo brayed at the guard.

"You better watch your mouth," the guard replied. "I'll write you up.''

Randazzo grabbed his crotch. "Here, write this up!" he yelled as the guard closed and locked the door.

There were greetings all around. Held had taken over the cubicle from the departing group. Sonny smiled and gripped Grimm's arm as they walked in. "This place brings back fond memories," she said.

"How's that?" Held asked.

"Hello, Aaron," Sonny said, kissing the attorney's cheek.

Randazzo appeared at the door. "I gotta talk to you, Sonny," he said.

The other attorneys and defendants milled around outside the cubicle as if drawn by the presence of Sonny and Aaron Held. The men seemed to be jockeying for position closest to Sonny. She has an ineffable star quality, thought Grimm, a sort of criminal charisma. Something about her seemed to promise excitement.

Grimm noticed it in the way she turned from Aaron Held and leveled her gaze on the stocky, insolent Randazzo. "I know that, Donnie," she said in a tone she wouldn't have used for Carmen. "In a moment."

Grimm excused himself, leaving Sonny and Held to talk while he met with Frank Hernandez.

"I picked up a piece of information I thought might interest you," Hernandez said, stepping aside with Grimm. He was a short, heavyset man with a pitted, pendulous face. "A contract agent for the DEA, a guy by the name of Manny Laplaca, Cuban out of Miami, was admitted to a hospital in Brooklyn about three weeks ago. He had a nine millimeter slug in his spine. Anything you might know about?"

"What hospital?" Grimm asked.

"I don't know, but I can find out. I got this from a good source inside DEA. From what my guy tells me, Laplaca was acting strictly off the shelf when he got plugged."

"But he was working for Zuluaga?"

Hernandez shrugged. "That's the implication, Arthur. Of course there's no proof."

"How about Zuluaga? Any word on where he is?"

"I didn't ask. I assume he's here in New York."

"Ask your man. I heard today he's no longer case agent. Supposedly he's been shunted off to another region. See what your source can find out about that."

Grimm thanked Hernandez and returned to the cubicle. Held was talking to Sonny about Judge Gass when Grimm rejoined them.

"For you, he might not be so bad," the attorney was saying. "Gass is one of those blue-blooded WASPs, a real snob. He's also a lecherous old dog and a male chauvinist. I've never known him to give out big time to a woman. His idea of women in the drug business is that they are victims being used by their husbands or boyfriends as mules or errand girls. He'll never accept that you're the boss.

"He hates Italians, blacks, Hispanics, Jews, and just about everyone else. But he'll like you. You're just his cup of tea. So be sexy, flirt with the old fart, and cry a lot. You'll have him coming in his robes."

"He also hates Vaggi," Grimm said.

"Exactly. And we will try to cultivate that hatred. We will use it to our advantage."

Held was seated facing the door. He had his legs crossed and he was bouncing his foot nervously and peering at Sonny from under a furrowed brow. Sonny looked over at Grimm, who was leaning against the small table he had fucked her on that morning.

"Now tell me what the Dragon Lady had to say. I've been dying to hear."

Grimm and Held explained the government's offer. Sonny was astounded.

"They'd give me bail?" she said incredulously. "And let me have my money back? Well, shit, Arthur, why didn't you ask her to give me the goods back as well."

When Grimm told her Vaggi had said the government would place her and Carmen in the Witness Protection Program and give them new identities, Sonny laughed her deep, resonant chortle.

"Oh, that's just ducky," she said. "You mean like those ghosts who walk around here with hoods over their heads. She wants me to turn in all these people for her, friends of mine, a former lover, and then she's going to protect me from them. That sounds worse than going to prison. Who'll protect me from myself?"

"Well, that's the question," Held said. "Most people in your position do not ask themselves that question."

"You tell Ms. Vaggi I happen to like the identity I've got now, thank you very much. Really, I'm insulted she would even conceive I would accept this deal."

"Most people in your position would jump at it," Grimm said.

"Perhaps. But that's not me. I don't snitch to save my own skin."

She grew angry when Grimm told her of Vaggi's reluctance to drop the charges against Rickie and Moon as part of the proposed deal. "What she'd really like is for you to testify against Rickie, too," Grimm said. "But she knows better than to ask."

"That bitch! She knows they haven't got a bloody thing to do with this. Tell Vaggi she can shove it."

"It's even more complicated than that," Grimm told her. "You see, they want Jack, they want Guy, they want Saul, and they want whoever else you can give them. Vaggi knows her case against Rickie is weak now that Karl Lundgren is out of the picture. So she's willing to trade. She has to. Jack is the real prize for her trophy cabinet. Meanwhile, Rickie is also high profile. She'd be famous if she could send him to prison. On the other hand, they hate to go up against someone like Rickie, with Aaron representing him, and lose.''

"Precisely," Held chimed in. "They know I'll make them eat it. And that's exactly how we handle this. We fight them all the way. If they want to play nasty, fine. When we win this for Rickie, Vaggi will be in deep shit.''

"Good. You can tell her where to stuff her deal. There's no way I'm going to become a government agent. My God, what sort of creep do they take me for? I may be a criminal, but I do have values. Tell Vaggi she can kiss my ass.''

"Let's not do that just yet," Held said. "Let's let Arthur play her along a bit and see what he can find out. This case is still developing. We learned today that Julie Zuluaga—remember him?''

"God, how could I forget him? He's the one who threatened me when I got busted. A real charmer.''

"Okay, he's off the case. There's a big stink to this, and if Arthur can uncover it, who knows what we may be able to accomplish.''

"Yes, but Aaron, that's so dangerous," Sonny protested. "I don't want anything else to happen to Arthur. These people are treacherous. Can't I just plead guilty and get it over with?''

"Patience, my dear. I don't think it's wise to give in too quickly.'' Held made a face and looked up at Grimm. "Arthur, what do you think?''

"I agree. We tell Vaggi you need time to think it over. Let them make the next move. In the meantime, we wait and see what happens with the motions. Try to get a feel for how Gass is going to act. Don't be in a hurry to plead. I doubt if that will defuse this case.''

Sonny let out a deep sigh. "All right. You gentlemen are the experts.'' She knitted her brow in a frown. "Please tell me you know what you're doing.''

Held chuckled. "Sonny, in a case like this, no one really knows what they're doing. Arthur and I just try to make educated guesses.''

As soon as Held stepped out of the room for a moment, Sonny stood and embraced Grimm.

"I loved this morning," she said. "That was wonderful. With visits like that, I could do thirty years, no problem."

"I'm getting a hard-on just thinking about it."

"Mmmmmm, I can feel it." She reached for his cock.

They kissed. "I've got to rush upstairs," Sonny said. "Judy and Carmen will be here any moment. I'm really not looking forward to having to tell Carmen she can't go live on your farm. She's got her little heart set on it."

"Well, think about it. Compromise," said Grimm. "Maybe she can come up on her vacations, at least until they ship you out."

"And when will that be?"

Grimm shrugged his good shoulder. "That depends."

"When will I see you again?"

"I'll try to get in over the weekend. Call me."

He leaned down to kiss her again and Sonny's tongue slithered into his mouth.

"God, this is so crazy," she said, pulling back and looking up at him. "My life is in a shambles and all I can think about is getting into your pants."

She's right, thought Grimm as he walked out of the federal jail for the second time that day. This is sheer madness. Nothing she tells me adds up. I'm obsessed with someone who's already dead. I should quit this case now before it's too late. The government will see to it that she spends the rest of her young life in prison.

Chapter Eleven

The restaurant was on the corner of 116th Street and Pleasant Avenue in the Italian enclave of East Harlem. Grimm arrived early, driven to the location by one of his men, who cruised around the block three times looking for surveillance stakeouts before dropping Grimm at the corner. Grimm was accompanied by the firm's electronics expert, Steve Silver, who spent close to an hour sweeping the restaurant for bugs. He used a piece of equipment known as a spectrum analyzer, a device that defines and traces every frequency traveling through or emanating from an immediate area. Silver then used another machine to check the phone lines for taps.

It was late morning on an overcast, windy Saturday. The restaurant was not officially open for business. While Silver conducted the sweep, Grimm sat at the bar with the owner and drank espresso. The owner's wife and two daughters were cooking, and a couple of neighborhood men lounged around watching the street. From the moment Grimm ducked in and sat down, an endless procession of Sicilian delicacies were placed before him.

Silver pronounced the restaurant bug free. He said, however, that he could not be sure about the phones at the telephone company offices. His equipment could trace the lines only as far as the main interchange, and taps were sometimes installed in what was known as the company's "security room." "As a rule, phones are no good," Silver said. "But you have no infinity transmitters installed here, which is the way they ordinarily do it. So the location itself is secure."

After a cup of coffee, Grimm made a call and summoned the driver, who was stationed at a phone booth some distance from the restaurant in case the place was under drive-by surveillance. A few minutes later, the car arrived to pick up Silver and his equipment.

"Paranoid, bo?" asked Virgil, the restaurant owner, a good-looking man in his early sixties. He reached in his pocket and pulled out a wad of bills. "Wha'd I owe ya'?"

"No. It's on me."

Soon after Silver departed, the principals in the sit-down began arriving. Grimm was in fact very paranoid, and he had suggested that the participants in the sit-down be driven to the restaurant and dropped off. First came Grimm's good friend, the mediator, Tommy Vegas, who was with a man Grimm knew to be the underboss of the Genovese family. Tommy was dressed as though he were about to go out jogging. He wore a burgundy and gray velour warm-up suit and white suede sneakers. Well past sixty, he had a head of pure white hair and a smooth, deeply tanned face. When he walked in and saw Grimm sitting at the bar, his face broke into a wide grin. Grimm stood and they hugged each other, taking care not to crush Grimm's injured shoulder, and kissed on both cheeks.

"You know Sally?" Tommy Vegas asked. "Sally, this is Arthur Grimm, a very good friend of mine."

It was a coded Mafia introduction. "Very good friend of mine," meant Tommy vouched for Grimm. A made man would have been introduced as "a very good friend of ours."

"C'mon back here," Virgil told them. "I got a nice table set up for youse."

The restaurant had a long, narrow front room with the bar running along the street side and booths against the wall. At the rear, another dining area with tables and chairs led off at an angle. It was an ideal layout for mobsters. Anyone coming in the restaurant would have to pass through the front section before they would be able to open fire at targets dining in the rear. Here two tables had been pushed together and laid out as though for a feast. As soon as the men sat down at the table, Virgil's wife and daughters brought out plates of food from the kitchen.

Tommy asked Grimm about his shoulder. Sally confirmed Frank Hernandez's information that Grimm had more than likely been shot by a Cuban named Manny Laplaca who did dirty work for Julie Zuluaga. Laplaca, Sally said, was in serious condition, his spine

severed, paralyzed from the waist down. He gave Grimm the name of
the hospital in Brooklyn where Laplaca was laid up.

"No guards on the room," said Sally. "You wanna do something,
jus' lemme know. We got two guys who drive ambulance over there."

"Anyway, bo," Tommy said, "the guy's worse off than dead. No
more chingaso for that spic cocksucker."

The men all roared. Grimm could sense their approval. Shortly, two
others Grimm knew to be ranking members of the Bonanno and
Colombo families came in and joined the table. It was a multi-partisan
gathering. These were the capos and lieutenants who handled narcotics
for the families so that the bosses could disavow any involvement with
drugs.

But not a word of business was discussed. Grimm was surprised at
how happy everyone seemed to be, and he was amazed by the quantities of food they put away. For the most part, Tommy held forth,
telling stories of life in Las Vegas. Tommy was an engaging raconteur
who commanded a great deal of respect in organized crime circles. He
had come to be regarded as one of the mob's ambassadors-at-large,
and was often called in to mediate at sit-downs where members of
more than one family were involved. Tommy sat at the end of the table
furthest from the front room and was the focus of attention.

Sally sat to Tommy's right. Sally was the highest ranking made man
at the table, and the man whose turf they were on. He was an ugly,
gruff man with blackheads on his cheeks and nose and a liverish
complexion. Grimm sat across the table from Sally, on Tommy's left,
because of his close relationship with Tommy and to signify the
importance of his role in the dynamics of the sit-down. Next to him sat
the Colombo representative, then the Bonannos' man. Grimm was
gratified to see that the sit-down was being conducted according to
strict protocol; it meant he would get a fair hearing.

Grimm surmised that each of the three families had a share in the
large shipment of heroin Jack and Saul had imported through California. The shipment was now in limbo because of the conflict with the
San Francisco smugglers, and because of the theft of the 6.5 million in
New York. Saul Diamond, Grimm noted with concern, had no representative at the meet. It was as though he were being tried in absentia.

They were apparently waiting for Jack and Guy Stash to arrive
before the actual business of the sit-down would get underway. Before
either of the principal partners came in, though, the Chinese delegation

descended on the restaurant. Grimm was making a trip to the men's room when he saw a dilapidated station wagon pull up with several Chinese men in plain suits. They looked like a group of waiters on their way to a restaurant in the suburbs. They flocked around a tall, youthful man in jeans, sneakers and a Lacoste sportshirt. This was Pang, the man Grimm had recognized in the group photo Doug Whelan showed him. Pang was a gregarious man with a booming voice who had a reputation as a stone killer.

"Hey, Gwimm!" Pang bellowed as he stepped into the restaurant. "Mudda-fucka! I no see you fo' long time."

Pang's pack of silent bodyguards remained in the front room. The young gang boss knew everyone at the table. He greeted them all with loud shouts and slaps on the back. Then, almost as though he'd been lying in wait until after Pang arrived, Guy Stash appeared, slipping in through the kitchen. He shook hands with everyone at the table, kissed Tommy and Sally, then went to the pay phone and made a call.

Guy barely acknowledged Grimm. It was obvious to everyone at the table that Guy had slighted him. What the fuck is this guy's problem? Grimm wondered. What did I ever do to upset this scumbag? With Guy's arrival the whole mood at the gathering changed, as though he had brought an atmosphere of suspicion and tension into the restaurant with him.

Guy looked even more uptight than usual. He had dark circles around his eyes, he had lost weight, and he looked ragged around the edges. He chain smoked and made snuffling sounds as though he'd been snorting coke. There was no question in Grimm's mind that Guy was under the gun. He had to assume that Guy, as Jack's junior partner and direct link with the Italian families, had taken responsibility for the investment capital raised by the New York distributors. Now he had been called on the carpet to explain why he was not able to produce the goods.

Ten minutes later, Jack Moriarty strolled in through the front door. At first Grimm didn't recognize him. Jack was wearing jeans, sneakers, a blue nylon windbreaker, dark glasses and a Yankees baseball cap. His normally ruddy face had been darkened with tanning lotion. Only when he removed the baseball cap exposing his thick mane of creamy silver and black hair, did Grimm know it was Jack.

It was a measure of the prominence Jack had in this world that once he arrived, the mood of the sit-down changed again. The focus of attention shifted from Tommy Vegas to the canny Irishman. Grimm understood Jack's standing to be due primarily to the fact that he was a big earner. Through his narcotics smuggling operation, millions were being made by the groups represented by the men at the table. Jack was the man with the connections all the way from Chaing Mai to Chinatown, from Palermo to East Harlem. He was overlord in the world's most dangerous trade.

He waltzed in looking like a DEA agent, which only added to his mystique. He was underground, on the lam. He could easily have excused himself from this gathering because of the high risk involved. Tommy Vegas could have met with him separately. But Jack had come in person, and the significance of this was not lost on anyone, least of all Grimm.

Now the real sit-down commenced. Tommy Vegas, in his role as mediator, resumed the focal position in the structured, almost ritualized mechanics of the assembly. Each party would be called on to present his version of events. Tommy Vegas would report to the bosses of the groups involved, and they would then decide how to settle the dispute.

Always insisting that he intended no disrespect to the others left at the table, Tommy Vegas would gesture to the person he wanted to speak with in private, and then would exit with that person to a room behind the dining area. Those left at the table continued eating, drinking, telling stories and laughing without a mention of what was being discussed in the back room.

Grimm and Tommy were the first ones to retire to the sit-down room. Tommy took his time lighting a big Cuban cigar, cutting off the end with gold clippers, then torching it with a gold lighter. Soon the air of the small office was clouded with cigar smoke. Tommy clenched the cigar in his teeth and smiled at Grimm.

"Good to see ya', bo." Tommy had tufts of white hair sprouting out from under the collar of his V-neck shirt. A cord looped around his neck and fastened to his glasses disappeared into the thick growth of hair on the back of his shoulders. "I agreed to sit on this thing 'cause I heard you was involved. So tell me, what's this all about?" He took the cigar out of his mouth and inspected the lit end. "You the only one here I figure to gimme the straight stuff."

Grimm told Tommy that he'd been asked by Aaron Held to pay a visit to Sonny at MCC the morning following the bust. Tommy said he'd read all about Grimm locating Rickie in California and returning him to New York, so Grimm explained how he tracked the Lincoln Town Car through the rental agency to the long-term parking area at Kennedy, and how he'd discovered Karl Lundgren's body in the trunk of the car.

"Where the fuck did this Zuluaga hard-on come from?" asked Tommy.

"They must've been following me."

Tommy grunted. "Could they'a had the car staked-out, bo?"

"They were too hot to see what was inside that trunk. They never could've sat on it."

"You mean the six-and-a-half mil."

"What they hoped was the six-and-a half mil. What turned out to be the dead guy. Zuluaga almost shit."

"Yeah, bo?" Tommy grinned. "Listen, good thing it wasn't the money. They would'a clipped you and stuck you in the trunk."

"Believe me, that crossed my mind."

"Okay, so you tell this to Jack, and he hires you to find out who whacked this kid and robbed the money. And you, bein' that you a nutcase, you take the job."

"Not exactly. Remember, I'm already working on this, hired by Aaron. Jack gave me a hundred thousand, which we agreed was to go toward Sonny's fee. In the meantime I told him I'd look into who took the money. But that was to be done on spec."

Next, Grimm told how he'd learned through his friends about the feud caused by the attempt to hide five hundred kilos of heroin in what was supposed to be a load of Thai sticks. This, he told Tommy, angered him because Jack had not told him what he was getting himself into.

"So what you're sayin' is that you want out, am I right, bo?" Tommy asked.

"Yes. I want out of any responsibility for trying to find out what happened to that money. I've agreed to represent the woman, Sonny, and I'll continue to do that. But I want no part of the rest of it."

Tommy laid a neat round ash from his cigar on a saucer. He looked at Grimm and nodded. "I don't see no problem with that. Probably that's a good idea, but lemme talk to Jack first. Now, what else you wanna tell me?"

"All right, I haven't even had a chance to tell this to Jack yet, but while I was looking into this, before I got shot, I was able to find out that this kid who was murdered—he took care of things for Sonny—anyway, he was a stone cold one hundred percent rat working undercover for the DEA.''

Tommy Vegas did not seem overly impressed with this bit of information. He raised his eyebrows and made an expression as if to say, So what else is new? Grimm got the distinct impression that Tommy already knew about Karl and had been testing Grimm.

Grimm did not tell him the previous evening he had obtained the results of the analyses made of the sweepings and swab samples he took from the Lincoln. An unusually high salt content was found in the smears from the outside of the car. Minute amounts of fine, powdered wood dust showed up in the interior sweepings. Traces of white sand were found in the mud caked under the fenders, in the sweepings from the front floor mats, and in the residue collected from the trunk. All indications showed that the car had been in close proximity to a salt water beach area within no more than a few days before the samples were taken.

One of Grimm's investigators had been to the radio communications company that leased Karl Lundgren his pager. He learned that Lundgren had received two calls on the machine between 5 and 7 P.M. on the Friday he was murdered, then a number of calls later to which there was no response. Both the earlier calls came from numbers traced to Manhattan public phones.

Grimm's man also found out that according to records, the Lincoln had been checked into the long-term parking lot at 9:53 P.M. The attendant there said he remembered the car, and though he couldn't recall what the person who left it looked like, he was sure a tall, good-looking English woman had not been in the car when it was delivered to the airport.

Grimm had decided not to share any of this information with Jack and the others at the sit-down first of all because it was inconclusive. It pointed to Saul Diamond and his man Gene Machine, but Grimm was not convinced. His sole purpose in attending the sit-down was to give formal notice that he was withdrawing from the investigation. As far as he was concerned, Jack had reneged on the deal by not telling him of the circumstances surrounding the importation of the heroin and the war brewing with the San Francisco smuggling group. Finally, Grimm suspected he was being manipulated, though he was not sure by whom.

"All right, bo, you did good, real good," Tommy said, winking at him. "Now, you in a hurry to go somewhere? 'Cause I wanna talk to you some more when I finish with these other guys. You mind hangin' around?"

Grimm did mind, but he said, "No, not at all."

Tommy stood. "You're all right, kid. Don't worry about nothin', you hear me? Nobody's got a beef with you—'cept maybe dese agents."

Tommy and Grimm returned to the dining area. Again assuring the others he intended no disrespect, Tommy asked Jack to leave the table and step into the back room with him.

With both Jack and Tommy gone from the table, Grimm felt estranged from the group. He reminisced with Pang about the days when the gang leader had been sequestered at MCC for refusing to testify before a grand jury. Pang had taken control of the kitchen during his stay at the federal jail, and it had become known as the best Chinese restaurant in town. Pang laughed uproariously as he recalled how he presided over corrupt guards.

"Oh, yeah, MCC—good jayu! Good jayu!" Pang howled.

Guy Stash huddled with Sally and the other two family underlings talking junk business. These were four of the biggest heroin wholesalers on the East Coast. Each of these men had his own crew to handle stashing, cutting, packaging and distributing goods to the black and Hispanic street dealers, and collections. Each group could probably handle upwards of twenty kilos per week. In addition to their local customers, they also had people coming in from places like Boston, Hartford, Philadelphia, Detroit.

For years, prominent New York crime bosses loudly proclaimed that they did not touch narcotics. Only in the most literal sense was this true. Within each of the five families, men like Guy Stash, Sally and the others managed the junk franchise. In turn, they kicked a healthy percentage of the profits up the line to the bosses. For this they received exclusive sanction to operate within specified areas. They got credit and credibility with the other mob-connected junk dealers, while disputes, rip-offs, bad debts and other problems, like the one that had precipitated this sit-down, were arbitrated in an effort to keep the business under control and to head off internecine wars.

Because Guy Stash was Jack's right-hand man, the others would look to him for their supply. If he was not able to come through, they would have to go to other, less reliable sources in order to keep their customers from going elsewhere. For a junk dealer, all other problems are secondary to maintaining a steady supply of quality merchandise from a trusted source. It was clear to Grimm as he listened to Guy that the supply had dried up and Guy was under tremendous pressure.

When Jack and Tommy Vegas finally reappeared, Tommy summoned Guy Stash. Jack struck Grimm as being mildly distracted, but not nearly as uncomfortable as Guy.

Jack was in his element. In his youth he had made his name as a tough street-fighter who was bolder and smarter than his Italian friends. Many of the wiseguys Jack hung around with still feared his capacity for swift, personal violence. Though seemingly sweet natured and friendly, he was known to have beaten to death men who crossed him. In this respect, he and Pang were the true equals in the room.

"Sally told you about this guy Laplaca?" Jack asked Grimm. He took him by the arm and moved him away from the others.

"Yeah."

"You want me to take care of it?"

"No, Jack. I don't want you to do anything,"

Jack scowled. "What's wrong, A.G.? You got a problem?"

"You know I do."

"Lissen, you got it all wrong, bo. Gimme a few minutes before you split. We'll talk about it." Jack gave him a bright, searching stare. "Be cool, A.G. There's a lot going on here you don't know about."

"Right. That's the problem. I don't like walking into something like this blind."

"Okay, okay, I hear you. I understand where you're comin' from, bo. Just gimme a chance to explain."

After Guy Stash came out, Tommy called for Sally and the other two crew bosses. Jack meanwhile sat with Pang and Guy. But within a few minutes, Tommy reappeared and asked Jack to join them, this time saying nothing to Pang and Guy who were left with Grimm at the table. Finally, the door to the rear room opened again and Pang was called in, leaving Grimm alone with Guy Stash.

This struck Grimm as highly unusual. He could conceive of no reason why Guy should be excluded from the inner sanctum. Grimm, as an outsider who had been called upon to do a specific job, and who now had withdrawn his services, had no need to be involved in any further discussions. But Guy was a principal, Jack's underboss.

Guy behaved as if Grimm weren't there. He sat at the end of the table smoking, frowning and jiggling his legs. Grimm had never seen Guy so agitated. He was sweating. His good-looking face was twisted into a grimace.

Within a few minutes, Jack came out of the back room and gave Guy some instructions. Guy went to the pay phone and made a few calls, he conferred with Jack again, then left without a word to anyone. When the other men emerged from the conference, everyone was on friendly terms. They all shook hands, kissed cheeks, and soon began dispersing. Tommy took Grimm by the arm and again led him into the back room.

"What you seen here today, bo, forget about it. *Capice?*" Tommy said.

"Of course."

Tommy smiled at him and nodded his head. "So tell me, how's life been treatin' ya'? Other than this shit."

"I can't complain. Business is good," Grimm answered. "This shoulder's taking a long time to heal, but other than that I'm okay."

"Hey, kid, be grateful you didn't get hit in the head. Brains don't heal so good."

Tommy sat back in his chair smoking a new cigar and eyeing Grimm appreciatively like a proud father. Grimm could feel the affection coming from the older man like a warm glow, and he let himself bask in it. Grimm couldn't have said what he had done, but it had obviously been the right thing.

"So now you this broad's lawyer, huh kid? How's that gonna work out? She gonna stand up?"

"I think so. She's strong—a lot stronger than most of the men in this."

Tommy chuckled. "Yeah, I know wha' choo mean, bo. I know her. Still, people change when they're facing a lot of time. Sonny's a smart lady. Not a bad lookin' broad, either. Jack brought her out to Vegas a couple 'a times. Tell ya' the truth, I think he was really in love with that broad. Flipped right out over her. She had him by the balls, only delicate like, a little squeeze here, a little twist there. Classy broad. I thought she was a weirdo till I talked to her. I don't go along with broads in the junk business, but I'll admit this one's got her head screwed on the right way."

Grimm was silent. He wanted to see where Tommy was going. He hadn't been brought back into the sit-down room to chat about Sonny.

"You gonna be able to do anything for her?" Tommy asked after a moment.

"I doubt it," Grimm said, shaking his head. "She's dead at trial. They want Jack so badly they're going to bury her for refusing to help. She knows that."

"You mean, even with dis rat cocksucker outta the way, that don't help her?"

"They've got a lot of other stuff. Tapes, money and goods in her possession."

"Yeah, now that don't seem right, for a smart broad like her, and with all the help she had, what's she doin' holdin' that shit? Somethin' don't sound right there."

"Well, I don't know. Maybe it was one of those last minute deals. Her man—the rat—he was indisposed."

"Yeah." Tommy laughed. "Right, bo—indisposed." He smiled at Grimm and puffed on his cigar.

"Bo, just between you an' me, I'll pretend I never heard it, who did him? Who got the money?"

"What makes you think I know?"

"Bo, I know you. I know how you operate. I'm sure you got a good idea."

"I've always got ideas. Ideas aren't proof."

Tommy chortled and sucked on his cigar. "Spoken like a true lawyer. You're good, kid. Now lissenna me, this ain't no courtroom. Somebody made a helluva good score here, an' got rid of the rat at the same time. I think you know who that somebody is." Tommy held the cigar with his thumb and forefingers like a dart, rolling it contemplatively and aiming it at Grimm.

"Tommy, I don't know, and that's the truth."

"See, kid, 'cause somebody's gotta cover that money. Jack's got a big problem. Pang's people ain't about to swallow this loss, so somebody's gotta eat it. That's why Jack was hopin' you could find out who robbed him. Now, you want out, and nobody's sayin' you gotta stay in. But, look at it from Jack's point of view. Nobody's got any goods. Nobody's makin' any money, which makes things even harder on Jack. This one score could'a made somebody rich and put Jack between a rock an' a hard place all in one neat move. What I'm sayin', if there's any way you can help Jack, you should think about it. *Capice?*"

Now Grimm understood why Guy Stash had been excluded from the final powwow: he was a prime suspect. With the revelation of Karl Lundgren's undercover role, Guy, as Lundgren's connection to the organization, had a lot of explaining to do. Apparently Guy had come up with the wrong answers; no wonder he hated Grimm. Tommy—and Jack—understood what all captains and lieutenants come to appreciate sooner or later: all else being equal, it's money that makes a man boss. Guy was a made man, Sicilian. With Guy's knowledge of Jack's operation, and with the Chinese in his pocket, if he could steal enough money from Jack to weaken him, no one would object if Jack turned up dead and Guy emerged as the new junk king.

Karl Lundgren had been killed with a single shot fired at close range at a point just behind the left ear. It was a typical execution-style murder carried out by someone the target probably knew and trusted. Karl was expecting to meet Guy and turn the money over to him. It was plausible. Grimm had no difficulty imagining Guy Stash killing Karl and taking the money, then trying to make it look as though someone else had done it. But the plan had gone awry because Guy certainly wasn't acting as though he had the money. And Jack was still very much in control.

"The fat man?" asked Tommy, though expecting no answer. "I got a problem with that. See, Saul's half a legitimate guy. He's got a business to run. I don't see him lookin' to go to war with Jack, d'you?"

"No, not at all," Grimm said. "He's crazy, but he's not stupid. Is Jack convinced it's Saul?"

"Jack don't know who it is. He wants like hell to find out. Right now his big worry is gettin' those goods in California cut loose."

"And he wants to be able to tell those people he's got me looking for the money."

Tommy shrugged. "He wants to be able to tell 'em somethin'."

Grimm was shaking his head. "No. I want out. I don't like it."

Tommy got up, and he and Grimm walked toward the door out into the front room of the restaurant. He took Grimm by the arm. "I gotta respect you for your decision, kid, an' I'm behind you. But, I also gotta say, should the information Jack's lookin' for come into your hands, I think it's only right, you should make sure he knows about it.''

Jack was seated at the bar with Virgil when Grimm and Tommy walked out. All the other participants in the sit-down had left.

Tommy put his arm around Jack's shoulders. "Okay, bo. You stay in touch the way we agreed. Just remember what I said. This kid's with me. Now he's Sonny's lawyer, that's all. I got the say-so to decide that much right now.''

"That's fine with me," Jack replied. "Me an' A.G. go back a long way. I got no beef with A.G. It was a misunderstanding, that's all.''

"Yeah, well now he's got dese agents takin' pot shots at him, an' we don't like that," Tommy said. Tommy nodded to Virgil, who went behind the bar and made a call. Within minutes there was a car out front. Tommy kissed both Jack and Grimm on their cheeks, telling them he'd look forward to seeing them in Las Vegas. When he'd left, Grimm and Jack took their drinks and moved from the bar to one of the booths along the wall.

"So what're we gonna do, A.G.?" Jack asked, his mouth drawn in that tight-lipped smile Grimm found so hard to interpret. "What's happenin' with my hundred Gs?''

"Are you serious? What d'you mean, what's happening with it? I gave it to Aaron, just like we agreed." Grimm answered him in complete seriousness.

Jack laughed. "Yeah, I know, good ole Aaron. He's got them deep pockets, right, bo? Ever notice how all these lawyers got suits with pockets down to the knees? Everything goes in those pockets. Nothin' ever comes out.''

"Jack, here's this woman standing up and taking all the weight, and you're worried about a hundred grand?''

"Bo, I'm only fuckin' with ya'. Don't take everything so serious. You think I give a damn about a hundred Gs? I need ten mil, yesterday.''

"Look, you put me in a bad position, Jack. You know I never would've agreed to have anything to do with this if you'd told me about what went down on the Coast. I don't appreciate that. Lance and Roger—''

"Hey! Hold it! Slow down a minute," Jack flared, cutting him off, his eyes flashing with anger. He leaned forward across the table and said, "Before you go sayin' somethin' you're gonna regret later, listen to me. Lemme explain what happened.'' Even with the artificial tan, Jack's mouth had gone white around the lips.

Grimm felt a sudden and intense hatred well up inside him. He had an almost overpowering urge to smash his fist in Jack's surly mouth. Fuck all these people, he thought. Every one of them, with their greed and treachery, their sleazy lives, their phony values. Looking at Jack's puffy face with its cosmetic tan, Grimm was filled with disgust and loathing as he thought of Jack and Sonny making love.

''How'm I supposed to know this lyin' fat fuck didn't tell those guys what was in that load?'' Jack was saying, his lips quivering as he fought to force a note of calm into his voice. ''It was Saul who negotiated the door. I know the cocksucker is sayin' he didn't know what was in there, but that's bullshit. You think I'm gonna risk blowin' somethin' this big just to cheat some guys out of a few million?''

''I don't know what to believe.''

Jack was holding up his hand. ''Wait. Hear me out. I'll tell ya' what really happened. I'm over there, A.G., right? Me an' Sonny, puttin' this trip together for a load of sticks. Sonny leaves me in Hong Kong an' comes back to see about settin' up the catch. Saul, Lance an' Sonny get together here in New York, an' Saul gives Lance a downstroke to grease things up, like a mil to show we're serious. Meanwhile my people in Bangkok, they've also been puttin' together a big load of junk for me on another thing, five hundred kis ready to roll. You know how that goes, nobody wants to sit on that shit. I guess the Thai Army made a big seizure, and they need to make it disappear. But my transportation falls apart, and there I am with no way to get those goods out of Thailand and over here. So I get in touch with Saul an' tell him, 'Talk to Lance. Tell him what we wanna do, an' make the deal. Whatever it takes.'

''The next thing Saul tells me is Lance wants it put together like this, packed like this which is no problem for us an' I get it all done. Saul tells me everything's together on this end. He says he paid Lance extra money. 'Send the package,' he tells me.

''Bo, how do you think I feel? I still find it hard to believe Saul would do this to me, to us, to me an' Sonny, 'cause she had a lot 'a bucks in this thing herself, close to three million in the Thai stick trip. Next thing I hear everything's all fucked up. I'm still over there waitin' to give the Chinese a big payment as soon as we know the load's in an'

SMACK GODDESS

everything's under control. I get in touch back here, an' Sonny's all flipped out. She says Lance is goin' nuts 'cause nobody ever told him about no junk. Seems the fat man gave him seven hundred and fifty grand and told him there might be something extra in the load, but never mentioned it was junk.

"Of course at this point, Saul goes into seclusion an' I can't reach him. No one can. Somehow, Sonny managed to smooth things over. They move some of the goods an' it looks like maybe everything's gonna work out. I come back, an' the shit really hits the fan. Sonny's pinched, this other guy's clipped, an' the money I need right away to square everyone up is gone."

"Whatever," Grimm said. "Still, you should've let me know what I was getting myself into. The whole thing is too full of lies for me. I'm not going to ally myself with anyone because as far as I'm concerned everyone's lying and I don't want anything to do with it."

"Okay. Listen, A.G., I don't want no beefs with choo, bo," Jack said. "We're friends. We been through too much together to let a little misunderstanding come between us. You just do what you gotta do. Watch out for Sonny. Make sure she gets whatever she needs. I'll take care 'a the rest 'a this shit."

Jack stood and waved to Virgil, who picked up the phone and dialed. Shortly, a sedan with two men in it pulled up in front of the restaurant. Jack put on his sunglasses and Yankees cap.

"I suppose Aaron's gonna be lookin' for some more money," he said, facing out to the street and zipping up his jacket.

"Maybe. We'll see how it goes."

"Jesus, a hunnert grand for a fuckin' plea ain't enough? You guys're unbelievable. What the fuck do you do with all your money?"

"Hey, Jack, we've got to fight this case as if we're going to trial. There's a lot of work involved. And Rickie's got to go to trial. So far the hundred from you is all we've got."

"What? Jesus Christ! Are you tellin' me Saul ain't given Aaron no money for Rickie?"

"Just the retainer, and that was gone long ago."

"I'll kill that—" Jack yelled, then quickly controlled himself. "Okay, bo, you tell Aaron I'll cover it if fatso don't. But you gotta gimme a few weeks. Lemme get these Chinks an' everybody else off my back first."

They shook hands, then hugged each other, though Grimm knew things would never be the same.

"You need a lift someplace, Arthur?" Virgil asked from behind the bar as Grimm stood watching Jack climb into the waiting car. "I can call somebody from the club down the street."

"No, thanks, Virg. I feel like walking, then I'll grab a taxi."

He left the restaurant and walked through a small park and across a playground. At least I'm out of the Karl Lundgren quagmire, he thought, feeling at once relieved and oddly deflated. From now on, it no longer matters to me who killed Lundgren and stole the six-and-a-half million. That's Jack's problem. I'm Sonny's lawyer, and that's it. As for the rest of it, the case is closed.

Sure, Grimm, he said to himself.

"All motions denied," pronounced the Honorable Dudley H. Gass from the bench. He gazed down at the congregation of lawyers, defendants and spectators. A dozen lawyers winced.

Aaron Held, as lead counsel, took the initiative and gently tried to coax the judge into hearing oral argument on some of the more meritorious defense motions. Gass meanwhile let his gaze rove around the packed courtroom. The judge appeared to be taking in the scene while tuning out Held's eloquent plea.

And what a scene it was. Rickie's fans were present in force, as were representatives of the media. A mob of spectators gathered at the rear of the courtroom, and more thronged in the foyer and hall.

"How can he do this?" Grimm asked as Held sat back down.

"Simple. He's a psychopath," Held said.

"This is gas warfare," Rickie blurted out loud enough for those around him to hear. Several spectators snickered and Held glared at his client.

Judge Gass, a tall, lean man with straight white hair, a ruddy complexion and craggy Yankee features, seemed to be more concerned with the crowd than with what the defense lawyers had to say. He peered out over the half-lenses of his spectacles and made a wide sweeping motion with one of his robed arms.

"Marshal!" he snapped. "We can't have these spectators standing around in the aisles. I want this court cleared of all but those who have seats."

The chief U.S. Marshal for the district rose from his seat just behind the defense table. A few deputies began clearing the room while spectators tried to squeeze into the already jammed benches.

"The Court has ruled," Gass stated. "You may expect a written ruling forthwith. I have heard all the argument I am going to hear on these motions. If you're not satisfied with the Court's ruling, then I suggest you take up your grievances with the Second Circuit Court of Appeals. That's what the appellate courts are for."

Gass glared at the lawyers as if daring one of them to say something. Even Vaggi looked cowed.

"We will now take a fifteen minute recess, during which time I intend to consult my calendar," the judge went on. "I suggest you gentlemen do the same. When we resume, we will decide upon a trial date. And we will stick to that date. I don't want to hear any excuses down the road that someone has a scheduling conflict. Is that understood?

"Marshal," Gass commanded without waiting for the attorneys to respond, "I want you to restrict the number of spectators. This is a courtroom, not a circus."

With that Gass rose from the bench.

"All rise!" called the bailiff.

"This does not bode well," Held muttered to Grimm as they stood.

There was a stunned silence in the courtroom as Judge Gass swooped down from the bench and strode off to his chambers. Then everyone began talking and moving about. The defense lawyers huddled around Aaron Held. Vaggi conferred with her assistant at the prosecution table.

Sonny looked at Grimm and said, "My God, what a nasty character," as the deputies moved in beside her.

The press converged on Rickie. "This isn't a courtroom, this is a gas chamber," Rickie said.

In the early editions, Rickie would be quoted as calling the judge "Deadly Gass."

Chapter Twelve

It was one of those quiet days in Manhattan, a weekend or holiday morning when everyone seems to have fled the city. As Grimm drove crosstown, whole blocks looked deserted. The empty, battered streets felt more intimate. He was aware of the colossal presence of the buildings.

Grimm too was fleeing, abandoning the vertical city for the undulant dunes of Southampton on what could be the last weekend of warm Indian summer weather before fall closed in. It was the day after Halloween. He wished he was on his way to the farm in Millbrook, alone, or with little Carmen. Instead, he was heading over to pick up Aaron Held and his wife Julia to attend one of Saul Diamond's famous bashes, a champagne brunch and dinner party that would last all weekend.

Many celebrity types were flying in from the Coast. The famous punk rock couple, Rickie Rude and his pregnant lover Suzi Sapphire, would also be there. This would be Rickie's first trip east since the pretrial hearing. Lately, he had been so busy recording a new album in L.A. that neither Held nor Grimm had been able to talk to him except briefly on the phone. Meanwhile, the tentative trial date approached. Held was anxious to begin preparing Rickie's defense. Still no fee was forthcoming.

This was to be a working weekend. Grimm and Held needed to sit down with Rickie to go over the defense strategy. They also wanted to confront Saul about the unpaid bill. Grimm hoped to get the business taken care of in time to make his usual Sunday morning visit with

Sonny. These trysts, what Sonny called her "sex therapy visits," had become a shared passion for them.

Usually they would be alone in the attorney conference room until after ten. Grimm was on good terms with the guard who worked the third floor, a white haired, lumbering black who was a veteran of nearly twenty years with the Bureau of Prisons. Shaking his hand one morning after being admitted, Grimm palmed him a fifty dollar bill. It disappeared into his pocket without a blink. Grimm could never be sure if the guard knew what he and Sonny were up to during those visits—the old man had a way of turning everything he said into a chuckle—but they could always hear the jangle of his keys letting them know he was coming, and he seemed to laugh and smile even more than usual when he let them out of the conference room.

Sonny now ran the Kosher and special diet kitchen in the basement of the prison. Her usual hours were from three in the morning until eleven, so when Grimm arrived, they called down for her and she was with him in minutes. From all appearances, and in her queenly manner, Sonny seemed to have taken over the place. The guards all knew her, and most seemed to like her; calling her "Miz Sonny," they treated her with the deference ordinarily reserved for organized crime bosses. Sonny was a force in the jail. She was buried alive in this building, yet even the people who worked there seemed to be drawn to her for direction.

Sonny would sashay into the conference room dressed in her kitchen whites and would have her pants off as soon as the door was closed behind them. She insisted on fucking before any business was discussed because she said it was impossible for her to concentrate as long as she was horny.

For Grimm, this was some of the most intense sex he'd ever known, a kind of inflamed and perilous athletics. Their large bodies seemed made for each other. He'd never made love with a woman who brought to sex such freedom of spirit and who found such pleasure in every moment of it. She loved to fuck, she loved the feeling of having him up inside her. She told him it had not always been that way for her. For years she'd been too strung out on business and junk to give herself to love. Now she was wet at the thought of him, alive to his touch.

They were doing everything possible given the space and circumstances. They were getting more and more heedless, wild. Grimm knew that if they kept it up, which they would, it was only a matter of time before they were caught. But they didn't care. They were afflicted with some kind of fever. Sonny would straddle him on the chair. He'd hold on to her hips and ass, bury his face in her breasts and go into a blind dazed fuck as if they were alone in the world. She felt so familiar, so right. Even her sweat had a known taste like well water from home. Whenever he fucked her, he had the sensation of being back in familiar surroundings, back where he belonged. Sometimes they both took off their pants and fucked on the floor as though it were perfectly natural. Or Sonny would lean across the table and stick her ass up. Grimm, to her rear, would go in to the hilt. Sometimes, Sonny would disappear under the table and suck his cock if there were other people outside. "Just so you don't get horny during the week," she'd say from under the table as she unzipped his fly.

They were goofy, always laughing and rolling around like kids.

"What would you say if someone came in right now and asked what we're doing?" Sonny said to him one morning when he was deep inside her.

"I'd invoke the attorney-client privilege," Grimm said and they both laughed so hard he could feel the walls of muscle inside Sonny contracting in spasms.

It was the laughter that nearly got them caught. The few close calls they'd had occurred when other lawyers or prisoners came in to check on all the noise.

There was tenderness, too. It was becoming obvious to both of them that beyond all the crazy fun, they were growing deeply attached to each other. Grimm was continually surprised at how comfortable he felt with her. He respected her strength and courage.

They took every day as it came, without a past, and never spoke of the future, except as it pertained to proceedings in the court case. She was going to prison, about that there could be no doubt. The limited time they had together, and the strangeness of the situation, added to the force of their love. It was all passion, passion at the edge of the abyss.

Grimm could only feel a kind of awe for the way Sonny was handling herself. As she grew physically stronger and healthier, her character seemed to strengthen and grow as well. She had quit cigarettes and even given up marijuana while she concentrated on getting her body in shape. She was taking yoga classes, meditating, reading two or three books a week, and participating in the exercise and consciousness raising group she'd helped organize on the women's unit. She was preparing special meals and sending them to all her friends on the various floors, managing a full-blown food smuggling operation, and putting her affairs in order.

"You're the busiest jailbird I've ever met," Grimm told her. Sonny said that keeping busy was her way of dealing with depression and loneliness. Her only complaint was she could not get enough of him.

Sonny was to plead guilty in front of Judge Gass in mid-November. On her behalf, Grimm had rejected all offers from the prosecutor's office that included cooperation with the government. Negotiations with Vita Vaggi had all but broken down. They had reached an impasse over the issue of Sonny's possible testimony for the defense at Rickie's trial. Vaggi, her hopes of securing indictments against Jack Moriarty, Guy Stash and Saul Diamond shattered, now focused all her wrath on prosecuting Rickie.

After Judge Gass ruled on the pretrial motions, Moon Landing's lawyer was able to obtain a hearing. He claimed that Vaggi had made misstatements of fact in her brief responding to Moon's motion to suppress the evidence found in his apartment—various small quantities of drugs. The suppression motion had been based on lack of probable cause to search Moon's apartment. At the hearing, Vaggi got trapped in a lie she was forced to resort to because DEA agent Zuluaga had made false representations in the affidavit used to obtain the search warrant.

When the lie became apparent, Judge Gass was irate. He came down hard on Vaggi, ordering the evidence seized in Moon's possession suppressed. He all but told Vaggi that because of her mishandling of the case, he was changing his ruling with regard to Moon and dismissing the indictment.

At this point, the remaining defendants, except for Rickie, had agreed to plead guilty in exchange for various recommendations from the government at sentencing. This left only Rickie to fight the charges. Vaggi was now trying to have Sonny's sentencing delayed until sometime after Rickie's trial. She insisted that her recommendation of fifteen years on the 848 count, the continuing criminal enterprise, which was to run concurrently with fifteen year sentences on the other counts, be contingent upon an agreement with Sonny that she would not testify on Rickie's behalf.

Sonny was outraged by this demand and instructed Grimm to turn the deal down flat. Vaggi retorted that she would ask for "a substantial period of incarceration" if Sonny helped Rickie. Grimm's only hope was to try to outmaneuver Vaggi by taking the issue directly before Judge Gass.

Grimm's shoulder was completely healed and he was almost back to full strength. As busy as he was with the Rude/Byrne-Downes case and his affair with Sonny, he still made time to work out regularly at the New York Athletic Club. He'd also been spending some time recently with Sonny's daughter, Carmen. Carmen seemed to have resigned herself to the idea that she was to go back to England while her mother went away to prison. Like Sonny, she never complained or felt sorry for herself. There were plans for her to spend a month at Grimm's farm during the summer when she came over to visit Sonny. Grimm adored the little girl. She was so bright and optimistic. Carmen had become a new source of joy in his life.

"Bad news, babe," Aaron Held said as he unfolded his long body into the front bucket seat of Grimm's car. Grimm kissed Held's wife, Julia, who sat in back, then pulled away from the couple's East Side townhouse. "I just got off the phone with Sonny," the lawyer continued. "Rumor has it that Brad Caine and Donnie Randazzo rolled over."

Grimm was alarmed. Caine and Randazzo, along with Micky Hoyos, were the only defendants other than Sonny who were still in custody. "You're shitting me," he said.

"I wish I were. Sonny says she saw Micky Hoyos this morning. She tried to reach you but you'd already left. Hoyos told her that both Caine and Randazzo disappeared suddenly from the units they were on. You know, the kind of moves they make in the middle of the night. The word is they're both down on the third floor in protective custody."

Grimm let this information sink in as he turned onto the East River Drive. "Have you contacted their lawyers yet?" he asked Held.

"Not yet. I thought I'd speak with you first."

"I suppose two out of twelve isn't bad," Julia Held said.

"Wrong, dear. I beg to differ. In this case it's bad. If Rickie were guilty, I would expect ten out of twelve to roll over. But this is an indication of how far Vaggi is prepared to go to get her conviction. Sonny assures me Caine and Randazzo are going to have to lie to put

Rickie in this conspiracy. You know how difficult it is to defend against lies. No, quite frankly I'm shocked Vaggi would stoop so low.''

"Maybe you've never been up against her in a case she wanted as badly as she wants this one," Grimm said.

"Of course," Julia agreed. "Not only does she want it, she's got to have this conviction. After all the time and money they have invested in this, if she loses, her career will suffer. Now listen, Arthur. I told Aaron a juicy bit of gossip I heard from a friend of mine who works with Vita.''

"Yes. Let's hear it," Grimm said.

"Vita is having an affair with an FBI man who's married and has four kids.''

Grimm looked at her in the rearview mirror. "Let me guess. His name is Doug Whelan." Julia was nodding, smiling. "President's Task Force on Organized Crime.''

"How astute of you. See, Aaron, I told you Arthur would know.''

Aaron Held said, "Good old Doug Whelan, who is now acting as a sort of unofficial case agent on this.''

"It seems like everything about this case is unofficial," Grimm said.

"Vita, of all people," Julia said. "With a married man, and a Catholic, no less. She must be losing her mind.''

"It's this case," Grimm said. "There's a kind of infectious madness about it.''

"Dominic Randazzo," Held mused aloud. "I must say, I'm a little surprised by that defection. What do you suppose he knows about Sonny's heavy friends?''

"It would seem to me that is the important question, and how he can put Rickie together with them.''

"I trust you'll look into that," the attorney said.

Grimm had not seen or heard from Jack Moriarty, or any of his people, since the Pleasant Avenue sit-down. He had been told, however, by his California friends, that all threats and intimations of war had been quelled. As often happens in such disputes, everything was forgiven in the name of money. Jack's charm and cash reserves had persuaded the San Francisco smugglers to open their stash coffers and the junk was flowing again. A six-and-a-half-million dollar loss had been absorbed, possibly written off as the steepest fee ever paid to silence an informant.

"Do you suppose Donnie Randazzo has any information on the untimely demise of Karl Lundgren?" Held asked as though picking up on Grimm's train of thought.

"I don't know," Grimm said. "But I'll bet that's how Vaggi got to him. They've been trying to lay that body off on everyone."

"The body." Held turned in his seat and faced Grimm. "Damnit, Arthur, what about the money? Don't you suppose anyone's interested in that? That's an awful lot of incentive. Aren't you even curious?"

"I'm off the case," Grimm said. "I'm a lawyer now. I'm no longer being paid to be curious."

"But surely you must have a theory," Julia said. "Who do you think did it?"

They were crossing the Triboro Bridge. Grimm slowed down to pay the toll. "Well, let me put it this way," he said, rolling down the window and handing a bill to the toll collector. "If I were a gambling man, which I'm not, I'd have to go with the odds, which are that somehow Saul managed it." As he drove away from the toll plaza, heading for Long Island, Grimm took a joint from his pocket. "Now, I'm not comfortable with that position. It could've just as easily been Jack's right-hand man, Guy Stash." Grimm depressed the cigarette lighter.

"But why would they want to steal money from themselves, Arthur?" Julia asked. "It was their money, wasn't it?"

Grimm lit the joint. "In a sense. But there's company money, so to speak, and then there's personal money. Whoever did it obviously discovered Lundgren was acting as an informant for the DEA. So they killed him, a reasonable solution. They probably felt they had the money coming as a sort of bonus."

"Knowing Jack Moriarty, he probably set the whole thing up himself," Aaron Held said.

"That's the FBI's theory," Grimm said, "or at least one they're working with. It has a few strong points, but I don't buy it. I will tell you one thing off the record, which I don't want repeated. Guy Stash is in dishonor, and it has something to do with this case. Jack may even have located the money." Grimm offered the joint to Held.

"No," Held said as he took the joint, "Saul did it. Not Saul personally, of course, but one of his gorillas. Guy Stash is in trouble because he let it happen.''

"Very possible," Grimm said.

Held puffed on the joint. "Then again, Zuluaga must have had his slimy hand in there somewhere.''

"Dear me . . . No, thank you, darling. Arthur's stuff is too strong for me," Julia said as she refused the joint. Held, holding it awkwardly between his thumb and forefinger as though it were some kind of insect, passed the joint back to Grimm. "You mean to say," Julia went on, "Saul's a murderer and we're going out to his country mansion for the weekend? How exciting.''

"What I want to know is why won't the fat son-of-a-bitch come off some of that money?'' Held asked and stared at Grimm. "Arthur, we're not leaving there without our fee.''

One thing could honestly be said for Saul Diamond, thought Grimm on more than one occasion during the long weekend: when it comes to throwing a party, no one would ever accuse him of being a cheapskate. At a rough guess, Grimm and Aaron Held figured the party tab would run over a quarter of a million, not including the coke and other illegal substances Saul made available.

Judy Roth, Saul's hardworking executive assistant, made an announcement, which was also printed on the back of the schedule of events each guest received, that the partygoers should eat and drink to their heart's content and without guilt because, said Judy, Saul and Diamond Star Enterprises had pledged to match the amount spent on the party to a charity for orphaned children. Saul was a real-life Santa to hundreds of New York orphans each year. He was a leading contributor to *The New York Times* Neediest Cases Fund. Curiously, though, when he owed a real debt, like Rickie's legal fees, it was an ordeal getting him to pay.

A seemingly endless procession of limousines arrived and departed Dune Castle throughout the weekend. Beginning with brunch Saturday morning, the party continued indefinitely, with guests coming and going, or staying over in the extra rooms and at a local inn Saul had booked. Most of the guests were music and movie business heavies, rock 'n' rollers, actors and actresses, directors, producers, promoters, and record and film company magnates. There were also artists and writers, journalists, including Rickie's friend Moon Landing, sports celebrities, publishers, and the usual batch of New York and L.A. professional partygoers. Mixed in with this crowd Grimm recognized a smattering of upper-echelon dope dealers who were careful to pay their respects to him and to Aaron Held.

The party was billed as a prenuptial celebration for Diamond Star's biggest moneymakers, Rickie Rude and Suzi Sapphire. As the world's premier punk couple, Rickie and Suzi were both peaking in popularity. Suzi had announced her pregnancy, " . . . another little punk on the planet . . . ," at the opening show of her national tour held in the Cow Palace in L.A. Suzi's month-long nationwide tour was due to wind up with a show at Madison Square Garden. Diamond Star Enterprises was promoting the show as the first public wedding of punk royalty. Rickie and Suzi were to be married on stage in a rock 'n' roll ceremony attended by thousands of fans. Pictures and articles about Rickie and Suzi appeared everywhere.

Rickie's new album, *Rude Awakening,* was soon to be released. One of the cuts from the album had come out as a single, and along with a controversial video was creating a furor in the entertainment world. The song, "The Ayatollah of Rock 'n' Rollah," shot up the charts into the Top Ten in spite of the fact that it had been banned from the air by a number of radio stations in different parts of the country. You couldn't walk past a newsstand in New York without seeing the wan, blue-eyed face of one or the other of them—and usually both—staring back. The current issue of *Time* magazine had a cover story on the self-styled Ayatollah, showing Rickie as he appeared in the video, with his punked-out Khomeini garb, above the caption, "Iconoclast or Criminal?" *People* magazine had both punks on the cover, and *Penthouse* ran a nude spread on Suzi which included the shots Karl Lundgren had taken of her sticking her ass out at the world.

Rickie was becoming the most talked about rock star since John Lennon. Rickie's new song was denounced by the leaders of the Moral Majority and other groups like MOM (Mothers Opposed to Marijuana). The groups called the video obscene and said it promoted drug use and espoused anti-Americanism. In the video, Rickie plays a punk leader known as Iatoldya Nomeanie, boss of a nation which is actually a state of mind called Irock ("You know, Irock, Irack, Iran"). He has captured and taken hostage all American female youth between the ages of thirteen and twenty, and makes demands to the President of America, one Ronald Rayguns, for the girls' release. Nomeanie is shown surrounded by semi-nude nubile girls as he sucks on a hookah filled with marijuana and hashish. He billows clouds of smoke like fog while he negotiates with the President via televiewer.

Rayguns, who looks like a demented cross between Reagan and Ronald McDonald, secretly plans with his advisors to destroy Irock. Rayguns and his mob keep bombing Third World countries where they think Nomeanie is operating. But after each explosion, the screen clears, smoke appears, and Rickie reappears with new demands, and the heavy weaponry of electric guitars.

Opinion among the critics was divided as to whether Rickie had finally succeeded in going beyond the limits of bad taste. Many said his content had become too provocative. Even some of his staunchest supporters found it hard to accept the Ayatollah incarnation. Still, it was a catchy tune, and the video was simply brilliant, scandalous though it may have been.

The B-side, called "Terra Incognita," another cut from the *Rude Awakening* album, was Rickie at his best on electric guitar; he evoked sounds from the instrument that hadn't been heard since Jimi Hendrix died, behind beautiful lyrics on a stranger-in-a-strange-land theme about a space traveler caught in a harsh dimension and longing for Mother Earth, which has been befouled, disemboweled, rendered lifeless.

Rickie, despite all the press and media coverage, refused to play the part of the superstar. In the few interviews and public statements he gave, he was as self-effacing as always, maintaining that his music was his vehicle of expression and that he was not advocating subversive activity. Following Aaron Held's advice, he reserved comment on the upcoming drug trial.

Cassy Steiger was at the Dune Castle party when Grimm and the Helds arrived early Saturday. She had come in from the Coast with Rickie and Suzi's entourage a few days before and was staying at the mansion while preparing to tape the Madison Square Garden extravaganza.

Grimm found Cassy at the estate's tennis courts. There was a buffet table and bar set up beside the courts. Grimm had a glass of champagne and watched Cassy and her partner easily beat their opponents.

"I see you're all healed," Cassy said when they had finished the set.

"C'mon, let's go for a swim," he said, and took her by the arm.

"Why didn't you call me and let me know you were in New York?" Grimm asked as they sat on the edge of the indoor pool.

"Was I suppose to?" She was hunched over, slowly kicking her lower legs in the water, all but the tips of her sleek, freckled breasts visible in the tiny bikini she had on.

"I thought we were friends."

Cassy looked at him. "We are friends. Man, you wanna hear how busy I been? We been doin' this feature-length documentary on Rickie and Suzi. Everybody's burnt out. I just hope I make it through this last gig."

Cassy looked back down at her legs, watching the bubbles she churned up. Grimm could see the muscles in her thighs flex as she kicked. Her legs and hips were well developed, and hard little triceps stood out at the backs of her arms. She was the first woman Grimm had known with a body he would describe as muscular and yet feminine. She seemed reluctant to look him in the eyes. Something's the matter with her, he thought.

"Did you catch the Ayatollah video yet?" she asked, still gazing down at the water in the pool.

"It's fantastic," he said. "I love it."

"Yeah." Cassy laughed. "Rickie's crazy, a genius. I'll tell ya' what, though, that video pissed a lotta people off. You should see the hate mail he's been gettin'."

"Look at me," Grimm said. He took hold of her chin and held her head so that he could look directly into her pale blue eyes. He looked at her deeply for a moment and then said, "Cassy, have you been doing coke?"

She frowned and compressed her lips. "Hey, what d'you want from me?" she said and shook her head free. "What I do is none 'a your business."

"I asked you a question, that's all."

"So who the fuck're you? My old man or somethin'? Don't try to lay any trips on me, Arthur, okay? You don't know what I been goin' through."

Grimm jumped down into the pool and moved around in front of her. He stood between her legs. "Will you please look at me?"

"Buzz off."

He put his hands on her thighs.

"Don't touch me."

"Cassy—"

"Leave me alone!"

"What happened, you forgot what that shit did to your brother? You want me to tell you about it?"

"I want you to leave me the fuck alone. That's all I want you to do."

Grimm started to move away from her but Cassy held him with her legs. "Hey, relax, will ya?" she said, finally looking at him. "We're talkin' a couple 'a hits now an' then. Nothin' serious, no pipe or nothin'. I been real tired, okay? So once in a while I do a line or two. No big thing."

"Oh, is that right?" he said and gave her a sarcastic sneer. "No big thing, huh? I might as well kiss your ass goodbye. Already you don't seem like the same person."

Cassy hung her head and began kicking her legs in the water again. "Fuck you, mister," she said in a sad, subdued voice. "I don't care if you don't wanna be my friend. I never liked you anyway."

"I'm sorry to hear that."

"You're full of shit."

"Maybe. But I always tried to be honest with you."

"You did? So how come I feel like this?" She looked up at him with pain in her eyes. "Jus' 'cause you don't feel nothin' doesn't mean emotions don't exist."

Grimm felt his heart sink. He had seen so many people destroy themselves with cocaine. And always they began by saying they didn't do much, it wasn't really a problem, just a few lines now and then. Next came the excuses: I'm tired, I'm trying to lose weight, I'm depressed, I fuck better on it. All of a sudden you saw them and they looked like they'd aged ten years in a year. Then their whole existence seemed to revolve around the next snort, the next hit on the pipe. He turned away from her.

"Arthur," Cassy cried. "So now I suppose you're jus' gonna walk way from me, huh? Shit, you're such a cold-blooded prick!"

"Just let me ask you this, does your brother know?"

"No. And you better not tell him, either," she snapped. "What the fuck kind 'a friend are you, anyway?"

He put his arms around her hips and pulled her into the pool. Cassy slid into the water with her long legs wrapped around him.

"Be nice to me, okay, Dad? Everybody needs a friend sometimes."

She looked up at him with a joyless smile. Grimm kissed her.

"There, now that's more like it," she said. "Promise me you'll always be my friend. Don't ever turn your back on me and walk away. Promise?"

"I promise," Grimm said.

Somehow they ended up in Cassy's room, in bed, making love. Grimm would always wonder exactly how it happened. It was spontaneous, no word was spoken. They left the pool and wandered into the cavernous house. The plan had been to put some clothes on and look for Rickie and Suzi. But by the time they got to Cassy's room, they were all over each other.

They stayed in bed until evening, dozing in each other's arms, then making love again. There was a fireworks display on the beach behind the mansion. Grimm woke with the first incandescent burst of colored light outside the bedroom window. Cassy, curled beside him, had her face pressed into the crook of his arm, mouth open. She slept heavily, wearily, like a child. Now you've gone and done it, he thought as he looked at her. Fucked your best friend's kid sister. Max is not going to go for this at all.

Her body made him think of a fawn. The long, smooth arms and legs were covered with fine, almost pure white down over tawny skin and russet dapples and freckles. The hair between her legs was burnt orange. Grimm had never made love with a redhead before and everything about her was different. Her nipples were bright pink and soft. She smelled clean, earthy, like the smell that hit you in the face when you got tackled and fell on freshly broken turf.

At first, Cassy had been awkward and tentative. It was all still new to her.

"Just relax," Grimm had told her, trying not to feel like a lecher. "Flow with it, sweetheart." He couldn't help thinking, Her brother's going to hate me. He thought she would go mad when he put his face in her cunt and started kissing it, licking it, rubbing his nose in it. She came ferociously and squeezed his head with her strong legs.

It was altogether different from the impetuous love he enjoyed with Sonny at the jail. Usually, he walked out of MCC feeling weak in the knees, as though Sonny had zapped him with a powerful jolt of current. With Cassy, it was more like an exchange of forces. He could feel the energy flowing out and then coming back into him.

Cassy held nothing back, unlike Sonny who, for all her abandon, always seemed to rein in some intangible core. Cassy seemed to melt into him. And he was absorbing her, drawing her in through the skin and membranes like a fine mist.

She awoke with a start at the first shuddering boom of the fireworks. She jerked awake with panic until she saw Grimm and realized what had caused the explosion.

"Oh, Arthur. Thank God. I wonder if I'll ever get over that you got shot on our first date?" She smiled and cuddled closer, then she reached between his legs and took hold of his cock deftly. "Mmmmm, mister. What have you done to your little girl? Spoiled her for life, now, haven't you?" she said, fondling him.

His cock stirred and he kissed her. "Happy?"

"Man, now I know what all the fuss is about. Nobody ever got me off like that."

When at last they got out of bed, dressed and reappeared at the party, it was as though everyone knew where they'd been and understood that now they were together. It was as though they gave off a new vibration.

Cassy assumed a whole new dimension in Grimm's mind. She was no longer Max's tomboy kid sister, no longer just the pretty, competent young woman whose near clairvoyant vigilance had saved his life. Now she was a lover. He wasn't even worried about confronting Max anymore. He'd been inside her. They were part of each other now.

They ate at a table with Rickie and Suzi, Moon Landing and his girlfriend, a Japanese writer who lived in San Francisco, and the Helds.

Rickie had changed his hairstyle. Gone was the spotted leopard pelt look. His hair was close to the same pale gold hue as Suzi's. He'd let it grow out on top and had shaved his skull to the rims of his ears so that the hair stuck up from the top of his head like a round tuft of frosted straw. It gave him a monkish look that fit with his new persona as mock religious ruler. As always he was amiable, warmly greeting anyone who came to the table to meet him. Rickie looked overwrought, though, and in need of a long rest before undertaking the stress of a criminal trial.

Like Grimm, Rickie was a marijuana maven. They both loved exotic cannabis, and whenever they got together, they would check out what the other was smoking. After dinner, Rickie lit up a joint, took a couple of deep hits, and passed it to Grimm. Dune Castle's chief domestic, Dr. Wu, and a flock of Chinese men and women sped around the room clearing tables, serving coffee and liqueurs. So far no one had seen Saul.

"How do you like it?" Rickie asked Grimm as he passed the joint on to Moon's date.

"Nice taste," Grimm said. "What is it?"

"Hawaiian," Rickie said. "Kona gold. Max gave it to me. I've got a quarter pound he gave me for you, too."

Aaron Held looked askance at the punk rock star. "Jesus, Rickie— please don't tell me you've been running around the country with pounds of marijuana. For God's sake, hire someone to carry your shit for you. Let's not make Vaggi's job any easier."

Rickie turned on him with his huge, dolorous blue eyes.

"You think I'm overreacting?" Held asked. "Arthur, shall we clue him in on the sort of people we're up against? You know Sonny's associates, Brad Caine and Donnie Randazzo?"

"Sure, I know them," Rickie answered with a faint smile.

"Well, they've rolled over. They're now working for the other side."

"Huh? What're you talking about?"

Held opened his eyes wide and stuck his face out at Rickie. "They rolled over," he said, rolling his eyeballs. "Vaggi flipped them. They're going to be witnesses for the prosecution and take the stand against you."

Rickie looked perplexed. "Testify against me? What're they going to say? I never did anything with them."

"Why don't we discuss this later," Grimm said. "No sense spoiling the party. Where's our gracious host, anyway?"

"In his office doin' lines an' talkin' shit on the phone, where else?" Suzi said. "He talks on the phone twenty four hours a day. He never comes outta that office."

"Listen, Arthur. I know this is a party and all that." Held stared at Grimm. "But the fact is we've got a trial coming up in January and Judge Gass is not going to give us a continuance, no matter how whacked-out Saul is. You've got to have a little chat with him."

"Wow," Rickie said, looking at Held and shaking his head. "I hear what you're sayin', Aaron. You mean this fat jerk hasn't paid you yet?"

Held scowled. "I realize this isn't the time or place, but I'm afraid that's exactly what I mean."

"Shit!" Rickie exclaimed and his pale cheeks flushed with anger. "He told me it was all taken care of."

"Well, it isn't. He keeps assuring us the check's in the mail. But for some reason it never arrives."

"A.G., do me a favor," Rickie said. "Pay him a visit. Do whatever you gotta do, but tell him if he doesn't pay this bill, he can forget about the Madison Square Garden show."

"Excuse me," Grimm said touching Cassy and getting up from the table. "I'll go have a word with him right now."

Grimm walked the length of the vast house until he came to the suite of offices that served as headquarters for Diamond Star Enterprises. He knocked on the door to Saul's office, but received no reply. The door was locked, so he walked along the hall to Judy Roth's office and, finding the door unlocked, went in.

On Judy's desk stood a console telephone with one button glowing steadily and another blinking. As Suzi had supposed, Saul was talking on the telephone. Grimm tried the door adjoining the two offices, but it was also locked. He put his ear to the door, but could hear nothing. He went back to Judy's desk, depressed the glowing button, then covered the mouthpiece and slowly lifted the receiver. At first, he heard only the hollow crackling sounds of an overseas connection, then Saul's basso profundo voice enquiring, "You still there?"

"Yeah, man," said a voice that sounded as though it belonged to an Hispanic male.

"Judy? That you, hon? Hold on a sec."

Grimm quickly replaced the receiver. He stepped back against the wall beside the door to Saul's office. A moment later, Grimm heard the door being unlocked. As it opened toward him, he grabbed hold of the handle and yanked, pulling Saul's bodyguard, Gene Machine, into the room.

"Hold it," Grimm said as Gene regained his balance and reached toward the small of his back for a weapon. He moved into the doorway so Saul could see him. "I just want to pay my respects to the host."

"A.G., c'mon in, pal. I should'a known it was you."

Saul waved Grimm into the office. He stabbed a button on the phone console with a finger as thick as a sausage, and resumed his conversation. Saul motioned Grimm to a chair as he spoke into the phone.

"That's not the point," Saul growled. "Don't worry about that. I told Ramón my people would take up the slack. You just take care of your end and let me take care of the rest. Look, call me back. I'm busy right now. Call me when you got something intelligent to say."

Grimm was looking at a framed photograph which hung among a display of awards, plaques, gold and platinum albums, and other pieces of memorabilia. The picture was of Saul dressed as Santa Claus and surrounded by awestruck children, the boys and girls of the Suffolk County orphanage Saul patronized.

Saul slammed down the receiver and turned toward Gene Machine. "Now listen, Machine, see if you can find Judy. Tell her to take all calls."

As soon as Gene Machine left the office, Saul took a piece of black marble from his desk drawer. He dumped out a vial of coke, then swooped down over the piece of marble and inhaled the little pile of powder. "Shit, A.G.," he said as he came up laughing, coughing, his eyes watering, "is that any way to break in here?"

"How else am I supposed to get to see you? You're like the Pope in here. What am I going to do, wait for you to give me an audience?"

Saul rumbled with laughter, his body quaking like a man with the hiccups. "The Pope, that's good, A.G. I been called a lot 'a things."

"Saul, let me ask you a question. Do you care whether or not Rickie gets convicted and goes to prison?"

"Jesus, A.G. Now what kind 'a dumb fucking question is that?"

"Then let me ask you another dumb question. Do you intend to pay Aaron's fee?"

"The fee. Aaron sent you in here to shake me down." Saul erupted from his chair. "Crooks. Fuckin' gangsters. That's all you lawyers are," he said as he piloted his huge body over to the bar. "What the fuck's he crying about? The publicity alone on this thing's worth a million bucks."

"C'mon, Saul. You know better than that. Aaron's got an office to run. He's been putting practically all his energy into Rickie's case. You promised me you'd pay, and you broke your word. It's Rickie's money. Rickie makes a fortune for you. He deserves the best defense money can buy."

"Of course he does. The kid's innocent. He doesn't even belong in this case." The promoter wiped his brow and poured two drinks from the pre-mixed batch of magaritas in the blender. He wore his silk robe.

"So pay Aaron his money and let him do his job," Grimm said as Saul handed him a drink. "You just hate to give Aaron money."

"Half a million balloons, Arthur! And I already gave him three hundred grand this year." He took a long drink of his margarita and moved back to his desk. "Who can afford such lawyer fees?" He chuckled.

Grimm said, "I'm not leaving this office until you come up with that money."

Saul's face went blank. "I don't have it right this minute. But I'll get it, A.G. You just gotta gimme some time, that's all."

"Rickie told me to tell you that unless you pay Aaron, he and Suzi will cancel the Madison Square Garden show."

Beads of sweat broke out on Saul's head. He sat back down and began rummaging in his desk looking for more coke. "He can't do that to me!"

Grimm got up and walked over to the fat man. "Saul, listen to me. I don't know what you're doing with Rickie's money, or with Suzi's money. That's not my business. You get together every cent you can find and give it to me toward Aaron's fee, or there'll be no Madison Square Garden show. Understand?"

The two men stared at each other. Saul's eyes glazed over and he looked away.

"All right. All right already," he said and went back to his search. "Jesus! You guys're unbelievable. Talk about heavy tactics. The wiseguys got nothing on you. What the fuck?" He snatched up the phone.

"Wu? Where's Miss Judy? I mean, where the fuck is everybody? I got no stash in here. Listen, when you see Miss Judy and Mr. Machine, tell them both to come to my office." He slammed down the phone.

"Judy's hiding my coke," he said and gave Grimm a desperate look. "She's worse than my wife, this kvetch. Nag, nag, nag. And now I got you and Aaron breathing down my neck. How the fuck am I supposed to get anything done around here? Now tell me, A.G., what's the story with Jack? You seen that Irish cocksucker lately?"

"I saw him at Virgil's. I haven't seen him since then."

"Sit down, please. You make me nervous. What is Jack tryin' to do to me, bro? Him an' his fuckin' greaseballs. Doesn't he know he can't trust those people?"

"Saul, there's six, almost seven million dollars missing. A guy got murdered who supposedly had that money with him. And there's every reason to believe the last stop the guy made was right here."

Saul's eyes narrowed. The fat of his face rippled as he glanced around. "Here? Who says he was here?"

"I say he was here."

After a tense pause, Saul said, "You told Jack this?"

Grimm shook his head. "No. I'm worried about you, Saul. I don't want to see you go to war."

"Is that what these low-life cocksuckers are threatening? They wanna go to war with me?"

There was a knock at the door and Gene Machine entered from Judy's office. Saul scribbled on a piece of paper and gave it to Gene. "Bring me that," he said. "An' bring me an ounce. Judy's been hiding my stash again. And find Aaron Held and Rickie an' tell 'em to come here. Then bring me those papers. And have Judy call me.

"Oh, man, see what I'm up against?" Saul gasped. "Yeah, okay, you're right. That guy was here. He brought me a pound 'a coke for my stash. But when he came out here he didn't have the money with him. He told me he couldn't fit it all in the car. He said he was gonna meet Guy Stash an' take him to the money. I had no idea the guy was a rat. I mean, before you found out, who knew that? When he left me, he was on his way to the airport. I still say agents clipped him an' kept the money for themselves."

"What time was it when he left here?"

"Eight, nine, who knows from time? Bo, he was gonna go straight to Kennedy an' meet Guy."

"Did he say where the money was?"

"No. I figured it was at the loft in SoHo. The dog was guarding the money. At least, that's what I thought. I mean, who wants to drive around with all that paper?"

The phone sounded and Saul snatched up the receiver. "Hi ya', hon. Everything all right? How's my mother? Is she enjoying the party? Good. Listen, Jude, come on up an' see me a minute, will ya', sweetie? I need to ask you something."

The door opened and Rickie came in followed by Aaron Held.

"She's the only one who knows what's goin' on around this nuthouse," Saul said as he replaced the receiver and looked up at Held and Rickie.

Saul got to his feet and waddled over to hug Rickie, his massive body nearly enveloping the tiny rock star. He and Aaron Held kissed gingerly on the cheek, then stepped back and eyed one another with a mixture of affection and suspicion.

"Lissen 'a me, you shyster," Saul said to Held. "Next time I invite you to my home for a party, don't go sendin' your muscle in here to shake me down." He laughed, mounds of blubber shaking beneath the Chinese robe. Then he went to his desk, took out a huge checkbook, and stood over it as he wrote out a check.

"The rest I'm gonna give you in cash," Saul said as he handed the check to Held. "I trust that won't present any problems."

Aaron Held looked at the check and rolled his eyes. He stood round-shouldered, hunched over the check.

"Don't worry, it's good," Saul said.

"I'm watching to see if the ink disappears," Held said with a sly smile. He folded the check and put it into his pocket with an almost ritualistic precision. Held lit an English Oval and he and Rickie sat down.

There was a soft knock at the door. Judy Roth came in followed by Gene Machine, who was carrying a briefcase. Saul tried to wave some kind of signal to Gene.

"Hello, Arthur, Aaron," Judy said, kissing them both. She turned to face her boss just as Gene Machine handed him a plastic baggie full of coke. Saul tried to slip the bag into his desk, but Judy saw him.

"No, Saul, I haven't been hiding your coke. I suggest you look up your nose."

"Good one, babe. Keep trying." Saul popped open the briefcase and looked inside. He whispered to Gene and to Judy, who leaned over the checkbook Saul had withdrawn the check from. Saul closed the briefcase and told Gene Machine to hand it to Held.

"Arthur, would you take care of that for me, please?" the lawyer said, waving his arm at the briefcase as though he were afraid of the contents. "I trust it's all there."

"How 'bout a couple 'a lines to celebrate?" Saul took the bag of coke from his desk. He looked up at Judy with a guilty expression on his face. "It's a party, hon."

"Yes. And somebody has got to see to the guests. Are you ever coming out of here?"

"Sure. Run along." Saul said. He dumped coke on the piece of marble and began carving long lines. "I'll be with you in just a minute."

With Judy gone, Saul stuck a crystal tube in his nostril and sucked up the lines like a vacuum cleaner. Rickie and Grimm, comfortable in their cannabis heads, declined, but Aaron Held stooped his tall frame over and noisily snorted two lines.

Rickie and Grimm looked at each other. Rickie gave a shrug of his slight shoulders and said, "My life is in the hands of maniacs."

"Now, Randazzo and Caine, what can they say to implicate you, Rickie?" Held sat back down and focused on Rickie. "Were you ever present when any drug transactions took place between either of them and Sonny?"

"Drug transactions? Aaron, to be around Sonny is to be around drug transactions. I don't know. I suppose so. Nothing heavy. The heavy shit she kept separate. But the business was always there. I never even paid any attention to it. People used to talk to her about drugs the way they talk to me about music."

"Where would these conversations take place? Can you remember any?"

"I used to run into them at her place. I'd see Brad at the club, Little Babylon. We got high. Smoke an occasional joint."

"Let me ask you this," Held continued, holding his cigarette aloft in one hand and running the other through his hair as he spoke. "Did you ever give either of them drugs or take money from them on Sonny's behalf?"

Rickie frowned and thought about this question. "No, I seriously doubt that. You know, anyone who knows me will tell you, I don't handle money. And the only drugs I touch are for my head, or for my friends. Sonny would never ask me to handle shit for her."

"Did you discuss drug deals with them? Or did they discuss drug deals with each other, or with Sonny, in your presence? I'm just trying to get an idea what Vaggi might have in mind with them."

"Again, that's really hard to say with any certainty. Sure, drug deals were always being discussed. But like I say, I was not really part of those conversations. Usually if Sonny was putting together something with somebody, and other people who weren't involved were around, out of respect, and discretion, she'd go into another room and talk to them in private. Let's say like I'm over at her place hangin' out and Donnie Randazzo comes over, which probably happened a couple of times. Now I know what he's there for. Business. But if he has something heavy he needs to discuss with Sonny, she'll take him in the other room.

"See, one thing you gotta understand, Aaron, Me an' Sonny, we're very close. I've know her for almost fifteen years. We love each other. We're like brother and sister. We trust each other completely."

"I see," Held said. "The problem is the government is going to try to turn that around and make it look like something illegal. To have a close relationship with a person who's a criminal, well, it can very easily be made to look like a criminal conspiracy. Conversations, telephone calls, meetings, this is the stuff of conspiracy. It's all simply a matter of perspective, of how the relationship is presented to a jury. You and Sonny were never lovers?"

Rickie smiled ruefully. "No. I mean, like I say, we love each other, but for some reason, we never got it on. A couple of times we came close. It was just close friendship, almost too close for lovers."

"Which is, you see, actually, worse," Held said.

"Why's that?"

"It's harder for a jury to comprehend and believe in that kind of a relationship. Right, Arthur?"

"Yes. They understand lovers. They understand business associates. But close friendship between a man and a woman, that's something the average person is going to be skeptical of. Keep in mind that these are very straight people."

"Well, fuck 'em. That's the way it is."

"You see the problem, Arthur?" Aaron Held asked.

"Just what we've talked about," Grimm said. "Sonny is the key."

"The government, Rickie," Held tried to explain, "is going to portray your relationship with Sonny in a certain way. Unless Sonny takes the stand and testifies that you had nothing to do with her drug operation, with Randazzo and Caine testifying, you'll get drowned in the overflow. They'll probably convict you."

"So where's the problem?" Saul grumbled. "Sonny takes the stand. It's the least she can do." He was looking at Grimm. "Am I right, A.G.? This is her beef, not Rickie's."

"It's everyone's beef," Grimm answered. "Look, Sonny's willing to testify. In fact, she wants to. But understand, if she takes the stand, the government will bury her at sentencing. With no testimony, I might be able to work out a deal for fifteen or twenty years. If she testifies, Vaggi will push for a minimum of forty."

"Forty years!" Rickie exclaimed.

"How can they get away with that shit?" Saul asked. He looked at Aaron Held as though for confirmation of what Grimm had said.

"Oh, they have their ways," Held said. "Vaggi will influence the judge. Gass will pay attention to her recommendation. Gass will understand that the government's case against Rickie hinges on Sonny's testimony."

"So what do we do?" Saul asked.

Rickie stood up. "Hold on just a second," he said. "Do you mean to tell me that if Sonny testifies she could get forty years with no parole?"

"It happens all the time," Grimm replied. "Don't forget, the same judge who hears her testimony is going to sentence her. He's going to punish her for helping you."

"Then she doesn't testify," Rickie said emphatically. "That ends that."

"Then we run a big risk—" Held was interrupted by the tone from Saul's telephone console.

"What the fuck?" Saul said, punching one of the buttons. "I thought I told you to take all calls, hon," he rumbled into the receiver. "What is it? Oh, all right, thanks, babe. Aaron, it's for you. Urgent."

Held grimaced as he stood up and went to the telephone.

"I'll take my chances," Rickie was saying to Grimm. "There's no way I'm going to let Sonny lay herself open for that kind of punishment."

Grimm half listened. He wanted to catch the gist of Held's telephone call. An urgent call for Held often meant Grimm would be called upon to do something. Saul was murmuring to Gene Machine, who stood beside the desk.

"It's a problem," Grimm said. "I'm trying to get around it."

"What?" Held cried. "That's incredible." He gaped at Grimm, his eyes bulging. "What the hell for?"

Now everyone was quiet. Held listened, then he muttered something into the phone and hung up as though in a daze. When he looked up, he had a mad grin on his face.

"Well?" said Saul.

"Now this calls for a real celebration," Held said, hovering over the lines on the piece of marble.

"C'mon, you prick!" Saul boomed at him. "Tell us!"

Held was laughing and gasping so hard he blew the coke all over Saul's desk. Then he stepped back and put his hands on his hips. His face was bright red and screwed up in a smirk of perverse delight. Grimm, Rickie, Saul and Gene Machine all gazed at the tall attorney and waited for him to say something.

"Vita Vaggi has been arrested," Held wheezed.

Grimm heard the words, but it took a moment for them to register. Vaggi arrested? His mind balked at the idea. He could not understand what it meant, but he knew he was not thrilled.

"Who was the young lady who answered the phone at your place this morning?" Bernie Wolfshein asked Grimm.

Grimm bounced the rubber ball on the court and slammed an overhead serve. Wolfshein dove to try to return the ball as it hit just inside the line and spun out.

"Nine-three," Grimm said. "That was Cassy Steiger," he told the agent as he retrieved the ball and tossed it back to him. "You know her. She was with me the night I got shot. You met her at the hospital."

Wolfshein flexed his knees, leaned forward, and stared straight ahead at the wall waiting for Grimm to serve again. He wore a pair of plastic athletic goggles and sweat bands around his curly haired head and hairy wrists. They were at the New York Athletic Club playing racquetball and Grimm was beating the DEA agent unmercifully.

"Long!" Wolfshein called as the ball bounced just beyond the back line. "Oh, right, the pretty redhead. Max Steiger's sister."

Yes, thought Grimm, Max's sister, and he served again. This time Wolfshein hit a low, hard return to Grimm's backhand. Grimm stretched out, picked the ball up just as it came off the court, and hit it back to the wall at a point so low it skidded across the floor on the rebound.

"Ten-three," Grimm said. "Game on the wall."

"Damn, I can't get anything by you today." Wolfshein took a couple of deep breaths. "Is that getting pretty serious? Is she live-in?"

In his mind's eye, Grimm saw Cassy, her head on his pillow,

smiling her healthy Southern California smile. "Well, as of right now she's . . . stay-in, you might say. Ready?"

The serve came right at Wolfshein, jamming him. He managed to jump back and get his racket on it, but the ball floated toward the wall and fell short.

"Game," Grimm said. "Want another?"

"I've had enough. You're too good for me today."

They gathered up their gear and left the courts. Grimm had been at the club since early afternoon. His left shoulder was still a little weak from the bullet wound and operation, but otherwise he was back to normal, feeling healthy and full of energy.

It was the middle of the week following the party for Rickie and Suzi at Dune Castle. Sonny's plea date had been postponed due to the crisis in the United States Attorney's Office caused by the arrest of Vita Vaggi. Vaggi was free on a personal recognizance bond, but there were strong doubts as to whether she would be able to continue prosecuting the Rude/Byrne-Downes case.

Aaron Held was elated by the turn of events. He felt that a new prosecutor at this late stage could only weaken the government's case.

Grimm was not so sure. When it came to the ways of the government, he was even more cynical than Held, and he reminded the attorney of what he'd often said regarding Vita Vaggi: compared to most of the Assistant United States Attorneys in the Southern District office, Vaggi was a saint.

Vaggi had been arrested around midnight on Halloween for leaving the scene of an accident, driving while intoxicated, and possession of controlled substances. The police found half a dozen Valium in her handbag. Bernie Wolfshein told Grimm that Vaggi had been at a Halloween party with Doug Whelan, the FBI agent from the President's Task Force on Organized Crime. She had driven her own car to the party and was joined there by Whelan, who arrived late from Washington. Vaggi had already had a few drinks by the time Whelan got there. An angry scene developed, with Vaggi attacking Whelan over misrepresentations concerning his marital status. Vaggi left the party in a rage. On the way home, she sideswiped another car as it emerged from a side street.

Perhaps because of the condition she was in, Vaggi made a decision she would regret for the rest of her life. She sped away from the scene.

She didn't get far. The right rear fender of the Japanese car she drove had been crushed in by the impact with the other vehicle, and it rubbed against the tire, causing a blowout within a few blocks of the accident. Two cops in a blue-and-white radio car found Vaggi slumped over the wheel of her car weeping uncontrollably.

"Vaggi called Whelan at the party," Wolfshein told Grimm, "and he went down to the precinct house and got her out."

The entire incident was hushed up. Stories appeared in a couple of the daily tabloids, but they reported only that the prosecutor had been involved in a minor accident. Vaggi's biggest problem was the narcotics charge. She claimed she had obtained the Valium under prescription, but the pills were found in a small, hand-painted pillbox and she was unable to produce proof that they were dispensed legally. Wolfshein told Grimm that Whelan had made a call "cop to cop" and managed to get the charges dropped. Vaggi was distraught over her liaison with Whelan, and had taken a temporary leave of absence from the U.S. Attorney's office.

The two friends sat soaking in the steam room after their game of racquetball. Wolfshein told Grimm that Ralph Vallone, Vaggi's boss, was undecided whether he should bounce Vaggi off the case.

"Who's he going to get to replace her?" Grimm said.

"Well, that's the problem. No one wants to take over a case like this midstream. And Vallone is not anxious to assign someone else who may not be able to get along with Vaggi's witnesses. It's a mess."

"Karl Lundgren, Julie Zuluaga, now Vaggi. Maybe there's a curse on this case."

"He asked me to help him," Wolfshein said.

"Who?"

"Ralph."

From the tone of Wolfshein's voice, Grimm knew what was coming. Still he asked, "Help him? How can you help Vallone?"

"Talk to you. Have you talk to Sonny Byrne-Downes and Held. See if we can't work something out. Right now you could just about write your own deal."

"Bernie, Sonny's not going to cooperate."

"There might be a new grand jury."

"What's that supposed to mean? A superseding indictment?"

Wolfshein shrugged. "Could be. Vallone's got to come up with something to save this case. If he assigns a new prosecutor, there's no telling what might happen. They might dismiss this indictment against Rude and put together a whole new case.''

"Look, Bernie, whatever happens, nothing changes our position. Sonny's not interested in crossing swords with Jack. Nor is Rickie. They'd rather take their chances with Dudley Gass.''

"Listen, Arthur, you may believe Rude is innocent. I'm not going to argue that with you. But WHO knows what goes on in this conspiracy.''

"Rickie doesn't know shit.''

"Nonsense,'' Wolfshein insisted. "He knows whatever Sonny knows.''

"I don't think so. Besides, does that make him guilty?''

"It might. That's for a jury to decide.''

"Exactly,'' Grimm said. "And that's why Rickie's going to trial.''

"All right. Have it your way. But remember, conspiracy is hard to beat. No one ever really knows what happened. It all comes down to what the jury wants to believe.''

They were quiet for a moment, then Wolfshein again brought up the subject of Cassy. "Isn't she awful young?'' he said.

"She's young,'' Grimm agreed.

"How's that work out?''

"So far it hasn't created any problems. We get along real well. The thing is, she's Max's sister. Max and I have been friends for a long time. I don't know, there's something almost incestuous about it.''

"Well, do you love her?'' Wolfshein asked. "That's the only important question. Everything else can be fixed.''

Grimm had asked himself this question a number of times over the past few days, ever since he and Cassy first made love at Dune Castle. He knew he loved being with her. She made him feel good, happy to be alive. The thought of hurting her filled him with dread.

"You know, Wolfie,'' he said, "I think I do.''

But he wasn't sure. What about Sonny? he asked himself. Could he love them both? He had never told anyone about his affair with Sonny. In a sense, it had never seemed quite real to him. In his mind now he resolved to call it quits with Sonny, not only because of how he felt about Cassy, but also because it was too crazy, too desperate. Besides the danger of getting caught, there was the harsh reality that Sonny would be in prison for at least the next fifteen or twenty years. He did not want to believe he had fallen for Cassy because Sonny was beyond his reach, but he had a dismaying sense of not knowing what his true feelings were.

PART THREE

The Trial of Rickie Rude

Chapter Thirteen

The trial of Rickie Rude began not quite two weeks into the new year, on the thirteenth of January. The Honorable Dudley H. Gass, United States District Court Judge, presided in the spacious Foley Square courtroom, which overflowed each day with Rickie's fans and legions of the media. Even during the protracted jury selection process, there were demonstrations outside the federal courthouse. "Rudies" rallied in support of their idol and clashed with police and militant anti-punks. City police and U.S. Marshals controlled the crowds. Barricades were set up to clear a walkway across the sidewalk and up the granite steps. In the center of it all, the self-styled Ayatollah of Rock 'n' Rollah teetered in the balance of the scales of American justice.

Because of Rickie's fame and the widespread publicity attending the case, it took the remainder of January to impanel the jury of five men and seven women, plus four alternates. The jurors ranged in age from mid forties to retirees above sixty, all but two from Westchester County. The government used all its peremptory challenges to eliminate anyone under forty or noticeably adrift of the mainstream.

This became the basis for Aaron Held's first objection. At Rickie's urging, Held complained to the judge that the jury was not composed of his client's peers. He accused the prosecution of bias toward "the young and the heterodox." The lawyer moved for a mistrial and suggested the formation of a new panel comprised of younger Manhattan residents. The prosecutor countered that city dwellers would be exposed to more press coverage and therefore require sequestration. It was untrue, said the government attorney, that the prosecution was purposely excluding the young. And besides, the Court was reminded, Rude himself was pushing forty.

"Motion denied," Gass intoned in his stentorian voice. "Mr. Held, the Court notes that jury panels are drawn from the rosters of registered voters. Juries are intended to be representative of the norm, not bohemians and misfits."

Thus the tone was set for the entire trial. There were two government prosecutors: Vita Vaggi, clinging to her position by her fingernails, and her young, awkward male assistant, named Gorth, who Aaron Held insisted on calling "Gorf." Held fought bitterly with Vaggi and Gorth about practically everything. The articulate, often scathingly sarcastic defense lawyer seemed intent on punishing Vaggi for retaining her hard-on grasp on her job, which rumor said was riding on the outcome of the Rude prosecution.

Vaggi, her nerves frayed as a result of her own problems, would at times appear to be overcome with rage and frustration. Gorth stumbled around near to her like a lovestruck teenager. Held was manic. One magazine writer covering the trial described the defense as a three-ring circus with Held as the ringmaster and Rickie as the clown.

Judge Dudley Gass despised Rickie from day one of the trial. Gass, a graduate of Harvard Law School, appeared appalled when he learned the defendant had attended Harvard as an undergraduate. The judge could barely look at Rickie without recoiling in disgust. Gass persisted in referring to Rickie as "the defendant," "that person," or "Mr. Rudinowski," even after the indictment was amended to reflect that Rickie's name had been legally changed to Rude. At one point shortly after the jury was impaneled, Rickie himself stood to object, saying no one would know who the judge was talking about if he kept calling him Richard Rudinowski.

"You'll not be called Rude in my courtroom," the judge asserted. "Rude is an absurd name. It's not a proper name."

"But Judge *Gass!*" Rickie pleaded and there was laughter from the spectators.

Each day, the judge looked for new ways to bar Rickie's supporters from the courtroom. He even tried to institute a dress code saying that some of the outfits—the spike hair-dos and ghoulish makeup—would be distracting to the jury and possibly prejudicial to the defense. In response to this, Rickie appeared in court the next day dressed in black judicial robes and dark glasses that had been cut in half to resemble Gass's spectacles.

By the first week in February, the actual trial finally got underway. The immediate Rude contingent, consisting of Aaron Held, his two assistants, Rickie, and the now quite pregnant Suzi Sapphire, would arrive at Foley Square in Aaron Held's limousine and hold impromptu news briefings on the courthouse steps. They were mobbed by reporters who recorded every detail of the famous punk couple's dress. Even Aaron Held's attire was scrupulously noted by the press.

Grimm, who drove his own car downtown and usually went to the jail next door to visit Sonny after court, resumed working as an investigator for the defense. This was done unofficially, to avoid any accusations of conflict of interest from the government, since he was still Sonny's attorney of record. For the duration of the trial, both Aaron Held and Grimm worked an average of eighteen to twenty hours a day.

In her opening statement, Vita Vaggi told the jury that this was a case that would "take them into another world. A strange world. A world of chauffeur-driven limousines and coast-to-coast commuting by private jet. A world of rock stars and Hollywood movie actors. But under the surface glitter, ladies and gentlemen, behind the bright lights, there is a seamy, and illegal, side to this particular world. And that is the world of international narcotics trafficking."

Vaggi declared that the government's evidence would show the defendant, "a world famous rock star," was also "a prime mover in a vast illegal network responsible for the importation and distribution of massive amounts of narcotics." Cautioning the jurors that some of the witnesses the government would call were "not the sort of people you would want to invite into your home for dinner," the prosecutor maintained it was necessary for the government to make use of such people when presenting its case because "these are the sort of people who inhabit this world."

The government would not rely solely upon the testimony of its cooperating witnesses, Vaggi continued. Through various other types of evidence, including tapes made of telephone conversations between the defendant and Sonia Byrnes-Downes, testimony of the witnesses would be corroborated by the defendant's own words intercepted through wiretaps. The jurors could also expect to be shown exhibits, documents and surveillance photos which would provide physical evidence of the defendant's role in this "highly sophisticated and well-organized criminal enterprise."

Finally, federal agents, agents of the Federal Bureau of Investigation and the Drug Enforcement Administration, would testify as to their findings compiled from months of surveillance and investigation.

"The evidence will show that the defendant Rickie Rude is an American success story that went wrong. Intelligent, talented, but utterly without respect for the law, and lacking all concern for the consequences of his actions."

Held stood to object, thought better of it and sat back down. Rickie sat gazing at Vaggi with a look of total fascination. Vaggi turned to direct the jury's attention toward him, and he bathed her with one of his spontaneous, celestial smiles.

"Not content with wealth and fame, Rickie Rude, the evidence will show, out of a complex combination of motives—greed, defiance, a desire to subvert the values of our nation—did knowingly conspire with others to traffic in controlled substances, namely huge amounts of deadly heroin. I am sure, ladies and gentlemen of the jury, that once you have seen and heard all the evidence to be presented to you in this courtroom, you will agree that such a person represents a serious threat to our society. Thank you."

Aaron Held's opening statement was an all-out attack on the government. This, said Held, was the case of an innocent man. "And what can you say about an innocent man? That he didn't do what the government says he did? That he doesn't belong in this courtroom faced with these charges? That the government made a terrible mistake?"

The lanky defense attorney leaned over the lectern and narrowed his gaze. "I only wish it were that simple," he said in a quiet, sorrowful tone. "No, ladies and gentlemen, this is no mistake. This is a calculated attempt at character assassination. Rickie Rude is a totally innocent man who is being prosecuted, I should say persecuted—"

Vaggi objected and Gass warned Held, who shot them both withering looks.

When the attorney turned back to the jury and began speaking again, his voice had softened.

"Ladies and gentlemen, Rickie Rude is a musician, a songwriter, a rock 'n' roll star who makes a huge amount of money and gives a great deal of it away to charity. Rickie Rude is not a criminal, he is not guilty of the charges brought by the government. Ms. Vaggi tries to blur the issue of motive. That's because, as you will learn, there is no motive. And there is no crime, not on the part of Rickie Rude. There is only the government's accusation of a crime. Remember this, it is important: the government is attempting to make a scapegoat out of Rickie Rude. They wish to discredit him and falsely identify him as a criminal, a drug dealer, because he is an outspoken critic of some of the government's policies. The government perceives Rickie Rude as a threat, not because of his alleged drug activities, but because his cry of concern carries to a large segment of society.

"Yes, the defense will prove that Rickie Rude is innocent of the charges the government has brought against him, that he has never been a participant in a drug distribution network, that he has never invested money in nor received the fruits of a drug conspiracy. But also, ladies and gentlemen, the defense will show that in this case it is the government that is guilty. Guilty of over-reaching. Guilty of cover-up and dirty tricks. Guilty of ineptitude and misrepresentation of the facts. Guilty of blind ambition. And guilty finally of perverting the very concepts of the American justice system."

Once the jury had been removed from the courtroom for the lunch recess, Vaggi objected to Held's entire opening as inflammatory. She moved for a mistrial on the grounds that Held had made false accusations against the prosecution, accusations he could not prove, and which, she believed, had prejudiced the jury unduly.

"Hogwash," Held said. "I'll prove every one of my accusations."

"These are opening statements, Ms. Vaggi," Judge Gass said, "The motion is denied. Let's get on with it."

After lunch, the government called its first witness, the real estate agent who managed the West Side brownstone where Sonny had been living at the time of the bust. Through this witness, a man in his mid-thirties who was obviously scared, Vaggi established that the building was owned by Rickie, through his company, Rude Productions. Two of the three apartments were occupied by tenants who had rental contracts and paid rent to the agent's company. Management fees, maintenance costs, taxes and other fees were paid out of the rents, with any leftover funds periodically credited to an account in the name of

Rude Productions. There was, however, no lease for the top floor flat and the agent testified that the company received no rent from the tenant, a Ms. Sonia Byrne-Downes, who lived in the apartment with her daughter.

"Did you ever question Mr. Rude as to the rental agreement he had with Sonia Byrne-Downes for the top floor apartment?" Vaggi asked the witness.

"No," the agent replied. He said Rude told him the top floor apartment was to be kept for his own use.

"For his own use?" Vaggi repeated. "Yet you testified it was occupied by Sonia Byrne-Downes and her daughter, correct?"

"Yes."

On cross-examination, Held asked the agent if he knew what Rickie did for a living.

"Sure," said the man. "He's a rock star."

"To your knowledge, is he a drug dealer?"

"Not that I know of."

Held then asked, "Did Mr. Rude ever mention to you that in his work it is necessary for him to travel a great deal?"

The agent replied that he understood from Rickie that he spent a lot of time in Los Angeles. He also knew Rickie went out on tour for weeks at a time.

Held then asked the leading question, "And did Mr. Rude tell you that because of his frequent trips out of town, he was going to let a friend of his live in the apartment when he wasn't around to sort of look after the place and keep it occupied?"

Vaggi objected to Held leading the witness, but Judge Gass, noting that this was cross-examination, overruled and allowed the question.

Yes, the agent agreed, this was his understanding of the arrangement Rickie had with Sonia Byrne-Downes.

On re-direct, Vaggi made the point that as far as the agent knew, Rickie never actually lived in the apartment. Her next witness was the manager of the Chelsea Hotel who told the jury Rickie had kept a suite at the hotel for over two years. He verified photocopies of hotel bills and records showing that Rickie paid for the suite during the period up to and after the August bust.

"Do you know Mr. Rude well?" Held asked on cross.

"Certainly. Quite well."

"To your knowledge, does Rickie Rude deal in drugs?"

"Absolutely not."

Held also elicited testimony from the manager that during the previous July and beginning of August, when the arrests took place, Rickie was in California.

Vaggi and Gorth then put on a series of FBI and DEA agents who gave testimony about the investigation, code-named "Operation Dope Star." Through these professional witnesses, Vaggi sought to present what Held called the government's "TV show scenario" of the case. To hear the agents tell it, Rickie's arrest had come as the result of dedicated, methodical police work.

Agents claimed they first became alerted to the activities of Sonia Byrne-Downes by New York City narcotics officers whose suspicions were aroused by the unusual amount of traffic in and out of the West Side residence. The street off Central Park West was at times blocked by limousines usually occupied by long-haired "hippie types" seen entering and leaving the brownstone. Agents checked the identity of the occupant of the top floor apartment where it had been established through surveillance that the freaky looking visitors were calling. They learned the flat was owned by Rude Productions and occupied by Sonia Byrne-Downes, a thirty-two-year-old British national with a history of drug convictions.

At this stage, said the agents, a special task force was assigned to the case. Agents set up twenty-four-hour surveillance on the brownstone, at first using vans and telephone company repair trucks, later moving into an apartment in a building on the corner opposite. People were photographed as they came and went. A number of known narcotics traffickers and suspects were identified. Byrne-Downes was followed to meetings with others on file as major narcotics dealers.

According to the official history of the case, which left out the spy in the camp, Karl Lundgren, the big break came when Joakim Lyndestrom, an attaché with the Swedish Embassy, was seized by Customs agents at Kennedy Airport when he attempted to enter the country carrying three kilos of pure cocaine in his diplomatic pouch. Lyndestrom immediately began cooperating with the authorities and named a woman, Jennifer Monsalvo, as his contact with the New York drug organization. Monsalvo, who was traveling on a separate flight, was allowed to clear through customs, though she was also suspected of carrying drugs, and followed from the airport by DEA agents. She led them directly to the West Side brownstone owned by the defendant.

No one was at the apartment when Monsalvo arrived, so she left and was subsequently arrested at a midtown hotel. Based on these facts, agents sought and obtained a court order for a wiretap to be installed on the phone in the apartment occupied by Byrne-Downes.

Here was the first major discrepancy in the government's case, another instance, Grimm suspected, of DEA agent Julio Zuluaga having falsified an affidavit in order to obtain a wiretap warrant. Sonny swore that Jenny Monsalvo had not gone from the airport to the apartment but straight to the hotel, as prearranged, where she was to wait until someone contacted her. Grimm located Monsalvo in a federal prison in Pleasanton, California, and in a phone conversation with her, verified Sonny's version of the events.

Monsalvo told Grimm she had been carrying three kilos of cocaine, which the DEA agents confiscated but never reported. Yes, she said, Zuluaga was the agent in charge. He had threatened and abused her as he attempted to get information about Sonny and the others, information which she did not in fact possess. Ultimately, confronted with Lyndestrom's testimony against her, Monsalvo had been persuaded to plead guilty to one count of conspiracy for which she was promised and did receive a sentence of three years in an Eastern District proceeding.

"Is she willing to testify?" asked Held when Grimm told him what he'd learned during a recess in the trial.

"She says she'd do anything to help Rickie and Sonny. Naturally, she's worried about what it might do to her chances for parole. She's going to have her lawyer contact me."

Over Held's objections as to relevance, Judge Gass allowed Vaggi to put in evidence the drugs, drug paraphernalia, money and other evidence seized during the raid on Sonny's apartment. Gass ruled that these exhibits were to be allowed in, subject to connection; if at the conclusion of their case the government failed in the Court's eyes to establish that a conspiracy existed, and that the defendant was a member of the conspiracy, then the jury would be instructed not to consider this evidence.

But the damage was done. This was a huge obstacle for the defense to overcome. Vaggi wheeled the evidence into the courtroom in a shopping cart. Agents told the jury the drugs and money had been found in the apartment owned by the defendant. Government chemists testified as to the purity of the drugs and stated that in their expert opinion heroin of comparable purity could be purchased only overseas at the source. Plastic bags full of off-white powder like plump, dirty little pillows were passed from juror to juror. Gorth held up big, clear, plastic bags stuffed with stacks of U.S. currency. Marshals and beefed-up security guards stood over the multimillion dollar cache the prosecutors spread out on the evidence table like a storefront display.

It was an impressive sight. Three-hundred-and-eighty thousand in tens, twenties, fifties and hundreds all bundled up and sealed in government evidence bags. The jurors did their best to appear impassive as they handled the bags full of cash and the forbidden white powder. One woman, a tiny Filipino who worked as a domestic in Westchester, wouldn't touch the heroin, and she passed the money gingerly as though she were afraid of it. A blue-haired matron, a retired high school principal who had been elected jury foreperson, cringed visibly as she returned the evidence packets to Gorth. Punks, freaks and journalists at the rear of the room craned their necks to get a look at the goods. The tension in the courtroom mounted as one of the agents testified that because of the rare purity of the drugs, their street value would amount to over twenty million dollars.

Held, in his cross-examination of each agent, did his best to weaken the impact of such devastating evidence by driving home the fact that the drugs and money had been discovered in Sonny's possession, not Rickie Rude's, that Rude was in California at the time of the raid and seizure, and that he surrendered voluntarily a few days after the bust. Though Gass continually cut Held's cross-examinations short, complaining the attorney was going over the same ground, Held was able to elicit from one agent the statement that Rickie had not been considered a suspect until late in the investigation.

Vaggi then called the agents who manned the surveillance post set up across the street from the West Side brownstone. They told of monitoring the electronic phone bugs and using zoom-lens camera equipment to photograph suspects. Poster-size blowups of pictures showing Sonny and Rickie together were set up on easels across from the jury box. Eight-by-ten inch glossy prints were handed among the jurors. During a recess, Grimm examined one blowup carefully. It was a touching shot of Rickie and Sonny arm-in-arm as they crossed the street to a waiting limousine. The grainy black and white image conveyed a mood of romantic decadence quite different from the pictures of Sonny and Jack. The pictures of Sonny and Rickie had no subtext of criminality. They instead evoked a sense of mythical affinity. Grimm thought he could make out the driver standing beside the stretch Cadillac. It was Gene Machine.

Surveillance agents testified that Rickie sometimes spent entire nights and portions of the following days at the apartment. The jury was left to draw their own conclusions. In the photos, Rickie and Sonny were almost always touching or holding each other. Through these witnesses the prosecutor portrayed a life-style completely alien to the citizens on the jury.

Next came the wiretap evidence. As the jurors listened to tapes through headphones and read from transcripts prepared by Vaggi's office, they heard Rickie and Sonny communicating in what might well have been their own private language. Whole passages were marked "unintelligible." Expert drug agents testified that the defendant and Byrne-Downes often resorted to what they termed "coded language" when talking about illegal activities. Apparently innocuous phrases such as "What's happening, sweetheart?," "What's going on?," or "How's everything?" could be interpreted to mean: What drugs are available? or How's business? Common words like "thing" were said to have illegal denotations, a "thing" being a drug or shipment of drugs. Thus a statement by Sonny to Rickie, "We have things to discuss," took on sinister meaning.

Vaggi lulled the jurors into a stupor with recordings of eccentric, disjointed calls. Even with the transcripts, it was impossible to understand what Sonny and Rickie were talking about. Nevertheless, the cumulative message was unmistakable: these people were not normal. Held objected over and over that the conversations were vague and irrelevant. Vaggi argued the relevance would be shown, and Judge Gass, though apparently as bored and mystified as the jury, allowed the government to continue.

Finally, after a full week of playing tapes interspersed with the testimony of drug agents, and over a month into the trial, Vaggi arrived at the period leading up to the raid of Sonny's apartment and her arrest. As established, Rickie was in California at the time, staying at no fixed location. Vaggi played a call from Rickie, answered by Carmen:

"Hello, Rickie."

"Hi ya,' sweetie pie. How's my favorite midget?"

"Fine, but I'm not a midget."

"Well, a small person. Anyway, where's Mom?"

"She's sleeping. Want me to wake her?"

"Hmmmmmm," says Rickie. "Yeah, doll. I guess you better. It's important."

A long pause, and then Sonny's deep voice: "Hello, darling."

An operator interrupts to tell Rickie to deposit more money. Rickie is heard speaking, unintelligibly, to someone else, then into the phone: "Sonny?"

"Yes, darling, I'm here. Is everything all right?"

"I don't know," Rickie mumbles. "Listen. No there's some problems out here. I ran into that guy, you know—"

"Sorry, darling. Who?"

"That—ah, black [unintelligible] guy. You know, your friend." The last words, your friend, were emphasized. Here a drug agent testified that the word "friend" was another code-word meaning drug contact.

Sonny pauses and then says, "Oh yes. I see. Listen, darling, perhaps I should call you back. Is he with you?"

"Yeah."

"And did you tell him he's supposed to come see me?"

"I told him. He said that stash guy would be there any time. He's got some problems out here. I don't know [unintelligible] the people up north."

"Stash guy," testified the agent, meant a man who was in charge of a cache of drugs, called "stash" by drug dealers. The meaning of this message, then, as interpreted by the agent, was that a person in control of a consignment of drugs was due to meet with Sonny in New York. Sonny next tells Rickie to give her the number of the pay phone and she'll go out and call him back. There's a pause. Muffled voices in the background.

"I'll call you at your office in about an hour," Rickie tells her. "In exactly an hour. You know which office I mean?"

"The one nearby?"

"Right."

An "office," the drug agent explained, was code for a public phone, in this case one located at a bar near Sonny's apartment. An undercover agent testified that he hung around the bar and tried to overhear Sonny's side of the conversation. Byrne-Downes, though, spotted him. She made an obscene gesture and told him to "fuck off." The agent told the jury Sonny appeared upset. She stuck her tongue out at him as she left the bar following the ten minute call. This call, the jury was led to infer, was strictly business, drug business. And the defendant Rickie Rude was smack in the middle of it.

If Vaggi had rested the government's case at this point, Grimm and Held later speculated, she might have had a winner. The jury might have voted to convict without having heard from the so-called cooperating witnesses. That one phone call was enough to establish the dubious connection necessary to illumine Rickie and Sonny's association in the worst possible light. So damning was the call that innocent gestures were now infected with the poison of conspiracy. It was, thought Grimm, a case of deflected guilt. Show the overwhelming involvement of Rickie's close friend, place them firmly in each other's lives, and what you come up with is an indelible taint. Aaron Held called this "the old bird-of-a-feather theory" of prosecution.

It was a subtle, amorphous prosecution, in its own way beautiful, thought Grimm, and difficult to attack. The fat little bags of junk, the awe-inspiring sight of all that cash. No matter how vigorously Held argued that the evidence had not been found in Rickie's possession, it was there. There also were the poster-sized pictures of Rickie basking in the illicit presence of the smack goddess. In the government's view, they were one. All those hours of taped telephone calls. They must have been talking about something. Furthermore, Vaggi was a model of prosecutorial diligence; she was merely doing her job; Held would have had a hard time proving government impropriety. So far, on the surface, the case against Rickie Rude appeared to be a straightforward criminal investigation culminating in a valid charge of conspiracy.

Held and Grimm agreed they had never seen a case quite like it. So many phantoms, so few real bogeymen. Julio Zuluaga, the rogue DEA agent, never came near the courtroom. Whelan too had disappeared into the woodwork. This was the first narcotics case Grimm had ever seen brought to trial without a case agent present in the courtroom.

Meanwhile, the ghost of the dead informant, Karl Lundgren, haunted the proceedings. There was so much Held could not go into, so many gray areas he had to avoid. Both the prosecution and the defense agreed to a stipulation prior to the start of testimony that the facts surrounding the murder of Lundgren were prejudicial and therefore off limits. Whenever Lundgren's name came up in testimony, he was left hanging in the atmosphere unexplained like an apparition.

With so many questions dangling, the jury looked to the defense rather than the government for answers. Vaggi, though nervous and sensitive, seemed sincere and totally above-board. Held, on the other hand, acted like something of a bully. His frustration at not being able to dig beneath the surface of the agents' glib lies and smug pretenses could easily be misconstrued as defense infirmity. And his zeal, at least until he could penetrate the government's facade, looked more like spite and malice directed at Vaggi personally. By the time the last of the government tapes were played, Vaggi had managed to project a case with the tempting reality of a mirage. A jury disposed to convict could have found it convincing.

But, as the defense was aware, the government intended to present a good deal more. Toward the end of the afternoon session on Friday, some weeks into the testimony of the government witnesses, Gorth handed out copies of supplemental discovery material, transcripts and reports of statements made by cooperating witnesses Dominic "Donnie Boy" Randazzo and Brad Caine. With the jury excused for the weekend, Vaggi announced to the Court that she intended to conclude her case with these final witnesses some time in the coming week. She said she would call Brad Caine to the stand as soon as Held was finished cross-examining the DEA agent presently testifying.

Judge Gass appeared to be consulting a calendar. "You're saying we'll have heard the government's case after two more witnesses, correct, Ms. Vaggi? Fine, that's just fine. And how long do you anticipate you'll need with them?" the judge asked, looking up. Then, without waiting for Vaggi's answer, he said, "Mr. Held, are you paying attention?"

Held glanced up from the stacks of papers he'd been scanning. He pushed them aside to one of his assistants, gave Grimm a lift of the eyebrows, and stood. "Of course, your Honor. I always pay heed when Ms. Vaggi speaks."

"I would estimate," Vaggi said, "depending on how long Mr. Held takes with his cross-examination, certainly the government should be ready to rest by the end of next week."

The judge again scowled at whatever he had before him on the bench. "That puts us into . . . Mr. Held, I suggest you be ready to put on your defense in approximately one week's time."

"Your Honor, am I to understand that Ms. Vaggi does not intend to call Special Agent Julio Zuluaga as a witness? Because if not, the defense would be—"

"I've been informed by the Drug Enforcement Administration that Agent Zuluaga is not available, your Honor. He's on foreign assignment," Vaggi interrupted.

"Haven't we seen enough agents, Mr. Held?" Gass asked.

"We mustn't accept quantity for quality, Judge. Zuluaga was the case agent in this investigation before he was shunted off somewhere to get him out of the way. I have several questions I believe only he can answer."

Gass sighed. "Can you give me an offer of proof? We've had a number of agents who impressed me as being well versed in the facts of this case, Mr. Held. If the man is unavailable, out of the country, I don't want to delay this trial. Ms. Vaggi, contact the DEA and ask them when they expect this agent to return. I'll consider Mr. Held's offer next week. Now, if there's nothing more, court is adjourned until Monday morning."

Held handed Grimm copies of the new discovery material. "Here, Arthur, take this over to Sonny," he said. "Have her read it through, then go over it with her. Also, get in touch with your pal Wolfshein. See if you can find out where that slime Zuluaga is hiding. I'm not sure I want to call him, but I'd love to catch them lying. I'll see you back at the hotel."

There was the usual crush of copy hungry reporters to be waded through, the whir and click of a dozen cameras. Grimm trailed along in the wake of the famous party. Held told reporters there would be no comment on the case proper until all the evidence was in. The defense mood was grave. But Rickie joked and smiled with reporters. He and Suzi waved to their fans. Then they all piled into the limo and it slid away from the crowd, whisking the besieged couple off to their suite at the Plaza Hotel.

"Hold me," Sonny said to Grimm. "Please, darling. I need to feel your strength."

He took her into his arms, embraced her, and she huddled against him as though she were taking shelter. "Was it dreadful today? The news made it sound horrible."

"They played that tape," Grimm said, stroking her soft, dark auburn hair, amazed to feel himself getting hard.

"That bloody tape!" Sonny stepped back and looked at him. "That's all Jack's fault, you know. He made Rickie call because he didn't want to call himself. He knew the bloody phone was tapped. Goddamm him. He had no right to involve Rickie." Her eyes glittered with anger.

"Sit down, Sonny," Grimm told her. "We'll get to that when the time comes." From his briefcase he took the copies of Randazzo's and Caine's statements and placed them on the table in front of her. "We've got to take it one step at a time. I want you to read this stuff over carefully. Next week, we start with Donny and Brad. Look for lies, look for inconsistencies, anything you can think of that we can use against these creeps to destroy them. Write it all down. I'll be in early tomorrow and we can go over it together."

Sonny glanced at the stacks of papers. She bunched her hands into fists, and when she looked up, Grimm saw tears welling in her eyes. "I can't believe this is happening. If Rickie gets convicted, I'll kill myself. It's all my goddamn fault. How could I be such a bloody fool?" Sonny sobbed and covered her face with her hands.

"Poor Suzi," she said. "I'll never forgive myself for ruining their lives. Finally they get it all together, she's going to have a baby . . . they're so happy . . . and now this."

Sonny dropped her hands and looked at him. Grimm resisted the urge to comfort her, to tell her it was all right. "I'm sorry," she said, sitting up and straightening her back. She reached across the table and took hold of his hands. "Forgive me. I won't be a crybaby."

"Just do your homework," Grimm said quietly. "This is far from over."

"How's the jury taking it, Arthur? You never tell me anything about the jury."

"Well, it's hard to tell. I can't read them at all. A jury's a curious animal. You never know what they'll do. Sometimes the ones that appear to be with you all the way, smiling at the defendant, laughing at the lawyer's jokes, in less than an hour they come back in with a conviction. This one, it's like they're all mannequins. They show nothing. They just sit there like stones."

"Is Rickie behaving himself? On the news they said he's been acting quite normal."

"He's trying. Aaron made him promise not to misbehave. Gass hasn't yelled at him all week."

Sonny managed a small smile. "Poor baby. It must be hard for him to sit there and listen to all that crap."

"You know," Grimm said, "I think he enjoys it."

She nodded. "Yes, I suppose he does. He's so crazy." She squeezed Grimm's hands. "But he mustn't go to prison, Arthur. I'll convince them he's innocent. Put me on the stand. Poor dear had nothing to do with my flow. I don't care how much time they give me, I'll not let Rickie go to prison for something he didn't do."

Grimm's plan to get Sonny sentenced before Rickie's trial had fallen through. At the pleading, he asked the Court for an expedited sentencing. He argued that the severe overcrowding and demeaning visiting conditions at the federal jail presented a hardship on Sonia and made it impossible for her to maintain her close ties with her daughter. Once Sonia was transferred to a regular prison, Grimm told Judge Gass, which could only take place after sentence was imposed, the visits would not be nearly so traumatic. Grimm put a child psychologist on the stand who testified that Carmen was unusually bright and sensitive and displayed a deep attachment to her mother, the sole parent.

As Aaron Held would say, it was a bullshit move, but difficult for the government to argue against. Gass was moved by the motherhood angle, he threw the defense a bone by ordering special visits for Sonny and Carmen in a less restrictive atmosphere. Twice weekly, Sonny was allowed to visit with her daughter in a room at the courthouse instead of at the prison. Vaggi's ungainly assistant, John Gorth, who argued at the pleading, agreed that the sentencing should take place as soon as possible, but he reminded the judge that Sonny was a British subject and therefore it might take some time for the Probation Department to gather the background material necessary to compose the presentence report.

Grimm knew he'd been outmaneuvered, but there was nothing he could do about it. Though Judge Gass had first scheduled the sentencing for before the Christmas holidays, it had been postponed twice because the Probation Department was supposedly waiting for reports from Scotland Yard and from Indian authorities concerning Sonny's prior arrests and her previous imprisonment in India. Now it was February and still the reports had not materialized. Grimm and everyone else knew they would not arrive until after Sonny was called to testify at the Rude trial.

So Sonny sat at the Metropolitan Correctional Center for months, all during the Christmas and New Year holidays, facing up to life in prison with no possibility of parole. The message to Sonny was clear: testify for Rude, and the probation presentence report will be so damning the government will be compelled to ask the judge for a minimum of forty years. And Judge Gass, after hearing Sonny's testimony on behalf of the rock 'n' roll singer, might just go along with the recommendation.

Grimm felt they'd won some small points with Judge Gass during the hearings. The supercilious old Yankee was impressed with Sonia Byrne-Downes. He liked what he saw of her in court, and he listened carefully to what Grimm and the psychologist said about her relationship with Carmen. She may have been a junk queen, but she was also from upper-crust British stock and was a devoted mother. If nothing else, the judge was curious.

Through it all the prisoner thrived. Right up until the time of the trial, when everyone in the Rude camp began to show signs of strain, Sonny remained strong. She was off the white powders, not that they were unavailable in the prison, but she had broken the cycle, found a new way to deal with her dread. One day, she confessed to Grimm that she believed she belonged in jail, at least for the time being. Her life, she said, had become too willful and at the same time removed from the needs of her inner self. She had been "naughty," as she put it, selfish, and her arrest and imprisonment had convinced her that it was time she changed the course of her life.

There had been no more of the sex therapy visits since before the engagement party for Rickie and Suzi at Dune Castle. Grimm told Sonny he was worried about getting caught with the sentencing hanging over them. Once the trial got underway, he had to cut his visits short and stick to business. Also, they both knew that his reluctance to fool around in the visiting room had to do with his growing attachment to Cassy Steiger. Since the weekend in Southampton, Grimm and Cassy had been practically living together. Sonny heard all about Cassy from Carmen and Judy Roth. She told Grimm she approved. "If Carmen and Judy like her, I know I would," she said to him. Like Grimm and Aaron Held, Sonny's major concern was Rickie's trial.

Still, Grimm knew in his limbs that his longing for her was far from satisfied. Happy as he was with Cassy, there was something about this woman that he could not get enough of, something he needed only she could provide.

"You know I love you, Sonny," Grimm told her as he watched the expression on her face while she skimmed through the pages of the statements, her gaze narrowed with concentration. She looked up at him and blinked her cat's eyes.

"I know you do, my love," she said with a distant look. "But you have to go, right?"

"I mean it. Whatever happens, whatever you need, anything at all, you can count on me."

They stared at each other for a long moment without speaking.

"Yes," Sonny said, looking past him. "I know that about you. I can feel it."

"Good." He touched her cheek, brushed his fingers across her lips. "Always remember it. And in the meantime, once this trial is over and you're sentenced—" He winked at her. "Maybe we can slip in a couple of X-rated visits."

"Mmmmmmmm," Sonny moaned and leered at him. "Now you're talking, counselor. But won't they ship me out immediately?"

Grimm leaned across the table to kiss her. "We'll think of some reason to keep you here for a week or two."

Sonny stroked his beard. "You're such a good man, Arthur. I'm so glad I know you."

He smiled at her. "Thanks. I'm glad I know you, too." He kissed her nose. "I'll be at the hotel with Rickie if I'm not home or at the office. Call me if you have any questions or you come up with some good stuff."

Cassy was in the bathroom taking a bath when Grimm walked into the apartment.

"Hi, honey," she said when he opened the door and looked in at her. "How'd it go today?"

"Rough. Did you watch the news?"

"Yeah. They were goin' on about some tape. Was it real bad?"

"Well, it wasn't good. I'll tell you about it. Finish your bath and let's have a drink. I've got to call the office."

Grimm went into his study and called his secretary. He was sitting at his desk writing down his messages when Cassy came in wrapped in a big towel. She placed a glass full of ice and vodka on the desk and sat on Grimm's lap.

"Thanks. Anything else? Yes, I'll take care of it. I'll call them over the weekend . . . No, not tonight. I'll be at the Plaza—"

"No, you won't," Cassy told him. "Rickie 'n' Suzi're comin' here. They're both wiped out and it's too hectic over there."

"Miki, cancel that," Grimm said into the phone. "I'll be here all night. But tell the service not to ring through unless it's Aaron or Sonny."

He hung up and kissed Cassy. "That's better. I wasn't looking forward to going out."

"Hey, I've got a surprise," she said. "But first tell me, was it real bad for Rickie today? Suzi sounded so depressed."

Grimm took a swallow of the drink and handed it to her. "It goes like that. Sometimes we have a good day, sometimes they do. Right now it's Vaggi's turn. But we'll get our chance. We haven't even started yet."

"But listen, no talkin' about the trial tonight, okay? Let's give it a rest. I got a nice veggie dinner happenin', those big Jap mushrooms you like. Then, my surprise."

Grimm undid the towel and was drying her. Her skin glistened with bath oil. He dried her nipples, then began sucking on one of them. His hand dropped to her crotch, still warm and wet from the bath.

Cassy breathed in his ear. "Man, that feels good. Horny, honey? Me too." She grinned at him and motioned with her head toward the bedroom. "C'mon, Dad, let's get it on. We got plenty 'a time. You know how slow Rickie 'n' Suzi are."

It had been this way since Cassy moved in with him. They lived on concentrated, healthy doses of each other punctuated by shorter, harder separations. Cassy was traveling between L.A. and New York like an airline stewardess. She had spent the Christmas holidays at the farm in Millbrook with Grimm and Carmen. The three of them were immensely happy together, all animal lovers, all vegetarians, all, in their own ways, self-centered, involved in their own interests, yet wrapped up together in something more like a little family than any of them had ever known. Early Christmas morning, when Carmen discovered the new saddle Grimm and Cassy had bought for her, with a bow tied around it and placed under the tree, she went up to their room, crawled onto the bed with them, and woke them with a big kiss.

With Grimm as her willing guide, Cassy was eagerly exploring the lush landscapes of sexual love. She'd been there before, but on tentative visits. Now she was comfortable enough to move in, occupy her desire, lay back and feel the contours of her own interior. She was fascinated by Grimm's cock. She loved to fondle it, stroke it, play with it as though it were a pet. "Listen, I grew up with five brothers," she told him by way of explanation.

Grimm and Rickie, Suzi and Cassy had all become close friends, drawn even closer now with the trial on. With Rickie and Grimm and Aaron Held often cloistered in Held's office sweating out the dynamics of the trial long after court adjourned for the day. Suzi and Cassy turned to each other for company. When Rickie and Suzi joined them for dinner that evening, they both looked utterly worn out from the emotional strain of the trial. Suzi seemed particularly affected by the stress. She was due to have her baby around the middle of March and already her small body looked as though it could hardly contain the new life growing within it a day longer.

"Now I know why they call it a trial," Suzi said. "It's worse than touring."

"Listen, you guys, I mean it. Fuck that trial," Cassy said. "Let's talk about somethin' else, please!" She got up and shook her fist at Grimm. "You promised! Anyway, I got a surprise. First we eat, then we kick back and watch the new movie, okay?"

Suzi had given up all drugs, pot, even coffee and cigarettes for the duration of her pregnancy. Once in a while, she would sip a glass of red wine. After the Madison Square Garden show, they had both gone into seclusion at a new home they bought on a piece of land adjoining Grimm's farm in Dutchess County. It was Grimm who turned them on to the place, a postmodern retreat built by some hippie master craftsmen, the same crew that had done the restoration work at Grimm's farm. Built on the side of a hill above a secluded valley and large pond on one hundred and thirty acres, it was Rickie and Suzi's first real home. They settled into the new house and didn't leave until just before the trial, when they encamped at the suite in the Plaza.

Rickie's latest album, *Rude Awakening,* which included the controversial "Ayatollah of Rock 'n' Rollah" cut, had been out since early December and was one of the hottest selling LPs in the country.

The Madison Square Garden show had gone down in rock 'n' roll history as one of the outstanding events of the punk phase. As he sat watching the video of the documentary Cassy had filmed, which contained sequences from the New York show, Grimm found it hard to reconcile Rickie's extraordinary stage presence with the small, peaceful man sprawled on the sofa across from him.

In the middle of the show, Max Steiger made an appearance. The audience filled the hall with cheering as they recognized Max sitting in a pool of light on top of a gigantic amplifier. Max's group, Instant Karma, joined him on stage and he and Suzi sang a few hard rock duets. In the film version they were now watching, Cassy and Max had edited in footage of the Vietnam War and scenes from the domestic peace movement.

Next Max played chords from Rickie's outer-space song, "Terra Incognita," which had become even more popular than the Ayatollah number. The audience went wild. Max was playing Rickie's music, and it could only mean the Prince of Punk himself was about to appear. The audience chanted: RICKIE! RICKIE! RICKIE! Spotlights flashed on and shone up into the dark reaches of the ceiling like beams searching the night sky. Then, as the crowd looked up, a funky space ship began to descend. A sign on the side read: URANUS OR BUST.

When the space ship finally touched down on stage near where Max was standing, it disintegrated in a pile of rubble. Max looked on as the alien climbed out from the wreckage. Rickie, in snakeskin boots and a tight red body suit with lots of zippers and an American flag patch on the shoulder, threw off pieces of the junked spacecraft, dusted himself off, looked around and walked over to Max.

The crowd was frantic. Rickie's entrance had stolen the show.

"Hey, man, don't I know you from somewhere?" Max asked into the microphone as he watched Rickie scan him for radiation.

One of the band members handed Rickie a mike. "Could be. Ever been to earth?" he asked and the band played a deafening chord. Then Rickie pranced over to the edge of the stage and gazed out at the crowd. "Used to be a nice place there once. YEAH!" he bellowed with his full-chested voice.

"YEAH!" the crowd roared back.

"BUT THEY TRASHED IT!"

Another roar in response.

The film cut to scenes of environmental devastation: the wastelands of East Jersey, polluted lakes and rivers, the brown miasma of smog over L.A. Then came a series of interviews and footage with Rickie and Suzi, and various friends and family.

Finally, the wedding. Max and Instant Karma played a punked-out electric guitar and synthesizer version of "Here Comes the Bride." The ceremony was performed by a friend of Rickie's. Instead of a ring, Suzi put a spiked collar and chain around Rickie's neck and pretended to drag him from the stage.

And so the Ayatollah of Rock 'n' Rollah and the Crown Princess of Punk were wed. When the film came to an end, and both Cassy and Grimm looked to Suzi and Rickie for their reactions, they found that the two punks were cuddled together fast asleep.

Monday morning when the government resumed its case, Vita Vaggi called Brad Caine to the stand. Caine was a partner in the popular Lower East Side rock club known as Little Babylon. He said he was thirty-seven years old and admitted to having been a drug dealer off and on for the past fifteen years. He was handsome, with large, wet looking brown eyes, and long thick dark hair. He was unable to look at Rickie.

How long had he known the defendant, Rickie Rude, asked the prosecutor. Caine told of having met Rickie for the first time four to five years ago at another, now defunct rock club where Rickie and his band were playing. On that occasion, he said he had given Rickie and some of his band members coke, heroin and marijuana for their personal use. Vaggi asked him if he knew a woman by the name of Sonia Byrne-Downes. Sure, Caine answered, he knew Sonny. And in what capacity did he know her? She was one of the biggest wholesale drug dealers in the city.

Vaggi leaned into the lectern. "Did there come a time when you met the defendant Rickie Rude again, Mr. Caine?"

"Yes."

"Would you relate to the jury the circumstances of that second meeting?"

"He came into my club about a year-and-a-half ago and we were introduced."

"Who introduced you to Mr. Rude this time?"

"Sonny."

With Vaggi coaxing him along, Caine told the jury that in time he learned that Rickie acted as a sort of behind-the-scenes advisor to Sonny, what Aaron Held would refer to mockingly in his cross-examination as her "hippie consigliari." Caine claimed both Sonny and Rickie told him this was Rickie's role. They made no bones about it. Rickie was an expert on drug quality, a taster, Caine said. He could touch a dab of heroin to the tip of his tongue and tell you how good it was and what it had been cut with. No one knew more about pot than Rickie. Caine said Sonny told him she always consulted Rickie before making a major move. He further claimed both Rickie and Sonny told him that Rickie worked investment capital through Sonny's dope trip which she paid back at a rate of five-to-one.

According to the witness, Rickie helped Sonny move drugs through his friends and associates in the rock scene. On a number of occasions, Caine testified, he had been present at Sonny's apartment on the West Side when the rock star came by to pick up quantities of drugs, mostly heroin, coke and marijuana, which he told them he was going to deliver to fellow rock 'n' rollers, movie stars and other celebrity types. Caine said he never saw Rickie pay Sonny for any of these drug packages. When he asked Sonny about this, she replied Rickie didn't need to pay "because he was her partner."

From their reading of the discovery material, Grimm and Aaron Held had known this was coming. The testimony sounded much more damaging when spoken at Vaggi's gentle prompting in the hushed courtroom before the jury. Caine was doing his best to come across as a sincere man who was there "to tell the truth," as he stated, in hopes that the judge would take his cooperation into consideration as a mitigating factor when it came time for his sentencing. Caine said that Vaggi had made him no promises of any sort. His agreement had come about as a result of a determination he'd made to change his life. Though he gave the impression he was not comfortable testifying against his friend, Caine was relaxed, confident and convincing.

The media gorged on Caine's evidence.

RUDE DRUG QUEEN'S "PARTNER"

said the *Post* quoting Caine. From all appearances, the defense was in serious trouble.

Vaggi kept Caine on the stand most of Monday and all of Tuesday morning before turning him over to Aaron Held. The defense had done their homework. Grimm, with invaluable help from Sonny, had spent the weekend gathering material in preparation for Held's cross-examination of Brad Caine. Sonny would have made a good lawyer herself, Grimm mused later as he organized the material. She had insight that cut through the lies and bullshit and she was able to identify subtle flaws in Caine's position. Caine's evidence amounted to his word against Rickie's; the defense's only hope was to convince the jury the witness was lying.

Sonny had a remarkable memory for someone who was supposedly strung-out on drugs most of the time. Best of all, she had access to sources of intelligence, both on the streets and inside the jail, that Held and Grimm would never have been able to tap into.

The lofty, long-haired attorney began gently with Brad Caine, putting him at ease. Caine's agreement with the government was discussed, Caine repeating that Vaggi had made him no promises. Held then dropped the subject. The attorney had a way of raising a point, leaving it there in midair to be returned to later. "We'll come back to that," he'd say ominously.

"Do you use drugs?" Held asked, seemingly out of nowhere.

"I used to," Caine replied, and he went on to tell of daily use of heroin and cocaine, Valium and other drugs.

"Are you on drugs now?" Held asked a few questions later.

Caine, as everyone knew, was in custody—actually, in the Federal Witness Security Program. The witness scowled and said, "No."

Held moved on. He spoke of Caine's fifteen year career as a drug dealer and elicited testimony that Caine had been arrested for drug offenses in the past. Two of those arrests had resulted in convictions, and Caine had been sentenced to prison as a result of the last one. He said he'd done time at the federal prison in Raybrook, New York.

"Was that before or after you met Rickie Rude?"

Caine seemed to be trying to remember. "Ah, after I met him the first time, but before I met him again at my club."

Which meeting took place, Held reestablished, about a year-and-a-half ago. How long ago had he been released from prison? the lawyer asked. Two years ago, the witness said.

Held glanced at his notes. "Hmmmmm, you didn't spend very long in prison, did you, Mr. Caine?"

"No."

"We'll come back to that," Held said, the warning tone in his voice. "And you went right back into the drug business when you were released, is that right?"

"Yeah, pretty much."

"Aren't you still on parole from that previous conviction?"

Caine admitted he was. Held left this line dangling and went on to ask the witness about his business interests and assets. What did he own, Held wanted to know, other than his interest in Little Babylon? Caine said he and his partner also had an art gallery on East 79th Street. Anything else? Caine thought about it for a moment.

Vaggi objected as to relevance, but Gass overruled when Held said he would show how Caine's assets were relevant. A car, Caine said, some jewelry, antiques, Persian carpets, gold. And had all this been paid for with drug profits? More or less, he did have an income from the club. Where did he get the money he used to buy into the club? Caine shrugged. Drug profits.

At this point, Held left the lectern and strode over to the defense table. "If I may have just a moment, your Honor."

Then he stopped mid-step and looked up at Caine as though suddenly thinking of another question. " By the way, you of course told the government prosecutor about all these assets, did you not, Mr. Caine?"

"Yeah, she knows."

"Certainly she knows," Held said gleefully as he reached out to retrieve a thick folder handed to him by one of his assistants. "This would be part of your new regimen demanding that you tell the truth, correct, Mr. Caine?"

Caine made no response. Held, leafing through the papers in the folder, said, "Now, let me back up just a moment, if you don't mind. You admit you've been dealing drugs for fifteen years, is that right?"

"Yes, sir," Caine answered with a sigh, sounding bored.

"And over that period you've used a number of aliases?"

"Right."

"Among them the name Thomas Bradford, I believe we established, which is actually your first name and middle name reversed, is that right?"

"That's right," Caine replied. Grimm watched the witness closely. He thought he saw him tense slightly.

Held was back at the lectern with the folder, still scanning the documents. "Did you file income taxes for these years, Mr. Caine?" Held asked.

"Yes, I filed."

"But they were fraudulent returns, were they not? I mean, you did not report your drug earnings, right?"

"Right," Caine agreed. Cheating on taxes seemed like a minor indiscretion compared with the gravity of the drug case.

Held looked up. "Do you expect to be prosecuted by the IRS as a result of this fraud?"

"No," Caine said. He explained this was part of his agreement with the government. No tax case.

"Oh, so you were made at least one promise?"

Caine said he hadn't looked at it that way.

"What about the Racketeering Influenced and Corrupt Organizations statute, known as RICO, which covers such activities as investing illegal funds in supposedly legitimate businesses like the club and art gallery? Have you been told that you face RICO charges?"

No again.

"Has Ms. Vaggi promised you that you will be able to retain your interest in these businesses as part of your agreement to testify against Rickie Rude?"

Caine seemed stumped. "We—I—" He looked to Vaggi, then up at the judge.

"Answer the question," Gass told him.

"I sold out, I'm selling out—"

Rickie laughed and was joined by snickering spectators. Held demanded in a grating voice, "You *sold* out, or you're *selling* out? Which is it, Mr. Caine?"

"I'm selling out," answered Caine.

"Haven't you already received a payment of—" Held looked at his papers. "One hundred and fifty thousand dollars from your partner?"

"Yes."

"And did Ms. Vaggi tell you that you will be required to forfeit to the government whatever money you receive?"

Caine shook his head. "No."

"She told you you could keep it?"

"Yes."

"So now we have another promise, which makes three so far. No tax case, no RICO charges, and you get to keep all your assets and whatever you make from the sale of your businesses. Correct so far, Mr. Caine?"

Held was gathering steam. His thin light brown hair came tumbling from behind his ears. His face grew animated, and his voice gained a kind of wrenching intensity. "Tell the jury about Transcam Incorporated, Mr. Caine."

Caine looked stunned. "What?"

"Transcam Corporation, incorporated in the state of Delaware," Held said, producing a sheaf of papers from the folder, papers which, Grimm knew, had nothing to do with Transcam. This was a bluff. Sonny had remembered being told about the company by Caine's partner, to whom Grimm had paid a visit over the weekend.

"Are you telling this court you know nothing about Transcam Corporation, Mr. Caine? Remember, you're under oath."

Caine, now visibly rattled, admitted he knew about the corporation. Grimm shot a glance at Vaggi, who looked bewildered.

"Who owns Transcam, Mr. Caine?"

"I don't know."

"You don't know? Is that the truth?"

"I'm not sure."

"But aren't you in fact, under the name Thomas Bradford—let's see." Held referred to his documents. "Yes, aren't you, as Bradford, president of the corporation?"

Caine was caught. Vaggi looked furious. Yes, the witness admitted, he was president, but he believed the corporation was owned by a Panamanian company.

"Oh, a *Panamanian company,* I see," Held said, his voice dripping with venom. "We'll get back to that. Tell us, please, what assets does Transcam have in this country?"

Then it all came out. A home on Fire Island, a forty-foot yacht, oceanfront property in Delaware, a building in Greenwich Village, cash deposits in banks totaling three-quarters of a million dollars.

"Did you tell Ms. Vaggi about these assets, Mr. Caine?"

"No."

"So you lied to her?"

"No, not really. I mean, those aren't my assets."

238 SMACK GODDESS

"Not yours? Mr. Caine, isn't it a fact that you and you alone are the owner of Transcam Corporation through the Panamanian front company?"

After a long pause during which Caine seemed to be trying to figure out how Held had got hold of this information, he said, "Yes."

"And is it not also true, Mr. Caine, that for the last six or seven years, even during the time you were in prison, you have been using this offshore company to launder your drug profits?"

Caine shrugged and nodded.

"The witness will answer the question," Judge Gass said.

"Yes," Caine said, "that's right."

"By the way, Mr. Caine, getting back to your last prison term. Would you tell the jury how you happened to get out after serving a little over nine months?"

Vaggi objected. Held said the question went to the witness' credibility, and Gass overruled.

"Didn't you cooperate with the government on that occasion also, Mr. Caine?"

"Yes."

"You not only cooperated by informing on others on that occasion, but you also set up and informed on both prisoners and prison guards while you were incarcerated at Raybrook. Didn't you, Mr. Caine?"

"Something like that," Caine said, becoming petulant.

"Something like that?" Held repeated with his voice scraping on Caine's nerves. "The fact is that you are very clever when it comes to making deals with people like Ms. Vaggi, aren't you, sir?"

Vaggi objected.

"Let me rephrase that," Held said. "Mr. Caine, isn't it true that you know exactly how to use the government by lying to them, supposedly helping them, when in reality the only person you're interested in helping is Brad Caine?"

"I'm interested in helping Brad Caine," the witness said. "But I'm not lying."

After the noon recess when Held was about to resume his cross-examination of Brad Caine, Vita Vaggi stood and addressed the Court. She said she wished to clear up one point that Mr. Held had raised during the morning session.

"Mr. Held, your Honor, asked the witness if he were on drugs, to which the witness responded no. In fact, there has been a misunderstanding here. Mr. Caine is taking prescription drugs for a medical problem he has. He assumed Mr. Held was talking about illegal drugs, which, of course, he is not taking. However, I wanted to clarify this point.''

"Thank you, Ms. Vaggi," Gass said, obviously dismissing the correction of Caine's testimony as inconsequential. "Mr. Held, are you ready to proceed?"

Held stood and cast a quick glimpse at Grimm. Later, he would say he couldn't believe Vaggi had stumbled into the trap they had laid for her. He worried momentarily that maybe there was something wrong with their information, but everything had been checked and rechecked. Vaggi had been given a ''tip,'' through a friend of Julia Held's who worked in the U.S. Attorney's office, that Held planned to raise the issue of Caine's prescription drug use.

Taking up his position at the lectern, it was all Held could do to keep from smiling. He stared at Vaggi for a moment, then opened and then closed the folder in front of him as if to signal the jury that this new information was more interesting than the questions he had prepared.

"So you *are* on drugs, Mr. Caine. Tell us, exactly what drugs are you taking?"

"Something for pain, an old back injury. And something for tension, to help me sleep."

"Specifically, sir," Held snapped. "Tell the jury what drugs you are taking."

Caine seemed unsure. "A painkiller and a tranquilizer."

"Are you trying to tell us you don't know the names of these drugs?"

"Not really. I know—"

"Wait. Just a moment. Did you not in fact demand specific drugs?"

"Not really. I mean, the ones they were giving me weren't doing any good."

"Mr. Caine," Held almost shouted, "is it not a fact that you went to the chief physician at the Metropolitan Correctional Center, where you are being held, and demanded that you be given a potent dosage of Valium and codeine?" Held looked directly at Vaggi when he said Valium.

"I told them the stuff they were giving me wasn't doing anything."

"No, no, that is not what you told them. You spoke to a Dr. Burack—"

"Objection, your Honor. Mr. Held is testifying for the witness."

"Sustained."

"Mr. Caine, did you not have a psychiatrist friend of yours, by the name of Dr. Stapleton, contact Dr. Burack at the jail and tell him to give you Valium and codeine in the dosage you wanted?"

"Yes, because the—"

"And what did Dr. Burack say?"

"He didn't say anything. He—"

"He refused to give you the drugs, didn't he, Mr. Caine? Didn't he tell you that Valium and codeine have a powerful synergistic effect that he felt would be detrimental to your well being?"

"Objection."

"Overruled."

"I can't remember," Caine said.

"You can't remember? Dr. Burack refused to give you the drugs, didn't he, Mr. Caine?"

"Yes."

"But you insisted on these drugs because you are well aware of the high you can get from this combination, right, Mr. Caine? You know all about drugs, having been an addict all these years, correct, sir?"

"Yes," Caine admitted.

"Now tell the jury what happened after Dr. Burack refused to give you the specific drugs you demanded."

Caine made no answer.

"You called Ms. Vaggi, didn't you, Mr. Caine?"

"Answer the question," Gass told him.

"Yes."

"You were so angry because the doctor wouldn't give you the drugs you wanted that you called Ms. Vaggi and told her about it. Is that right?"

"Yes."

"And what did Ms. Vaggi say?"

"She said she'd see what she could do."

"What *did* Ms. Vaggi do?"

Caine shrugged. "I don't know. Ask her—"

"You don't know!" Held screamed. "Is that the truth, Mr. Caine?"

Caine looked at Vaggi. She started to get up, but Held brandished an official looking piece of paper and addressed the Court. "Your Honor, this witness has lied repeatedly. I have here a copy of the Court Order, signed by a United States Magistrate, who is an officer of this Court. This Order, which was obtained by Ms. Vaggi at this witness's request, directs the medical staff at the MCC to provide Mr. Caine with the drugs he demanded. Mr. Caine also asked for and received a copy of this Order and used it to procure drugs from the medical staff at the jail over objections from the chief physician, Dr. Burack, who is prepared to testify to this. Mr. Caine is well aware of the lengths that the government prosecutor went to to provide him with these dangerous drugs. I move this Court to impeach the witness, strike his entire testimony, and have him cited for perjury.''

Vaggi stood. ''Your Honor—''

But Gass ignored her. He took Held's copy of the Order and read it. Then he turned to Caine and asked, ''Did you receive a copy of this Order, sir?''

Again Caine gave a limp shrug. ''I knew something happened. Yeah, I got a copy of the Order, but that's all I knew. I mean, she doesn't tell me everything she does.''

Gass looked to Vaggi for her explanation. Grimm and Held had seen it all a hundred times before. The judge was showing her a way out. The prosecutor told the Court that Caine's doctor, Dr. Stapleton, called her and asked that she intervene with the medical staff at the jail in an effort to relieve Caine's suffering. ''He was in pain,'' she said. ''And extremely anxious. He wasn't able to sleep at night. His doctor informed me that the physician at the MCC was being overly cautious, that these substances are commonly prescribed for such treatment as Mr. Caine requires.''

Here Held threw what he would later describe as one of the lowest blows of his career. ''Well, your Honor, when it comes to Valium, we can't be expected to take Ms. Vaggi's word. I plan to call my own witnesses on this matter.''

The reference to Valium went over the heads of all but those who knew of Vaggi's own troubles with the drug. Vaggi went red in the face, then turned to glower at Held, who sneered back at her.

Gass was obviously concerned by Held's revelations and the accusations he made about the witness. Held and Grimm knew that he would be particularly angry with Vaggi because she had gone to a magistrate to get the Order while Gass was away over the holidays. The implication was that Gass didn't know what was going on in his own court. He handed the Order to his clerk. Despite his displeasure, he did his best to explain it to the jury.

Judge Gass denied Held's motion to impeach the witness. Caine, he said, could not be expected to know exactly what steps Ms. Vaggi had taken on his behalf, only the results, which he admitted. The jury would make their own determination as to his truthfulness.

But Held wasn't through. He had them on the run. He asked Caine if it had been part of his agreement with the government that he was to be given drugs in exchange for his testimony against Rickie Rude. Caine gave an evasive answer, something to the effect that Vaggi had agreed to do whatever she could to help him.

"Mr. Caine, did you threaten Ms. Vaggi that if you didn't receive the drugs you wanted you would refuse to testify?"

Everyone, including Gass and Vaggi, seemed to be wondering how Held got his information. What they didn't know was that Caine had a big mouth. He liked to brag to guards at the jail who worked the so-called "snitch unit" on the third floor where he was housed, never dreaming that Sonny was an integral link in the gossip mill at MCC. In fact, as Grimm would learn, Sonny had at least two guards at the MCC on her payroll. She paid them for information as well as other goodies they provided.

"Look, I was upset." Caine gave Vaggi a despairing look. "She threatened me."

Held looked astonished. "What? The government prosecutor, Ms. Vaggi, threatened you?" he said, his voice quavering with disbelief.

"I didn't want to testify at this trial. I was upset, I was tense. She threatened me. She said if I refused to testify—"

"Yes? Go on, Mr. Caine. If you refused to testify, what did Ms. Vaggi threaten to do?"

Caine seemed to catch hold of himself. "It could be—when I got sentenced, it could go against me."

Caine's credibility was shot. Held kept him on the stand the rest of the day, taking him back over his direct testimony and tangling him up in a number of significant inconsistencies. It hardly mattered. By this time, no one believed much of what he had to say.

"Mr. Caine, with a deal like you got, and with all of your skill as a practiced liar, can you give us one good reason why we should believe you?" Held asked him at the end of the session.

Caine answered peevishly, "I don't care if *you* believe me or not. It happens to be the truth."

On redirect, Vaggi was able to do little to resurrect her witness. When Judge Gass dismissed him, Caine looked directly at Rickie for the first time. Rickie smiled at him. "See how badly he fucked up," Rickie said to Held. "He didn't really want to hurt me."

Court was adjourned for the day. Reporters flocked around the defense team.

"Aaron, that was great. You destroyed the lyin' sack 'a shit," Suzi Sapphire said and Held beamed.

"Stunk up the courtroom with him," Rickie agreed.

PROSECUTOR GAVE WITNESS DRUGS

announced the evening edition of the *Post*.

Dominic "Donnie Boy" Randazzo would prove a harder nut to crack, though the meat inside was sweet. His direct testimony lasted two days and proceeded along similar lines as Caine's. Held immediately established an atmosphere of intense acrimony between himself and the witness by repeatedly objecting to the form and style of Randazzo's answers to Vaggi's questions.

"Your Honor," Held implored the judge, "would you please instruct this witness simply to answer the questions put to him and to stop his long-winded editorializing."

Randazzo told the jury that he first met Rickie at Sonny's apartment when he went there to transact drug business. He said Sonny openly consulted with Rickie, and that she would do nothing without Rickie's approval. In time, said the witness, Sonny's personal use of drugs, particularly heroin, began to interfere with her ability to conduct business. This upset Rickie. Randazzo told the jury he went to Rickie and complained about Sonny's drug problem and her deteriorating work habits. Rickie supposedly responded that he would "straighten her out."

Shortly thereafter, Randazzo went on, Sonny introduced him to a man named Karl Lundgren, known as "Loose Karl," and told him that he could contact Lundgren when he needed to pick up drugs or make payments. When he asked Sonny how she knew Lundgren could be trusted, she replied, "Don't worry, he's cool. He's been with Rickie for a long time."

Held called for a conference with the judge at the sidebar. Vaggi, he told Judge Gass, when they were out of earshot of the jury and spectators, had violated the agreed stipulation to leave the dead informant Karl Lundgren out of testimony. How was he, Held, supposed to cross-examine the witness on the subject of Lundgren when it had been decided that the jury was not to learn what happened to the man?

"Your Honor," Vaggi whispered, "I have no intention of asking this witness questions relating to the murder of Karl Lundgren, which is the substance of the agreement Mr. Held and I made with the Court. That the circumstances surrounding Lundgren's murder, the fact of the murder itself, and the inference that the defendant benefited from the murder—"

"Just a moment, Ms. Vaggi," Held cut in, hissing at her. "There isn't a shred of evidence to suggest—"

"Mr. Held, Ms. Vaggi is not suggesting anything of the kind, merely stating that the jury might infer that the defendant had much to gain by eliminating a possible witness against him," Gass interrupted.

"Exactly, your Honor," Vaggi agreed. "And this is why the government stipulated that this information would be kept from the jury. However, mention of Lundgren and some testimony as to his function within the organization is, to a certain degree, unavoidable in establishing the defendant's proprietary role."

Judge Gass concurred, but warned the prosecutor that she was venturing out on thin ice. As long as the murder was not brought up, the jury could know about Lundgren.

"And his double role as an undercover informant, your Honor?" Held asked. "Does the government intend to reveal this also?"

"No, your Honor, the government does not. That would raise the question of what happened to him," Vaggi assured the Court.

"Your Honor," Held asserted, "I think Ms. Vaggi is cutting it awfully close here. I think we're on dangerous ground, and I'd like to restate for the record my opposition to any mention of Karl Lundgren for the reasons previously mentioned when the matter was first raised."

"All right, your objection is noted, Mr. Held. Ms. Vaggi, be careful."

End of conference. Had Vaggi been able to see the smile on Held's face as he looked at Grimm while walking back to the defense table, she might have realized she'd strayed into another of his ambushes.

From that point on, resumed the witness, he took care of most of his business with Karl Lundgren, Sonny's assistant, while getting together with her from time to time to go over the accounts and to discuss future business. The jury learned about the SoHo loft where Randazzo claimed he often went to meet Lundgren and pick up drugs or deliver money.

"Can you tell us, Mr. Randazzo, was there a name printed on the nameplate above the buzzer to the loft?" Vaggi asked the witness.

"Yeah."

"And what was that name?"

"Rude Productions," Randazzo answered. He went on to explain that the loft was what is known in the drug business as a "stash pad," a place to keep drugs and large amounts of money so they would not be in the actual dealer's possession.

Randazzo testified, once Lundgren came on the scene business again settled into a stable pattern. He told of calling Karl on the electronic pager, then arranging to meet with him. Once in a while, though, it was necessary for Randazzo to meet directly with Sonny. These meetings nearly always took place at the West Side apartment, and Rickie was often present. Vaggi wrapped up Randazzo's direct testimony with a series of questions on the nature of drug discussions Randazzo claimed he'd had with Rickie. Here Vaggi raised the specter of what Held would call her "*National Enquirer* version of the defendant."

Rickie, Randazzo told the jury, Judge Gass and the enthralled spectators, liked to pontificate on the political ramifications of the traffic in illegal drugs. Held objected to this line as irrelevant and prejudicial, but Vaggi asserted it went to the question of intent and was therefore highly relevant. Gass let it in. Randazzo claimed Rickie told him that his real interest in the drug business was in fostering the spread of the drug culture. Rickie was into drugs, he said, because he saw them as a powerful subversive influence, like rock music, aimed at weakening the government's control over certain elements of the society. Randazzo even went so far as to state that Rickie told him he donated drug profits to various radical underground organizations. He quoted Rickie as saying, "Drug users make bad citizens."

The newspapers had a field day with this testimony. Here was Rickie, the self-proclaimed Ayatollah of Rock 'n' Rollah, plotting revolution financed with dope dollars. The *Post* ran a front page still of

Rickie from the Ayatollah video, a shot of him puffing on his water pipe under the headline:

DOPE DICTATOR!

In a skull session at Aaron Held's East Side office that evening, Held and Grimm decided that Vaggi was making a last ditch attempt to save her case by straying into the thorny Lundgren material The mention in evidence of the SoHo loft called for a strategic response. Throwing in the sensational smear tactic was Vaggi's way of getting back at Held for the fun he'd had at her expense over Caine's drug prescriptions. It was also no doubt calculated to further prejudice Judge Gass against Rickie.

"And now to make it all backfire!" Held said with a gleam in his eye.

Grimm was sure Randazzo was lying about having been to the SoHo loft. Sonny confirmed this. No one, she told him, except Lundgren, Rickie and Suzi and herself knew about the loft. Grimm was now convinced that even the DEA had not known about the stash pad until he led them there from the news conference. So he immediately began devising a plan for Held to demonstrate to the jury that Randazzo was lying, repeating information fed to him by Vaggi, who probably got it from Whelan's people. Grimm and Aaron Held tossed the idea back and forth, Held adding dramatic embellishments, what he called "crowd pleasers."

Because Vaggi could not produce Karl Lundgren, the defense reasoned, it would have made better sense for her to have left him out of the case altogether. The murdered Lundgren and his sub-rosa role as an informant for the DEA cracked the door on another whole dimension to the conspiracy. Once the door was ajar, the jury would expect to be taken in and given a look around. But Vaggi couldn't afford to do this because Rickie's presence was nowhere to be found once the focus was shifted to this area of the case.

For here was the land of Jack Moriarty, the treacherous terrain of Guy Stash and Julie Zuluaga. Sonia Byrne-Downes stood guard at the door like a goddess. No one could get through unless she gave the nod. Vaggi had to understand that by forcing the defense to call Sonny to the stand, she risked her entire case on her ability to break Sonny as a witness.

Chapter Fourteen

A criminal investigation has a kind of internal rhythm all its own. Grimm was thinking as he drove downtown to court early the next day, in some investigations you perceive what happened and why almost as soon as you know the salient facts. Then it's merely a matter of running down the evidence, proving objectively what you already know. But then there are other cases, the enigmas like Rude/Byrne-Downes, that resist being solved, may never be entirely resolved, and cannot be forced to reveal their secrets until the inner timing is right.

Like so many other things in life, it was all a matter of learning patience. Sometimes you had to sit back and let things happen. Once again he thought that what he did for a living most resembled a kind of abstract, real-life game of chess. He was most engaged, most alive, when he had time to think only of what his next move would be.

They were moving onto the offensive. Before the first defense witness was called, Aaron Held's cross-examination of Donnie Randazzo would begin the onslaught. Here was an opportunity to deliver a crushing body blow to Vaggi's case from which she might never recover. If Held could discredit Randazzo even half as effectively as he had Brad Caine, Rickie could walk.

Grimm had been at work on the plan most of the night. He'd even enlisted Cassy and Carmen to help. Once the idea began to take form, Grimm got in touch with his foreman at the farm in Millbrook, and he told him to load Myrtle, Karl Lundgren's bulldog, into a van and bring her down to the city. Cassy and Carmen took her to a studio and sat her down for a photo session. Cover girl material she was not, but Grimm hoped she would provide the kind of graphic evidence they felt they needed to destroy the smug Randazzo.

Meanwhile, Grimm had made an excursion uptown to East Harlem to meet with Dominic Randazzo's ex-partner. Grimm knew that Randazzo, a cocky would-be button guy, was not about to be intimidated by Aaron Held. His wits had been honed over years of dodging the law. He knew how to lie to cops, so it was not a difficult step for him to take to lie for cops. And Randazzo knew all about glib criminal lawyers. To him Held was a Jewboy mouthpiece with a slick tongue who was basically full of shit. To crumble Randazzo's tough-guy facade, they would need to go for the vitals.

Every criminal turned government witness who takes the stand and testifies against former friends, business partners, and in some cases relatives or lovers, does it from a complex rationale made up of selfish motives and secret fears. Grimm had studied dozens of rats over the years as they sat on the witness stand and spilled their guts. Sometimes they did it to get revenge for real or imagined suffering they had endured. Often they were failures opting for the easiest way out, or manipulators like Caine who were able to convince themselves that their freedom was worth more than that of the people they testified against. Some were simply afraid of the government and the prospect of spending years behind bars.

But freedom, or fear of imprisonment, was not always the critical factor. Like Randazzo and Caine, most government witnesses were in and out of jail all their lives. It was the deal, seeing what they could get from the government, that counted. Grimm remembered one case where a 250-pound onetime mob bone-crusher, who was serving natural life with the State for multiple murders, testified under an agreement with the government wherein his punk lover would be transferred with him to another prison so they could live together. Grimm could not think of one turncoat witness he believed had testified from a genuine sense of civic responsibility or a need to tell the truth.

Also, Grimm knew, they almost always lied. Despite all their claims to the contrary, they couldn't help it, the vast majority of them were men for whom lying is second nature. If ninety percent of what they said was true, only the best of them knew where to stop before making statements a good defense lawyer could use to hang them. They lied sometimes just to make what they said sound more interesting. Not a few seemed to get off on being the center of attention.

The problem was that jurors, even when they hated the rats and disbelieved most of what they had to say, generally forgot about them when it came time for deliberations and tended to swallow the government's case as an undifferentiated whole. The prosecution operated under the theory that if you sling enough shit, some of it is bound to stick. Only a bloody kill, a stinking disembowelment that made the government look dishonest for suborning perjury, strengthened the defense. Such had been Held's cross-examination of Brad Caine.

One surefire method of exposing a stool pigeon and setting him up for the kill was to unravel his rationale, forcing a crisis on the stand. Suddenly the witness would feel alone and afraid.

Despised by their own and resented, used and then tossed aside by the cops and prosecutors once they had served their purpose, these government witnesses became a kind of mutant breed, underworld creatures who could never metamorphose into true-blue citizens. They almost always ended badly, reverting to desperate crime, drinking or drugging themselves to death. There is no role that collapses more completely than that of accuser. The Federal Witness Protection Program may have a good record as far as safeguarding their flock from would-be assassins. The suicide rate, however, is less encouraging.

Though by no means unheard of, and becoming more common every day, it was still fairly unusual for a tough guy of Randazzo's ilk to defect and become a stool pigeon. Grimm needed to know why Randazzo had chosen to roll over. To understand this, he needed to know how the rat fit into the overall picture. It didn't take him long to find out.

Through his organized crime contacts, he was introduced to a slouching, bearded young man named Funzi, a Bonnano family associate. Funzi told Grimm that Randazzo's access to superior goods through his connection to Sonny's flow had gone to his head. He also succeeded in poisoning the old neighborhood against him by cheating Funzi on a couple of deals and generally riling local bosses. He left Harlem and moved to an apartment on the West Side. There he tried to insinuate himself into the chic international dope and showbiz set dominated by Sonny and her friends. Randazzo, Funzi said, had fantasies of taking over Sonny's business trip. He claimed he was fucking her. He said he was going to make her fall in love with him, then put her out to pasture with a steady supply of junk for her personal habit. There had been a bullet rolling around with Randazzo's name on it since well before the bust, Grimm was told. The only reason Randazzo hadn't turned up dead a long time ago was that he had protection from on high.

"Who?" Grimm asked Funzi. But the hulking junk dealer was shaking his hairy head even before Grimm uttered the question. Funzi said he wouldn't name names. "Okay," said Grimm. "I'll say the name. If I'm right, you don't say anything. Guy Stash."

Funzi said nothing.

Held began his cross-examination of Randazzo in a way Grimm had never seen the wily criminal attorney proceed before. Usually he was impersonal and all business until he worked his way under the witness's skin. But with Randazzo he was ruthless. He jumped right back into the rancor he'd stirred up during the direct with his angry objections and cutting insults. The stocky, light haired and blue eyed first generation Sicilian-American immediately struck a defensive attitude.

The lawyer started on Randazzo's background. Wasn't it true that he'd been run out of his old neighborhood because he had a reputation as a liar and a cheat? Randazzo bristled. No, not at all. He'd moved because he was afraid of local heat.

"But you can never go back there, correct, Mr. Randazzo?" Held said, trying to strip away his self-satisfied front.

"Now now, maybe."

"Not now, not before now. Not since you got caught cheating your old partner, isn't that right?" Then, on Grimm's advice, Held dropped a load in Randazzo's lap.

"Do you know a man by the name of Gaetano Stasio, Mr. Randazzo? Better known as Guy Stash?"

Vaggi leapt to her feet and asked the judge for a bench conference. At the sidebar, she told Judge Gass that Held was straying into an area that was part of an ongoing investigation, a secret grand jury probe that would be compromised by exposure at this time. She offered to show the judge, in chambers, evidence to verify her claim.

In a voice loud enough for Randazzo to overhear, Held argued that he needed to show that the witness, at the direction of Stasio, "who is this man's boss, purposely set up by Sonia Byrne-Downes by delivering drugs and money to her at a time when he knew she was about to be arrested.'' Held added that the witness was now concocting evidence against the defendant in order to aid Stasio in his attempt to promote a "coup within the wholesale narcotics industry in this city." Gass scowled and said he didn't follow. Held assured him he would clarify the issue for the judge and jury through witnesses he intended to call to rebut Randazzo's testimony.

Vaggi looked shaken. She complained that Held was talking too loudly and asked that the witness be excused. Held, whose understanding of Grimm's theory of the internal strife within the Moriarty organization was necessarily limited, got the impression Vaggi had no idea what he was talking about. Gass called a recess. He said he would meet with the prosecutor in chambers so that she could show him why the witness's relationship with Guy Stash should not be allowed in evidence.

Vaggi glared at Grimm as she returned from the bench. She knew this kind of information could come only from Grimm's sources.

"Well?" Held asked Grimm as the courtroom emptied. "How did he react? Are we on to something?"

"He looked like he was ready to crawl under the rug," Grimm said. "When he heard the name Stasio, he almost shit."

The defense was not surprised, nor particularly disappointed, when Gass announced his ruling that Held would not be allowed to cross-examine the witness on his association with Gaetano Stasio, since this was not evidence that had been part of the direct testimony, and the government had convinced him that such information, if made public, could jeopardize an ongoing investigation and possibly endanger agents' lives. But the defense's purposes had been accomplished. The witness was scared out of his wits.

When the jury was returned to the courtroom and Held resumed his cross-examination, he could rattle Randazzo without mentioning Guy Stash's name. The defense lawyer narrowed the focus of his questioning to the day of the August bust. Held asked the witness why he had taken the three kilos of heroin and 450,000 in cash and delivered it to Ms. Byrne-Downes personally when he told the jury he took care of such details with Lundgren?

"I was leaving town," Randazzo answered. "I wanted to balance out the account before I left."

"I see. And that is the amount you owed Ms. Byrne-Downes, 450,000 is that correct, Mr. Randazzo?"

"Yeah. Once I gave her back the three kis I didn't sell, that's what I owed."

"You're certain you gave her 450,000?"

"Yeah, exactly 450."

"How much do you make on a kilo of heroin, Mr. Randazzo?"

The witness shrugged. "Depends on what I do with it. Fifty, maybe a hundred grand."

Held looked impressed. "A hundred thousand per kilo. That's a lot of money. Why didn't you sell the three kilos instead of returning them to Ms. Byrne-Downes?"

"I told you, I wanted to get out of town." Randazzo was sweating.

"And did you get out of town?"

No answer.

"Mr. Randazzo, I didn't hear your answer. Did you leave town?"

"I was gonna . . ."

"Weren't you arrested at your apartment the next day?"

"Yeah."

"Why didn't you give the drugs and money to Mr. Lundgren? You told us Sonny Byrne-Downes had instructed you to handle your business with Mr. Lundgren instead of with her, right, Mr. Randazzo?"

Randazzo, beginning to squirm, thought for a moment, then answered, "I couldn't reach him."

"Did you try? Did you call him on the pager?"

"Yeah, a couple 'a times."

Held was nodding, his long hair dangling over his collar. From his folder full of papers, he produced what Grimm knew were the records of calls made to Lundgren's pager number and copies of the messages left on the day of his murder.

"Can you tell us what time you called Lundgren and the message you left?"

Randazzo said he couldn't remember.

"Why were you in such a hurry to leave town, Mr. Randazzo?"

"It was the weekend. It was hot in New York. I was goin' to Atlantic City for a few days."

"Wasn't it in fact because you were informed ahead of time that the arrests were about to take place?"

"No. I didn't know nothin' about no arrests."

"You wanted to get out of town rather than stick around and make an extra quarter of a million dollars?"

"Yeah," Randazzo said, "that's right."

Held addressed the Court. "Your Honor, I have here copies of records obtained from the Radioman Communications Company. These records reflect all the calls made to Karl Lundgren's pager on the day in question, that is, September 13th of last year, the day of the arrest of Sonia Byrne-Downes and one day before this witness was arrested. With the Court's permission, I would like these records marked and entered as a defense exhibit."

Judge Gass and Vaggi inspected the records. Held said that if necessary he could produce someone from Radioman to attest to the records, but Vaggi and the judge agreed to accept them. Once the records had been tagged as a defense exhibit, Held asked for permission to approach the witness. He handed Randazzo the pager company records.

"Mr. Randazzo, I am showing you records of all calls placed to Karl Lundgren's pager, and copies of the messages left, on the day you say you tried to reach him twice to get him to take the heroin and money from you. Will you please look at the records and show us where they reflect the calls you say you made."

There were no such calls. Grimm knew the records by heart. Like most drug operations, there was no action before noon. Then there were two calls from Sonny leaving West Side pay phone callback numbers. Later there was a call from Queens from Micky Hoyos. Around 7:15 P.M., there was another call from Sonny, then nothing until late evening. Randazzo stared at the records. Finally, he handed them back and said, "Maybe I called him at his place. Or I could 'a called him the day before. I forget."

"Did the loft have a phone? That is, Lundgren's place in SoHo. Was there a phone?"

"I think so. I can't remember."

"How many times did you visit Lundgren at the loft?"

"I don't know exactly. Maybe five or six times. Maybe more."

Held strode back to the defense table. He handed the pager records to the clerk, stopped and looked around the courtroom significantly, and grinned at Grimm who was seated in the first row of the spectators' benches with Cassy, Carmen and Suzi Sapphire. Cassy had beside her a large poster-size rectangular package wrapped in brown paper.

Taking up his position at the lectern again, Held asked Randazzo questions about Karl Lundgren's loft. Where was it located? SoHo. Address? Randazzo said he couldn't remember the exact address, but it was on a side street off West Broadway. Describe the building. Nothing unusual about it, typical medium-size building of the kind that contains lofts refurbished as artists' studios and living areas. How many lofts were there in the building? Four, Randazzo believed. He added that Lundgren lived on the second floor, one level above the street. Again the witness stated that the name Rude Productions appeared on the nameplate above the buzzer to Lundgren's loft.

"And did Mr. Lundgren live at the loft?" Held asked.

"Yeah."

"Alone? With a wife? Girlfriend? Roommate?"

"No. He lived there alone."

"You're sure about that, Mr. Randazzo?"

The witness hesitated. He looked at Vaggi and said, "I never saw nobody else there." He looked back at Held. "He never mentioned about nobody else livin' there."

"How was the place decorated?"

"I don't notice those things. Lot's 'a pictures. The guy was a photographer. You know, pictures and posters of rock stars, that kind'a stuff."

"You're sure he lived there alone? What about pets? A cat or dog?"

"Maybe. I don't remember seein' no pet."

"Mr. Randazzo, do you know what an English bulldog looks like?"

"Yeah."

"You're familiar with the breed?"

"Yeah, I've seen 'em."

"Could you describe the outstanding characteristics of the English bulldog?"

Randazzo shrugged and made a face. "I dunno. Short, kind'a bowlegged. Pushed-in nose, kind'a smashed-in lookin' face."

This was Grimm's cue. He stood and began removing the brown wrapping paper from the package Cassy and Carmen had brought into the courtroom.

Gass, Vaggi, the jury and everyone else in the room watched Grimm. In an obvious parody of Vaggi's use of the blown-up surveillance photos of Rickie and Sonny, Held took the unwrapped, poster-sized cardboard from Grimm and, keeping it faced toward the wall, walked over to the easel Vaggi had used to display the surveillance shots. He turned the poster around and mounted it on the easel for everyone to see. The brooding countenance of Myrtle, Lundgren's bulldog, stared out from the giant color photograph. There were a few gasps, then a twitter of laughter rippled through the courtroom.

"Do you recognize this dog, Mr. Randazzo?" Held asked.

Randazzo looked as though he knew he was in trouble. "It's a bulldog."

"Exactly, sir. Have you ever seen this particular bulldog before?"

"I don't know. Maybe."

"You don't remember this dog?"

"No. Not that I know of."

"Is this Mr. Lundgren's dog?"

Randazzo was getting flustered, he didn't know whether to say yes or no. Grimm saw him glancing at Vaggi, but the prosecutor couldn't help him. She knew no more about Myrtle than Randazzo did. Sonny had told Grimm that Karl always left Myrtle at the loft to guard the stash when he went out to make deliveries or pickups, just as he had on the day he was murdered. Had Julio Zuluaga been in court, he might have remembered seeing Myrtle with Grimm the day Grimm discovered Lundgren's body at Kennedy Airport. So the feds had no way of knowing about Myrtle. She had been living at Grimm's farm since soon after he took her from the loft.

"Could be," Randazzo said. "I dunno."

"In all your visits to the SoHo loft, the five or six times, possibly more, I believe you told the jury you visited there, on any of those occasions, did you ever encounter this bulldog?" Held stabbed at the picture with his long forefinger.

"Not that I remember," Randazzo said after a long pause.

Abruptly, Held concluded his cross-examination. "I have no further questions, your Honor."

It was already late in the afternoon when Dominic Randazzo stepped down from the witness stand. On redirect, Vaggi had asked a few questions to try to clarify areas of Randazzo's testimony Held had managed to sully. But she made no mention of the bulldog, whose magnified image glared at the jury as Randazzo disappeared in a cloud of doubt. Who, everyone wondered, could forget a face like that?

There was a restive atmosphere in the courtroom as Vita Vaggi stood and announced, "The government rests, your Honor." Held's cross-examination of Randazzo left everyone feeling perplexed and dissatisfied, which is exactly the effect the defense lawyer hoped for. He wanted the government to rest on a note of uncertainty, a sense of something having been left out. Judge Gass excused the jury, as usual admonishing them not to discuss the case amongst themselves or with anyone else, and to avoid reading about it in newspapers or watching news stories on TV. He told them, in the morning the defense would begin presentation of its case.

With the jury out of the room, Held made a motion to dismiss the indictment against Rickie. The government, the attorney argued, had failed to prove the existence of a conspiracy of which the defendant was a member, therefore the drugs, money and other evidence seized from Sonny must not be allowed in against Rickie. In eloquent reasoning, Held paced back and forth as he ticked off the "insurmountable faults and weaknesses of the government's case."

"Your Honor," Held concluded, "the prosecution of Rickie Rude is a sham, a flagrant attempt to convict an innocent man on nothing more substantial than guilt by association."

Vaggi countered that Held was conveniently leaving out the taped telephone conversations between Rickie and Sonny which she averred proved the existence of a conspiracy and the willful, knowing participation of the defendant. Even without the testimonies of Caine and Randazzo, the prosecutor said, enough evidence existed to allow the jury to decide whether the defendant joined the conspiracy. The judge, making mention of the phone call from Rickie in California, sided with the government and denied Held's motion.

"Now, Mr. Held, is the defense ready to proceed with its first witness at nine-forty-five tomorrow?"

Held stood slowly. "Yes, judge, we are ready." He turned to face the spectators' areas as though looking for someone. "As long as the Marshals can have Sonia Byrne-Downes available," Held declared in a loud voice as he turned back to the bench, "the defense is ready to proceed."

At once, journalists began to bolt for the door. As soon as Gass adjourned and stalked from the bench, the courtroom erupted in pandemonium. Reporters thronged around the defense team and shouted questions at Held and the diminutive defendant. Rickie and Suzi hugged each other. Grimm had to smile when he saw a couple of the courtroom artists approach the giant photo of Myrtle and begin making sketches.

Held, Rickie and Suzi practically had to fight their way out of the courthouse and down the wide granite steps to the attorney's waiting limo. There was a mood of elation as the day clearly belonged to the defense. Rickie and his lawyer were all smiles for the public. Donnie Randazzo's failure to recognize the bulldog had taken on disproportionate significance. The government's case was faltering. Aaron Held had a difficult time containing his excitement. On the sidewalk, he and Grimm both burst out laughing and threw their arms around each other.

"That was wild," Held exclaimed. "Did you see the look on Vaggi's face when she got a load of Myrtle?"

"Like, what the fuck is that?" Rickie said. "Brilliant, A.G. Brilliant. Pure Perry Mason."

Suzi, looking drained, stood on her tiptoes in front of Grimm. "Give us a kiss, you big nut. That was incredible."

"Whoa. Wait a minute," Held said. "What about me?"

They all laughed and hugged the lawyer.

"You going over to see Sonny?" Rickie asked Grimm.

Grimm checked his watch. "Yes. The coast should be clear by now. You coming, Aaron?"

"I'll be there as soon as possible," Held said. "Come along, Cassy. We'll give you and Carmen a lift uptown."

Grimm kissed Carmen and Cassy and said he'd see them later.

"Give Sonny our love," Rickie said. "Tell her we'll see her tomorrow."

They all climbed into the stretch Caddy leaving Grimm on the sidewalk amid the crowds of journalists, celebrity gawkers and Rudies. He walked around the back of the courthouse to the federal jail and checked in to see his client.

Sonny sat across the table from Grimm in one of the cubicles in the attorney visiting room. Her eyes looked unusually clear and sparkly, her skin as pale and smooth as porcelain. She was dressed in her blue institutional smock and slacks.

"Your hands are freezing," Grimm told her. "Nervous, baby?"

"You'll be there, darling. As long as I can see your face, I'll manage. Where's Aaron?"

"He's coming. Don't worry, you can handle Vaggi."

"Oh, I'm not worried about that bitch. She doesn't scare me. It's the jury I worry about. I want them to believe me."

"They will."

"You'll bring Carmen?"

"Of course. She wouldn't miss it for the world."

Sonny smiled. "She must've been delighted that her friend Myrtle was such a big hit." Now she laughed. "Arthur, you're crazy."

"What can I tell you? It worked." He kissed her cold fingers.

Sonny stroked his beard and said, "Do you suppose you would have liked me if we'd met before . . . all this shit?" She gave him a reflective look.

"Why wouldn't I have liked you?"

"Well." She thought about it. "I wasn't the same person then. The shit makes you, indifferent, I suppose. And then there was the business. It was all such an ego trip. I don't know if you would've liked me or not. I was a strange woman."

"What are you like now?"

After a moment she said, "I don't know. Perhaps I haven't really changed, though I do feel quite different. Relaxed. Centered. I see things a lot more clearly now. I look back on the person I was then and I ask myself, why in God's name did I behave like that?"

"Like what?"

"It's difficult to explain. I suppose it's a kind of arrogance or megalomania. I never allowed myself to stop and think about what I was doing. When you're in the position I was in, you're the most popular person in town. Everyone is fighting to get next to you."

"It seems to me that hasn't changed."

She smiled, "No, but my attitude has. I used to believe I could do no wrong."

"And now what do you believe?"

"Now?" Sonny sighed and shook her head. "Now I believe I was not a good person. I did a lot of bad things. And I was never satisfied, never at peace with myself. Something was missing. Perhaps if I'd had you. What do you think? If we had met and fallen in love, would we have been happy with each other?"

Grimm gave her a long look. "Maybe," he said.

Sonny smiled again. "You," she said. "Yes, that's right. Maybe. For a while, in any case. My little Carmencita and I, close as we are, we sometimes felt terribly lonely. We obviously needed the charming, mysterious Mr. Grimm to take us under his strong wing and love us, protect us. Could you do that, darling? Would you?"

"Gladly," Grimm said.

"It's fun to think about, isn't it? Pity we'll never know."

JUNK QUEEN TO TESTIFY

said the morning headlines.

"Mr. Held, are you ready to call your first witness?" Judge Gass asked.

It was ten-fifteen in the morning. There was a vibrant air of expectation in the courtroom as Held rose from his chair.

"Yes, thank you, your Honor," the lawyer replied. "The defense calls Sonia Byrne-Downes."

This was the moment everyone had been waiting for. After so much testimony concerning her, Sonny had begun to take on near mythic proportions in the minds of those following the trial. People wanted to see her. Everyone was anxious to know what she had to say about Rickie.

Grimm, Cassy and Carmen had arrived at the courthouse early. They were seated in their usual spot with Suzi in the front middle of the row of spectators' benches reserved for the defense. By the time Judge Gass mounted his dais, the courtroom was already filled to capacity and the Marshals and security guards were turning people away. Now everyone stared at the thick, molded, wooden door leading to the witness room. The bailiff opened the door and Sonny was brought in.

She was dressed in a long, gray woolen skirt and a snug-fitting black turtleneck sweater. She wore no jewelry and what little makeup she had on seemed to accentuate her sharp cheekbones and large, bright eyes. She wore a light violet lipstick on her wide, sensual mouth. The birthmark over the corner of her eye was plainly visible, again giving her a sense of raw vulnerability. Her auburn hair was lustrous and wavy. Seeing her walk toward the witness stand, Grimm felt a pang of desire.

"God, she's beautiful," Cassy said. "What a face!"

What she had was great poise. Grimm thought he could never get tired of looking at her. She stood half turned toward the judge, who was not immune to her renown. He stared at her over the top of his spectacles and she looked straight over at the jury as she was sworn in. She took her seat and Gass told her she could adjust the microphone. Then he leaned across and showed her how it was done. He asked her to please keep her voice up and address her answers to the jury.

"Yes, I will. Thank you, your Honor," she said in the deep inflections of her patrician British accent. Grimm could see glimpses of Carmen in her. It was breeding, thought Grimm, the integrity of bloodlines.

Knowing everyone in the room was intrigued by her, Aaron Held indulged the general curiosity by taking Sonny through a brief biographical sketch. She said she'd been born June 10th, 1950, in London, England. Her father was a civil servant with the Foreign Service, her mother of Irish descent. Sonny said she had been educated in England and at the Sorbonne in Paris. Married once, husband deceased. Children? Yes, one daughter, eleven years old. Was her daughter present in the courtroom? Yes. Held asked Carmen to stand so the jury could get a look at her.

Sonny explained that when she was a little girl growing up, her father had been posted at different times to Ethiopia, the Sudan, the West Indies, and finally India. She was sent to boarding school in England, but spent her holidays with her family living in these countries. As a teenager, she began smuggling small amounts of hashish from India to England and sharing it with her schoolmates. At nineteen, while living in Paris, she married. Her husband died a year later, just a month before the birth of her child.

Her first trip to the United States came in the early Seventies. In 1976, she was arrested and spent a year in prison in Delhi, India, for smuggling hashish. She returned to New York in 1977 and had lived here on and off since. Her daughter attended the Ethel Burnham School for Girls. Aaron Held asked her now she supported herself.

"Selling drugs," Sonny answered matter-of-factly.

The lawyer moved on. Her long relationship with the defendant, Rickie Rude, was discussed. How long had she known Rickie? Nearly fifteen years. They first met in London in 1967. Held asked her to relate to the jury the circumstances of that meeting. Sonny recalled that Rickie was performing as a folk singer in the British Isles. At that time, he was known as Rick Rudd. He was quite popular in England, a sort of working-class hero. It was there that he began to change his image, due to contact with the skinheads, the forerunners of the punk movement. Rickie had been thrown out of his hotel, and had no place to stay in London. Sonny was living at the time in a large flat just off the King's Road in the Chelsea section of the city. Rickie was invited to stay there and he moved in, living with Sonny and her then fiancé and other friends and relatives who moved in and out. Rickie stayed with them for several months until late 1967 when he left for the Continent.

What kind of relationship did they have? Were they lovers? No. They were very close friends but not physically intimate. Sonny had been living with the man who was later to become her husband, father of her daughter. Her relationship with Rickie had always been one of deep mutual trust and understanding, she explained. Through good times and bad times they could always depend on each other. Rickie had been poor in those days—by choice. What money he made he gave away. He preferred to live a kind of hippie vagabond existence. Sometimes he would get stuck in places with no money—Paris, Amsterdam, Madrid. Then Sonny would either send him money or give him names of friends of hers he could look up for a place to stay and a meal. He stayed with her again in Paris for a few weeks in early 1969, just after her husband's death and right around the time Carmen was born.

Later, even as Rickie became more successful, he continued his nomadic life-style, shunning the accumulation of wealth and material possessions. He lived in cheap hotels or friends' homes. His main concern in life was his music. He expressed fear that money and the trappings of fame would destroy him, as he believed it had so many artists he admired.

When Rickie and Sonny got together again in New York in the mid-Seventies, Sonny told the jury, she tried to get him to invest some of the money he was making in property. He resisted it, but she acted as a sort of informal business advisor to him. Sonny said she was also good friends with Saul Diamond's executive assistant, Judy Roth. Together, she and Judy helped Rickie organize his finances. By the Eighties, Rickie was making serious money. He purchased a condominium in Florida for his mother, and he sent money to his brothers and sisters. He bought buildings in Manhattan, the West Side brownstone and the loft in SoHo. But Rickie still refused to handle money. He continued to live in hotels, the Chelsea at this time, and changed his life-style hardly at all.

"Now, Ms. Byrne-Downes, were you paid a fee for acting as an informal business consultant and investment counselor to Rickie Rude?" Held inquired.

"No," Sonny answered, "We're friends, we don't try to make money from each other. I did it because Judy and I felt Rickie needed help. He was making a lot of money, but he was always broke because he gave it all away."

"To your knowledge, Ms. Byrne-Downes, does Rickie give away a large percentage of his earnings to charities?"

"Vast amounts. As I said, Rickie does not believe in the accumulation of personal wealth."

Did Rickie know what business she was in? Held asked. Yes, she never attempted to hide it from him. All the time she had known him, she had been in the drug business. Held asked her to explain to the jury how she happened to become a drug dealer. Sonny blinked her huge, luminous eyes and replied that, as she'd stated before, she began by smuggling small amounts of hash from India, where it was plentiful, to England when she returned to school from her holidays. This was during the Sixties, a time of great social change in England as well as in America. The Beatles and the Rolling Stones. Drugs. Youth groups known then as the Mods and the Rockers. Later, hippies. Sonny came of age in the midst of all this upheaval. In India, drugs, particularly cannabis, were nothing new. One could buy hash easily and cheaply.

At first, she shared the hash with her friends. In time, though, she and the other girls began selling some of it and using the money to buy clothes, records, and to travel about. Eventually, she became intrigued by the independence the money afforded her. Soon, she was employing girls as couriers, sending them to India to pick up hash from her sources there, paying them a fee, then consigning the shipments to dealers in London who sold it for her. The business flourished. Sonny said she'd always been good with figures.

In India, in London and on the Continent, she was meeting young people from all over the world. Hippies from America and Canada, long-haired kids from the Netherlands, Scandinavia, Australia. They were all looking for hash. Sonny said she began making trips to Nepal, to the Hindu Kush in Afghanistan, to the Bekaa Valley in the Lebanon.

In these places, she made contact with the local growers who provided her with the best quality hashish. Usually she arranged to have the hash smuggled to England or Holland, but sometimes she sold it to other hash smugglers who took it to different parts of the world. She was dealing in small amounts, no more than fifteen or twenty kilos at a time.

"The business sort of took over my life," she told the jury.

In Paris in 1968, she married and got pregnant. Her husband moved in radical political circles. They were in France during the student rebellion. Sonny attended the Sorbonne for a year, and for a time, her drug activities declined.

After her husband's death, she returned to London, now with her baby girl. She was twenty-one years old. She got back into hash smuggling full time. She went to India and started shipping hash to Europe, later Canada and the States, using a variety of smuggling methods and increasing the quantities. She was moving about continually. Through all these years, she and Rickie remained in touch. Whenever she was in the States, or when Rickie was in London, they would get together. After her prison term in India, she more or less resettled in New York.

It was on her advice that Rickie purchased the West Side brownstone. Rickie, who liked living in hotels, particularly the Chelsea, asked her if she would like to move into the top floor flat of the brownstone and sort of keep an eye on the place for him. He was on the road much of the time, recording on the West Coast, touring the country with his band. Carmen was going to school in Manhattan, and so they lived in the flat rent-free with the understanding that Rickie was welcome to stay there whenever and for however long he wished if life at the Chelsea got too hectic. This part of her testimony paralleled that of the real estate agent who testified for the government.

"Could you have afforded to pay rent?" Held asked.

"Certainly. I offered, but Rickie wouldn't hear of it."

"Did Rickie know you were dealing drugs out of the apartment?"

"But I wasn't," Sonny protested. "I lived there with my daughter. The business was all handled elsewhere."

Now Held began taking Sonny through the evidence Vaggi had introduced with testimony by the various drug and FBI agents. The drugs, she said, the heroin, cocaine and other drugs seized at the apartment belonged to her and her alone. The same was true of the money. It was all hers. Rickie had no involvement whatsoever in her drug business. If he wanted drugs for his own personal use, she would simply give them to him free of charge.

"And did Rickie often ask you for drugs?"

"No. Pot—marijuana—once in a while. For the last few years, Rickie has been staying away from hard drugs. He likes marijuana."

Had he ever been a drug addict? Held asked. An addict, no, not in her opinion. A heavy user, perhaps, at times in the past. Rickie, like herself, had grown up in and around the drug culture, but he had no understanding of, nor any interest in, the drug business.

Sonny then explained the supposed coded language in the taped telephone conversations between herself and Rickie. "That blonde girl," was not code for a shipment of drugs. It was a reference to Suzi Sapphire, Rickie's wife, whom he met, in a roundabout way, through Sonny. Suzi was asked to stand and display her white gold hair. "How's the kid?" meant exactly that: How was her kid, Carmen. Carmen and Rickie were great friends, Sonny explained. Sonny went through a dozen or more equally dubious examples of crypto drug talk. Held did not ask her to explain the crucial call from Rickie in California, leaving that for Vaggi.

Sonny disputed point by point the testimonies of the cooperating government witnesses, Caine and Randazzo. No, she said, Rickie had never been present at any business discussions or drug transactions at the West Side apartment for the good reason that such dealings had never taken place there. Randazzo and Caine were lying, Sonny declared. She did not do business at home where she lived with her young daughter. She had been in the business for a long time, and she knew how to keep her dealings private, confidential, and out of the home. It was all set up and administered through a system of stash pads, communications through beepers and pay phones, with deliveries and payoffs handled by runners.

"How was it then, Ms. Byrne-Downes, that you happened to have three kilos of heroin and nearly half a million dollars in cash in your apartment at the time of your arrest?"

"Against my wishes, Dominic Randazzo, who came to the flat unannounced, insisted I take the money and goods from him. I was furious. He said he was hot, the police were watching him, so he wanted to give me everything he owed and whatever he had of mine so he could leave town until he cooled off.''

''Didn't you employ a man named Karl Lundgren to take care of pick-ups and deliveries for you?''

''Yes, Karl was one of my runners. Karl ordinarily handled Donnie. I told Donnie to call Karl on the pager and give the stuff to him. He refused. He said he couldn't wait around for Karl. He just appeared on my doorstep and handed me the package.''

''By the way, Ms. Byrne-Downes, would you tell the jury how much money Mr. Randazzo gave you on September 13th?''

''Yes. He gave me $450,000.''

Held was watching the clock. He'd had Sonny on the stand all day, and he wanted to wrap up her direct testimony so as to leave Vaggi with only enough time to begin her cross before the session adjourned for the day.

''You're absolutely sure of the amount?''

''I'm positive. He gave me 450,000. I had another few thousand of my own there as well.''

''I see. And when you were arrested later the same day, how much money did you have in your possession at the apartment when the agents made their raid?''

''The same amount. The 450,000 Donnie gave me and another 3,500. All together, 453,500.''

Held appeared to be studying his notes. He frowned and looked up at Sonny. ''If I may have just a moment, your Honor. There appears to be a discrepancy here.'' The lawyer asked the clerk to give him Government Exhibit e-12, a notebook containing figures which was found in Sonny's possession at the time of her arrest, and which was alleged by the prosecution to contain records of drug transactions. ''May I approach the witness, your Honor?''

''You may, Mr. Held.''

Held leaned over the side of the witness box. ''Ms. Byrne-Downes, I am showing you Government Exhibit e-12, a notebook with figures in it, and I ask you if you recognize this notebook?''

''Yes,'' she answered. ''It's mine.''

''And is this your handwriting?''

''It is.''

''Would you tell the jury what the figures in the book represent?''

"Payments made to me. I would sometimes meet people I worked with and take money from them. Then I'd meet with Karl and give the money to him to hold. Those are my records."

"And what does this figure here represent?"

Sonny squinted at the book. "That would be the payment made by Donnie Randazzo. 450K means 450,000. Minus three means deduct the three kilos returned. Nine dash thirteen is the date. The letter D signifies the transaction was with Donnie."

"Thank you, Ms. Byrne-Downes." Held walked across the courtroom and gave the notebook to the jury foreperson. Then he marched to the lectern and turned back to the witness.

"Ms. Byrne-Downes, could you tell us how it is that when the agents arrested you, they only recovered 380,000?"

"Objection, your Honor," said Vaggi. "Mr. Held is asking the witness to speculate—"

"I certainly am not doing anything of the kind, your Honor. The witness was there. I'm not asking her to speculate at all. I want her to relate what she knows to have happened to cause the discrepancy of over $70,000 between the amount she says she had on hand and the amount the agents claim they seized."

"Overruled. The witness may answer as to what she observed, what she knows to have happened by her observations." Gass turned to Sonny and asked, "How much money did the agents take from you, Ms. Byrne-Downes?"

"They took all of it, your Honor. All 453,500."

"And do you know of your own observations what happened to the roughly 70,000 not received in evidence?"

"I know they took it with them. How they managed to lose 70,000, I could only speculate about that."

Judge Gass looked disturbed. "Can you recall the names of any of the agents who arrested you, Ms. Byrne-Downes?" the judge asked.

"I remember one of them, the one who was in charge. His name was Julio Zuluaga."

Judge Gass made some notes and turned the witness back over to Aaron Held.

"Ms. Byrne-Downes, please tell the jury in your own words about the arrangement you and Karl Lundgren had with Rickie Rude concerning the loft located in the SoHo district of Manhattan."

"Well, actually, I wasn't involved in the loft. Karl rented it from

Rude Productions, which is the company Judy Roth set up to hold Rickie's property. The company owns the building. Karl leased the loft from the company.''

"For what purpose?"

"Karl was a photographer and graphic artist. He designed record album jackets. He did promotional posters, things of that sort. He lived in the studio and he worked there.''

"Was the loft used as a stash pad or as an office for your drug operation?''

"No, it was not. I insisted on that.''

"Was there a phone at the loft, Ms. Byrne-Downes?''

"No. Karl used the beeper.''

Held was walking toward the easel where the poster-size photo of Myrtle had been turned to face the wall. "Did Mr. Lundgren live alone, do you know?''

"Yes. He and his dog, Myrtle.''

"What kind of dog is Myrtle, Ms. Byrne-Downes?''

"She's an English bulldog.''

Held turned the photo around. "Is this Myrtle?''

Sonny regarded the enlarged picture. "It certainly looks like her. The coloring and markings are identical. That's Myrtle's collar. I would have to say it is Myrtle.''

"Ms. Byrne-Downes, did you go to the loft often?''

"Not often, no. Once in a while I'd pass by to see what Karl was working on.''

"Was Myrtle always there when you stopped by?''

"Yes, always. Karl had a lot of valuable equipment in the loft. Myrtle was his watch dog.''

"Would you say it was impossible to go to the loft to see Karl Lundgren without encountering his dog, Myrtle?''

"Quite impossible," Sonny said. "Myrtle followed Karl around the studio. They were inseparable.''

"I have just a few more questions, Judge Gass," Held announced to the Court as he walked from the easel back to the lectern. It was five minutes to four.

"Do you know a woman by the name of Jennifer Monsalvo, Ms. Byrne-Downes?''

"Yes, I do.''

"How did you come to know her?''

"Jenny worked for me. She was a courier. She got busted last year."

"Was she working for you when she got arrested?"

"Yes."

"Now, would you please relate to the jury your knowledge of the circumstances of that bust?"

"Jenny made a trip to Colombia. Her partner, a man she worked with, a Swede I've never met, got busted by Customs at Kennedy Airport. He was carrying cocaine, and he gave up Jenny, he told on her. Drug agents arrested her at the hotel she was staying at."

"And was Ms. Monsalvo carrying drugs at the time she was arrested?"

"Yes, about five pounds of cocaine."

"And, as you recall, what instructions did Ms. Monsalvo follow upon her arrival in New York?"

"She went straight from the airport to the hotel where she was to wait for someone to contact her. I was using what we call 'watchers' at the airport, people who watch the flight come in to see if the couriers make it through. We knew the Swede didn't make it, and we tried to warn Jenny, but the agents were all over her. So we left a message for her at the hotel telling her she had company."

"Did Ms. Monsalvo go from the airport to your place on the West Side, to your knowledge?"

"No."

"You're sure of that?"

"Absolutely sure. Jenny had no idea where I was living."

After a few more questions about the Monsalvo affair, which contradicted the agents' testimonies as to how they obtained the warrants to tap Sonny's phone, gaping holes were left in the government's version of the investigation. Held then wrapped up Sonny's direct testimony with a series of concise, pointed questions aimed at knocking the bottom out of the case against Rickie Rude.

"In all the years you have known Rickie Rude, Ms. Byrne-Downes, have you ever known him to be involved in the drug business, either yours or anyone else's?"

"No. Never."

"Have you ever conspired with, confederated with or joined in a plan with Rickie Rude to import or distribute illegal drugs?"

"No, sir, I have not."

"Has Rickie Rude ever given you money to invest in drug smuggling schemes?"

"No."

"Have you ever given Rickie Rude either drugs or money as return for investments or as reward for help given you?"

"No."

Held gave a slight bow of his long, beautifully tailored torso, his fly-away hair in disarray. "Thank you very much, Ms. Byrne-Downes," the lawyer said sweetly. He turned to the prosecutor's table.

"Your witness, Ms. Vaggi."

The Dragon Lady meets The Smack Goddess, Grimm thought. Here was a contest worthy of an arena. Sonny had been cool on direct, if anything, too cool. She was on her best British behavior, her accent a trifle more pronounced than when she talked to Grimm. He feared she might be coming over as too much in control, arrogant, overbearing, manipulative. He realized with a slight shock she was all of those things. Vaggi, meanwhile, had adopted the part of the much-abused, dedicated and no-nonsense drug prosecutor striving to protect American society from the corrupt alien likes of Sonia Byrne-Downes. And it was effective. Her attitude communicated that these people were dangerously clever. Grimm was certain that not a few people in the room would have liked to see Sonny humbled.

After a few low-key introductory questions, Vaggi startled the audience with a shocker.

"Ms. Byrne-Downes, you told us your husband is deceased. How did he die?"

"Your Honor," Held said wearily, "I object."

"Relevancy, Mr. Held?"

"Yes, Judge. What could this inquiry possibly have to do with Rickie Rude?"

The judge looked to Vaggi for an answer.

"Background on the witness, your Honor. It goes to the witness's character, and therefore her credibility," she began but the judge was already nodding.

"Yes, I'm going to let it in. Objection overruled. You may continue, Ms. Vaggi."

Grimm and Held had decided to leave this out of the direct. They knew Vaggi wouldn't be able to resist going for the jugular. They also knew Carmen would be present in the courtroom when Vaggi asked this question. It was a tactical decision they hoped would show the prosecutor's vicious streak.

Sonny was staring at Vaggi with a look so full of hatred Grimm thought the prosecutor would wilt. But Vaggi bore up under the harsh gaze and actually seemed to gain a kind of malicious strength.

"I killed him," Sonny said. "Is that what you wanted to hear, Ms. Vaggi?"

Several people gasped in unison. There was an undercurrent of murmuring. Vaggi looked as though she'd been checked by the ruthless sincerity of Sonny's response. The two women continued staring at each other. They were the same age, both intelligent, urbane. Their divergent careers had brought them to a showdown of wits in this courtroom. Sonny was already condemned; she had about her an air of someone who is making a final stand at the edge of a precipice. She had nothing to lose but her self-respect. Vaggi, though, was still trying to claw her way out of the pit she'd slipped into while negotiating this treacherous case. Both women were there to pay the wages of ambition.

"How did you happen to kill your husband, Ms. Byrne-Downes?" Vaggi asked, her voice tuned with a jeer as if to say it might have been easy for a woman like Sonny.

Held made his dramatic point by turning to look at Carmen, and Grimm noticed several jurors take the cue and do the same. There was the little girl sitting upright, wide-eyed, gazing at her mother as though she were bracing herself for an unpleasant event, like a brave kid getting psyched-up to have a booster shot.

"I shot him," Sonny said bitterly. "My husband was a violent man. He sometimes lost his temper and beat me." She looked directly at her child as she spoke. "I was pregnant. Finally, I—there was a struggle and I shot him."

Vaggi would have been wiser to have left out the entire line of inquiry. Sonny's bruised look suddenly made sense. Though Grimm knew she was born with the mark over her eye, it now became symbolic, the stamp of the battered woman who had risen up and defended herself and the nascent life in her womb, the life now perched on the edge of the bench watching her. Held slumped in his seat and stared down at his hands. He stole a glance at the jury. Grimm wondered when Vaggi would begin to recognize the traps they laid for her.

For the remainder of that first session, Vaggi attempted to portray Sonny as a cold, hardened criminal who was there to protect Rickie, by lying, for reasons of her own. What reasons? Through her questions, Vaggi wanted to lead the jury to infer that a conspiracy existed between Rickie and Sonny, a conspiracy of arcane allegiance, and that the goals of the conspiracy were manifold. She would have them believe Sonny conspired with Rickie to create a financial empire fueled with drug profits washed through the musician's business enterprises. The rest of the afternoon, Vaggi's questions were all about money.

And the figures were astronomical, though Grimm knew Sonny was underestimating them. With Sonny's record book to guide her, Vaggi extracted testimony to the effect that the witness handled gross profits in the tens of millions over her career. Where had all the money gone? It was the cardinal question to ask a dope dealer. A basic axiom of drug investigations is to follow the money. The course of the cash will delineate the structure of the conspiracy. Vaggi was on to something, but she didn't know what.

Sonny was too clever to let Vaggi lure her into a cul de sac. When asked how much she personally netted in an average year, Sonny replied that in her business there was no such thing as an average year. Drug smuggling was like high-stakes gambling, Sonny said. Sometimes your boat came in and you hit, other times you lost it all. What assets did she own? Just some paintings, Sonny said, worth a few hundred thousand, which had been seized by the government. She claimed she'd never had a bank account in her life. Vaggi tried to make it look as though it had been Sonny's money that was put up to purchase the West Side brownstone, but Sonny insisted she left the financing of the building in the hands of Judy Roth, who paid with Rickie's money.

"Are you asking this jury to accept the premise that you've accumulated nothing after all the millions of dollars you've made dealing drugs?" Vaggi asked incredulously.

"No. As I said, I had 453,500 in cash, and about another half million in goods. At the time I was arrested, I had perhaps another three or four hundred thousand owed to me. Altogether, I had somewhere between a million-and-a-half and two million. That was mine. But you people got all that.''

It was no good. All the talk of money and they had ended back at the missing seventy grand. Vaggi couldn't overcome the unhappy fact that her case had been sabotaged by corrupt agents. That evening the late edition of the *Post* ran the headline:

FEDS STOLE 70K SAYS JUNK QUEEN

It seemed as though Grimm and Cassy had only just finished making love. He was lying with her in his arms, the smell of her red hair in his nose, he had dozed off and now the phone was ringing. But when he looked at the glowing figures of the digital clock beside the bed, he saw it was almost four in the morning. He grabbed the receiver.

''A.G.,'' said the voice on the other end. Grimm placed it immediately, and he tensed. It was Jack Moriarty. He sounded drunk or high on coke, probably both. ''I gotta talk to ya', bo.''

Jack gave him a number, said he was out in Tommy's neck of the woods, which Grimm took to mean Nevada.

''Who was it?'' Cassy asked as he moved off the bed.

''I've got to go out for a few minutes, baby,'' he said and leaned over to kiss her. ''I'll be right back.'' But as he dressed, he could feel Cassy's eyes watching him as he strapped on his gun.

How convenient, he thought as he left the building, if these cocksuckers are looking to whack me out. On the sidewalk there was no one. No cars came along the street with gunmen slouched inside. Healthy paranoia, thought Grimm, and he braced himself to walk through the brittle cold to a pay phone on the corner of Columbus Avenue.

''Lissen,'' Jack said when Grimm reached him, ''what the fuck're you an' Aaron tryin' ta do?'' He was drunk, his speech now slurred.

''What are you talking about?''

''You know what I'm talkin' about, it's in all the papers, for chrissake. What ya' got my girl on the stand for, A.G.? What're ya', fuckin' nuts?''

Grimm was so enraged he had to stop himself from ripping the receiver off the phone and throwing it in the street. Bad enough that he had to be awakened at the crack of dawn and ordered from his warm bed into the freezing cold, but then to have to listen to some drunk tell him and Aaron how to run their business, it was too much. Grimm felt like telling Moriarty to go fuck himself. He struggled to control his anger.

"Jack," he tried to explain, summoning all the patience he could find, "Sonny insisted on taking the stand. And we had to put her on. What do you want us to do, let Rickie get convicted?"

"What convicted? Shit, anybody could beat that case. They're full 'a shit. What's Rickie got to do with the junk business? They got no case. You put her on'a stand. Jesus, A.G., I don' gotta tell ya' what's gonna happen. Think of the shit they're gonna bring out."

Grimm felt like telling him they did have a case, and that it was his fault for making Rickie call Sonny on a tapped phone. Then he realized with a wave of disgust that Jack wasn't worried about Sonny at all. Nor did he care about what happened to Rickie. His only concern was for what she might reveal about his operation.

"Look, I don't tell you how to run your business, you don't tell me how to run mine. Aaron and I know what we're doing. So does Sonny. Now just relax, Jack. Don't worry. Nobody's going to hurt you."

For a moment, there was no response. Grimm could hear the sounds of a party in the background. He was on the verge of hanging up.

"A.G., you don't unnerstand—"

"No, you don't understand. I understand. Aaron understands. Rickie is on trial in a drug conspiracy case in the Southern District of New York. They have a ninety-eight percent conviction rate. Conspiracy is the vaguest, easiest charge in the book to prove. They do have a case against him or he wouldn't be on trial. We have a job to do, and we don't need you or anybody else telling us how to do it. You just worry about yourself."

"What the fuck is that supposed to mean?"

"It means, you've got nothing to worry about on this end. As far as Sonny and Rickie are concerned, when it comes to them talking about . . . whatever, they won't. We've taken care of all that. We got the judge to rule that certain areas can't be opened up. Rickie and Sonny are together. They—"

"They're together, all right. You know them so good, huh, pal?"

"I know them well enough to know they're not going to say or do anything to hurt you."

"I know that bitch better'n you ever will."

"Then you know you've got nothing to worry about."

"Don't get hostile with me, A.G. I looked out for you on this."

God, thought Grimm, I'd like to smack his pug face. "I'm not getting hostile with you, Jack. I'm telling you not to worry. We have everything under control. Now do me a favor, take it easy. Enjoy yourself and stop worrying. Call me when you're straight."

"I will, bo. I wanna see you."

"Good. I'll talk to you," Grimm said and hung up.

Back at the apartment, he was much too worked up to try to go back to sleep. He went to his study and rolled a joint. Nothing quite like catching that first morning buzz to put it all in perspective. Another hour or so and it would be time to get up anyway. He had scheduled an early meeting with his friend Bernie Wolfshein of DEA.

Then Cassy, naked, peeked around the door of the study. "Everything all right?" she asked and stepped inside the room.

"Come over here and sit on my lap," Grimm told her, the THC beginning to work its wonders. Life was good again.

"Who was it?" Cassy purred into his beard.

"Just some drunk," Grimm said. But he knew it was incidents like this that would ultimately come between them. The nocturnal trips to the pay phone. The gun strapped to his side. The unsavory side of his life.

What's interesting about this case, thought Grimm later that morning, is all the material the jury will never know about, the real facts they will never learn. He was reminded of what a DEA agent told him once before he was about to testify at a drug trial. "We're going to get up there and tell our lies, then you're going to get up there and tell your lies. It's just a question of whose lies the jury believes."

Over coffee that morning at the Conservatory in the Mayflower Hotel, Wolfshein had told him that Special Agent Julio Zuluaga had been "cut loose" by the Agency. Zuluaga had been suspended pending the outcome of an internal investigation. He was unofficial now, a rogue cop. "Was he ever official?" Grimm asked and Wolfshein shrugged. So the jury would never have the pleasure of meeting Julie Zoo and hearing his version of the events, nor would they understand the significance of the deficiency.

Also they would never meet the man about whom they'd heard so much: Karl Lundgren. They saw a picture of his dog, they heard about his job and his home, but his murder was an unsolved mystery the jury would not be called upon to contemplate. Grimm had to believe such an absence would not go unnoticed. And the ambiguous six-and-a-half million dollars, that may or may not have existed, may or may not have been stolen, the jury would never learn of that, just as they would never hear of the attempt on Grimm's life. Jack Moriarty, Guy Stash, Saul Diamond, here were the real forces behind this case, men the jury would not judge. And the heroin war that had nearly erupted between the California smugglers and the New York gangsters and moneymen, the war still smoldering within Moriarty's organization, none of this would be revealed to the placid souls of Westchester who were now taking their seats in the jury box.

Instead, they were charged with the responsibility of deciding the guilt or innocence of a highly visible public figure who many people believed stood as a symbol for just about everything that was wrong with America. It was a symbolic trial, just as the drug issue was a kind of symbolic politics.

But despite the optimism of the defense at this point in the trial, Grimm was worried. He was worried because he knew Rickie was guilty. Not guilty in any real sense, not a drug dealer, but technically guilty of the crime of conspiracy.

All Vaggi had to do was show that Rickie knew a conspiracy existed, and that he knowingly, intentionally furthered the ends of the conspiracy. She had already proven that. The one tape-recorded telephone conversation was enough to get Rickie fifteen years in prison. He was aware of Sonny's business, he knew Jack Moriarty's position, and he was caught acting as a go-between.

If Rickie had been anyone other than who he was, and if the government had not had such a stake in trying him. Grimm doubted they would have prosecuted. If Vaggi had felt more confident and not been under such pressure, she might have concentrated on the real evidence she could produce and resisted the overreach of employing false testimony. Ironically, if the government had been honest, Grimm believed, Rickie wouldn't have stood a chance.

Now the defense could only hope the jury might excuse Rickie his close association with Sonny to censure the government's behavior in resorting to lying witnesses. It was a tough way to win a trial.

Chapter Fifteen

John Gorth, Vita Vaggi's earnest assistant, was alone at the prosecution table when the jury was brought in. The door to the witness room opened and Sonny entered accompanied by two deputy marshals. For her second day on the witness stand she wore a blue knit dress with long sleeves and a high rolled collar. Her long, pale face gave her a staid Victorian look.

Judge Gass was already seated upon the bench. He was at work shuffling papers and making notes when he looked up over his spectacles and saw Sonny take her seat in the witness box. Grimm thought he noticed the judge give her a slight nod.

"Good morning, ladies and gentlemen," the judge said, turning to greet the jurors. "I trust you all passed a pleasant evening. Counsel, are we ready to proceed? Mr. Gorth, where is Ms. Vaggi?" The judge spoke the question that was on everyone's mind.

"Your Honor, I expect her here any moment. There was—ah, she had an early meeting. I believe the government has an application to make before we proceed with the cross-examination."

Gass apologized and excused the jury. Held turned and beckoned Grimm to the defense table.

"What's going on here?" Held whispered.

"I have no idea," Grimm said.

There was a disturbance at the rear of the room. The crowd at the doors parted and Vita Vaggi walked in with two men. One of the men was her boss, United States Attorney Ralph Vallone.

"Here we go. Check this out," Held said, looking past Grimm and nodding toward the doors. "The heavies are here."

Grimm turned and felt a sinking sensation in the pit of his stomach. He suddenly remembered his call from Jack Moriarty; it was as though Jack had divined the government had something like this in store for Sonny. Grimm recognized the other man with Vaggi and Vallone as Michael Leonard, a Special Assistant U.S. Attorney who was Chief of the Organized Crime Division. Big guns, thought Grimm, brought in to back up the weakening prosecution.

Vallone, a lean, intense man with thinning dark hair, was a media darling. The newspeople in the courtroom immediately perked up. A deputy marshal stood from his seat in the front row of the spectators' benches and Vallone sat down. Leonard and Vaggi continued on to the prosecution table.

"Good morning, your Honor. I'm sorry I'm late." Vaggi addressed the bench. "With the Court's permission, Mr. Michael Leonard, who I'm sure is familiar to your Honor, will be joining counsel for the government this morning."

Gass peered at Vaggi and Leonard over the rims of his glasses. "Ms. Vaggi, I understand you have an application to make before we proceed with the cross-examination."

"Yes, your Honor. The government wishes to question the witness without the jury present as to matters relating to the bifurcated structure of the investigation in this case which, on the one hand, led to the arrest of the defendant, and which on the other hand, is ongoing. As your Honor is aware, it is the government's position that the ongoing aspect of the investigation is of a highly sensitive and potentially prejudicial nature and must be kept confidential at all costs."

Judge Gass was frowning. Aaron Held was on his feet before Vaggi had even finished.

"Just a moment, Mr. Held," Vaggi barked at him.

"Your Honor—Ms. Vaggi, you don't tell me when to speak." Held turned and glared at the prosecutor. "This is highly irregular and the defense objects strenuously."

"Counsel." Gass pounced on them. "Please, let's not bicker. Let us be patient, please. This trial has been taxing on everyone's nerves, I quite understand, but—"

"Your Honor, if I may. I must say I find this most disturbing."

Held swung his arm around like a boom and leveled his long finger at
Vaggi. "Your Honor will recall what happened when I attempted to
examine one of the government's witnesses, Dominic Randazzo, concerning a Mr. Gaetano Stasio. Ms. Vaggi had a fit. How can she
possibly propose to subject the defense's witness to an examination on
matters she wants kept secret? This is preposterous, your Honor. I do
not need to instruct the Court on the impropriety of this application.
There are statutes and rules governing the proper procedures to be
utilized when the government seeks to question a witness. They may
subpoena the witness before a grand jury. If the witness refuses to
testify, they may immunize the witness and compel the testimony. Ms.
Vaggi, and certainly the gentleman with her, Mr. Leonard, are well
aware of these procedures. I suggest what this amounts to is a thinly
disguised attempt on behalf of the prosecution to intimidate the defense's witness." As he said this, Held turned and looked at Vallone
seated prominently in the front of the courtroom.

"Your Honor," Held went on without hesitation, turning back to
the bench and walking from behind the defense table, "what we are
concerned with here in this courtroom is a burden of proof the government has assumed with regard to Rickie Rude. We are not to concern
ourselves with some Mafia pizza pie in the sky. I submit that this trial
is losing focus and is in danger of disintegration. The government must
be required to concentrate upon their prosecution of Rickie Rude,
shamefully inadequate as it may be. I object vehemently to any
questions being put to this witness about any subject matter which is
not related to the material opened on direct examination, i.e. the
relationship of Ms. Byrne-Downes to the defendant."

Held had struck a raw nerve, the coherence of the trial of Rickie
Rude. There was an apparent sense that the government's case had
been badly damaged by Sonny's testimony. By assuming responsibility for the drugs, money and other evidence, and by exonerating
Rickie of any involvement in her business activities, Sonny had virtually removed the shadow of doubt cast by the prosecution. The
government was desperate to discredit the witness.

Judge Gass meanwhile was overwrought by the stress of the trial and
in fear of a mistrial or reversible error. He knew that Vallone and
Leonard were there to shore up Vaggi's case by unnerving the witness.
They wanted to take advantage of this opportunity to question Sonny
about her organized crime affiliations. But it was too late. The defense

maneuver earlier with Donnie Boy Randazzo had succeeded in desig-
nating this area of inquiry out of bounds. Gass had ruled Held could
not question Donnie Randazzo about his relationship with Guy Stash.
The judge couldn't reverse that ruling now without compromising the
supposed objectivity of the Court.

So ruled the judge. "Yes, Mr. Held, the Court agrees. Ms. Vaggi,
you will proceed with your examination of the witness and stick with
the relationship between her and the defendant. I shall sustain any
objections Mr. Held has to questions that deviate from the framework
established during the direct testimony." Gass turned and looked at
Sonny.

"This witness," he continued, "stands convicted of serious crimes
and is due to be sentenced expeditiously. Mr. Held is quite correct. If
you wish to question her about matters that are extraneous to this case,
call her before the grand jury. Now, bailiff, bring in the jury. Let us
continue."

Grimm saw Held sigh with relief as he sat back down beside Rickie.
Vaggi took up her position at the lectern and began a relentless assault
on Sonny's character. With questions that were not at all typical of her
dignified courtroom manner, Vaggi tried to impeach Sonny's honesty
by characterizing her as a drug addict, a criminal and a vamp who
made her way in the world by exploiting men.

"Ms. Byrne-Downes, isn't it true that all your lovers are criminals?"

"Objection."

"Sustained."

But the prosecutor was able to make little headway against the
refined, protective British aplomb Sonny wore like a charmed mantle.
She was the essence of cool. If the jury never quite warmed up to her,
there was nevertheless the feeling that they believed her.

Only once did Vaggi appear to have Sonny in trouble. She got her to
repeat her testimony averring the West Side apartment was not used as
a location for drug transactions. Then the prosecutor produced a batch
of surveillance photos showing drug dealers, among them Brad Caine
and Donnie Randazzo, entering or leaving the brownstone. What,
Vaggi demanded, was Brad Caine doing at her apartment if not
conducting drug transactions?

Grimm noticed Sonny's eyes lose focus fleetingly as she searched
for an answer. "I bought several paintings from Brad's gallery," she

said, barely faltering. "He came around to collect money from me. Also, we had a social relationship. He was a friend."

"And Dominic Randazzo? Why did he visit you at the apartment if not to transact drug business?"

"Donnie," Sonny snorted. "Donnie was a pest. He was a groupie. He hung around just hoping to get a look at Rickie."

Vaggi showed her a number of other photos, pictures of drug dealers and celebrities arriving and departing from the West Side building. Among those pictured were all the original defendants in the case, others who had not been charged, and even a famous British rock star who had recently been hospitalized for treatment of a heroin habit. All good friends, Sonny declared. They came to visit but not to buy drugs. Weak, thought Grimm, but it flew.

When at last Vaggi came to the incriminating phone call Rickie placed to Sonny from California, she loaded on the weight. Who, she insisted, was the other person with Rickie when he called her from the L.A. pay phone?

"That was one of my ex-boyfriends," Sonny said with a sardonic smile.

"A boyfriend?" Vaggi's eyes went up. "What is his name?"

"Objection," Held interrupted. "The question is irrelevant and off limits. Again Ms. Vaggi is attempting to sidetrack the witness. I don't see what Ms. Byrne-Downes' love life has to do with this case."

"Your Honor," Vaggi cooed, trying to contain her anger, "the call in question is in evidence. The jury has heard the tape. Nothing about this call can be deemed irrelevant."

"Go ahead, Ms. Vaggi. The objection is overruled. However, I will remind you, keep to the subject."

"His name," Sonny declared, "is John Moriarty."

Grimm felt Mike Leonard and Vaggi stiffen at the mention of Jack's name, as though the prosecution finally saw the true quarry straying into their sights. "And what does Mr. Moriarty do for a living, Ms. Byrne-Downes?" the prosecutor asked.

Sonny shifted uncomfortably in her seat. "He's a businessman."

"Is he in the drug business?"

Grimm tensed. This was getting sensitive. He looked at Aaron Held and saw the attorney was looking down at his papers as though the line of Vaggi's questions was not worthy of his attention.

"Yes," Sonny replied.

Grimm saw Held look up at Sonny. She had just placed Rickie back in the middle of the conspiracy. She had also implicated Jack Moriarty. Vaggi went on to ask her specific questions about the call. She handed the witness a copy of the transcript of the conversation and directed the jury to the proper pages in their papers.

How the hell is she going to get out of this? Grimm was wondering.

"To what was Mr. Rude referring when he told you there were 'some problems out here'?"

"A quarrel," Sonny answered.

"A quarrel between whom?"

"Between myself and Mr. Moriarty."

"Was the quarrel about drugs?"

"No."

"What was the quarrel about, Ms. Byrne-Downes?"

"Your Honor," Held complained, "do we need to know all this? It may have a certain entertainment interest, but I don't see what it has to do with the defendant."

"Overruled."

"The quarrel was about my relationship with two brothers who live in Northern California," Sonny said. She went on to explain that this was what was meant by the reference Rickie made to "people up north."

Vaggi scowled at the witness. "Why didn't Mr. Moriarty phone you himself?"

"Mr. Moriarty and I had a fight and broke up over my friendship with these men. At the time of the call, Mr. Moriarty was in a jealous rage. He knew if he phoned himself I would hang up. So he used Rickie to make the call."

Vaggi squinted at the witness in disbelief. "Ms. Byrne-Downes, why did you feel it was necessary to go out to a pay phone to talk to Mr. Moriarty?"

"Mr. Moriarty was a fugitive. He knew my phone was tapped. He would only speak to me on public telephones."

"And what did you mean when you told Mr. Rude—I'm looking at line seventeen on page sixty-six—'And did you tell him he's supposed to come see me?'"

Sonny looked down at her transcript. "Exactly that," she replied, looking up at the jury. "Jack had been bothering Rickie. He was trying to use Rickie to patch things up between us. I told Rickie to have Jack come see me and leave him alone."

"On line twenty-one of the same page, Ms. Byrne-Downes, where Mr. Rude says to you, 'He said that stash guy would be there any time,' to whom is Mr. Rude referring?"

Held objected and asked for a conference at the sidebar.

"Gaetano Stasio again, Mr. Held?" the judge asked when they were huddled beside the bench.

"I believe so, your Honor. I must say I think Ms. Vaggi is precluded from going into this area of inquiry by the Court's earlier ruling."

"Your Honor—" Vaggi began but Judge Gass cut her off.

"Yes, I agree." The judge turned to the court reporter. "Strike that last question," he said. "Proceed, Ms. Vaggi."

Grimm could see Gass was furious. Vaggi asked a few more questions, but she was stumped. Sonny insisted the contents of the call were not drug-related. The prosecutor had a whispered conference with Michael Leonard at the prosecution table, and then, soon after the late recess, she informed the judge she had no more questions.

On redirect, Held asked Sonny if she had ever been prosecuted, or even charged, for the shooting of her husband.

"No," Sonny said. "The authorities in France determined that I had acted in self-defense."

"How many months pregnant were you at the time, Ms. Byrne-Downes?"

"Eight months."

"And did you fear for the safety of your unborn child?" Held asked.

"Yes," said Sonny. "Of course I did."

"I have no further questions, your Honor."

Judge Gass turned to Sonny. "Thank you, Ms. Byrne-Downes," he said. "You may step down."

Grimm felt his whole body go slack as Sonny dismounted the witness stand and was led from the courtroom. He realized his shirt beneath his jacket was drenched with nervous sweat. There was an almost palpable air of the relief of tension in the room as the door closed behind Sonny and Judge Gass excused the jury with his daily reminders to avoid any discussion or news stories about the case.

"Well?" Held asked as the courtroom cleared. "Did they believe her?"

Grimm looked over at the prosecution table. Vaggi, Gorth, Michael Leonard and Ralph Vallone had their heads together. If the look on the United States Attorney's face was any indication of how Sonny's testimony had weathered Vaggi's cross-examination, Grimm would have to say Sonny carried the day. Vallone did not look at all pleased.

The next witness called by the defense was Judy Roth. She took the stand first thing the following day.

Judy told the jury she was the Executive Administrator of Diamond Star Enterprises, the theatrical management company that handled Rickie Rude's professional career. Judy corroborated Sonny's testimony concerning Rickie's finances and the purchases of the Manhattan real estate as well as the condo in St. Petersburg, Florida, bought for Rickie's mother. Through Judy, the defense introduced deeds and other documents, including the lease between Karl Lundgren and Rude Productions for the loft in SoHo, rental receipts, bank statements and cancelled checks.

"How long have you been with Diamond Star Enterprises, Ms. Roth?" Held inquired of the witness.

"Since October of 1972," Judy answered.

"And were you working at Diamond Star when Rickie Rude was signed on as one of the company's properties?"

"Yes, I was."

"So you have known and been associated with Rickie Rude in a business capacity for a long time."

"Yes, that's correct."

"Have you ever known Mr. Rude to be active in the illegal drug trade?"

"No, absolutely not."

Held asked Judy if she knew how much Rickie was worth. She replied that it was difficult to give an exact figure as his earnings fluctuated. "Is it fair to say Mr. Rude is a multimillion dollar property for Diamond Star?"

"Certainly." Judy went on to refer to Rickie's tax returns and said the rock star in the prior year had realized earnings from royalties alone that were in the millions of dollars. His latest album, *Rude Awakening,* had already sold over five million copies and would continue to sell well. Then there were also the personal appearances, videos, and any number of residual deals. While it was true, Judy affirmed, that Rickie gave away a large percentage of his income, he was nevertheless a wealthy man.

Finally, through Judy, Held introduced evidence about Rickie's recent marriage to Suzi Sapphire, another Diamond Star property. Suzi, Judy told the jury, was also well on her way toward becoming a major star in her own right. She was due to have a baby soon and this, said Judy, was the main reason Rickie had decided to settle down and give up his vagabond lifestyle.

"Ms. Roth, you know Sonny Byrne-Downes, do you?"

"Yes, I know Sonny."

"And to your knowledge, is Rickie Rude, or has he ever been, a partner of Sonny Byrne-Downes in the drug business?"

"No way. Rickie is not business oriented."

"How would you describe the relationship between Rickie and Sonny?"

"I'd say they are old, dear friends. They've been through some hard times together, so they're just real close."

Vaggi, when she got up to cross-examine, tried to malign Sonny through Judy Roth.

Is Sonny Byrne-Downes an honest woman, to your knowledge, Ms. Roth?"

"Yes, she's honest."

"But didn't you just tell us you know her as a professional criminal? A drug dealer?"

"Yes, she's a drug dealer. The two are not necessarily mutually exclusive, Ms. Vaggi. From all I know of Sonny, she's an honest person."

"Would you say that drug dealers are greedy?"

Held objected and Gass sustained.

"Let me rephrase that. Is Sonny, in your opinion, a greedy person?"

"Sonny has never struck me as being greedy."

"But she is a drug dealer?"

"Objection, your Honor. Asked and answered."

When Judy Roth stepped down from the witness stand, Held asked for a recess. As it was late in the day, Judge Gass excused the jury with his customary admonitions. He said he understood how difficult it was for them to avoid listening to or reading stories about the trial since the coverage was so extensive, but he said he felt he could trust them and he did not want to impose the added inconvenience of sequestration which, he said, might become necessary once deliberations were under way.

"Your Honor, I have just one more witness," Aaron Held announced once the jury had left. "Mr. Rude has advised me he wishes to testify."

There was a flurry of activity in the courtroom as journalists headed for the door. Judge Gass asked Held how long he anticipated the defendant's direct examination would take.

"I should imagine the better part of a whole day," answered the defense lawyer. "A lot of this ground has been covered by Ms. Byrne-Downes, and I won't be repeating her evidence. However, I do wish to go into Mr. Rude's history somewhat."

"So we can plan on closing arguments by Thursday or Friday at the latest. Does that sound about right?" the judge commented, looking much relieved that the end of the trial was in sight. He addressed Vaggi, "Is there anything else?"

"Yes, there is, your Honor," the prosecutor said. "Mr. Seiler of the Probation Department has advised me that the presentence report on Byrne-Downes is complete. As I notice Mr. Grimm is in the courtroom, may I suggest we set a date for the Byrne-Downes sentencing?"

The trial is going badly for the government, Grimm thought. Here is Vaggi's chance to get revenge. Judge Gass conferred with his clerk. "The Court is in receipt of the Probation presentence report. Mr. Grimm, have you and your client seen the report yet?"

Standing, Grimm moved into the arena and said, "No, judge. This is the first I've heard of it being complete. I know Ms. Byrne-Downes will want an opportunity to review the report with counsel in advance of the sentencing."

"And that is her right, certainly. The Marshals will please arrange to have Ms. Byrne-Downes brought to the offices of the Probation Department at the earliest possible convenience so that she can read the report with you present, Mr. Grimm. The Court is aware that Ms. Byrne-Downes has been held at the MCC for quite some time now, and of the hardship this has entailed. So, shall we set the sentencing for next week? Say Monday morning before the regular session begins? Is Monday morning at half past nine agreeable?''

"Monday morning," Sonny gasped. "Oh, God, Arthur, I'm terrified. I just know they're going to make me pay for helping Rickie. What if I get life?''

"No, sweetheart. You won't get life. I think Gass likes you.''

But what did it matter, Grimm was thinking, thirty, forty years with no parole. That was the same as life. By the time she got out, Carmen would be middle-aged.

"Let's not talk about it," Sonny said. "It's too depressing. Tell me, what do you think? Will Rickie win? That's all that really matters.''

"He has a good chance. You were convincing. At this point, I'd give him about an eighty percent chance of winning an acquittal. A lot will depend on how he does on the stand. It's risky letting him testify. Aaron was ready to rest with Judy. But Rickie wants to testify and I agree with him. I think it's essential. No jury wants to acquit someone who's afraid to get up there and tell his side of the story. If Rickie's half as good as you and Judy were, I'd say we've got a winner.''

Sonny reached across the table and took hold of his bearded face. "He'll be better," she said, her eyes shining. "He's much more lovable. God, I was so nervous. Could you tell?''

"No. I was amazed at how relaxed you looked. The only time I thought I saw you freak a little bit was when Vaggi asked you about the pictures and all the traffic in and out of the apartment.''

"Believe me, I was sweating the whole time. It's quite a rush, committing perjury.''

"Happens all the time. All Vaggi's witnesses lied through their teeth." Grimm kissed her. "Aaron's come up with another great idea.''

"Yes? Tell me about it.''

"Later." They kissed again, long and deep, Sonny's tongue wallowing in his mouth.

"I've got to run," he told her. "Tomorrow the Marshals are going to take you across the street so you can read the presentence report. I'll see you there.''

Sonny's glorious eyes widened. "So it's Monday, then. Hanging day.''

The presentence report, a fifty-page document prepared by the Federal Probation Department upon which Judge Gass would base his sentence, was bad, one of the worst Grimm had ever seen. This was the official version of Sonia Byrne-Downes and her crimes against society.

She was portrayed as a ruthless, greedy master criminal and expert drug smuggler who would stop at nothing to get what she wanted. Here was a woman, said the report, born to a life with all the advantages one could hope for, but instead of becoming a decent, hardworking and law-abiding member of society, she had put her attributes and advantages to use in dedicating herself to a life of crime. She was "a criminal mastermind and ringleader of a far-flung international conspiracy responsible for smuggling and distributing massive quantities of narcotics in the United States, Canada and Europe."

The killing of Sonny's husband in France read like a cold-blooded murder. There was no mention of the fact she had been hospitalized twice as a result of the beatings he'd inflicted on her. And the corpse of Karl Lundgren, so well concealed from the jury, was all but laid on Sonny's doorstep. She was a professional criminal who'd never had a legitimate job in her life. She had never paid taxes. Yet she traveled all over the world, lived in luxury wherever she went, and did exactly as she pleased. The report merely noted she had a daughter, aged eleven.

Worse still, the report went on, Byrne-Downes showed absolutely no remorse. Only a fraction of her ill-gotten gains had been recovered by the government. Byrne-Downes had repeatedly rebuffed offers to demonstrate her capacity for rehabilitation by turning against her partners in crime and helping the government. She admitted she had lovers who were gangsters sought by federal authorities, yet instead of recognizing her social obligations by aiding the government in apprehending her cohorts, she continued to ally herself with the forces of the underworld. Her prior record, including the arrest and incarceration in Delhi (which, the report said, was alleged to have ended upon payment of a substantial bribe to Indian authorities rather than upon expiration of term) proved that she was beyond hope, incorrigible, fit only for severe punishment and complete incapacitation in the form of long-term imprisonment.

Grimm and Sonny were sitting at a table in the outer office of the Probation Department, each reading a copy of the report. To Grimm's astonishment, Sonny began stroking the inside of his thigh and running her hand over his cock under the table as they read. He smiled at her. "They're right. You are incorrigible," he told her and they laughed.

"Please, Arthur," she pleaded. "Come see me Saturday morning. Love me. I need you. This may be our last chance. They may ship me out right after I'm sentenced."

He did visit her, both Saturday and Sunday and they fucked each other for all they were worth in the attorney visiting room. It was just like the old days before Grimm took up with Cassy and before he started worrying about getting caught. Somehow none of that seemed to matter anymore. Cassy had gone out to the Coast on business for a week or so. Grimm was able to postpone feeling guilty about cheating on her. He told himself these were exigent circumstances; he might never see the woman again. He went around in a haze all weekend, smoked to the gills with Rickie, fucked to the bottom of the well with Sonny. It was like the last days of the world.

"Dear God, how I'm going to miss you," Sonny told him. "You know, I'd give up my life of crime for you."

"Would you really?"

"Well, put it this way, I'd try."

Grimm stayed at the Plaza suite with Rickie and Suzi over the weekend. He and Aaron Held took Rickie through rehearsals of his direct examination, then Held would act the part of Vaggi and cross-examine him. Rickie said he was glad Held was his lawyer and not the prosecutor. Suzi wasn't feeling well. Sunday evening, they all relaxed and went out to dinner. Rickie felt that he was ready. Aaron Held said he was ready. Later that evening, Sonny called from the jail and said that she was ready.

Judge Gass seemed more nervous than usual as he prepared to impose sentence on Sonny. The courtroom was jam packed. Rickie was scheduled to begin his direct testimony at ten, but he had come early for Sonny's sentencing. Grimm saw Ralph Vallone and his sidekick Michael Leonard sit in the front row of the spectators' benches where the judge could not miss them. Vallone moved amid a bevy of reporters. Held had not yet arrived. Grimm was alone seated at the defense table.

There was some sort of delay in fetching Sonny from the Marshals' bullpen. Gass was already on the bench, his hands fluttering through papers. Vaggi too seemed deep in study of official documents. Only Grimm sat idly looking around. He had not prepared a statement for the Court in mitigation of sentence. What was there to say? Again the government had all the grounds. Grimm wondered what it would take to call the whole thing off. All Sonny would have to do was give in, agree to let them turn her into a rat. At last the defendant was brought into the courtroom.

She appeared flushed. She was wearing a gray suit and simple white blouse open at the collar, looking only a little less austere than Vaggi.

"Those bloody idiots over at MCC," she whispered to Grimm. "They locked me in the hole last night. The lieutenant said they had information I was planning an escape. Can you believe it? Meanwhile, everyone at the jail thinks I got cold feet and decided to become a snitch."

"Don't worry about it," Grimm said. "I'll speak to the warden."

"I'm not worried. I'm pissed," Sonny said and was overheard by those near her, including Vaggi.

"In the matter of the United States versus Sonia Byrne-Downes," said Judge Gass's clerk.

"Is the government ready?" the judge asked.

Vaggi stood as straight as an arrow. "Yes, your Honor. The government is ready."

Gass turned to Grimm. "Is the defendant ready?"

There was a hush in the room. Grimm stood and Sonny got to her feet beside him.

"Yes, your Honor, the defendant Sonia Byrne-Downes is ready."

Gass wouldn't look at Sonny, or at Grimm for that matter. Grimm could feel his stomach tightening in a knot. The judge is much too nervous, he thought, something is wrong.

"Has the defendant read the presentence report?" asked the judge.

"She has, your Honor," answered Grimm.

Gass finally looked at him. "Mr. Grimm, is there any legal reason why this defendant should not be sentenced at this time?"

"No, your Honor, no legal reason."

"Well, is there any information in the probation report with which you or the defendant wish to take issue?"

"Not specifically. Factually the report is accurate. However I would like the opportunity to address the Court on the matter of Ms. Byrne-

Downes' character, which I believe the report has slanted. It has maligned and misrepresented the sort of person she is and her motives for becoming involved in the life she chose.''

Grimm felt he had to pierce the judge's tension. From the way Gass was acting, it was clear that heavy pressure, however subtle, was being brought to bear on the judge. Not so subtle was the fact that Vallone had deigned to be present at the sentencing, and that he was surrounded by reporters. The import was clear, the government wanted to see Sonny "thrilled," the jailhouse slang for the imposition of a particularly harsh sentence. The idea was to hurt Sonny so severely that Rickie and all his freak followers would cower before the might of Uncle Sam.

"You will be given a chance to speak on behalf of your client, Mr. Grimm," Judge Gass said. "Ms. Vaggi, is the government's version of the crimes this defendant stands convicted of accurate?"

"It is, your Honor. The government feels the Probation Department report accurately portrays Byrne-Downes' role in the conspiracy."

"Does the defendant have anything she wishes to say to the Court before I pass the sentence?" the judge asked, still looking everywhere but at Sonny.

"No, your Honor. I've asked Mr. Grimm to speak for me. You heard me testify, I feel you have a good idea of the sort of person I am."

Sonny looked straight at Judge Gass, she spoke loudly and clearly. Still Gass would not return her gaze. Grimm thought he had never seen the tough old judge so worked up, not even when he was fuming at Rickie. His hands trembled violently as his fingers fretted with papers on his desk.

"The Court will hear from counsel for the defendant."

"Judge, the verdict is not yet in on Rickie Rude," Grimm began, his voice gathering force. "From Sonia Byrne-Downes' point of view, it is impossible for her to separate her fate from that of the person she counts as her best friend in life. Sonia made a brave and unselfish decision when she chose to testify on behalf of Rickie Rude. Her first concern is that the truth of her friend's innocence be known."

Grimm could sense Vaggi was about to object. He quickly changed the course of his oration. "Your Honor, I met Sonia the morning following her arrest, and in the time since, as sometimes happens with a lawyer and client, I have come to know this woman well." Just how well, Grimm was thinking, no one would ever know.

"The other day Sonia told me she feels she is no longer the same person she was when she was on the street. She now realizes how far she'd let her life slip out of control because of her involvement with drugs. As you impose sentence, I ask you to consider both the purpose and the effect of long-term imprisonment.

"What is the purpose of imprisonment?" Grimm asked rhetorically. "Punishment and incapacitation. We remove people from society to punish them because they do not respect the laws that bind our society, and to stop them from engaging in illegal activity. But we do not lose hope. Those of us who love these people—their families, their friends and loved ones"—Grimm turned and pointed to where Rickie sat with Suzi and Carmen—"hope they will change their behavior and rejoin us as free people. Ours is not an unforgiving society. This is a society that prides itself on its compassion as well as its sense of justice. So the question we must ask ourselves is: how much imprisonment is enough?

"Prison changes people, your Honor. I have known many people who have gone to prison for varying lengths of time. I have not known anyone who was not changed by the experience of imprisonment. From what I have seen, during the first few years positive changes may take place. But after four or five years in prison it is a clear case of diminishing returns. After five or six years in prison, irreparable harm is done to even the strongest personalities. In other words, your Honor, a sentence which requires service of more than six or seven years is in fact a life sentence.

"Sonia Byrne-Downes is a brave woman. She chose to come to her friend's defense when she knew it would only hurt her. She is an intelligent woman, a strong woman who has come to terms with her past and determined to change and become a better person. I have seen these changes taking place over the last six months.

"Judge Gass, I believe you know in your heart Sonia is not the depraved, incorrigible woman this report makes her out to be." Grimm held the probation report aloft, then he let it drop into the wastepaper basket beside the defense table. "This report is trash. You met Sonia in this courtroom. You heard her testify. You met her daughter, Carmen. You know also of the deep and abiding friendship between Sonia and Rickie Rude. I suggest to you that these are not the feelings of a greedy parasite. Sonia is a woman whose life still has much value despite the mistakes she has made.

"You also know that any sentence you impose under the continuing criminal enterprise statute is non-parolable. Sonia will have to serve every day of it. I urge the Court to take into consideration this defendant's willingness to plead guilty and to accept responsibility for her wrongdoing. I also urge you to consider Sonia's character and her capacity for rehabilitation. Sonia is a person who should not be shut away from us forever. In view of Sonia Byrne-Downes' acknowledgment of her guilt, I ask you to sentence her to a ten-year term of imprisonment. Give her an opportunity to pay for her mistakes and to rejoin us as a better person so that we may learn from her example. Thank you."

Grimm sat down. The judge was scribbling notes, he peered over the rims of his spectacles as though he were not sure Grimm had finished.

"Thank you, Mr. Grimm. The Court will hear from the government."

Vaggi's manner was subdued. She rose from the prosecution table and addressed the Court with a kind of quiet concern as though deeply troubled by what she had to do. The room was still with attention.

"Your Honor, the government does not ordinarily advise the Court in the matter of sentencing. In this case, however, I wish to speak briefly with regard to this defendant and make a specific recommendation as to the length of sentence.

"Sonia Byrne-Downes is precisely the kind of career criminal Congress had in mind when it enacted the continuing criminal enterprise statute," Vaggi declared. She looked at Sonny, then back up at the judge. Gass glanced around the room. "A major criminal, your Honor, a Class One violator, manager of a network capable of regularly acquiring and distributing in this country quantities of many pounds, multi-kilos of pure heroin and cocaine and multi-ton loads of marijuana and hashish. This is a woman who, by her own admission, has devoted her entire life since her teenage years to trafficking in drugs.

"Mr. Grimm asks us to consider the purpose of imprisonment. The reason we build prisons, your Honor, is to protect society from people like Sonia Byrne-Downes. Mr. Grimm characterizes the defendant as a courageous woman, a loyal friend, an intelligent woman who let her life slip out of control. I would ask the Court to consider her victims, the countless lives destroyed by her activities. I would ask those who love Sonia Byrne-Downes to bear in mind the devastating effect drugs have on our society.

"Further, your Honor, this defendant has not demonstrated the least hint of remorse for her crimes. She has refused to assist the government. The best efforts of the government have been unsuccessful in recovering any of the huge profits reaped by this woman. I submit her actions do not exhibit a capacity for rehabilitation but rather just the opposite.

"Perhaps it is true that Byrne-Downes has a strong character. It is usually the case that major criminals have strong characters. The problem is she has used this strength of character to implement a massive criminal conspiracy.

"Because of the wide-ranging dimensions of this conspiracy, your Honor," Vaggi began winding up, "and because of this defendant's admitted role as the key individual in this drug ring, also because Byrne-Downes has shown no remorse for her actions, the government feels compelled to recommend that Sonia Byrne-Downes receive the maximum penalty available under the law: life imprisonment with no possibility of parole."

There was a funereal quiet in the courtroom. Gass nodded and thanked the prosecutor.

"Well, Mr. Grimm, I have heard some eloquent arguments as to why imprisonment doesn't work," Judge Gass began his remarks. "And, to a degree, I will say I share some of your reservations as to the efficacy of long-term imprisonment. However, in this case I'm inclined to agree with the government, up to a point, when it comes to disposing of criminals such as this defendant.

"Sonia Byrne-Downes, you are an attractive, well-educated woman from a good background and you have no excuse for having adopted a criminal life-style. I suspect that there is more to your motives than greed. I base this on having listened carefully to your testimony. I believe you acted out of a craving for excitement, and this is a very dangerous impetus.

"The Court notes the fact that you pled guilty, and in doing so, you saved the government substantial time and resources. Also, you have appeared as a witness in the trial of Mr. Rude, a witness for the defense. This fact shall in no way affect the determination of sentence except that it has given me an opportunity to learn about you and to make certain judgments based on your comportment on the witness stand and your testimony.

"Furthermore, the Court has taken judicial notice of the fact that you are a single parent of a sensitive and gifted young daughter who loves you very much. During the time you've been held at the MCC, I allowed you special visiting privileges to lessen the pain of your incarceration on your child. I must say, in response to Mr. Grimm's comments, I also feel badly for the families of those who do not respect the law.

"But what all this really boils down to, it seems to me, Ms. Byrne-Downes, is that you have done nothing to help yourself. You seem determined, for reasons of your own, to bear the full weight of this vast enterprise. You hold the key, Ms. Byrne-Downes. The government is anxious for you to cooperate with them in this matter. There are still many people engaging in this activity, the government feels you could be helpful in putting some of them out of commission. Is there something you wish to tell the Court with regard to your refusal to assist the government?"

"Your Honor," Sonny offered, "I have cooperated in every way I know how. I pled guilty, I admitted responsibility, and I testified truthfully. I don't believe it's my job to be a policeman."

"Are you afraid for your life, or your daughter's life, Ms. Byrne-Downes?"

"It's not a question of fear. It's a question of what I believe. I couldn't live with myself if I tried to get out of this by becoming a snitch."

Now Judge Gass was looking at her. He seemed struck by the ingenuousness of Sonny's response. Grimm felt a pang of hope that she was getting through to him.

"Well, Ms. Byrne-Downes, you have a rare sense of loyalty, rare from those of your particular stripe, that is. But you must understand that you also have a social obligation. The trafficking in narcotics is a terrible threat to our society. Do you understand the gravity of your offenses?"

"I do, your Honor. I must say, when Ms. Vaggi accuses me of destroying people's lives, that hurts. I never consciously intended to hurt anyone. I now realize through my own experience and through meeting others in prison whose lives have been ruined by their use of drugs how serious this problem is. I am not proud of my actions, your Honor."

Gass lifted his bushy white eyebrows. Sonny moved him, Grimm was certain. The judge seemed at a loss, divided in his feelings for Sonny.

Gass cleared his throat. "It is my duty to impose a penalty which is commensurate with the gravity of the offenses and with your admitted role in this enterprise. The sentence I impose must also have a deterrence value. It should cause others to stop and think before they embark on a scheme to import these kinds of substances into this country.

"Also, as I remarked, you have shown no willingness to cooperate with the government in their efforts to combat this activity. Therefore, it is the judgment of this Court, that as to Count Four, the continuing criminal enterprise count, it is adjudged that the defendant, Sonia Byrne-Downes, is hereby committed to the custody of the Attorney General or his authorized representative for a period of thirty years. Also, as to this Count, the Court imposes a fine of one hundred thousand dollars.

"On Counts One, Two and Three respectively the sentence is fifteen years on each count, all terms to run concurrently with the thirty-year sentence imposed on Count Four. Also, on Count Three, the substantive possession count, this count is to include a provision of lifetime Special Parole, which means that, should you violate the terms of parole upon release from prison, you will have an automatic life sentence.

"Now, Ms. Byrne-Downes, the Court does not wish to leave you without a ray of hope. Therefore, should you decide to cooperate with the government in this matter, you have one hundred and twenty days to apply to the Court for a reduction of your sentence. The Court will then consider reducing your sentence based on the nature and extent of your cooperation. If you are interested in getting out of prison any time in the not too distant future, I suggest you give this a lot of careful consideration.

"If there is nothing further, the defendant is remanded. Court will stand in adjournment for thirty minutes."

Sonny's expression remained unchanged. The deputy Marshals immediately began moving in around her, ready to escort her back to MCC. She squeezed Grimm's hand.

"You were wonderful. Will I see you later?" she asked.

"I'll be over right after court."

Carmen came up and hugged her mother. The little girl was in tears. Rickie and Suzi gathered round. They were all crying and hugging Sonny as the Marshals stepped in and hustled her from the courtroom.

Aaron Held, who had come in while Judge Gass was passing sentence, now made his way through the crowd to the defense table. Following behind him, with his two assistants, was an elderly woman wearing a heavy, drab overcoat and a kerchief on her head.

"Mom!" Rickie cried when he saw her. The reporters heard and fell on them.

Held winked at Grimm. "Wait'll the jury gets a load of her."

"Did you hear the sentence?" Grimm asked. "Did you hear the judge?"

"My friend," Aaron Held said, holding up his forefinger, "one thing I will say for the Honorable Dudley Gass: he tells it like it is." The lawyer began unpacking his briefcase, piling the defense table with transcripts and documents. He looked over at Vaggi, who was hunched into her work.

"Vaggi is out for blood," Held said. "They all are. I think Gass was prepared to go higher. Sonny changed his mind. Now come on, help me get ready. We'll discuss Sonny later. Let's slam this thing where it will hurt them most."

The first day of Rickie's testimony, everyone agreed, was a huge success. Rickie was lovable, there was no other way to explain it. Once the jurors got over his weird appearance, they opened up and listened to him talk. The women were particularly charmed by him. One reporter called him "bright eyed and bushy tailed," and the description was apt. He had an air of boyish insouciance as he related the circumstances of his childhood in a Polish neighborhood of Northeast Chicago.

"Are your parents still alive?" Aaron Held asked.

"My mom is. My father died when I was seven."

"Where does your mother live?"

"St. Petersburg, Florida."

"In the home you purchased for her?"

"It's a condo, yeah."

"That you bought for her?"

"Hey, it was the least I could do. My mom's my biggest fan."

"Mr. Rude, do you see your mother here in court today?"

"Yup, she's here. Hi, Mom." Rickie gave his mother a little wave.

Held turned to her. "Mrs. Rudinowski, please stand so the jury can see you."

She had taken off her overcoat and kerchief. She was raw-boned, arthritic, a plain old lady who looked like a charwoman who had cleaned office buildings all her life. She looked at her son, then gazed at the jury. Her eyes were the same vivid blue as Rickie's.

Rickie told of an impoverished childhood in the Chicago ghetto. There were six children who survived, he said, four girls and two boys, with Rickie in the middle. Another boy had died as an infant, an older brother had been killed in the war. When Rickie's father died, one of the other sons quit school and went to work to help support the family. Two of the daughters were already working, another had married but her husband was also killed in Vietnam, leaving her with two babies. Rickie showed musical and intellectual promise from an early age. His father, a violinist, loved classical music, so the kids grew up to the sounds of the masters. Rickie was the best student of all the children, and his mother was determined he would be allowed to stay in school. She devoted herself to his future.

Throughout grade school, junior and senior high Rickie played in school bands and took music lessons. He had a precocious talent. Poor as the family was, his father started him on piano lessons when he was four years old. By the time he was ten, Rickie was recognized as a musical prodigy. In junior high, he skipped a grade; he graduated from high school two years early after winning a full scholarship to Harvard.

When he arrived in Cambridge, he was sixteen years old and already an accomplished poet and songwriter who put the words of poems to music and played acoustic guitar and harmonica in the style made popular by Bob Dylan. This was the early Sixties, the beatnik and hipster era.

Calling himself Rick Rudd, Rickie was soon finding work performing in Harvard Square and Boston clubs and coffee houses like the famous Club 47 where Joan Baez, Tom Rush, Pete Seeger and many others played. After graduation from Harvard, Rickie cut his first album, a low-budget independent production made at a studio in Roxbury, Massachusetts.

The album, *Roomy Nations*, showing Rickie's penchant for puns and his internationalist theme, was later picked up and distributed by Columbia Records. Though not at first a big seller in the United States, the album established Rickie as a folksinger and songwriter with a small cult following in cities like Boston, New York and San Francisco. In the United Kingdom, the album made the charts. Rickie went on his first concert tour of the British Isles in late 1966. He was twenty-two years old.

Held displayed the album cover from *Roomy Nations*. He asked that it be marked for identification and admitted as evidence. Vaggi objected as to relevance, but Held argued successfully that anything pertaining to the defendant's career was relevant. The jury was handed the album cover showing Rickie looking like a young boy. Considering the life he'd led, the witness on the stand hadn't changed all that much. On the album, Rickie was pictured standing on the grassy banks of the Charles River, the red brick buildings of Harvard University in the background. He had a guitar slung over his shoulder, was dressed in jeans and a blue denim workshirt, and was surrounded by a gaggle of ducks and pigeons like a beat St. Francis of Assisi.

Rickie's testimony corroborated Sonny's on their relationship. "I love her," he informed the jury. She was the most loyal friend he'd ever had.

"Did you know she was in the drug business?" Held asked.

"I never thought of it as a business. Nobody did. Everybody smoked pot. It was more like a way of life."

Rickie's career began to take off. His style changed through contact with different groups and movements in youth culture and rock 'n' roll. He became more electrified, more up-tempo. Then he met the impresario Saul Diamond in London in the early Seventies and together they created his new image. He was metamorphosed into Rickie Rude. The Prince of Punk was born. In 1974, his new group, Brain Damage, was formed and their first album, *Frontal Lobotomy,* was released. Next came a second album with Brain Damage, then Moon Landing's "White Noise" article, the feature film, and superstardom.

"I was an overnight success," Rickie said. "It's just that the night lasted ten years."

Rickie looked small and childlike sitting in the witness box beside Judge Gass. He had a forlorn look, like a lonely kid who wanders onto the schoolyard and hangs around hoping the other kids will play with him. By the end of the first day of testimony even the judge seemed to be touched by the "punk Pollack kid from Chi-town."

That evening, Grimm was able to smuggle a pint of vodka into MCC and he and Sonny polished it off in spiked sodas while commiserating in the attorney visiting room.

"Did you mean what you told the judge," Grimm asked her, "about being ashamed of yourself?"

"Yes. You know, it's one thing sitting around snorting coke and heroin with the Beautiful People. It's quite another to come in here and see all this." Sonny gestured to indicate the prison. "I wish I'd stuck with hash and marijuana, I'd feel a lot better about myself."

"Gass would've given you a lot less time, too."

Sonny sighed. "Oh, well. It's too late to start feeling sorry for myself, and my victims, as Vaggi calls them. I don't know, Arthur. I have my moments when I really feel miserable. Why couldn't I have met you five years ago, fallen madly in love, as I am now, and gone off to live with you and Carmen happily ever after?" She was smiling, but tears were running down her face.

Soon they were horny and wanted to fuck. The outer salon was crowded with lawyers and prisoners who kept poking their heads into the cubicle to express their condolences. Finally, both drunk, they managed it. Grimm stood with his back to the door blocking the window. He held the door handle behind his back while Sonny dropped his pants.

Then she knelt in front of him and lovingly sucked his cock. "Mmmmmmm, you taste so good," she said, looking up at him.

Sonny stripped down to her T-shirt, socks and sneakers. When she took her panties off she tossed them aside and did a little pirouette.

They fucked standing. Grimm's back slammed against the door with each thrust into her. Sonny seemed to impale herself on him, she rode him as if she were trying to rip herself apart.

"Make it good, my love," she moaned. "I've never been so horny in all my life."

Grimm's knees buckled and he came with a long shudder. Sonny began to come with him. She cried out. At that point, neither of them cared what happened. Sonny was going off to prison for the better part of the next thirty years, but at that moment they were coming. She had played heavily, risked everything, and she had lost. It was all part of the game, all part of the life she had chosen.

Grimm held her ass in his arms and staggered over to the table.

"Don't worry, darling," she said as he set her down. "I'll think of something."

Sonny picked up her lace panties from the floor and tucked them into his pocket. "A keepsake to remember me by."

Aaron Held wound up Rickie's direct testimony by mid-morning of the next day. He brought Rickie up to the present, including his marriage to Suzi Sapphire, who Held had stand and display her pregnant belly for the jury. The California phone call was disposed of in a few questions. Rickie said he ran into the man he knew as Jack Moriarty at La Scala restaurant in Los Angeles. He was a former boyfriend of Sonny's. Rickie said he believed the phone call was about some sort of lover's spat. Held drew it all to a conclusion with a categoric denial by the defendant of any willful, knowing participation in a drug conspiracy.

In her cross-examination, Vita Vaggi was masterful. She attacked Rickie's sincerity, and in the process she exposed his cleverness. Vaggi's questioning showed that Rickie was too intelligent, too aware not to have been fully cognizant of what was going on around him.

Approaching him at first hesitantly, like a starstruck interviewer, she gradually melted his defenses by getting him to talk about his beliefs. Grimm and Held both saw it coming; they had warned Rickie against waxing philosophic. But Rickie thrived on metaphysics, politics and social commentary. This was what his music was all about, and it meant more to him than money.

Held repeatedly objected to Vaggi's questions about Rickie's political views. Gass overruled, stating the defendant's beliefs went to the question of motive. At the sidebar, the judge told Held he would allow the line of questioning to show the defendant's state of mind. Vaggi intended to show the jury that while helping Sonny, Rickie was aware that what she was doing was illegal, and that Rickie had done it out of a belief that widespread drug use would precipitate revolution. It was the Ayatollah theory again. Held gave Rickie a sharp look of forewarning as he passed by the witness stand on his way to the defense table.

Vaggi kept her questioning low-key, never attacking the witness as Held had done with Caine and Randazzo.

"Mr. Rude, are you an anarchist?" the prosecutor asked.

"Objection."

"Overruled. The witness may answer."

"I would describe myself as a radical libertarian," Rickie replied.

"I see. And in your stance as a radical libertarian, do you believe in overthrowing the government?"

"Your Honor," Held pleaded. "The defendant is not charged with sedition."

"Proceed, Ms. Vaggi."

"No, not by force. I believe in evolution."

Unlike Held, Vaggi was in no position to pass over the Ayatollah phase of Rickie's career. She wanted to show the jury that Rickie should be presumed guilty because of his radical views. Vaggi even proposed to show the Ayatollah video for the jury, provoking further angry objections from Aaron Held.

"It is the man and his actions that are on trial, not his art."

Gass excused the jury and called for a recess. He said he would view the video in chambers with counsel and rule on its relevancy.

When court reconvened, Judge Gass announced that the jury would not be shown the video. However, as Held had placed other albums by the defendant in evidence, Vaggi would be allowed to do the same with *Rude Awakening,* the cover of which was a picture of Rickie in his Ayatollah of Rock 'n' Rollah costume.

"Is this your latest record album, entitled *Rude Awakening,* Mr. Rude?"

"Yes."

"And did you compose the song, 'The Ayatollah of Rock 'n' Rollah'?"

Yes again, said the defendant.

"In the song, Mr. Rude, do you portray yourself as Ayatollah Khomeini?"

Held was on his feet. He shook his head wearily. "Your Honor, this is absurd."

"Is that an objection, Mr. Held?"

"It is. I object."

"Overruled."

"Well," Rickie said, "not exactly. I call myself Iatoldya Nomeanie, spiritual leader of a mythical land known as Irock."

"Tell the jury about Irock, Mr. Rude."

"Your Honor, I object. The question is far too vague."

"Sustained. Ask specific questions, Ms. Vaggi."

"Specifically, Mr. Rude, do the people of Irock take drugs?"

"Only if they wish," Rickie responded.

"I see. Thank you, Mr. Rude. I have no further questions."

"Re-direct, Mr. Held?" the judge asked.

Held stood and walked to the lectern. "Thank you, your Honor. I have just one question." He turned and addressed the defendant.

"Mr. Rude, Irock, is this supposed to be an actual country?"

"No. Irock is a state of mind."

Chapter Sixteen

The trial had entered its sixth week when Aaron Held rested the defense. Closing arguments took another day, then on Friday, Judge Gass charged the jury and deliberations began. Over objections from Held, the judge ordered that the jurors were to be sequestered until a verdict was reached. Friday evening, the defense team withdrew to Rickie and Suzi's suite at the Plaza to wait.

The same contrast in style between Aaron Held and Vita Vaggi that had prevailed through the trial was most apparent during summations. Held was brilliant, frenetic, bombastic. A showman. Lawyers and courtroom regulars in the audience marveled at his performance. Grimm feared it was a bit too intense for this sober jury. Held was like a symphony orchestra conductor, his long hair flying, his arms flapping, carried away by the music of his words and the melody of his logic.

Vita Vaggi, on the other hand, gave the jury the verbal equivalent of Easy Listening. There was nothing remarkable or obtrusive about her delivery. Yet she was effective. She knew how to talk to this jury and they had no trouble understanding her. Her seriousness, her sedate dress and dignified poise, brought with it the vast impersonal force of the United States Government. Without articulating it, Vaggi's oration carried the same heavy ballast that poured from Judge Gass. If Vaggi had been at the nadir during her cross-examination of Sonny, Grimm considered, her case had been gathering persuasive momentum ever since.

"This is not Irock, ladies and gentlemen of the jury," declared the prosecutor. "This is not some mythical land of drug-induced euphoria where anything goes. This is the United States of America. This is a nation of laws. Congress enacts laws and the government enforces them to protect society.

"And in this country, rich or poor, famous or unknown, no one is above the law. Those who flout the laws of this country must be held accountable no matter how rich or famous they are. By your verdict, ladies and gentlemen, by finding Rickie Rude guilty of the crime of conspiracy to possess with intent to distribute narcotics, you will be sending a message to the world that this is a nation of responsible citizens where each and every person is held accountable to the laws of the land."

Vaggi reviewed the evidence of the many federal agents who had testified. She went over the surveillance photos, the physical evidence, the wiretaps. Here was a real investigation, she said, which had uncovered a real conspiracy with real heroin, real money and real criminals. This was not, as the defense would like the jury to believe, a case of government paranoia. She played the tape of the California phone call again. "Does that sound like a conversation about a lover's quarrel?" The jury heard both Sonia Byrne-Downes and the defendant testify as to their relationship. Vaggi concluded by saying that it was up to the jury to determine whether Byrne-Downes had told the truth or lied to protect her friend.

Aaron Held chastised the government and Vaggi for conducting what he termed a "celebrity witch hunt." He accused the prosecutor's office and the FBI and DEA of a "conspiracy to get famous," and said the case against Rickie was a "shoddy fabrication" the government attempted to prove by using government witnesses who were no more than "hired guns, hired liars."

The defense lawyer maintained that Rickie was an innocent associate, at worst a close friend of the principal conspirator, but a non-participant in the actual conspiracy.

"In America," Held said, "as the government prosecutor pointed out, we are a nation governed by laws. And the law says a man is to be presumed innocent until he has been proven guilty beyond a reasonable doubt. A man cannot be assumed to be guilty just because he has a friend who is involved in illegal activities. Nor even because he has an unusual life-style.

"The case against Rickie Rude is a fiasco, a government production that flopped. Had the owner of the building where Sonia Byrne-Downes lived been anyone other than Rickie Rude, you people would not have had to sit here for six weeks listening to a pack of lies. The government never would have gone to trial if Sonia Byrne-Downes' landlord had not been a famous and controversial rock star.

"Remember what I told you at the outset of this trial, ladies and gentlemen." Held paused and walked from the lectern over behind Rickie seated at the defense table. "This is the case of an innocent man. Sonia Byrne-Downes is not on trial here. Rickie Rude is. Remember that as you retire to deliberate. Remember the facts of this case as they pertain to Rickie Rude. Remember the testimony of Sonia Byrne-Downes, who has no deal with the government wherein she is rewarded for her performance on the stand. Remember also the testimonies of Judy Roth and Rickie Rude himself. Remember the major point they all agreed on. Rickie Rude did not participate in Sonia Byrne-Downes' illegal activities. Rickie Rude is not a criminal."

Finally it was Judge Gass' charge to the jury that most troubled the defense. These were the last words left ringing in the ears of the jurors as they withdrew to the jury room to begin their official function as the finders of fact. To the jurors, the judge's words carried the weight of law.

From the defense standpoint, the charge was a disaster. All that was necessary, said the judge, was for the jury to find that a conspiracy existed, which had been shown, and that the defendant knowingly and intentionally participated in it. "A single act may be the basis for drawing an actor within the ambit of the conspiracy," Judge Gass instructed. "The extent of his participation has no bearing on his guilt or innocence.

"This Court charges you that it is *not necessary* for a defendant to receive any monetary benefit from his participation in the conspiracy *or to have* a *financial stake* in the outcome as long as *he in fact participated in it.*"

The judge went on to discuss the indictment and the overt acts set forth. He told the jury that "the offense of conspiracy is complete when an unlawful agreement is made and *any* overt act is done by a conspirator to effect the object of the conspiracy.

"The overt act *need not* be a criminal act in and of itself, or an act which itself constitutes *an object of the conspiracy*. It may be an act which is *innocent on its face,* but it must be of such a character that it *furthers or promotes, aids* and *assists in accomplishing a purpose of the conspiracy* charged in the indictment.''

Rickie was named in only one overt act, said the judge, a telephone call made from a Los Angeles public telephone to Sonia Byrne-Downes at her residence in New York in July of the previous year. Now Gass told them that if they were convinced beyond a reasonable doubt that the content of that call acted to further the ends of the conspiracy, then they had to find the defendant guilty as charged.

On that note, at four fifty-three on Friday afternoon, the case went to the jury. The waiting began.

Saturday at two-thirty in the afternoon, after deliberating a total of ten-and-a-half hours, the jury sent a note to Judge Gass. They said they wanted to hear the recording of the California call yet again, and they also wished to have Sonny's testimony relating to the phone call read back to them from the transcript. Judge Gass summoned the parties.

Rickie, Grimm and Suzi drove downtown to the courthouse in Grimm's car. Aaron Held, who had been waiting at the courthouse, met them there. Held was excited. The jury, he believed, was focused on the phone call and now they were looking to Sonny's testimony to convince them Rickie was innocent.

The whole city of New York seemed to have moved into Foley Square for the weekend. There were tour buses lined up near the courthouse. The trial of Rickie Rude was a bigger draw than China-town and Little Italy. Police manned the barricades on the sidewalk and lined the cordoned-off walkway up the steps into the building. The various media representatives had set up camp in the streets to await the verdict. There were a number of large mobile TV broadcasting vans parked in the square.

The faces of the jurors were as impassive as they had been during the trial as they listened to the tape of the telephone call, and to the Court Reporter as he read the transcript of Sonny's testimony. It was all over in twenty minutes and the jurors went back to their delibera-tions. Rickie swore one of the ladies in the second row smiled at him as they filed out of the court. When not deliberating, the jurors were sequestered at a hotel in an undisclosed location. Because of the crowds at the courthouse, the judge had agreed to let Rickie await the verdict at his hotel.

The waiting continued.

Rickie wanted to see Sonny before she was shipped off to prison. *The New York Times Magazine* was doing a cover story on Rickie and the trial, so when the writer contacted Grimm to ask for an interview with Sonny, Grimm called the warden at MCC and arranged a special co-defendants' meeting and media visit in a private conference room at the jail. From the courthouse, Rickie and Grimm went next door and checked into the prison. Aaron Held took Suzi Sapphire back to the hotel in his limo. Grimm and Rickie were met by the *Times* writer and a photographer in the lobby of the jail.

"Hey, baby," Rickie greeted Sonny when she was brought into the conference room. "You got my cell ready?"

"I'll ask the warden to let us cell together," Sonny answered as they hugged each other. "But that's nonsense. You're going to beat this case. Everyone says so." She ruffled Rickie's hair and kissed his head.

"Everyone doesn't know dear old Deadly Gass," Rickie murmured.

They posed for the photographer nose-to-nose with their arms around each other's necks. Grimm sat aside and watched Sonny and Rickie together. He was immediately struck by the level of their intimacy.

At the same time, there were veiled sexual nuances to their responses to each other. It was, thought Grimm, the sex of not fucking. They had never gone to bed together because the circumstances were never quite right. It was obvious Rickie adored Sonny. She possessed him, she held him in thrall. For her, he was a kind of eternal suitor, and her love was uncomplicated because she had never slept with him. Grimm could not help but wonder at the murky karmic elements that had coalesced to bring these two extraordinary souls together.

When asked why the rock star had not been able to steer Sonny away from her life of crime, Rickie answered that "Everyone has to do what they have to do. No one can tell someone else how to live their life. That may sound like a platitude, but it's not so simple in practice. In a way, that's what this trial is all about."

Grimm was left with the thought that we do not always choose our friends. It was as though life picked them for you, as though events conspired to tangle you up in someone else's life. Rickie and Sonny

were in harmony. Had the jury been able to see them together as they
were now, thought the investigator, they would have had little difficulty pronouncing Rickie's fate. He was guilty, all right, guilty of
having been caught up in this woman's powerful orbit. But there was
nothing he could do about it, and he is not the only one, Grimm
thought.

No one could relax. The weekend felt like one long, unbearably
tense pause in the proceedings. Grimm hung around the hotel with
Rickie and Suzi. Cassy was in L.A., trying to leave so she could return
to New York. Moon Landing was in and out of the suite at the Plaza,
as were other friends of Rickie's and Suzi's. Saturday night Judy Roth,
Aaron Held and his wife Julia came over for dinner. The jury had
retired for the night to continue their deliberations in the morning.
    "Jesus!" Held said. "What is taking them so long? One defendant
charged with one count. I hope to God they're not deadlocked."
    "They're probably having a ball living it up in a fancy hotel at the
government's expense," Julia said. "There won't be a verdict until
Monday."
    "Oh, no," Suzi groaned. "I don't know if I can make it till
Monday."
    Cassy called to say she would be arriving in New York Monday and
planned to stay with Suzi until after the baby was born. Her brother
Max told Rickie that all his friends on the Coast were praying for him.
Saul Diamond called and told Rickie that the odds in Las Vegas were
five-to-two for acquittal.
    "Yeah?" Rickie said. "How much did you get down?"
    "Sweetheart, I bet the whole shebang," the promoter answered.
They waited.

Sunday at noon, the jury sent in another message. They said they
felt hopelessly deadlocked, but they had two questions for the judge.
They wanted him to define "conspiracy" and "conspirator" for them.
Again Judge Gass ordered the parties to convene in the courtroom.
Held called Grimm at the Plaza and told him to get Rickie down to the
courthouse.
    "Vaggi is going to ask for an Allen charge," Held said as they
joined him at the defense table. "I wish we had some idea which way
they're leaning."

222222

222

"And what, may I ask, is an Allen charge?" Rickie asked.

"Gass, if he agrees, will instruct the jury that they must find in favor of the majority," Held told him.

"Oh, man, that's fucked up. What's the sense in all that crap about a unanimous verdict if the old fart can tell them what to do? This whole thing is bullshit," Rickie lamented.

But Judge Gass declined to give the Allen charge. Instead, he consoled the jury and answered their questions. A conspiracy, he said, was, as he had instructed, an unlawful agreement, and a conspirator was anyone who knowingly joined or furthered that agreement. The judge congratulated them on the fine job they were doing. "Just keep trying," Gass said. "I'm sure you'll be able to reach a verdict if you just keep at it."

Grimm said he saw one of the males and one of the females smile at the defense as the jurors trooped out to resume deliberations. For the first time in the trial, he felt an emotional charge coming from the jury. It was as though they had suddenly come alive. Held said he felt it too.

"They're with us," Held declared. "The majority is for acquittal. The one thing we don't want at this point is a mistrial."

At 9:00 P.M. Sunday night when they quit deliberating for the day, the jury foreperson sent a message to the judge to say that they felt they were close to reaching a verdict. Sunday night dragged into Monday morning.

Monday afternoon at one o'clock, Grimm answered the phone in the Plaza suite.

"We have a verdict," Held said, his voice taut with anxiety. "Get Rickie down here immediately."

Oh, shit, Grimm thought, wouldn't you know it. The first and only time he had let Rickie out of his sight since the deliberations began, and the jury was in with their verdict. Figuring the jurors would have quit for lunch, Grimm had stayed at the suite to man the phones while Rickie and Suzi went out for a walk in the park across the street. He told them to be back by 1:00, but neither of them was exactly punctual. Still, in Suzi's condition she couldn't walk for long.

Grimm went down to the lobby and spoke with the bell captain. He had his car brought around from the parking garage. The bell captain cleared a spot for him at the taxi stand in front of the hotel on Central

Park South. Parked there he couldn't miss Rickie and Suzi on their return to the hotel.

Fuck it, he thought as he sat in the car waiting. No sense getting all bent out of shape. They can't do anything without the defendant, so they'll just have to wait until we get there. We can always blame it on traffic. After all, the jury had kept them waiting for three days.

It was a beautifully clear and bright winter's day. Grimm thought he might as well smoke a joint. He searched around in his pockets to see if he had anything rolled up.

Then he caught sight of them walking along the sidewalk near the horse-drawn carriages lined up across the street from the hotel. Grimm turned around in his seat to watch as they came toward him. They were walking arm-in-arm. They looked happy just to be holding each other and walking along the sidewalk. Rickie was talking to Suzi and smiling as though he hadn't a care in the world. He spotted Grimm while they were making their way across the street, and he waved.

"Hey, big guy. What's up?" Rickie asked as he and Suzi came alongside the car.

"Get in, kids," Grimm said. "We've got a verdict."

Rickie and Suzi looked at each other.

"Yikes," Rickie said as he opened the rear door for Suzi, then got into the front. "You mean like, this is it? Tonight I could be in the slammer?" He grinned at Grimm. "Hey, A.G., maybe I should'a packed my toothbrush."

"No. They give you toothbrushes," Grimm said.

"C'mon, you guys. What're you talkin' about?" Suzi piped up. "You're gonna be with me tonight. You're gonna win this trial."

"Well, pal, so what do we got to smoke? Huh, A.G.?" Rickie asked when they stopped for a red light. "You don't expect me to go in there straight, do you?"

Grimm had some joints of Thai pot in a baggie. He handed it to Rickie, who took out two joints and lit one for each of them. They smoked in silence as Grimm sped downtown.

News of the imminent verdict had leaked. Foley Square was swamped with tourists, fans, anti-Rudies, newspeople, lawyers, cops, federal agents. All milled around aimlessly awaiting Rickie's arrival. Grimm pulled the Jag up to the curb at the foot of the wide granite steps leading to the pillared facade of the United States Courthouse. The cops had most of the crowd restrained behind the police lines, but the moment the car drew up and stopped, newsmen and cameramen surged forward and clustered around. They peered into the car and were shouting questions at Rickie before he'd even opened the door.

"Here we go," Rickie said, looking over at Grimm and giving him a wink. "Stoned again."

Rickie popped open the car door and began to move out. Grimm saw Andrew Devlin, one of Aaron Held's assistants, running down the courthouse steps toward the car. "Look, there's Andy," Grimm said. "I'll park and be right with you. You and Suzi head on in with Andy. Don't get hung up with the reporters."

Fans straining at the police barricades were screaming Rickie's name. "FREE RUDE!" they chanted. Others were calling to Suzi, who smiled and waved to them. The newsmen were all around now, asking questions and shoving microphones in their faces. Photographers and news cameramen zeroed in on them. Devlin spoke a few words to Rickie, then he leaned in the open passenger's door of the Jag. Rickie was talking to reporters, Suzi at his side.

"Hmmmm, smells good in here," Devlin said, sniffing the air.

"What's going on in there?" Grimm asked.

"Everybody's freaking out. Aaron's going nuts. The judge is all flipped out. The usual. I've got to get Rickie in there. The jury's ready to come in."

"Yeah," Grimm said. "I'll be right—"

At that moment, Grimm looked through the windshield and saw a man moving through the crowd toward them. He was a tall, light-skinned black wearing a loose green Army flak jacket and a red bandana tied around his head. Around his neck hung a camera and light meter, and on his shoulder he carried a mini-cam video camera. For an instant, Grimm's eye met his.

That is no cameraman, said a voice in Grimm's head. That's a gunman.

Rickie and Suzi were still standing on the sidewalk just beyond the open car door. They were hemmed in by journalists and photographers. The black man with the red bandana shouldered his way through the crowd. He had almost reached Rickie and Suzi when he happened to glance into the car and see Grimm staring at him. Now he swung the camera on his shoulder toward the car.

Grimm grabbed Devlin by the back of his neck and shoved him down on the floor below the dash. At the same time he lunged across the seat reaching for the sidewalk through the open door. As he felt the material of Suzi's coat in his fingers, he grabbed her off her feet, pulling her in the car toward him. Grimm was screaming at Rickie: "GET DOWN! GET DOWN! LOOK OUT!"

As Grimm pulled Suzi toward him, he looked up and saw the mini-cam erupt in automatic gunfire. The windshield fragmented into millions of cracks. Grimm could feel the slugs tearing into the car seats as he tried to cover Suzi with his body. He looked up out the open car door in time to see Rickie's head turn to look at him, then suddenly his head twitched and jerked violently on his neck. A piece of Rickie's forehead ripped away like a hunk of clay. A fine pink mist filled the air.

People were crying out. In an instant, there was blood everywhere. Rickie had fallen to the sidewalk. Grimm still had both Devlin and Suzi crushed beneath him on the floor and front seat of the car. The crowd was in panic. People were screaming and fleeing in all directions. Grimm opened the driver's door and got out.

He looked over and saw the gunman drop his disguised weapon and turn to run. Grimm was moving toward the front of the car, about to give chase when he saw a uniformed cop and two plainclothes agents drawing their guns.

"Don't kill him!" Grimm yelled.

The black man was hit with gunfire from the three pistols. His legs skittered out from under him. His body tumbled wildly and lay sprawled over the curb.

Grimm saw one of the agents run up and shoot the man twice in the head. Grimm turned away. He looked back at the passenger's side of the car. There was Suzi, covered with blood, crouched on the sidewalk holding Rickie.

Chapter Seventeen

Sonny was exhausted. She had been up since three in the morning working in the Kosher kitchen. Still no verdict from that bloody jury! Christ, what could be taking so long? Outside her cell she could hear the Nigerian women screaming at the Puerto Rican women, who screamed back. Over all the yelling and screaming, she heard the soap operas blaring on the TV set in the multi-purpose room.

She was so tired she just wanted to crawl into her bunk and rest for ten minutes before she braved the trip to the shower. That lecherous little greaseball of a hack was on duty. She knew he'd be lurking around trying to get a look at her tits while she showered. What is it I hate most about this experience? she wondered idly. The noise? The lack of privacy? The humiliation?

Lately, she had been working sixteen hours a day to keep busy and get off the unit, especially since Rickie's jury had been out. They kept her in the hole one day because of the escape attempt rumor, but Arthur had called the warden and straightened that out.

No, she thought as she stood and stripped off her dirty kitchen whites, she couldn't stand her greasy hair and the smell of cooked food clinging to her a moment longer. She had to bathe. Then she would have a nice hot cup of tea. She hoped Arthur might come to see her tonight, but she doubted it. He'd be at the hotel with Rickie and Suzi maintaining the vigil, unless there was a verdict.

The noise grew louder. Sonny felt the door to her cell open behind her. She turned and saw her friend Leslie standing in the tier staring in at her. Leslie looked like a zombie.

"What is it, Les?" Sonny asked. "What's the matter? Is it guilty?"

Her friend, who was normally outgoing and talkative, stood there dumbstruck.

"Come in, Les," Sonny told her. "Close the door. Can't you see I'm not dressed?"

"Sonny," Leslie said dully. "Oh, God. Oh, God, Sonny."

Sonny took hold of her friend's shoulders. "What is it, Les? Tell me."

"On the news," she said. "It's on TV. Rickie's been shot."

"Byrne-Downes! Byrne-Downes!"

Sonny heard the little butch cop yelling her name. Fuck you, she thought. I'm not moving. If you want me, you can get off your fat ass and come get me.

Her cell was in semi-darkness. She stared at the hands of her watch. It was well past midnight. Why would that bitch be calling me at this hour? she wondered. It was too early for work and too late for anything else.

She had not really slept. Mind and body were leaden with grief.

Sonny lay on her bunk weeping silently. She could take anything, but not life without Rickie. Dear God, please don't let him die.

The police speculated that the gunman was either a deranged fan or fanatic anti-Rudie. Arthur, when she finally reached him, refused to talk about it on the phone. He was at Bellevue where Rickie was undergoing emergency brain surgery. Two bullets had penetrated Rickie's skull. A third hit him in the neck. Suzi too was in the hospital, though miraculously she had not been hit by the gunfire. The shock had caused her to go into labor. She had given birth to a healthy nine-pound baby boy, but was still weak and traumatized, still in intensive care. Three other people, all newsmen, were injured in the attack. According to the TV reports, the gunman was shot to death by police as he attempted to flee. Judge Gass had declared a mistrial. Though the jury had reached a verdict, the result had not been announced to the public.

Arthur promised he would see her in the morning. Meanwhile, she could only hope and pray for Rickie's recovery. Was it all her fault? Her mind cowered from the thought.

Sonny heard the familiar sound of keys jangling. Why can't they leave me alone?

The cell door swung open with a bang. A stocky black female guard snapped on the light and swaggered in.

"Byrne-Downes, get up. Pack your shit. You're shippin' out."

Sonny sat up. Her eyes were swollen, her vision blurry from crying.

The guard held up a collapsed cardboard carton. "Here. Just one box. That's all you're allowed. Move it. They're waitin' on you down in Receiving and Discharge."

Sonny knew better than to argue. She got off the bunk, started to pack, then gave up and sat staring at the wall. Half an hour later, a lieutenant and the Internal Security guard came on the unit to get her. She was on good terms with the lieutenant, a heavy-set, dark-skinned black who always had big yellow stains ringing the armpits of his white shirts. Sonny made him sandwiches when he came down to inspect the kitchen. The two cops stood in the door to her cell.

"C'mon, Byrne-Downes, let's move it," the lieutenant said.

"Where am I going?"

He shrugged his heavy shoulders. "Marshals're comin' to get you. VIP service."

"I see," Sonny said. "May I please make a phone call to my attorney?"

"Sorry, ma'am. No phone calls. Security. They want you downstairs right away."

Hurry up and wait, thought Sonny. By daybreak, she was still sitting in one of the filthy, freezing bullpens down on the third floor waiting for the marshals to come for her. She had been huddled on the cold steel bench for hours shivering until a cop she knew was kind enough to bring her a blanket. It had taken all of twenty minutes to inventory her belongings and dress her out in traveling clothes. The hack in the property room had written "Alderson, W. VA." on the box containing her stuff so she supposed she was being taken to the women's penitentiary in West Virginia.

While she sat in the cold, dark room, a deep sense of calm came over her, almost a stupor. Sonny let her mind dwell on Rickie, the one person with whom she felt a true affinity. Arthur was different. What she felt for Arthur was dominated by her passion, the physical need she felt to draw him into her.

Now she was up to dealing with the question of blame. Were they afraid he would turn on them if he got convicted? Or was this their way of trying to get to her?

Sonny had met Saul through Rickie, and it was Saul who put her together with Jack. Before Jack, she had been her own person; before Jack, she never would have gone near a junk scam.

Jack had tried to possess her. Not only her body but her mind. He wanted to take over her flow and turn it into a smack trip. And she let him. It wasn't greed, it wasn't ego. It was boredom and loneliness.

Together, she and Rickie had decided to get away from those people. Without ever actually planning it, they instigated their own secret rebellion. It was one of those junked-out fantasies, those horror stories that have a way of coming true.

Rickie had taught her to go beyond ego and money, to live life for the experience first. She knew he was right, she understood him, but for her it was different. Rickie had his art, his music. She had nothing to show for all those trips she'd done, all those crazy years of risk. For her, the money made life more interesting, it was a kind of symbolic energy, and Sonny's money had been stolen from her by men like Saul Diamond and Jack: business partners, scammers, lovers, men who for some reason thought they were smarter than she was, men who convinced themselves that her share of the profits belonged to them.

And that was the sickness of it all: it was her fault for letting them think they could control her trip in the first place. So her payoff was always left till last when the owners and distributors had already raked off the big profits. Or her share was bled off into new projects, new scams she would then be depended upon to make happen. Saul and Jack saw fit to take her money and use it as though it were their own.

That whole last movie, the Thai trip, never could have happened without her to put it together. Then once again they tried to screw her. She trusted Jack, and he changed the deal on her. Only God knew what double-dealing games Saul was playing, old moneybags himself, running around investing the same four or five million—at least half of which was hers, though she'd never actually seen it in one place— using the same dubious fortune to seed half a dozen different deals. Well, finally she had seen all that money come together, and when she found out that Karl Lundgren and Guy Stash were about to betray her, she decided to take it. It was hers anyway. Sonny never would have believed how treacherous Guy and his people were if she hadn't discovered it for herself. And Karl, a rat. She had to act. She had to get even and get out.

But they knew her weakness: her love for Rickie. They knew they could control her through him. And, once more, she had let it be so. The junk had ruined her thinking, it had anesthesized her. How could she be so unconsious not to realize they would go after Rickie if they couldn't get her?

At last the marshals came for her just as the other prisoners were being brought down for court. She had been sitting in the bullpen for over six hours. But Sonny said nothing to the two deputy marshals, a man and a woman, who came to collect her. They looped a chain around her waist, cuffed her hands, then attached the handcuffs to the chain in front allowing just enough slack for her to reach her mouth. Around her ankles they clamped leg shackles so that she had to shuffle along in half-step. The prisoners who had been brought down for court gawked at her as the deputies led her from the bullpen. The three of them rode the elevator down to street level and exited the prison through the garage.

It was the first time Sonny had been outdoors in months. Her eyes smarted from the intensity of real light. The marshals were brusque, all business.

They shoved her into the rear of a tan government sedan with no handles on the inside rear doors. Plainclothes cops and agents stood around the car looking from one end of the alley to the other as though they were waiting for something to happen. This is jolly, Sonny thought, if someone is trying to kill me, these idiots have decided to make it easy by leaving me here like a sitting duck.

They had been waiting for nearly an hour when Sonny saw two men coming along the alley from the street. One was tall, a good-looking man with silver gray hair. The other was dark and trim. Both wore suits and Sonny felt sure they were upper-echelon FBI agents.

Now everyone started moving. Uniformed cops got into their cars, while others carrying riot guns took up positions on the sidewalk. The two deputy marshals who had come into MCC got into the front seat and started the engine. The plainclothes cops and the FBI men remained standing on the sidewalk just outside the car.

Still they did not leave. What the fuck are they waiting for now? Sonny wondered. God, how I hate bloody cops.

From the back seat of the car, she could see out to the street MCC faced. As she sat there gazing at the crowd, her heart suddenly leapt at the sight of a man walking down the street toward the prison. That could only be one person, she thought. Only one man I know with that long-legged, swaying stride, shoulders swinging. It was Arthur. She sat up and stared at the approaching figure, those slim hips, the broad shoulders, the strong looking neck. He was wearing sunglasses, like the cops. But he was no cop, not her man. The height, that full black beard, it was definitely him. He looked rumpled and out of sorts as though he'd been up all night. Probably just coming from the hospital now, she thought. Oh, God, please let him have good news.

"I say . . . " Sonny began, realizing how silly she sounded.

The female deputy noticed Sonny looking at someone, and she became alert. Just as Sonny started to speak, she saw Arthur walk up to a parked car with two men in it. Jesus, thought Sonny as she recognized one of the men, the one behind the wheel; it's that scumbag DEA agent Julie Zuluaga. First of all, what's he doing here? And second, why is Arthur talking to him?

In the next moment, she saw Arthur pounding his fist on the window of the car and shouting at Zuluaga. The marshals and cops all turned to look.

"That's my lawyer," Sonny said. "I must speak with him."

The female deputy swung around and glared at her. "Sit back and shut up," she yelled.

The tall, silver-haired man knocked on the window of the car and nodded. As the sedan pulled away from the curb, a blue-and-white swung in behind it and another led the way. They drove in tandem to the end of the short alleyway.

Arthur was no more than thirty or forty feet from her. Sonny wanted to knock on the window to get his attention, but the chain around her waist and cuffed to her wrists prevented her. She ignored the deputy and sat on the edge of the seat craning her neck to see what was going on. Arthur was totally absorbed in hassling Zuluaga. The DEA agent had opened the door, heaving it against Grimm's leg. In a fit of anger, he was trying to get out of the car. Sonny was struck by how big Arthur looked standing next to the car. Goddamn, he's going to kill that guy, Sonny thought. As the marshals' sedan pulled out of the alley and turned onto the street, she saw the other man with Zuluaga get out of the car.

They drove right past them. Helplessly, Sonny looked out the window at Arthur as the sedan picked up speed. Even if she yelled, he would never hear her. He was in a full-pitched battle with Zuluaga now. He had him by his jacket and he was hitting him in the face. Sonny looked back over her shoulder and saw the two FBI agents walking briskly toward Zuluaga's car.

PART FOUR

Flight

Chapter Eighteen

This is not so much a case as it is a cause, thought Grimm. He understood there would never be a clear end to his involvement in Rude/Byrne-Downes. The affair would go on, in one dimension or other, forever.

The message had come into the answering service late the night before: "Gene Machine at MCC. Please come see me." It occurred to Grimm that he did not know Machine's real name. He called Aaron Held at his office.

"Who?" said Held.

"Gene Machine. The guy who works for Saul."

"I have no idea," Held said. "I didn't know he had a real name."

"Well, he does, and he's been arrested. He's at MCC."

"In that case," Held responded after a moment, "I suggest you call Saul."

After Rickie's trial, Aaron Held was the most celebrated criminal lawyer in New York. Although there was never an official verdict in the case, as Judge Gass declared a mistrial and ordered the jurors not to speak with the press, Held's defense of the rock star was pronounced a brilliant display of the trial lawyer's art. Some jurors had been hounded by reporters until they agreed to make statements. According to various press reports, the jury had arrived at a verdict of not guilty. There were other stories that insisted the verdict had been guilty. In a sense, the jury was still out. Rickie persisted in controversy.

In public statements, Held chastised the U.S. Attorney's Office for bringing an indictment against Rickie in the first place. He claimed the case against his client had been manufactured by overzealous prosecutors acting in bad faith. Soon after the trial, Vita Vaggi quit. Even Ralph Vallone came under fire for signing his name to what was generally considered a malicious prosecution. Sonny's testimony had cleared Rickie. He was martyred in the media.

But it was a bitter victory. Held was shattered by the attack on Rickie. Grimm had been concerned the attorney was on the verge of an emotional breakdown. Held recovered by throwing himself back into his work. Unlike Grimm, Held was able to remove himself from Rude/Byrne-Downes and go on to new campaigns. He was preparing to go to trial on a big Mafia racketeering case.

Grimm, though, could not just walk away. His client had been spirited out of New York and relocated to the women's penitentiary in West Virginia. There she was placed in maximum security lockdown status until Grimm intervened. He got a court order from Judge Gass directing that Sonny be allowed in population. There were continuous rumblings of grand jury proceedings emanating from Vallone's office, and Grimm's name was one of those being bandied about as a possible witness. Sonny might be called back to New York to testify at any time. The FBI was said to be investigating the possible connection between the murder of Karl Lundgren and the attack on Rickie. Grimm was certain Gene Machine's arrest had something to do with the continuing investigation.

The FBI questioned Grimm a number of times following the attempt on Rickie's life at the foot of the courthouse steps. The gunman, who was shot to death within moments of the attack by men identified as federal drug agents, was a thirty-two-year-old ex-con who had done time in Attica for armed robbery.

So far no motive had been discovered. The feds were saying publicly they believed the man was a maniac, another Hinkley or John Chapman acting out some deranged fantasy. The gunman was not known to have organized crime or radical political connections. Privately, agents theorized Rickie had been shot to prevent him from telling government authorities what he knew about the Jack Moriarty organization. Grimm's friend Bernie Wolfshein told him that the gunman had done time in Lewisburg when Jack and Guy Stash were there.

Grimm tried to reach Saul at the Southampton mansion, but learned the promoter was out of town. Judy Roth had moved from Saul's to a place of her own in the city. Grimm called her at her apartment and found that Saul had gone to the Coast three days earlier. Grimm asked Judy if she'd heard Gene Machine was in jail.

"Oh, God, no," she said. "Now what?"

"When did you last see him?" Grimm asked.

"The day Saul left. Gene drove him to the airport."

"Next time you talk to him, tell him Gene's been picked up. I'm on my way to see him now. Ask Saul to leave a number where I can reach him."

Gene's name, Judy told him, was Eugene Marchand.

In the lobby of the federal detention center, Grimm checked his weapon and filled out the attorney visiting forms. This was his first visit to MCC since Sonny's departure. Through the plate glass partition of the attorney visiting room, Grimm could see Gene Machine waiting for him. He was leaning against the wall beside the soda machine, his arms folded across his chest.

The small conference cubicles were all taken. Grimm and Gene Machine shook hands, then sat at a table near the soda machine.

"So, what're you pinched for?" Grimm asked.

"Parole violation," Gene answered. "I still owe the feds some time on my '78 beef. I get a call from my P.O., this was yesterday. He tells me he needs to see me. So I go down, and the feds are there. They say they got me for associating with known felons. I was seen at a stakeout on Mulberry Street. A bullshit technical violation."

Gene paused, then said, "But what they really want to talk about is Karl Lundgren. They're still tryin' to figure out who clipped that piece of shit."

"What did you tell them?"

Gene gave him a thin smile. "I said I thought it was probably suicide."

"Do you want a lawyer?"

He nodded. "You know, right?"

Grimm sat forward and leaned on the table. "What I know isn't important. What do you want me to do?"

"A couple 'a things. I need you to contact Saul."

"That's done. I should be talking with him this afternoon."

"Tell him everything's cool on this end. I don't want him to freak when he hears they pinched me. Understand what I'm saying?"

"Yes," Grimm said.

"What kind of money are we talkin' about?"

"No money," Grimm said.

"I really don't think they got much, otherwise they'd just charge me. This is a squeeze."

Machine gave him a steady look. Grimm sat back and waited while the ex-Marine measured him. "Sonny told you I'm with her, right?"

Grimm shook his head. "She didn't tell me anything."

"But you know. All along, I worked for her. I was going to take care of something for her but"—he looked around—"as you can see, I'm in no position to do anything right now. Sonny needs your help."

"Sonny knows I'll do whatever I can for her."

"Yeah, right." Gene placed his left arm on the surface of the table, then he rolled his forearm until his hand stood on its edge to signify a wall. With his other hand, he walked his fingers along until he came to the wall. "This is her problem," Gene said. His right hand sprang over the wall. "Now what? See what I'm saying?"

Grimm nodded.

"Good. Somebody will be in touch with you," Gene said. "Somebody you know and trust. They'll fill you in on the details."

The trusted someone Gene Machine had said would be in touch turned out to be the writer, Moon Landing. Grimm was in his office late one afternoon about a week after he had spoken with Machine at MCC when Moon dropped by.

"I've been drinking heavily," Moon said, although he appeared sober. "I haven't slept in days. I'm not cut out for this secret agent shit."

Moon put a gym bag on Grimm's desk. "There's 250 grand. I'm supposed to ask if that's enough."

"That should cover it."

A few days later, he heard from Moon again. Grimm planned to go to the farm for the weekend, and whenever he was in Millbrook, he spent as much time as possible with Suzi. Suzi had been living in seclusion since the shooting and the birth of her child. Moon called to ask if he could have a lift to Suzi's place in the country.

Judy Roth and Cassy Steiger also stayed with Suzi and the baby in the months following the Foley Square attack. Grimm and Cassy were trying to maintain their coast-to-coast constrained love affair, though Grimm sensed a tension between them which he believed was a result of the horror everyone felt over what had happened to Rickie. It was something he intended to deal with, like so many other things, as soon as he could find the time.

Rickie never regained consciousness. He was, for all intents and purposes, dead. He was being kept alive by life support systems at the government's insistence. Even if he were to come out of the coma, which was highly improbable, the doctors said that the brain damage was so extensive he would always be a vegetable. Suzi was suing to have the machines shut off so that Rickie could die, but because Vallone's office refused to dismiss the criminal indictment, the punk's fate remained in legal limbo.

Judy Roth was staying with Suzi for a few days. They prepared a big meal for Moon and Grimm. Grimm and Suzi had become close during the trial, and after the debacle in Foley Square it was as though they were wed in grief.

For now, Suzi only wanted to remain in the country and nurture her baby. She told Grimm she had doubts as to whether she would ever return to the rock 'n' roll life. Other than one trip she'd made with Judy to West Virginia to visit Sonny and show her the baby, Suzi rarely left the country retreat. She hadn't been back to New York since she'd been released from the hospital. "I don't know if I'll ever be able to deal with crowds again," she told them. "The thought of it terrifies me."

Her baby was a healthy, fat kid with a big, round head and Rickie's crystal clear blue eyes. Suzi named him Spike. He had a happy disposition and almost never cried. Grimm doted on the baby. Everyone remarked that little Spike seemed to love Arthur.

"Sure he loves A.G.," Suzi said, handing the baby to Grimm. "Spike thinks A.G.'s his daddy, right Spike? Yeah, we found the tough guy's soft spot, didn't we, kid?"

Judy showed them photos of Sonny taken during the visit. Sonny was dressed in leotards and a tank top, "her running getup," Judy said. "You wouldn't believe the shape she's in. She runs five miles a day every day." Sonny's rich auburn hair had grown out, she wore it swept back and tossed over her shoulder. In the pictures, she was leaning against a wooden rail fence holding the baby and looking at him with an expression of tenderness and sorrow.

"Here." Judy handed Grimm a manila envelope. Inside were some maps of the desolate, rolling hills and mountains of West Virginia.

There was also a hand-drawn diagram of the isolated women's prison. "From what she tells me," Judy said, looking over Grimm's shoulder as he studied the maps, "the whole thing is really the second phase: getting her out of the area, escaping the surrounding countryside."

"Yeah, the perimeter fence is no big deal," Suzi added. "It's an eight-and-a-half foot chainlink fence with strands of barbed wire at the top. Sonny says she's got that. Every morning, she goes out running, right around six. As soon as they open the compound, she's out on the jogging track. The compound is sixty-nine buildings on ninety-six acres of land."

"Getting out of the compound is the easy part," Judy went on. "She says there are a few spots where she can climb right over the fence, or under it. The important part of the whole trip is the actual flight from the area. I guess you know who will take care of that. Sonny said if 250 grand isn't enough, she'll have Moon bring you some more."

"See, here's how it goes," Suzi told him. "Right after count clears, around six, they open the compound for breakfast and it's open for the rest of the day. They don't count again until four in the afternoon. She works in the recreation department, in the arts and crafts room, but she's off all weekend. So from six in the mornin' till four in the afternoon, nobody'll miss her. They won't even know she split."

Early the following Monday, Grimm was on his way to California. In Los Angeles, he checked into a room near the airport at the Sheraton La Reina Hotel. He did not bother to unpack since he had no intention of staying. He took off his jacket and shoes and lay on the bed resting when he heard a knock at the door.

Through the peephole, Grimm saw a man standing in the hallway. He was of average height, slim, with short brown hair and a neatly trimmed beard. He wore an inexpensive brown suit and round tortoise-shell glasses. The only noticeable thing about him was the large red Samsonite suitcase he carried.

Grimm opened the door and the two men stood grinning at each other for a moment before the man stepped into the room. They embraced and hugged each other, then clasped hands in the Brother-hood handshake. Neither of them spoke until Grimm turned on the TV.

"I hardly recognized you," Grimm said.

"That's the idea."

The man swung the red suitcase up onto the bed and opened it. He removed two small, zippered plastic bags. Each contained an expensive-looking woman's wig: one was black and straight with bangs, and the other was blond, short and curly.

"How do you like her? Little Orphan Annie or the Mata Hari look?"

Next, he showed Grimm two complete woman's outfits and a bag full of make-up, cosmetics and underwear. In a leather zip case were two full sets of identification—one U.S. and one Canadian—and credit cards and other miscellaneous papers.

"And these briefs will hold up?" Grimm said, leafing through the passports.

"Bro, these are real chicks. Dead chicks, but real. Both of 'em died when they were little kids. Never had passports. We did all the homework, even had the death certificates pulled. Guaranteed solid. We wouldn't sell you no bogus briefs unless we knew they were righteous."

"What about the pictures?" Grimm asked.

"We got equipment in the motorhome. As soon as we get her aboard, we snap her with the different wigs, stamp and seal the pictures, and presto, instant I.D. She's ready to boogie."

Grimm got out the maps and diagrams Judy and Suzi had given him. He showed the man one of the recent photographs of Sonny. They spread the maps out on the bed and went over the details.

"Here, Columbus, Ohio, this is where we meet with the motorhome," the man told him. "We'll be using a stolen van to make the pickup."

Grimm pointed to an old logging road that ran along the southeast border of the federal lands reservation where the women's prison was located. "Make sure you're somewhere along this stretch of road by six-fifteen or six-twenty. Hide yourselves. The pickup time has to be kept to a minimum because of the bounty hunters. She'll come along this road between six-thirty and seven. Once you make contact, get her out of there right away."

"A.G., relax. We got women with us who did time in that joint. We know all about the counts and the bounty hunters. All she's got to do is show up. We'll take care of the rest." The man was a member of the Brotherhood of Eternal Love who had escaped from federal custody nearly ten years earlier. He had been on the lam ever since.

"We'll have our cut-out vehicle here." He pointed to a spot on the map. "We disguise her, dump the van, then head for the motorhome in Ohio. Just tell me where you want the client delivered."

"Take her to Detroit. Check in to the Ramada at the airport. Use the name C.W. Newmark. The Canadians will contact you no later than Monday morning."

"Got it. Now, have you got what I need?"

Grimm went to his suitcase and took out twenty-five packs of one hundred hundred-dollar bills, the 250,000 Moon had given him. He gave it to the man. "If something goes wrong and it doesn't go down on Saturday, get a new vehicle and try again Sunday at the same time. If she still doesn't show, abort and contact me through the usual way."

He wrote a number on a slip of paper and handed it to him. "I'll be at this number next Monday, one week from today, from noon on East Coast time. I'll wait to hear from you."

The man looked at the slip of paper for a moment, then tore it up and went into the bathroom to flush the scraps down the toilet.

"No evidence, right, A.G. Isn't that the first rule? Okay, bro. I guess that's about it. Any messages for the passenger?"

Grimm thought about it. He smiled and said, "Yeah. Tell her I said she's incorrigible. She'll know what I mean."

So much for that, Grimm thought once his friend had left and gone to the airline terminal to catch his flight back East. There was nothing more he could do now except wait.

He changed his clothes and got ready to leave. The assignment was in the hands of the best people in the business, many of them fugitives themselves. If they failed then chances were it wasn't meant to happen.

Grimm took the Browning Hi-Power from his luggage and strapped it on under a lightweight jacket. Meanwhile, he had other business to attend to. Places to go and people to see. Things to get done in the hazy L.A. sun. In the hotel lobby, he rented a car and drove north to Beverly Hills.

Chapter Nineteen

Saul Diamond was ensconced in one of the plush flamingo pink bungalows at the Beverly Hills Hotel. He had been there for three weeks by the time Grimm arrived. He was in L.A. to try to save a movie deal that had been teetering on the edge of disaster since the disappearance of the six-and-a-half million almost a year before. Grimm was assured there were any number of other irons in the fire, including a book-movie deal about the life of Rickie Rude, who was still lingering somewhere between life and death.

Grimm knew all these deals could have been negotiated over the phone from Saul's Southampton mansion, which was how he had been doing business ever since his weight reached 350 pounds. With the outbreak of hostilities among Saul, Jack Moriarty and the different drug clans, Saul had been barricaded at Dune Castle surrounded by heavily armed bodyguards.

This move to L.A., this foray into what could only be considered enemy territory, signified a major shift in the fat man's logistics. Either peace had been declared or something extremely tempting lured Saul from his Long Island fortress.

The fact that Jack Moriarty was also on the Coast, probably in the L.A. vicinity, hardly seemed coincidental. For the past week, Grimm had been receiving messages from Jack saying he wanted to meet. Grimm was told to name a location, though preferably not in the New York area. When he reached Jack pay phone-to-pay phone, he had dialed a Southern California area code. In the meantime, Saul begged Grimm to come see him; he offered large cash retainers for as yet unspecified assignments. When Gene Machine got busted, leaving Sonny's project unfinished, Grimm knew there was every reason for him to make one of his extended visits to the West Coast.

He told himself it was business that brought him to L.A., but in his heart Grimm knew he missed Cassy badly. He longed to spend a few quiet days with her so they could try to get to the bottom of the rift growing between them. Yet he hadn't even told her he was coming to L.A. He hadn't even called her or returned her calls in over a week. With one hand, he was shoving her away; with the other, he was groping for her in the dark.

Since Rickie had been shot, Grimm felt himself withdrawing more and more from intimate relationships. He had allowed himself to love Rickie, and now Rickie was gone. He had let himself fall in love with Sonny even when he knew he could not have her. Now he was afraid his feelings for Cassy would bring them only pain. As long as he was alone, he was not vulnerable. More importantly, if he did not allow himself to become someone else's source of happiness, then he could never let that person down.

Grimm feared he would infect Cassy's healthy young life with the violence and corruption that seemed to infuse his existence. He thrived on this life of danger, but it was no life to share, not with a woman like Cassy. Better to push her away now gently than to have to tear himself from her after it was too late. Better not to anger Max and lose another friend. Even as these thoughts went through his mind, he knew he would go to her.

Saul was insulated by the usual retinue of bodyguards, assistants, hangers-on. True to form, the obese promoter sat at a desk talking on the telephone when Grimm entered the bungalow.

A tall, thin and deeply tanned man wearing a Hawaiian shirt opened the door, then went out onto the patio where there were a few women in bathing suits and men wearing loose shirts Grimm was sure concealed guns. There was a bar in the room with a blender full of Saul's relished pale green margaritas. Grimm knew the bag of coke could not be far away. Saul had simply transplanted his milieu and modus operandi from Southampton to Beverly Hills.

The instant Saul slammed down the receiver the phone rang again.

"Jesus H. Christ," Saul rumbled and heaved from his chair. "Sylvia," he called out to the patio. "I'm not answering that."

Saul wore a navy blue Turkish towel beach suit, the top open exposing his immense girth. His legs were so fat the trunks rode up in the crotch and his thighs were chafed raw where they rubbed together as he walked. He came out from behind the desk and lumbered toward Grimm.

"About fuckin' time you got your ass out here, A.G.," Saul began. His voice seemed to have grown even more gravelly. Dark bags drooped from under his eyes. He looked tired and full of woe.

A woman in a bikini came in from the patio and answered the phone. "I'm sorry, Mr. Diamond is not available at the moment," she said with a professional tone. "Would you like to leave a message and I'll have him call you back?"

Saul was hugging Grimm. He clung to him and seemed reluctant to let him go. When Grimm stepped back and looked at him, he could see there were tears in Saul's murky eyes.

"That was a guy named Benny Glickman," said the woman at Saul's desk as she cradled the receiver. "He wants you to call him as soon as possible."

"Thanks, doll. Sylvia, say hello to A.G. Then call the front desk and tell 'em to hold all calls 'til further notice."

Saul waddled over to the bar and switched on the blender. "You realize the last time I saw you was the night of Rickie 'n Suzi's party," he said above the whirring of the machine. Saul shook his head and wiped tears from his eyes. "I just can't get over it, A.G. Christ, I miss that little guy."

Grimm and Sylvia both looked at Saul. He reached into the pocket of his beach jacket and took out a bag of coke. "Here," he said, handing the bag to Sylvia. "Keep everyone out on the patio for a while, hon."

Saul poured drinks. He handed one to Grimm and went back to his desk. As soon as Sylvia had left the room, he said, "Why would anyone want to hurt Rickie, A.G.? That I don't understand. Was it because of the Ayatollah video?"

"No," Grimm replied. "I don't believe it had anything to do with Rickie's music or his image. Nor was the gunman just some nut."

"Then who? Why? You really think it could of been agents?"

"Saul, I saw them kill the guy who shot Rickie right in front of the courthouse. They knew he was coming. They were there to make sure he didn't live to talk about it."

"Listen," Saul said, "you know all along I been sayin' it was agents behind this thing. The same people who tried to clip you. Zuluaga an' his crew. Jack never wanted to believe me. He still thinks I had Karl whacked and robbed that money. But what I don't understand is why? Why would they want to kill Rickie?"

Grimm replied, "For one thing, they were afraid if he got convicted he'd roll over and tell everything he knew."

"Rickie didn't know nothin'. You know that. Rickie wasn't involved."

"No, that's not true. He wasn't involved, but he knew. That much the government had right. Sonny told Rickie everything. He was her alter ego. He never cared about the money. He wasn't involved in the business. But he was fascinated by Sonny's trip. Vaggi had it right when she accused him of interest in the political dimension of what Sonny was about."

"What could he know that was worth whackin' him over?"

"I just told you," Grimm said, "whatever Sonny knew, Rickie knew. Sonny kept no secrets from him. That's why the government put him in this case in the first place. They wanted to use him to put pressure on Sonny, and they figured if he got convicted they could squeeze him and maybe he'd open up on you, Jack, Guy Stash and the wiseguys, the people in San Francisco. Rickie also knew who killed Karl Lundgren. He knew who stole the six-and-a-half million. And he knew why."

Saul gazed at him. His face clouded. "You tellin' me he knew Karl was a rat? Even before you found out? How could he know? Then you must be sayin' Sonny knew, too."

"Of course she knew," Grimm said. "And you knew. Suzi. She found out what Karl was up to. He may even have told her. Karl was supporting Suzi for a while before she got on her feet. He gave her money, he was in love with her. They were from the same hometown in Connecticut. He felt he'd discovered her. Then he turned you and Rickie on to Suzi, and he lost her. He was bitter. He was going to make sure you and Rickie got busted. But Suzi found out what he was up to. She told Rickie, and naturally he told Sonny. They also told you."

"A.G.," Saul began. He looked around nervously. "Listen, no one was sure. Suzi heard somethin' from some people, scammers she knows from Connecticut. Sonny wanted to check it out. She was tryin.'

to reach Jack. All that other shit was goin' down out here, you know, with The Brothers. Then, I don't know what happened. The bust came down. It was chaos."

"Saul, don't try to bullshit me. You know what happened. Gene Machine killed Karl. Jack knows it, too. And by now the feds have a pretty good idea it was Machine. They have no evidence, but that's the real reason they picked him up. They're hoping he'll roll over on you."

"Okay. But I didn't tell Machine to kill Karl. And I didn't get the money. It's like I told you, I swear. When Karl came out to Dune Castle, he didn't have the money. We still weren't sure about him—at least, I wasn't. I wanted Jack to handle it. But Machine confronted Karl and he admitted it. See, Machine did time on that old beef, the 'Final Analysis' trip, and he realized it was Karl who gave it up. Yeah, Machine killed him. The money was supposed to be at the loft in SoHo. Machine was gonna take Karl back there and get the money. But when they got there, it wasn't there. Machine lost it and whacked Karl. It had to be Zuluaga. Zuluaga must'a got that money. That was all part of their plan."

Saul kept shooting nervous glances out at the people on the patio as though he were afraid they might hear what he was saying. The sounds of voices and laughter drifted in. Grimm could see a long-legged, dark-skinned woman stretched out on a chaise longue. She was wearing big sunglasses and appeared to be reading a script. The slim man in the Hawaiian shirt moved around offering coke.

"What is it you want me to do?" Grimm asked him after a moment.

"You gotta help me. Listen, you gotta reach out for Jack for me. See if you can set up a meet. It's crazy for him an' me to be at each other's throats. Tell him I didn't rob that money. Okay? It's the truth. So Machine whacked Karl. The guy was a rat. He was gonna give everybody up. But Jack should make peace. I got somethin' very heavy about to happen out here. There's millions in it for all of us, me, Jack, you, whoever. Talk to him. Convince him he should talk to me. All I want is peace and future business between him an' me. We gotta put a stop to all this crazy shit before somethin' else bad happens. Will you do this for me?"

"All I can do is talk to him," Grimm said.

"That's all I'm askin'. I know he's out here somewhere. You know how to reach him? Where he's at?"

"I can get a message to him."

"An' he'll meet with you, bro. Look, I want you to meet somebody. Adrianna!" Saul stood and shouted out to the patio. "Wait'll you see this one, A.G. I got a very heavy move I'm about to make with her an' her old man. Jack could get in an' make himself a serious pay check. I wanna hire you to handle security. I'll give you points. Adrianna," he called again. "Come on in here a minute, sweetheart. Meet my friend, A.G."

It was the tall, dark-skinned woman. Grimm watched her sleek brown legs uncross, then, when she stood and walked toward him, even with the sunglasses on, he knew they had already met. He recognized the dark, toffee-colored complexion and the luxuriant head of dark hair. It was Adrianna Gavíria. Grimm had been introduced to her and her Colombian husband at the party for Rickie and Suzi in Southampton.

She took off her sunglasses and held out a long, brown hand. "But we've met," she said. "I remember you."

Grimm was standing. "You would not be easy to forget," he said, taking her hand.

"Thank you." She smiled. "Nice to see you again."

"Adrianna an' her husband're thinkin' of investin' some money in a movie project I got goin'," Saul said. "A.G. is a good friend 'a Max Steiger," he told Adrianna. "He goes with Max's sister, Cassy."

"Yes, of course. I met Cassy at the party."

"Right." Saul turned to Grimm. "We're hopin' to get Max an' his people to work with us. I'm givin' a little dinner party tomorrow night. Why don't you join us?"

"Maybe I will," Grimm said. "I'll let you know."

"Well, I do hope we see each other again, Mr. Grimm," Adrianna Gavíria said. "Excuse me."

And with that, she stepped back out onto the patio.

"Classy broad," Saul said as they watched her leave. "Her brother an' her old man are really heavy. Colombians. They got millions in cash they need to wash. An' they got tons of coke. Tons, bro. I can make a move right now with these people for like unlimited amounts."

Grimm held up his hand. "Saul, I don't want to hear about it."

"But I need Jack to help with distribution. An' I wanna hire you to oversee security. With Machine locked up—"

But Grimm was shaking his head. "No," he said. "That's not my line. I'll talk to Jack for you. I'll tell him you want peace and you want to meet with him. No more."

"Great. Fine. An' tell him, for Christ's sake, tell him I didn't rob that money. Please."

"I'll tell him."

Saul was visibly pleased. "That's my man, A.G. I knew I could depend on you. That's why I love you." He waddled over and hugged Grimm.

"How 'bout Max? You gonna see Max an' Cassy?"

"I'm going to see Cassy," Grimm told him.

"Listen, give her my love. Tell her she an' Max should stay in touch. I sent them a copy of the script. Call me. Come to dinner tomorrow night."

He waved at Grimm. "I love you, A.G.," Saul said as he turned toward the patio and his other guests.

It was a short drive from the hotel to the campus of U.C.L.A. Cassy was competing in the Pacific Athletic Conference Singles Tennis Championships. Grimm had called her office at To The Max Productions and learned she was scheduled to play a preliminary round that afternoon. When he reached the university, he pulled in behind a row of palm trees and sat smoking a joint while he watched the cars and studied the faces of the drivers coming in the entrance after him.

Cassy struggled to come from behind in the second set of her match. She looked tense and fatigued. And much too thin. Watching her from the stands, Grimm had a sinking fear she was doing coke again.

It was a humid day and both women were soaked with sweat. All tied at 5-5, covering the court beautifully and hitting deep ground-strokes, Cassy broke serve and went on to win the second set 7-5.

During the last set, Cassy's concentration seemed to improve. Her serve was a powerful weapon. Taking an early lead, she went on to win the set and match.

"You're sopping," Grimm said, putting his arms around her. "Just the way I like you." He smiled. "How do you feel?"

"You," she said. "I mean, you just show up. No call. No messages."

"You look tired, baby."

"I haven't been sleepin' too good. Lonely. Sex starved. It's about a certain guy I know who treats me like dirt."

"Who? I'll kill him."

"You, asshole. How come you never call me? What did I ever do to deserve this?"

"Nothing. I'm sorry. I've been busy."

"Arthur, please, don't gimme that busy crap. When aren't you busy? If you've decided to cool it with me, at least have enough respect to let me know."

"What're you doing now?" he asked.

She shrugged. "I'm gonna go in an' take a shower an' change."

"Then what?"

She knitted her brow. "Go home, I guess. What're you gonna do?"

"Go with you."

Grimm locked the rental car and left it at the U.C.L.A. parking lot. He drove Cassy in her Ferrari up the coast to the house in Malibu. Max, she told him, was at the ranch in Big Sur. She didn't expect him back until the weekend.

"So I've got you all to myself," Grimm said.

They spent a quiet evening at home. Cassy gave him no reason to believe she was doing coke. She was relaxed, ate well, and did not make frequent trips to the bathroom. So Grimm did not question her about it. He attributed her thin body to the intense training she'd been doing. After dinner, they took the dog for a walk on the beach.

"You know, if you weren't so big," Cassy told him, "I'd kick the shit out of you." She stopped walking and scowled at him. "I couldn't believe it when you didn't call me back. Listen, Arthur, let's tell each other the truth. Can we have that kind of relationship? No lies. No pretending."

"We have that kind of relationship," he said.

"Do we? You mean it?"

"I've never lied to you."

"Yeah. But you don't tell me everything."

"That's different."

"Tell me one thing. Do you love me?"

"Yes," he said. "I do."

"Well then, what's the problem? How come you act so weird sometimes?"

"Baby, this is me. I have my other life. My business. I keep telling you, it has nothing to do with you."

Cassy took his arm and they began walking again. "Will it always be like this?'' she asked, squeezing his hand. "Can't you just be normal? You could be a lawyer. You're a good lawyer, honey.''

Grimm did not answer. He was looking out at the ocean.

"This horrible thing with Rickie. God, Arthur, it's all so sick. And you almost got shot again. Suzi . . . What kind of life is that? Who're these people doin' this? Can't you get away from them?''

In bed that night, he made love to her slowly, gently, for a long time. Cassy seemed to be able to shut everything out of her mind and relax. Grimm could feel her enjoyment in every gesture, every caress. She loved having her body stroked and touched. I could marry her, he thought suddenly as he felt her come and looked down at her face. Her eyes were shut tight. For an instant she looked like Max in rapture when he played guitar. We could have children. We could be a family. She'd make a great mother, a great wife.

Now he was coming. He felt his seed loose in her. I could change, he told himself. I could settle down and live a different life with her, a better life. I could become a better person.

But as he moved off her and slowly withdrew, the doubts returned.

Chapter Twenty

It was the dogs she feared most, not the men. Sonny had heard all about those dogs. Bloodhounds, like *The Hound of the Baskervilles*, sniffing, slobbering, mantracking dogs. The women sometimes heard the dogs in the distance baying as they chased wild animals. The dogs worried her. Men she could deal with.

Sonny stood off the edge of her bunk and took a deep breath. It was morning. *The* morning. The day that would decide her fate. Anxiously she looked out the window. Thank God, a beautiful spring day. No fog. If there had been fog, as there often was in the morning this time of year, they would keep the women locked in their units until after it lifted. And then it would be too late.

How wonderful to feel the muscles of her thighs and buttocks flexing with the firm elasticity of an athlete, she thought as she bent all the way over to lace her fancy new running shoes. Such suppleness, she could lay her wrists flat on the floor. That was one thing she would say for this godforsaken place, for her it had been a health spa.

She was ready, she knew it in her stomach. It was five-thirty in the morning. The sun was already up bringing another long, hazy blue day to the mountains of West Virginia. There was nothing more for her to do. Her cell looked exactly as it would any other weekend morning when there was no room inspection: bed unmade, the desk cluttered with books and papers, her locker door standing open with the pictures of Rickie pasted inside. Dear God, please don't let me start thinking of Rickie now or I may lose the courage to go out there and run, and to keep running.

If her friend Mandy did her job and put the dummy in her bunk that afternoon before the four o'clock count, and they counted the dummy, Sonny would be out of the country before they realized she was gone. If all goes according to plan, she thought, by this time tomorrow I'll be in Toronto, on my way to Montreal. And from there, Mexico City. Mexico, the very name had the ring of freedom.

Her fingers felt cold and stiff, her stomach queasy. But her face was composed with venerable British stoicism. Sangfroid, she thought, we Brits are known for our cool, even when inside we're scared shitless.

Sonny found her place in the common area and began her ritual fifteen minutes of stretching. This was her best time of day, early morning, when all the "screaming meemies," as Sonny called the other women, were still asleep. She wore a brand new running outfit, dark green tights, neat little shorts and a halter top under a zip-front sweatshirt, all shades of green to blend with the landscape.

Soon after she began her stretching, the jitters in her tummy eased. The trick is not to think about it, she reminded herself as she extended her long, muscular leg in the hurdler's stretch. In another dimension, what is to be has already happened. She had visualized every phase of her flight, seen it all in her mind with such clarity she believed in her escape just as she believed in the energy flowing along her spine. She experienced the opening of her groin, then a powerful surge of energy seemed to uncoil and burst like a blossom at the base of her skull.

I can do anything, she told herself. Jesus, who needs drugs when you can feel this good? Whatever happens, she said to herself, promise me you will never allow yourself to forget how good, how alive you feel at this moment.

"Unit officers, release your inmates," came the announcement over the P.A. Sonny took a few minutes to finish her stretching.

Few of the other women were up yet. Sonny heard someone shuffling along in a pair of slippers. God, how she hated the sound of scuffing feet.

"Good morning," she said with a haughty nod as she passed the unit officer on her way to the door. Good, it was Miss Pack—"Ms. Pac-Man," the women called her. Laziness incarnate.

Sonny stepped into the cool, moist air. She felt at once braced and terrified by the realness of the morning and what she was about to do. Her mind seemed to run off in all directions. Relax, she told herself. Get centered. Run.

Her legs stretched out as though they were winged and carried her above the earth. She seemed to fly. She was lighter than the spring air. A disembodied spirit.

The mountains, her old friends, pondered her flight; they seemed to understand they could not keep her. Sonny loved the mountains, she would miss their sedate company. Sometimes they were private and wrapped away in clouds, preening or sulking, the clouds changing like a limitless wardrobe. Other days they seemed to stalk closer, obtrusive, standing out in sharp relief as though naked and imposing on her space.

Today the mountains were chiaroscuro, both bright and shady as the billowy clouds floated past like airships. She hardly felt her feet touch the ground as she ran off into the blue expanse. It was so simple, one day you were a prisoner, and the next day you were free: a decision you made.

The jogging trail took her up and down hill. Sonny felt the sudden release of adrenaline like a rush. She was in her stride. No one was on the track, no one was about. She saw a few women going from the units to the dining hall. She could see indistinct bodies moving to and fro at the rear gate, men in gray, hacks, tired and dull-witted at the end of the graveyard shift.

As she mounted one rise, Sonny glimpsed Control Center. It was a squat stone fortress-like building attached to the Administration Hall. There, or so the prisoners were led to believe, intelligent beings watched over their movements. But Sonny had studied her keepers, and she doubted their vigilance. Lethargy was the order of the day. Tedium was the prevailing mood.

Nothing serious ever happened in this place. There were fights over who was and who was not giving up pussy; there were fights over drugs; a lot of cursing went on; but these women were not contemplating escape. The few who might were kept in the maximum security unit and not allowed out onto the compound, as Sonny had been for the first two months she was here. The women joked that the fence was there to keep the snakes and mountain lions out. In truth many of these women, even when they were released, came back, because they had nowhere else to go.

A huge alarm horn was mounted on the roof of Control Center. It was painted bright red and looked like the speaker of an old fashioned gramophone. The horn made her think of the dogs, and for a moment her stomach tensed again. If a prisoner were missing at count time, then that alarm horn would go off. And what a god-awful noise it made, a great bellowing sound like the croak of a giant bullfrog. The horn could be heard for miles echoing throughout the valley and alerting the bounty hunters with their hound dogs. Sonny had heard the alarm go off once and the sound vibrated in her bowels. A woman failed to appear for the 4:00 P.M. count so the alarm was sounded. They found her later in the power house, unconscious from an overdose.

Women wandered off from time to time, but they never got far. The big deterrent was the location. They were in the middle of nowhere surrounded by miles of rough wilderness, rivers and swamps full of snakes, forests full of bears, to say nothing of the hillbilly bounty hunters with their convict-sniffing dogs. Any woman crazy enough to run off from this place could not get away unless she had outside help who knew exactly what they were doing.

Oh God, Arthur, please don't let me down. Be the one man in my life who really is there when I need him.

All the omens were auspicious. The planets in their heavenly concourse aligned to energize her will. Mandy tossed the I Ching, she lay the Tarot cards and found further augery of success. Arthur's people, whoever they were—Sonny suspected they were from the Brotherhood or possibly Weather Undergound—sent the coolest messages. One of the few men she knew with real guts and loyalty to boot, Gene Machine—himself now a prisoner—blessed the operation.

Above all, she loved and trusted Arthur. In the end, the feeling she came back to was that if her love and belief in Arthur were misplaced, then she might as well stay in prison because there was nothing out there worth escaping for, except her darling Carmen. She loved her baby and longed to be with her. But now, with Rickie gone, she had to believe in Arthur. Otherwise life was meaningless.

She was running. Sonny knew at once the violence of her lungs and the pounding of her heart. She felt a cool sheen on her brow. She was running as she ran every morning, running on the jogging track along the fence, up hill, down hill, in the fresh mountain air.

The perimeter road outside the fence veered away to circumvent the granite boulders and thick brush at the rear of the compound. Her friend Mandy operated the bulldozer they were using to clear this area. The previous day when the cop wasn't looking, Mandy ripped the underpinnings along the bottom of the fence with the blade of the bulldozer. She then moved a pile of brush to cover the rent. Sonny could see the brush pile thirty, now twenty-five yards farther along the track. Each loping stride brought her nearer.

The fence was a single chainlink cyclone with three strands of barbed wire strung along the top. No concertina wire, none of the weight-sensitive "snitch wire" like they used in the fences at the men's prisons. She was now at the farthest end of the compound from Control Center. They would have to be watching her with binoculars, and even at that, once the jogging track dipped down into the gully where Mandy made the breach in the fence, she would be hidden from their sight. Only if the whole plan were somehow compromised, or if Mandy had snitched her out, would they be aware of what she was doing.

Running down the last hill she came to a walk as she left the jogging track. Casually she strode behind the brush pile. The only danger she faced was if the Outside Patrol truck drove by on the perimeter road.

Under the brush at the back of the pile, she found the pair of leather work gloves Mandy left for her. The fence was two yards from the brush. She could see the spot where Mandy spoiled the footing. Sonny got down and crawled to the fence. She gripped it with her gloved hands and ripped it toward her. The bottom of the fence came up like a springed hatch, she had to prop the fence with a sapling from the brush pile, lie down in the mud, then wriggle under it. Sonny dragged the length of her body free, sprung the fence and pulled it back in place.

That was it. She was out. It seemed incredible that she could be outside the fence with everything else unchanged. The spring day was exactly the same either side of the fence.

The easy part was over. Sonny got to her knees, pushed up, and without so much as a glance behind at the prison she headed off into the heavy undergrowth and granite outcroppings. Only her friends, the mountains, watched.

Now began what Sonny thought of as stage two of her flight. She was like an astronaut riding a rocket on some mission into space. Liftoff had occurred, she was free of the launch pad. But she still had to clear the atmosphere. This was the risky part because from here on she was totally dependent on luck, conditions beyond her control, and the loyalty of others.

She was moving, hurtling through space. Her direction was toward the sun, east, down along the woodsy declivity to the banks of the Green River. She was in dense forest now, she was alone with her pounding, brazen heart. Only the dogs could find her in such thick woods. God, woman, she thought, but you are mad.

When she reached the river, she traveled downstream along the near bank. Her gloved hands grappling with the brush, she moved like a yeti through the wilderness. Then before her the river swung away, spread out and flattened over a bed of stone and gravel.

She was not twenty minutes outside the fence. Were they to discover her missing and sound the alarm, she was sure to be caught. No way to traverse these hinterlands and get away with man and hound tracking her. She slid down the embankment and plodded into the freezing cold river. When she reached the middle, she stood still for a moment and listened. She gazed up into the blue depths of the sky.

The water rose to her thighs, the stones beneath her feet felt slippery. Her legs were numb with the cold. Sonny turned and trod carefully for fear of twisting an ankle. She was covered with mud, her face glistened with sweat and was smeared with traces of blood where the whiplash of branches had scratched her. Her eyes stung. She felt strong, tireless. Her mind was alive with the task at hand. Cross the river. Get to the other side. Make good this escape.

Against the opposite bank of the river, big gray and green boulders gave way to more woods. Sonny climbed over the rocks and pulled herself up the steep bank until she reached the floor of a pine forest. Her map, memorized, guided her along the east bank of the river through thinner pine woods continuing downstream until she came to marshland. Here she had to stop and turn deeper into the woods away from the river. Skirting the edge of a swamp with its thick growth of low, slender alder, she came at last to the old logging road.

For the first time since she left the the prison, she checked her watch. Six fifty-two. She'd been outside the compound for fifty minutes. She was right on schedule.

There would be no more need for the gloves. She took them off and tucked them under the waistband of her shorts, leaving no trace behind for the sniffing monsters. Smooth sailing from here, old girl, she told herself. Sonny was in orbit, circling around Scarface Mountain, as the locals called her favorite peak with its granite-sided summit protruding like a man's profile from the woodlands southeast of the compound.

Nothing for her to do now but walk, stroll along this narrow

overgrown path until—what? Well, Sonia, you crazy person, fine fix
you've got yourself into now. What if these characters don't show?
What if they got drunk and stoned last night and overslept? If they
catch me now, they'll give me another five years and lock me away
somewhere far from the light of day.

Sonny walked on, feeling at once foolish and fearless.

The logging road, she knew, led to a gravel seasonal two-lane road
that was the first vestige of encroaching civilization on the vast federal
lands reservation. Hillbillies and their dogs traveled in pickup trucks
along this road, infrequently, true, but nonetheless, alarm or not, if
they were to see a woman covered in mud and sweat sauntering along
this way they would stop and chase her, loose their hounds; they would
know she could only be an escapee from the woman's penitentiary.

What it comes down to is this, she told herself matter-of-factly,
either I meet with Arthur's people before I reach the gravel state road,
or I'm fucked. It's as simple as that. Because, even if they don't
discover I'm gone until tomorrow, without a ride out of these back-
woods, there will be no further flight, no break with onerous gravity. I
will come crashing back to earth.

Chapter Twenty-one

The women's semifinal match was to be played at three o'clock Saturday afternoon. Grimm and Cassy left Malibu around eleven after a restful morning. Grimm called the L.A. office in Century City and checked the answering service, but there were no messages from anyone he thought might be Jack Moriarty. All week he had been leaving messages for Jack; the illusive fugitive was apparently incommunicado. Nor were there calls from his Brotherhood friend. It was already afternoon back East. Though Grimm had been trying not to think about the escape, he kept seeing images in his mind of Sonny running through dense forest.

When they got to U.C.L.A., Grimm took a seat at mid-court and watched Cassy as she warmed up. She was relaxed and hitting the ball with more confidence and power than she had during her previous matches. After winning the first set 6-1, she was ahead 3-love in the second set when Grimm looked up across court to see Jack standing with an attractive young blonde watching the match.

It took Grimm a moment to recognize him, Jack looked as though he had lost at least twenty pounds. All the puffy bloatedness was gone from his face, and he appeared younger and more handsome, but also drawn and tense. The woman with him had long, sun-streaked dirty blonde hair and a deep, even tan. She was a Southern California girl dressed in faded cutoff jeans and a white camisole top. They both carried motorcycle helmets.

Dressed in slacks and a polo shirt, unarmed, Grimm felt exposed.

"Looks like she's wailing the piss outta this chick," Jack said as

Grimm walked over to them. He gave him one of his thin-lipped smiles.

"You look great," Grimm told him as they shook hands.

Jack slapped his hands on his shrunken midriff. "Twenny-five pounds I dropped, bo. Gave up eatin' red meat. Quit the hard booze. All I do now is eat vegetables and drink wine. An' I been workin' out. Hey, lissen. Meet Val. Val, I want you to meet a good friend of mine. This is Arthur, A.G., we call him. That's his girlfriend out there givin' that other kid a tennis lesson."

"Hi," Val said and smiled as she gave him her hand. She was wearing a Lady's Gold Rolex, several jade bracelets, and diamond stud earrings. Though she was young, no more than Cassy's age, there was a self-assured poise in the way she carried herself. When she took out a pack of Dunhill cigarettes and lit one with a gold and malachite lighter, Grimm knew she was in the business.

They were all watching the match. Cassy closed out the set 6-love. She shook hands with her opponent and glanced around looking for Grimm.

"You remember Jack?" Grimm asked as he hugged Cassy and congratulated her.

"Jack. Wait a sec. You mean, from Saul's way back when? Sure. Man, you lost weight. You look fantastic."

Jack beamed. "Thanks. You play great tennis."

"And this is Jack's friend, Val," Grimm said.

"Hi, Val. Cassy Steiger."

Cassy excused herself and went off to shower and change. Grimm and Jack left Val at courtside watching a men's match while they walked over to the parking lot so Jack could show Grimm his motorcycle.

"I'm not even going to ask you how you knew I was here," Grimm said.

"Bo, you'd be surprised."

"You had me followed."

"Wrong. Not me. King Farouk."

Jack leaned on the seat of the motorcycle. He took off his sunglasses and looked at Grimm with his pale eyes. His thin lips were drawn back over his expensive dental work. His face thinner, the cleft in his chin seemed more pronounced. "Surprised?" he asked.

"Not really. I knew he was up to something."

"Yeah, right. What did that fat fuck say to you, anyway?"

"He says he wants a meet. He told me to tell you he wants peace."

Jack laughed. He ran his hand through his thick, silvery hair. "He's got a lot 'a balls, I'll say that much for him. Peace? That lyin' bastard. So why's he tryin' to set me up to clip me? Did he tell you that?"

"No. He's trying to do some big coke scam. He's been bugging me all week to contact you."

"He's tryin' to use you to flush me out. You meet a guy with him, tall dude with a tan?"

"Wears a Hawaiian shirt?"

"I don't know what he wears, it's what he packs. This guy does work. He's outta Florida. Supposed to be one 'a the best in the business. Saul wants to use you to draw me out so this guy can clip me." Jack gazed at Grimm. "Nice guy, huh? Your buddy, Saul."

"You're sure?"

"C'mon, A.G. You know me a long time. You know how I operate."

Yes, Grimm thought, I believe I do. Jack was a master at cultivating spies. Sometimes he was so deft that even the spy was unaware who was manipulating him.

Jack sighed. "You wanna know somethin', A.G.? I'm so sick 'a guys tryin' to make a sucker outta me. Why can't people just do what they say they're gonna do? You know, if I had twenny loyal guys I could take over this whole fuckin' country. Nobody could stop me. But who can find guys like this? The women are better. If I had twenny guys with the guts of Sonny, or this kid Val, forget about it. It's like, with the men their fuckin' egos always gotta get in the way."

"And with the women, it's their hearts," Grimm said.

The women, Cassy and Val, were walking toward them, talking and laughing.

"Check this out," Jack said, nodding his head at them, "bosom buddies already. Now that's what's happenin', A.G. That's what it's all about, those two right there. Younger women, faster motorcycles, and bigger crocodiles, right, bo? But see, with guys like you an' me, the crocodiles don't come big enough."

They made plans to meet for dinner that evening in Bel Air at a restaurant Val suggested. Jack said he had something important to discuss with Grimm.

At dinner, Jack was entertaining, full of wine and good cheer, lavishing attention on Val and Cassy.

"See," Jack said during a conversation about tennis, "where I grew up kids played stickball. I never tried tennis 'til a month ago. Val made me play. But I'm the kind 'a guy that really gets into whatever I'm doin'."

"What he means is that he's a fanatic," Val said.

"Okay, a fanatic. Tennis, fishin', whatever, I go all out. Even smugglin'. Does that sound nuts?"

"When you figure how much time they're going to give you for it, yes," Grimm said.

Jack laughed and his eyes twinkled. "First they gotta catch me."

"If you don't catch yourself," Val put in. She looked at Grimm. "I been tryin' to tell him, but he won't listen to me. It's time to split. Everybody who stays in the U.S. goes to jail."

"Where'm I gonna go? Where's safe? Listen, when these people're after you, one place is as safe as another. It's all in how you make your moves."

"With the money you got, you could buy a whole country," Val said. She was flushed from the wine and the excitement. "Be real, Jack. You're just too plugged in to leave."

If there had been any doubts in Grimm's mind as to what Val did with her time, they were dispelled during the course of the evening. Twice while they ate, she was called to the phone, and twice more she looked at her watch, took out a purse bulging with quarters, excused herself and went to the pay phone. Not only is she in the business, he thought, but there's a big load of something in town and she's moving it. For Jack, this was standard operating procedure. He probably brought the load in, deposited it with Val and her people, then shacked up with her while the goods were converted into money. Grimm suspected the product was coke.

Jack was so different without his New York gangster friends around, Grimm almost liked him again. He was witty, attentive and laid back. He and Val invited Grimm and Cassy back to their hotel, but they refused because Cassy had to get to bed early and rest up for the finals.

"We'll be there," Jack said. "My money's on you."

Outside in the parking lot Jack took hold of Grimm's arm and led him aside. Cassy and Val were standing next to Val's Mercedes making plans to get together.

"A.G., I got a proposition for you," Jack said, his arm around Grimm's shoulders. "This is guaranteed to blow your mind."

Jack squeezed Grimm's shoulders and looked at him with his eyes shining. "I never told nobody about this, A.G. Not even Sonny. Guy Stash don't even know. But I'm gonna bring you in 'cause you the only guy I know I can trust on this whole goddamn planet."

His lips seemed to disappear as his mouth tightened and his manner became all New York tough guy again. "What I got is a 24-carat gold contact inside the U.S. Attorney's Office."

Grimm was shocked. Jack's eyes were gleaming and his face had lit up.

"You heard me," he went on. "And I ain't talkin' about no lightweight secretary or clerk. We're talking' a bona fide fuckin' prosecutor! An Assistant U.S. Attorney. I own the sucker. Him an' his girlfriend, who also works in the office. Stone cold coke freaks."

Jack grinned and laughed out loud. He looked over at Val and Cassy, but they were absorbed in their own conversation. "Are you holdin' on to your balls?" Jack asked.

"You never cease to amaze me," was all Grimm could think to say.

"The information I get from this source is so solid, A.G., that's how come I been able to keep from gettin' pinched all this time. Twenny-five grand a month it cost me, plus bonuses and coke. Here's my problem. I'm too hot. I can't meet with this person no more. I want you to act as my go between. You're perfect. Semi-legit." Jack grinned. "I'll pay you the same I give them. That's like 300 grand a year. All you gotta do is meet with the guy, say once a month, then relay the information to me."

Grimm knew he should say no, should refuse to listen to another word. Getting mixed up with such a highly placed traitor, especially a cocaine addict, could only mean serious trouble down the road. It was exactly the sort of thing he had promised himself that he would eliminate from his life.

But it was so tempting, and the money was right. To a man in Grimm's line of work, such a contact was priceless.

"It could backfire," Grimm said, imagining the unknown contact weeping his tale of addiction and corruption before a grand jury. "They call it obstruction of justice."

"Sure, I know," Jack agreed. "This ain't no walk in the park. Why do you think I'm willin' to pay you that kind'a dough? I need some-body who ain't gonna fuck this up."

"Let me think about it," Grimm said, looking over at Cassy.

Grimm swore he would discuss it with no one. He told Jack he would sleep on it and let him know at the tennis match next day.

All night he could think of little less. Cassy could see he was preoccupied and she asked him what was wrong. But Grimm couldn't tell her. He saw it as a choice between the life he imagined he could live with her and the possibility of winding up with a bullet in his head or in prison or disbarred, all he had ever worked for lost. There was nothing new about any of these possibilities. Such were the risks he lived with.

On the other hand, if he took the assignment, he would gain an unheard of advantage. It would be like trading on Wall Street with the best insider information. It was wicked, but he could find no taboo in his personal set of values that precluded him from making use of spies, counterspies, moles or informants. That was simply good tradecraft. The government couldn't make a case without their rats. Why shouldn't he have at least one?

Lying in bed early the ncxt morning in Max's house in Malibu, Grimm listened to the surf while Cassy lay sleeping, clinging to his side. He still had not made up his mind. His thoughts turned to Sonny. Was she free?

That question seemed to make all the difference.

Just as the finals were about to begin, Max Steiger arrived at the U.C.L.A. tennis courts in his converted Greyhound bus, his latest consort and an entourage in tow. Max's new girlfriend, the actress Diana DeBurgh, was a raven-haired beauty of twenty-four. Grimm noticed Max stiffen when he recognized Jack.

"So, where's the champ?" Max wanted to know.

Grimm pointed to the practice courts. "She's warming up."

"Let's go over and wish her luck," Max said, taking Grimm by the arm.

"You mind tellin' me what Jack's doin' here?" Max demanded as they walked toward the court where Cassy was hitting volleys with a teammate. The tone of Max's voice was sharp with disapproval.

"He's a tennis fan," Grimm said.

"He's also on the FBI's Ten Most-Wanted list. Wasn't it you who told me I don't need that kind of heat?"

Grimm stopped walking and looked at him. "This is a public place,

Max. It's not the same as having him in your home," he said, though he knew Max was right.

The rock star knit his brow and frowned. It was an expression he and Cassy shared. "I don't like it. I don't want him around . . ." He trailed off, looking at his sister.

"Why? What's wrong with Jack all of a sudden?"

Max turned his eyes back on Grimm. "I need to tell you, after what happened to Rickie?"

"You think Jack had something to do with that?"

"A.G., where is your head at? This is what happens when you get mixed up with people like Jack and Guy Stash. These are gangsters, they're in the goddamn junk business."

"True. What about Saul? What business is he in?"

"I warned you about Saul almost a year ago, when the bust first came down. I won't have anything to do with him anymore. Everything he touches turns to shit. He fucked over Rickie, he fucked over Suzi. I hear he fucked Sonny, and he tried to fuck Jack and Guy Stash." Max took hold of Grimm's arm again and continued walking.

"You know where I'm coming from, A.G. I've had it with these people, and I don't want them around my sister. What did we always say, back in the old days? Remember? Coke, junk, that shit brings nothing but negativity. It's bad karma. People die. Why do I need to tell you this when you're the one who showed it to me?"

They stood on the edge of the practice court watching Cassy warm up.

"Hey, Red. Ready to kick some ass?" Max called to his sister. She looked over, grinned, and came trotting up to them.

"Hiya, bro," she said and they hugged.

"How do you feel?" Max asked.

"Great," she said, slipping her arm around Grimm's hips. "My big guy's here. And now you. You know I'm stoked."

It was a close match, but Cassy was never really in trouble. She managed to dominate most points and won the match in straight sets, 6-4, 7-5, beating a senior from Stanford to retain her PAC title. Watching her play, Grimm fell in love with her all over again. She was a beautiful athlete. Never had he felt so divided. He was in love with Cassy—and yet, another part of him was miles away, in flight, with Sonny.

"Party time!" Max announced after the match when they were all standing with Cassy congratulating her on the victory. Someone went to the motorhome and broke out bottles of champagne. Cassy drank from her trophy cup. While she went off to change, the celebrations continued in the parking lot. Max invited everyone to the house in Malibu to continue the festivities.

Jack said he and Val wouldn't be able to make it as they were booked on a flight leaving LAX that evening. "I'm gonna see you later, right, A.G.?" he asked Grimm, as they parted at the tennis courts. He told Grimm to stop by his bungalow at the Chateau Marmont in Hollywood around seven. "So I can give you that thing—the address." Then he and Val mounted the motorcycle and rode away.

Grimm drove the rental car from Malibu into Hollywood. He went alone. Cassy was upset with him for leaving in the middle of her party. Though Grimm had not agreed to take the assignment as go-between for Jack and his Justice Department contact, somehow they both understood he would. When it came to his dealings with Jack, Grimm had always been aware of a subtle lack of will on his part. Unless Grimm actively tried to resist the man's influence, Jack held sway as if by unstated agreement. It was Jack's cunning, his skill at duplicity that daunted Grimm.

"Hi. C'mon in," Val said, as she opened the door to the bungalow. The air in the room smelled of killer weed.

She sat on the edge of the king-size bed. "Jack'll be with you in a sec. He's takin' a shower." Val retrieved a half-smoked joint from the ashtray. She wore a simple yellow and white summer dress and yellow pumps. She looked more like a well dressed young co-ed than a drug dealer. There were several suitcases near the door.

"I really like Cassy," Val said as she exhaled the pungent smoke and handed him the joint. "I hope the four of us can get together sometime. Maybe go on a trip," she drawled. "I really think this guy should get outta Dodge and stay out." She jerked her thumb toward the bathroom. The hissing sounds of a shower stopped.

Just then the phone rang. Val continued to stare at Grimm for a few seconds, then she picked up the receiver.

"Oh, hi, Adrianna," she said into the phone. She was still looking at Grimm. "Huh, hon? Oh, no, we been out all day. Yeah, but he's in the bathroom. We're leavin' in around fifteen minutes. He told me to tell you we'll meet you at Hector's plane. Sure, hon. I'll tell him.''

As Val hung up, Jack came out of the bathroom. He was dressed only in a pair of bikini briefs.

"That was Adrianna," Val told him. "She wants you to call her."

Jack's eyes met Grimm's.

"Doesn't he look good?" Val said, snapping the elastic waistband in Jack's underpants. "Now all he's gotta do is tighten this up." She ran her small, tan hands around his midsection.

"Lissen, baby. Gimme about five minutes with A.G. Run down to the front desk and check us outta this joint."

"Wild kid," Jack said after she'd left the room. "Smokes pot like you do." He began pulling on clothes as they talked.

"You're gonna do this for me, right, bo?"

"What's going to happen to Saul?"

"You picked up on that." Jack reached for his trousers. "Never mind Saul. Saul, Guy, how I handle the people in my organization who try to fuck me, that's nothin' to do with nobody but me."

"Meanwhile, Guy's still walking around."

Jack zipped up his pants and looked at him. "A.G., I don't need to tell you, there's politics involved here. Guy's got this." Jack made a small circle with his thumb and forefinger and held it to his chest to signify a badge. "He's got a whole crew to contend with. But don't worry, I know he tried to take me out. I know he was workin' with Zuluaga. I know all about Guy Stash. And I'll handle it. When the timing's right, when he least expects it, and when it'll hurt him most, that's when I'll do Guy." He stabbed himself in the chest with his finger. "Me. I'll do Mr. Stash myself. I made him, and I'll destroy him."

"But why Saul, Jack? He's a mess. He—"

"Why Saul?" Jack sighed. He sat down and began putting on his shoes. "This whole fuckin' thing's Saul's fault. All of it. If he hadn't tried to cheat me, none 'a this would'a happened. I had everything under control. I knew Karl was no good. I knew Karl and Guy were workin' with Zuluaga. Bo, you understand, I'm gettin' my information from *them*. From the government, for christsake."

That there had been a conspiracy between the DEA Group Supervisor, Julio Zuluaga, and Jack's right-hand man, Guy Stash, was an idea that had been taking form in Grimm's mind since early in the case, and he had strong suspicions at least as far back as the East Harlem sit-down. He could think of no other explanation for the lapse in surveillance on Karl Lundgren the day he was murdered. Zuluaga may have been a corrupt cop, but he was too smart and too good at what he did to allow a fish as big as Guy Stash to slip through his hands unless there was some complicity between them which promised an even bigger catch.

Guy Stash had shopped his boss to the DEA. The plan was for Stash and Zuluaga to carve up the six-and-a-half million. Zuluaga would present Jack, and no doubt Saul as well, to the U.S. Attorney's Office, leaving Guy to fill the slot as New York's junk overlord.

Grimm confirmed his notions of the alliance during the trial through Aaron Held's cross-examination of Donnie Randazzo. From the outset the investigator had been troubled by the fact that an old hand like Sonny got caught holding all that hard evidence, the money and drugs Randazzo gave her. She had been set up by someone who knew the bust was about to go down. When Randazzo's ex-partner, Funzi, tacitly verified Guy Stash's control over Donnie Boy, Grimm again saw the hidden hand of Zuluaga at work. Zuluaga and Guy expected the discovery of money and drugs in Sonny's possession to divert attention while they made off with the fortune needed to pay the San Francisco smugglers so they could have the rest of the goods released. Guy—and Zuluaga—would then own Jack's trip.

But Grimm was also aware the plan had failed. Someone beat Guy Stash and Zuluaga to the money. The great New York heroin coup had backfired. Zuluaga was so embarrassed when he lost the six-and-a-half million, he had to steal seventy thousand back from Sonny just to pay his men off.

"You still don't wanna believe Saul stole that money, huh, bo?" Jack said, looking at him as he tied his shoes.

Grimm shook his head. "No, I don't believe it."

"So lemme ask you this. Who whacked Karl?"

"Gene Machine."

Jack stood up. "Right. An' we both know who Gene Machine works for."

"Well," Grimm said, "we think we do."

Jack raised his eyebrows and gazed at Grimm. He smiled and nodded his head. "You're pretty smart, A.G." He put his hand on

Grimm's shoulder and squeezed. "But listen to me, bo. Saul's history.
You met Adrianna? Saul owes Adrianna's old man a million-and-
a-half from the last trip. Saul uses other people's money like it's his
own. For years he's been robbin' from Rickie, from Sonny, from me,
from whoever he does business with. So maybe he didn't get that
money. Maybe there was no money. Maybe the whole thing was a
trap." Jack grinned. "Hey, maybe Sonny pulled a fast one on everybody. She's cute. She's the one person I know who could'a pulled off
somethin' like that. If she did"—he shrugged—"good luck to her.
Too bad she won't be on the street to enjoy it." Jack laughed bitterly.
"She'll have a hell of a time tryin' to spend six mil at the prison
commissary." He laughed so hard his face turned red and he started to
cough. "By the time she gets out, she'll be so old, she won't have time
to spend it."

When he stopped laughing, Jack walked over to one of the suitcases,
took out an elaborate, hand-tooled leather folder and gave it to Grimm.

"Anyway, whatever, no one can help Saul now. Saul, Guy, they're
dead men. That's the way it goes in this business. You fuck up, you
die. And don't worry about Zuluaga, either. Don't worry about any of
it. Let me worry. You just hold on to this folder. This is the key. Val
will be in touch. All my messages will come through her. She'll tell
you where she wants to meet you and when. You go there with this
folder. When my man sees this folder, he'll know you're his contact."

"What do I do with the information he gives me?" Grimm asked.

Jack pointed to his head. "It goes up here, bo. In your noodle. Then
you relay it to me through Val. She'll handle all payments. Sometimes
I might send you questions to ask this guy. But never nothin' in
writing."

"What about questions of my own?"

Jack's thin lips eased back in a smile. "I knew you were gonna ask
me that. Okay, listen. Just clear the info with me first. And don't tell
nobody nothin'. Not even Held. This is just between you, me and the
guy." He laughed. "Bo, I wish I could be there to see the look on your
face when you find out who this guy is."

"Wait a minute, I know this person?"

Jack shrugged. "What, you don't know all them prosecutors?"

"Who is it, Jack? Before we go any further, I want to know."

"Guess," Jack said. "I'll bet you five grand you can't guess."

"Give me a hint."

"No hints."

"I'm not doing it unless I know who it is."

"Okay." Jack reached for the folder, but Grimm held it back.

"See how well I know you, bo," Jack said, laughing. "You know, you got it as bad as I do, pal. You're wired to this life. It's worse than any drug."

Jack opened the door to the bungalow and they stepped out together. Val was leaning against her car smoking a cigarette and talking to a bellboy.

"I'm outta here, bo," Jack said. "I gotta make a quick call, then we're gone. Give my best to Cassy. You'll be hearin' from Val."

Grimm walked off to the rental car, waving to Val as he left.

Driving from the hotel, off into the hazy-neon-tinged dusk of Hollywood, Grimm began to feel sick and panicky. He broke into a sweat. He couldn't get Saul out of his mind. What am I going to do? he kept asking himself. Just go back to the party at Max's knowing a man I consider a friend is about to walk into a trap and die?

He thought of Saul, he remembered the picture of him on the wall in his office at Dune Castle: Saul dressed as Santa Claus and surrounded by orphans. Part of him believed Jack was right. Saul deserved to die. He keeps ruining other people's lives. And yet, Grimm had always liked Saul in an odd way. He was such a puzzle: generous, and a cheat; a man who had worked hard all his life, hustled, driven himself to get where he was, and at the same time subverting everything he did. But if Saul's life was worthless, what value did any life have, even his own? The question that troubled Grimm most was whether he really cared one way or another about Saul, about his life.

Soon, Grimm found himself riding the streets of Beverly Hills. He saw the famous pink hotel nestled amid the palm trees on the hill. Part of him insisted there was value to Saul's life, to all life. Grimm decided to save the man's life, for whatever it was worth. He would take it up with Jack later.

Saul, though, was not there. No one was in either of the adjoining bungalows his party occupied. The man at the front desk said he had not checked out. Grimm stood in the porte-cochere and handed the parking attendant a fifty dollar bill. Saul, he was told, left in a limousine an hour earlier. Alone? No, with a tall, thin man and an attractive dark-skinned lady.

Grimm went to a pay phone and called Judy Roth in New York.

"What's wrong, Arthur?" Judy asked.

"I can't find Saul."

"He's at the hotel. I just spoke with him a couple of hours ago."

"No, he's not. I'm at the hotel."

"He probably went out to dinner." Judy was silent a moment. "Is everything all right?"

"I don't think so," Grimm said.

"Arthur, he sounded so strange, strained. And he told me how much he loves me, and how he loves his mother. He said if anything happens to him, I should be sure to take care of Fanny and his sisters. He's never talked to me like that before. It was so weird."

There was nothing more Grimm could do. He got back in his car and drove to Max's in Malibu.

Early Monday morning, Grimm and Cassy went to his offices in Century City. Cassy was miffed because he missed most of her party. She was tired and hungover and couldn't understand why he was dragging her around at such an hour.

Grimm put the leather, hand-tooled folder Jack had given him in his safe. As the secretaries and law partners began arriving, he introduced Cassy. They sat in the office drinking coffee and gazed out the large windows at the smog shrouded hills surrounding the valley.

At nine forty-five West Coast time, Grimm's call came through.

"Hey, guy," said the man on the other end. "We delivered that package. Your friend says thanks."

"Thank you," Grimm said.

"Bro, it's our pleasure."

Chapter Twenty-two

Sonny's escape had been front page news from the moment it was revealed she had fled. Prison officials reported they found a dummy in her bed, complete with cuttings of her hair glued to a head of papier-maché. They characterized the escape as "well planned and well executed," and they speculated that she must have had outside help in getting free from the isolated facility. Standing on a street corner in Los Angeles, Grimm had experienced a sense of déjà vu when he picked up a copy of the *Los Angeles Times* and saw Sonny's big, melancholy doe eyes staring at him from the front page.

N.Y. HEROIN QUEEN ESCAPES

read the caption under her photo. Long may she run, Grimm thought.

Then this news was upstaged by the reported disappearance of Saul Diamond, the four hundred pound rock 'n' roll impresario who vanished from his Beverly Hills hotel suite while on a business trip to Los Angeles. The connection between Sonny, Saul and Rickie was rehashed. Police said they were investigating the possibility that Sonny's escape and Saul's disappearance were somehow related. Rickie Rude, the media reminded the world, was still neither dead nor alive, existing in a kind of technological afterlife due to the legal battle over his custody.

In New York, soon after his return from California, Grimm was visited by deputies from the U.S. Marshal's Service, the agency with jurisdiction over fugitives and escapees from federal custody. They wanted to question Grimm about contact he'd had with his client after she was moved to the women's penitentiary in West Virginia. It was curious, one of the deputies remarked. that Grimm had been responsible for obtaining the court order from Judge Gass directing that Sonny be removed from maximum security and allowed into general population.

"Not curious at all," Grimm said. "I'm her lawyer."

Then there were inquiries from the FBI and Los Angeles detectives looking into the disappearance and suspected homicide of Saul Diamond. The detectives knew Grimm had been to the hotel asking for Saul the night he disappeared. Two weeks later, Saul's semi-nude, badly decomposed body was found by rangers in a canyon at a national forest sixty-five miles north of Los Angeles. The coroner's report said there were signs that a fierce struggle had taken place. Death resulted from multiple gunshot wounds in the head. When questioned, Grimm had a difficult time accounting for the two hours he'd spent at the Chateau Marmont with Val and Jack and riding around looking for Saul.

To make matters worse, the police visited Max and Cassy Steiger and grilled them about Grimm's comings and goings from the Malibu victory party. Grimm's friendship with the Steigers was further strained. It seemed everyone suspected that he was involved in the murder of Saul, and he couldn't even convince himself that he was not. A sense of guilt permeated his relations.

He worked on new cases, he spent weekends at the farm in Millbrook, but it was as though he were living by rote. He had the sense he was biding his time until something catastrophic happened. Even his friend, Bernie Wolfshein, seemed leery of being seen in public with Grimm.

"You're a hot item, pal," Wolfshein told him one afternoon when they met in Central Park not far from the brownstone owned by Rickie Rude. "I don't know how you guys do it, but you and Held always manage to land in the thick of things. Held comes out smelling like a rose. You, well, let's just say you come out smelling."

"What's going to happen with Rickie? Can't you do something, Wolf? Suzi, the poor kid, she wants it to end. She wants to bury him."

"Believe me, I'm doing everything I can. It's up to Vallone, and no one tells him what to do. They have a lot of time and money invested.

Certain individuals were hoping for big brownie points. Everyone wanted in on the act, and you know how that goes. The level of professionalism has been badly compromised.''

"It was a dishonest prosecution. They should have just dropped it.''

Wolfshein sighed and pushed his glasses back up his nose. "Politics, pal.''

"Shoddy justice, Wolf.''

"Look, you help me find Moriarty, I'm sure we can do something.''

"I don't believe you said that. You mean we're reduced to bargaining over a vegetable?''

Wolfshein shrugged. "Arthur, be careful,'' the agent said. "I worry about you.'' He turned and walked away.

That same evening, jarring Grimm's sense of synchronicity, he received a call on his answering service from a woman who left a message for him to call a San Francisco attorney's office. When Grimm returned the call, asking for a Ms. Michelle Grande, he was connected with Jack's friend, Val. They made plans to meet in New York.

Grimm had the hand-tooled leather folder spread conspicuously before him. He was working on *The New York Times* crossword puzzle and sipping a drink at a table in an East Side bar.

This was the signal. His contact, Jack's mole in the Justice Department, was supposed to spot the folder and make himself known. Grimm was tense with curiosity. As much as any other motive, it was his inquisitive nature that had caused him to take this assignment.

The folder proved unnecessary. Grimm was looking up at the entrance when a young man walked in the bar and stumbled as he bumped into a departing couple. Grimm's first impulse was to hide the folder and leave. But John Gorth, Vita Vaggi's former assistant, had recognized him. They looked at each other and both knew there could be only one explanation for their being in this place at this time.

The tiny island of Spanish Wells had been settled by British fishermen from Bermuda. It was the only all-white cay in the far-flung Bahamian archipelago, said the wizened old boatman who took Grimm across the channel. Nearly all the blond haired, blue eyed inhabitants were related and lived on the island like one big happy family.

Grimm was wedged into the rear of the small dory in a flimsy plywood superstructure that made the boat look like a top-heavy child's toy. As Spanish Wells had no airport, Grimm had flown into neighboring North Eleuthera from Pompano, Florida on an unscheduled, undocumented flight. He was met and escorted through Customs by two Bahamian policemen who delivered him to the quay where the old man in his mock Popeye tugboat waited.

He recognized the sandy spits of land and tufts of stunted palm trees as the backdrop in government surveillance photos he'd been shown of Jack and Sonny. So he could assume the heat knew about this hideaway. But, as Val had put it at their last meeting in New York when she gave him instructions on how to get here, it was cool because Jack had everyone from the top down to the local constabulary in his pocket.

Val was waiting for Grimm on the wharf when the motorboat docked. She sat on the fender of a small English station wagon. She wore dark glasses with white plastic frames and had a cigarette stuck in the middle of her mouth.

"Hi, A.G." Val waved and giggled as he shouldered his way out of the boat. "Isn't that the goofiest lookin' thing you ever saw? You look like Bluto sittin' in there."

Grimm and Val had decided they liked each other. They were both apprehensive about the alliance they had joined in Jack's service, and they had taken to giving each other small, reassuring hugs whenever they met or parted.

They loaded Grimm's bags into the rear of the station wagon.

"I was hopin' you might'a brought Cassy," Val said as she started the engine and pulled away from the dock. "What goes on with you two, anyway?" she asked when Grimm made no reply.

"We've pretty much decided to part company," Grimm answered indifferently.

Val let it drop. She took him on a tour of the island, up the low bluff above the channel to North Eleuthera, along the sloping groves of cay lime, grapefruit, coconut palm and banana trees, through the narrow, one-way streets and past the neat, clean shops and houses of the town. She looked like one of the natives, her hair was even lighter and her skin looked as tan and creamy as a model's in a Caribbean holiday advertisement. She wore a white skirt hiked up to the tops of her thighs, sandals, and a loose peasant blouse. Her lips and fingernails were painted Chinese red. In her hip Southern California jargon, she prattled on about life on the lam with America's most-wanted drug outlaw.

"He's not doin' too good," Val told Grimm.

"Why, what's wrong?"

"You'll see. He's drinkin' a lot, an' he's sick. He's been on a bad one ever since he found out Sonny escaped from prison."

They arrived back at the opposite end of the deep water canal from where Grimm had landed. Val parked alongside a concrete jetty and boathouse. She produced a joint from her cigarette pack and lit it with the malachite lighter.

"He acts like he's worried about her bringin' him more heat," Val said, exhaling and handing the joint to Grimm. "I don't believe it."

"Sonny's not about to come running to him."

"Right. Anyway, there's no such thing as more heat than he's already got."

Val got out of the car. "Grab your stuff," she said. "Our ride'll be here any minute."

Grimm took his suitcases and followed her onto the dock. She kicked off her sandals, sat down and dangled her feet in the water.

"Grimm," she said, taking off her glasses and looking up at him, "you're weird."

"What makes you say that?"

"Cassy's a good kid."

"I know she is."

He remained standing, basking his jaded senses in the beauty of the surroundings. The water in the canal was so clear it was white along the shore and transparent down to the bright aqua depths. Palm fronds rustled in the afternoon trade winds. The light sparkled on the water and glittered off Val's gold watch as she reached for the joint.

"A gal's gotta know where she stands," she said.

Grimm gazed into her bloodshot eyes. "Val, what would you say if I told you Cassy thinks I murdered Saul Diamond? She thinks I just got up and left her party, went out and killed a man who was a friend, then went back and made love to her like it was all in a day's work. I don't know how to get her to believe that's not what happened."

Val flushed. Her tan face mottled. "No. She doesn't think that. I talked to her since then."

"What did she say?"

"She's confused. You never tell her anything."

"C'mon. What am I going to tell her?"

"Yeah, I know. I have the same trouble. It's hard to relate to someone who's not in the biz. So, retire. You're already rich, right?"

"Sounds like a good idea." Grimm smiled at her. "I'll tell you what, we'll both retire. Right after we finish whatever it is we're doing."

A cigarette boat picked them up and took them to Jack's private island. It was a hilly, slender isle with a natural harbor known as Royal Cay. Two blond brothers from Spanish Wells piloted the speedboat.

Grimm was shocked when he saw Jack. It had been close to four months since their last meeting in California, and Jack looked as though he had been on a continuous binge. His face was bloated and colored high pink. He was so drunk when Grimm arrived it was hopeless to think of getting down to any sort of business. The brothers explained they had been out fishing all day and Jack had succumbed to the effects of white rum in the hot sun.

Val flicked her eyebrows. "This is every day," she said as she showed Grimm to his room.

The house was a one-story villa overgrown with brightly colored flowering shrubs. The walls were made of rustic stone and stucco. Woven reed carpets were scattered on the red tile floors. The house stood at the edge of the beach with nothing but dazzling white sands and arching palm trees between the grounds and the horizon. It was the only home on the island.

"What a beautiful place," Grimm said as he looked out from the guest room.

"Paradise," Val said. "It's every scammer's dream come true. Hungry?"

"I must admit, I could eat," Grimm said.

"Good. Me too. I'm gonna try to get"—she nodded her head in the direction of the patio where Jack drank and fumed beside the pool—"to eat something. Maybe it'll sober him up." She pursed her red lips and squinted.

"What can I tell ya', A.G.? He's on a real bummer. This guy's got more money than God, but does it look like he's enjoying it? Ever since he heard about Sonny, he's been a different person. He'll be sober for a couple of hours in the morning. Then all he does is snort coke, scream at everybody and give orders until he gets shit-faced again."

Jack was one of those marauding drunks who never seem to pass out. He was like an angry god, full of wrath, spewing hate directed at no one and everyone. Grimm wasn't even sure Jack recognized him.

He refused to eat, he shoved aside the food brought to him by Val— a delicious raw conch salad, fried grouper fingers and french fries. Grimm ate Jack's serving as well as his own. Jack glared at him and at Val while he drank what he didn't spill of glasses of white rum over ice and a wedge of lime. Later, he was up reeling around looking for hidden microphones and prowling government agents. His mood vacillated between extreme paranoia and despair. Grimm could see that Jack was lost in the frantic maze of cocaine and alcohol psychosis.

About the only sense Grimm could make from Jack's ranting was that he felt both betrayed and threatened by Sonny's escape. He imagined she had been aided by federal authorities who were in collusion with her in a plot to trap him. Then the scenario would shift and he imagined himself pursued by Guy Stash and Mafia bosses who coveted his wealth and power and sought to avenge the theft of the six-and-a-half million. Val assured Grimm these fears were hallucinations. She said there had been no word from Sonny since the escape, nor were there any threats or rumors of underworld vendettas. Still, Jack had little else on his mind from the moment he learned Sonny was free.

"I think he's still in love with her," Val said.

A segment of the long evening ended abruptly when Jack fell off his chair and they saw he had been sitting in a puddle of blood. Dark blood soaked the seat of his bathing suit and ran down the backs of his legs.

"Piles," Val said. "His 'rhoids are in an uproar."

The sight of his own blood seemed to sober him up. Jack allowed himself to be led off to his bedroom by one of the brothers with Val in attendance.

"He's a mess," Val said when she rejoined Grimm. "I been tryin' to get him to see a doctor in Miami, but he's a stubborn bastard."

It was an endless night, and one Grimm would never forget. He had come at Jack's insistence, to discuss the latest intelligence acquired from Assistant U.S. Attorney John Gorth, and also to be instructed as to information Jack wanted from the mole. Ever since Grimm had let himself be lured into this unholy allegiance he had felt unclean and exposed to insidious danger. Now he was repelled. He felt like a jackal hanging around to feed off the carrion of corrupt lives.

Grimm went to him later, toward dawn. Jack lay on his stomach on a rattan day bed on the patio near the swimming pool. He was still drinking, but he had reached a state beyond drunkenness; he was lucid, though stewing in bile. His rear end was swaddled in a towel like a baby in diapers.

Sick as he obviously was, and would later admit, all his thoughts were of Sonny.

"She robbed that six million from me, A.G. Plus who knows how much more. I'm gonna kill her if it's the last thing I do."

"You didn't seem to mind as long as she was in prison," Grimm said. "What's bothering you? Is your pride hurt?"

Jack glared at him with his faded blue eyes. There was no sparkle left in them; they glowered with smoldering hate. "You helped her escape, didn't you? You put it together."

"I had nothing to do with it," Grimm lied. His voice sounded true but he could feel his mouth betraying him.

"You lyin' cocksucker," Jack snarled with his bloodless lips. "Tell me where she is or I'll kill you, too."

They were alone on the patio. Everyone else was asleep in other parts of the house. Jack had ordered Val to her own bedroom. He said he couldn't stand to look at her after she had ministered to his hemorrhoids. Grimm, himself a little drunk, tired and full of self-loathing, snapped. He had an instant reaction, not so much a thought as an impulse, to kill Jack.

He stood and grabbed him by the hair. He yanked Jack's head back from the pillow where it rested, and then he hit him in the mouth, backhanded, with such force Jack's lips split, his head snapped and his eyes goggled as he went sprawling from the bed to the floor.

Still in a rage, Grimm went over to where Jack lay dazed and bloodied. He intended to kill him, he felt if he stopped now Jack would never allow him to leave alive. In a flash, he saw the whole thing in his mind. He would break Jack's neck, kill him quietly in the early morning, then drag him to the boat, leave, and dump the body at sea. Grimm felt the visceral control that came over him when he knew he was about to kill. He got down on his knees beside Jack.

Jack gazed at him. "You're in love with her, aren't you?" he said. Incredibly, faced with death, he could think only of Sonny. "But you can't have her. Nobody can have her but me. You understand?"

Grimm felt the will to kill him drain away. All he was left with was pity.

"I'll find her," Jack said with his bleeding mouth as Grimm helped him back onto the bed. "I'll make her right. Nobody gets away with what she did to me."

"Leave it alone, Jack."

"No. You leave her alone, A.G. I mean it. She's my woman."

"She's not yours. She never was and she never will be."

He sneered. "She'll never be yours, either. Sonny loves nobody but Sonny. She'll give you no peace. She destroys every man who loves her."

"If you go looking for her, I'll kill you," Grimm said.

Jack laughed at him. "Fuck you," he said. "You think I give a fuck? I'm dyin' anyway. Sonny put some goddamn Irish curse on me. She made my asshole fall out." Jack cackled.

"Bring her to me," he said, staring at Grimm with a demented look. "Drag her back by the cunt hairs an' I'll give you anything you want. Just bring her to me so I can abuse her."

"You already abused her. Whatever Sonny did to you, you deserved it. You set her up."

"I never set her up!" Jack yelled. His face colored dark red with anger. "Guy Stash set her up."

"But you let it happen. That's just as bad. You knew Lundgren and Guy were working with Zuluaga, and you left Sonny out there to get busted. You did nothing to protect her."

"Goddamn it, I told you. I had it all under control. I was gonna get her outta there. It was me they wanted. They never would'a busted Sonny 'til they got me. The only reason Zuluaga went after Sonny was because they clipped Karl and stole the money. When they lost their rat, they panicked. Look, I knew what was goin' on, but I needed proof. I needed to catch Zuluaga and Guy in bed together so I could show the old men and get permission to kill Guy without bringin' on a war. I had a beautiful trap set for them. I knew every move they were makin'. But somehow Sonny got wind of what was goin' on and she moved before it was ready."

Grimm shook his head. "You threw her to the dogs. Sonny was loyal to you. As soon as you knew the kind of danger she was in, you should have done everything in your power to help her. Sonny stuck by you even after you and Saul changed the deal on her. You cheated her, and she put her reputation on the line with her people in San Francisco to save the trip. No, I see it all now, Jack. You let Sonny get busted because you couldn't have her. You knew she didn't love you. You wanted to make her suffer.''

Jack's eyes glazed over. He seemed to retreat, to call in all his anger and hatred and hunker down within himself as if expecting a long seige. Grimm felt Jack knew he was right. He had betrayed and lost the one thing he wanted most in life. Not just Sonny the woman, the physical and emotional entity, but also the strength her respect bestowed on him. He had abandoned the one person he knew he could trust.

They talked until after sunrise. Jack said it was impossible for him to sleep. "I feel like somethin' crawled up inside me and died," he said. "All them years in the penitentiary did this to me. The fear and the loneliness. The hate. You hold it all in for so long it rots your insides.''

"And you wanted that for Sonny?''

"Yes. I wanted her to go through what I did. I wanted to punish her. I wanted to see if it would break her.''

Grimm sat with him like his confessor. Jack was the most open he had ever been. A solemn feeling of warmth, even of love, grew between them and filled the mood as the sky began to pale and the new day broke over the island.

"I can't go on with this Gorth business," Grimm told him. "It's too hairy.''

"Even for you, bo?'' Jack said with a chuckle. "I never would'a believed I'd hear them words from A.G.''

"Even for me.''

"Don't worry about it,'' Jack said. "It's all over, anyway. I'm cashin' in my chips.''

"What're you going to do?''

Jack stared at him for a moment without answering. "A.G., you know where she is. You're gonna see her.''

"Jack—''

"Hear me out. Just tell her for me, she's the best. Tell her I love her. I'll always love her. Tell her I'm sorry an' I never meant to do her no harm.''

"I don't know where she is,'' Grimm told him.

Jack nodded. He propped his head on his hand to take another swig of rum. "You're a friend, A.G. You're one 'a the few people I really care about. But you're a lousy liar.''

Grimm reached out and put his hand on Jack's shoulder. He put his arm around his neck, then leaned over and hugged him. They kissed cheeks.

"You'll stay in touch, right bo? I'll have Val call."

"You old pirate," Grimm said. "I never knew whether I loved you or hated you. I still don't know."

"Good. That's the way it should be," Jack said and he pushed him away.

The blond brothers took Grimm from Royal Cay to Nassau in the speedboat. Val went along to make some calls and do some shopping.

"Ask me why I'm still here," she said to him as they parted on the quay at the Paradise Island Yacht Basin.

Grimm was looking off across the roadstead. "He hasn't told you where all the money is yet," he said and smiled at her.

Val laughed. "Creep." She wrinkled her nose at him. "I'll never tell."

"Get him to a doctor, Val."

"I been beggin' him to go to a doctor. He won't listen to me."

Grimm put his arm around her and she hugged him. "We're all done," he said. "We can retire now."

Val looked up at him with hope in her eyes. "For real?"

"Honest. No more weirdness."

Grimm got into a taxi and told the driver to take him to a hotel. Val was standing at a public phone in front of the yacht club. She looked up and waved goodbye to Grimm as the taxi drove away.

Chapter Twenty-three

From the air, the first thing that struck Grimm about the island of Jamaica was how mountainous it was. Lush green blankets like quilts of dense growth covered the heaving, undulating landscape. The mountains were shades of green slashed with red dirt roads. Compared with the Bahamas, the low sandy spits of land from which he'd just come, Jamaica was a country, a full-blown land.

He was arriving on an Air Jamaica flight from Nassau to Kingston. Before leaving the Bahamas, he had shaved off his beard, had his hair cut short, and spent a few days lounging around the beach and hotel swimming pool sunning himself. This was Grimm's first trip to Jamaica. He made it through Customs and Immigration without a hitch, then sailed out into the jelled masses of languid, black-skinned men, women and children clotted around the airport arrivals terminal.

Kingston teemed with the idle poor. The smell of the air was laced with rotting verdure and the briny odors of people sweating out an existence. The slow moving bodies and staring eyes insisted on poverty. Only the cars sped around. The road from the airport skirted a wide, drab bay empty of all but broken pilings protruding from the yellowish-brown water. The taxi driver told Grimm that the new Prime Minister was intent on improving relations with the United States, which, everyone hoped, would mean more dollars flowing to the island.

"Smiles are returning to the faces of some," he said in a lilting patois. "But we must wait to see if he is a good man, or just another robber."

Grimm checked into the Kingston Pegasus Hotel, a deluxe high rise in a verdant oasis of wide, tree-lined streets and walled-in villas that seemed to be separated by an invisible barrier from the sweltering, fetid city. The first thing he did after getting settled in his room was to go for a swim. This was beginning to feel like a vacation. He was enjoying the luxury of having no appointments to keep, no list of phone calls to make, no heaps of paperwork to wade through.

In New York, agents dogged him. His phones were tapped; he was under constant surveillance. So it was with a feeling of breaking out that he had escaped from the city and begun the circuitous trek and island-hopping hegira that brought him here. It felt good to be alone in an alien land where he could move behind a protective non-identity. He was a world away from federal courthouses, prison visiting rooms, and grand jury subpoenas.

Back in his room, he stood on the small balcony overlooking the city. Here was the land of Rastafari, a religion that regarded marijuana as sacrament. Grimm felt like a pilgrim. A smoky haze hung in the twilight, lights twinkled in the surrounding hills. The jungle city dozed.

Before dawn the next morning, there was a soft knock at the door to Grimm's hotel room.

"Luv, broder," said a tall, slim black man when Grimm opened the door. He wore a gold and green knitted tam stuffed with braids of hair. "I am Broder Norman."

There was no way anyone could follow Norman on the ground. Grimm was scared at first but soon gave up worrying; he figured that if his destiny was to get crushed to death in a speeding car with this Rasta, then so be it. With the sun coming up behind them, they drove west along the south coast of the island, then turned inland.

All of a sudden Brother Norman slowed down. They were climbing into the mountains, and the road became a narrow swath through tropical rain forest. Rastas owned big communal farms in the surrounding parish, Norman explained. He said the farms provided fruits and vegetables which were hauled into Kingston and sold to the poor at reduced prices. They could afford to sell their produce at as little as one-third the going price and still survive because their principal crop was the ganja they loaded into boats and airplanes to be shipped to the United States.

"Yeah, mon. Ganja feeds the people of Jamaica," Brother Norman said. "Without ganja, my people would starve."

Deep in the mountains, they stopped in front of a small, neat yellow house surrounded by fruit trees and plants and a white picket fence. Brother Norman got out and told Grimm to follow. He went to a tree and picked a mango for each of them. They ate the fruit as they walked along a path leading into the bush behind the house.

There was an almost unreal brilliance to the colors of the plants, the blossoms on the trees, the shrubs and wildflowers growing by the side of the path. They rounded a turning in the trail and came out on the edge of a ridge overlooking a shallow, bowl-shaped valley.

The entire hollow had been cleared and planted with marijuana. The bushy young plants stood shoulder-high and were an iridescent lime green with thick, long tops. Norman stood gazing at the plantation like a proud father. Grimm could see young girls wending their way in and out of the rows of plants as they pruned the large shade leaves and gathered them in sacks. White beehives were stacked about the field like doll houses.

The plants were fragrant in the hot sun. Norman plucked a bud from the fleshy top of a plant and crushed it in his fingers, held the bud to his nose, closed his eyes and breathed the smell.

"Jah," the Rasta droned. "Ganja, mon. Ganja is Jah's gift to monkind." He opened his eyes and gazed at Grimm, offering the crushed bud to his nose. "It's a serious t'ing. Dem crazy baldheads, dem try to kill us for a plant Jah created."

The young bud had a spicy, fruity smell like cinnamon and lemon. As they were leaving the valley, Norman turned and made a sweeping gesture.

"All for 'er, mon. When you see big boss lady, you tell 'er, Broder Norman give all St. Anne's parish ganja to white lady boss. Yeah, mon. Fill all de boats, mon. Every airplane. All de best Jamaican ganja. We 'ave tree 'undred plantation like dis one. I give all to 'er, mon. No problem."

It was late in the afternoon by the time they arrived in the western coastal village of Negril. Norman drove through the small town and up to a cluster of bungalow-style hotels, restaurants and cafés clinging to the rock cliffs above the sea. He stopped the car by the gates in front of a hotel called Xtabe. Two large rottweilers and a German shepherd bounded out and stood at the fence bellowing at them. Norman looked at Grimm, raised his forefinger and wagged it. Then a short, power-fully built white man wearing only bathing trunks came out from one of the bungalows behind the fence. He quieted the dogs before step-ping through the gate.

"Jah be with you, mon," Norman said, grinning at Grimm. "Luv, broder." And he sped away.

The white man introduced himself as Hank. He had a dark tan and a head covered with bushy gray curls. His accent was unmistakably East Coast, closer to Boston than New York. He took Grimm's bags and led him across the road and up a path to one of the small bungalows hidden among the trees and shrubs.

"You're welcome to stay here," Hank told him. "Let me know if you need anything. There's a place down the road, you can't miss it. It's a Negril landmark called Rick's Café. There's a sort of tradition around here, people go to Rick's to have a few drinks and mellow out while they watch the sunset. You should check it out. You never know who might show up."

A mixed crowd—Americans, Germans, white and black Jamaicans, tourists and islanders, Rastas and hippies—gathered at Rick's Café to watch the sun go down into the Caribbean.

Grimm arrived early and sat at the bar. He drank white rum and fruit juice and thought about the morbid connection between the name of the place and the friend he'd so recently lost. Each drink was accom-panied by a token embossed with a marijuana leaf and the words, "Rick's Café. Negril, Jamaica." What was she thinking about when she chose this place? he wondered.

Reggae music thumped in the background. The smell of ganja smoke wafted on the sea breeze. Grimm was watching the bloody sunset as it seeped along the horizon. Laughter and soft voices came from the parties seated on the terrace. He picked up his drink and was about to sip it when he looked over and saw a young girl in a bikini standing near the kitchen just inside the entrance. She was carefully studying the faces of the people in the café. Now they were looking at each other.

The little girl's mouth fell open. "Oh!" she cried and ran up to him.

Grimm came off the bar stool as she threw her arms around his neck and he swooped her off her feet.

"Arthur," she said, kissing him. "You look so different. I hardly know you."

"And you, my darling. You look different too, so tan and lovely. So healthy."

They smiled at each other and kissed again. Then she took him by the hand and led him out into the street. Grimm's stomach fluttered in anticipation. Carmen walked him to a new, black Rover sedan.

"Granny," the little girl announced as she opened the car door, "I found him—but I almost didn't. He shaved his beard and he looks very different. This is Mummy's lawyer, Granny, and my friend, Arthur Grimm."

"How do you do, Mr. Grimm?" said the woman behind the wheel. "I'm Sybil Byrne-Downes, Sonia's mother."

She had the same long, strong looking limbs and large feet and hands as her daughter. Her hair was white, her skin was clear and smooth. Grimm estimated she was in her mid-to-late sixties, still quite fit and vigorous, her gaze sharp and steady. She seemed to size him up in a glance, as if to confirm what she'd been told about him.

He sat in front with Sonny's mother. Carmen sat in back perched between the bucket seats, her arm around Grimm's neck. They collected his luggage from the bungalow, then drove out of town. Mrs. Byrne-Downes negotiated the rough, pot-holed roads with all the skill of someone used to driving in places like India and Ethiopia.

"Granny, remember I told you about the farm Arthur has in New York? That's where I wanted to work looking after the horses."

"I certainly do remember. And I believe I could tell you the names, ages and bloodlines of all the horses, as well," said Sybil Byrne-Downes, smiling at her granddaughter.

"You'll never guess what, Arthur. I've got two horses. Well, actually, one horse and one foal all my own. The mare was pregnant when Mummy got her for me. We saw her have the foal."

"That's exciting," Grimm said. "What did you name the foal?"

"Mummy named him Rasta. He has red hair."

"We weren't certain what day you'd be arriving," said Mrs. Byrne-Downes in her impeccable English. "For the past several days, we've been stopping by the café each evening."

"Oh!" Carmen exclaimed. "Mummy's going to be so happy."

"Quite honestly, I don't know who's been more excited, Sonia or Carmen. You're a very popular man, Mr. Grimm."

They drove southeast, back in the direction of Kingston, then turned due south heading for the coast. Soon they passed through a town called Savannah-La-Mar, then followed the signs toward Little London. The road became a gravel lane at the outskirts of the village. Sybil Byrne-Downes had to slow the car to get around the deep ruts and mud puddles. Outside it was pitch black. Groups of country people straggled by the roadside, their black faces worn with fatigue.

After several more turnings, the road became a single lane track through overgrown brush. Finally, they came to a tiny village built up outside a large stone wall standing out at each side of the road. A tall wood and iron gate blocked their way. Grimm noticed shards of broken glass like sharp colored teeth stuck along the top of the wall. Set into a stone column holding the gate was a brass plaque that had turned green in the sea air. Grimm was able to make out the word "Innisfree."

Two burly Jamaicans carrying shotguns came out of a building next to the wall and peered into the Rover.

"Good evening, Nevil," Mrs. Byrne-Downes said to the man nearest.

"Everyt'ing all right, mom?" he asked, looking at Grimm.

"Everything's fine, thank you."

He waved to the other man who opened slowly first one, then the other side of the gate and stepped back to let them pass. The road improved as they wound through fields, low rolling hills and a grove of coconut palms, and then came to an open expanse where a number of small buildings stood scattered around the beach beside a crescent shaped cove.

The moon had begun to rise and it was lighter outside. One of the first things Grimm noticed as his eyes took in the scene was a forty-foot sloop moored in the bay.

Gold moonlight reflected off the surface of the sea like a shimmering highway to the horizon. As the car pulled to a stop, Grimm looked away from the shore and caught a glimpse of Sonny standing in the shadows near one of the buildings. She had her arms folded, hugging herself beneath her breasts. She was leaning forward slightly with her head cocked to one side.

"Mummy. He's here," Carmen called through the window and Sonny stepped from the shadows. Grimm could feel his heart pounding.

She was smiling, her whole face lit up in the moonlight as she came toward the side of the car and looked in at him. For a moment neither of them spoke. They just looked at each other.

"You're certain it's him?" Sonny asked Carmen.

"Oh, Mummy. Of course it's him. He's shaved his beard."

But by then Grimm was out of the car and they were laughing, hugging and kissing each other.

"Is this real?" Sonny asked, looking up at him with tears in her eyes. "Pinch me. Tell me this is real."

"It's as real as anything gets," Grimm said, and once more he realized there was nothing he would not do just to be able to look into her astonishing eyes.

They put his luggage into one of the bungalows, the one that contained Sonny and Carmen's bedrooms. The compound was made up of six detached buildings huddled beside the beach. Three were what Sonny called "the cottages," with bedrooms and baths. Sonny's parents were staying in one of the cottages, and servants lived in the third. The largest building, in the middle of the others, held the dining room and adjoining kitchen. Sonny had converted one of the other buildings into a studio where she and Carmen were doing some painting. The last one was used for storage.

In the bedroom, they rolled around on the bed kissing each other.

"Welcome to Innisfree," Sonny said. "Tomorrow we'll take you on the grand tour." She touched his cheek. "I can't get over how different you look without your beard."

"This is my disguise," he said.

"You look so young. I'm not sure I like you as much without it. And the short hair—you look like a bloody cop."

"God forbid. I'll grow it back."

"Has there been a lot of heat?"

"They've been all over me."

"I'm sorry, darling. But, never mind. We're safe here. God, how I love you. How I have longed for this moment."

"And me," Grimm said. "Sometimes I thought I'd never see you again."

"Were you surprised when you got my message?"

"Just happy. Very happy."

"Mmmmmmm, I wish I could devour you right at this moment."
She kissed him on his nose, his forehead, his cheeks and eyes. "But
I'm afraid we'll have to wait until after we've had dinner. My father is
very anxious to meet you. Do you realize, my darling, tonight we will
sleep together in a real bed?"

One look at Edward Byrne-Downes and Grimm knew the man was a
drinker. He was tall, with a full head of thick, wavy, iron gray hair. He
had a long face with a fine web of broken capillaries netted over his
slightly bulbous nose and fleshy cheeks. His handshake was firm and
his speech precise. He wore a white shirt open at the collar with a
spotted silk cravat tied around his thick neck. He was standing with a
drink in one hand, puffing on a pipe and studying a chessboard when
Grimm walked into the room with Sonny.

After Sonny introduced them and they shook hands, the first question Edward Byrne-Downes asked him was whether he played chess.
The man seemed starved for male company.

"Carmen is my only match," he said as he poured Grimm a drink.

Innisfree, Grimm learned during the course of the meal, was originally a sugarcane plantation that had been turned into an exclusive
retreat. During the previous political regime on the island, the place
had gone into decline and was bought by a Colombian drug smuggling
cartel who used the airstrip located on the property as a refueling stop.
The 165-acre estate had been deeded to a company owned by Sonny
six years ago to cover a large debt.

Sonny's father had once served as the British Vice-Consul to Jamaica. He and his wife maintained a villa on the North Coast in the village
of Runaway Bay. Edward arranged for the transfer of Innisfree to a
Caymen Island holding company, and then, as a project to keep him
busy in retirement, he set about supervising the restoration of the
estate. There was a large old plantation manor house that was still
under renovation.

"Believe Sonia's quite safe here," Edward assured Grimm. He
spoke with the clipped manner of a British Army officer, puffing his
cheeks and blurting his words. "Long as she avoids places Americans
are known to congregate, doubt they'll discover she's on the island."

He explained that he enjoyed excellent relations with high-ranking officials of both political parties, as well as the head of CID, the island's top police officer, who, he intimated, was prepared to alert him should the Americans decide to come snooping around.

They sat on the terrace of the dining bungalow at a table looking out to the cove. The food was prepared and served by a Jamaican couple who lived on the compound, although Sonny oversaw every detail. The main course was a local fish cooked in sweet-and-sour sauce made from mangoes, papaya, and coconut milk, with wild rice and breadfruit. After the meal, they drank cups of the strong homegrown Blue Mountain coffee and cognac in crystal snifters.

The Byrne-Downes family seemed so fastidious and traditional, Grimm was struck by their aristocratic disregard for the law. It was as though they were above all that.

"We were contacted by a chap from Scotland Yard," Edward said as they discussed the aftermath of Sonny's escape. "Fellow told us Sonia had run off. Didn't seem too worried about it, rather just wanted to let us know."

After they finished eating and talking, Carmen wanted to show Grimm her horses. He and Sonny walked with Carmen to a fenced-in field where the mare stood beside her sleeping foal. The moon was high and shed a soft glow over the bay. When the foal heard them approach, he lifted his head.

"Hello, Rastaman," Carmen called to him.

They walked back along the beach. Carmen ran ahead to get ready for bed.

"Let's stop here a moment, darling," Sonny said. They sat on the sand and shared a joint in the moonlight. Their eyes fell on the sailboat moored in the cove. Grimm could just make out the name on the transom. "Freudian Sloop. Key West," it said.

"That's the boat Gene Machine was working on at Saul's," Grimm said.

"Yes," Sonny answered. She hugged his arm and rested her head on his shoulder. "Arthur, I'm sorry I had to fib to you in the beginning. I—well, how was I to know you are so clever? Then I fell in love with you. I wanted to tell you the truth, but I was afraid you'd have nothing more to do with me. Then, you seemed to find out everything in any case. Are you angry, my love?"

He looked at her face. The birthmark seemed less noticeable because of her tan, but the eerie agate eye sparkled in the moonlight. Can I ever believe anything this woman tells me? he wondered.

"Jack knows you stole the money," he told her.

Sonny stiffened. She lifted her head and looked at him. "Arthur, that was my money. Saul and Jack have been taking my money for years. I told Jack not once but a thousand times I was fed up with the way he and Saul kept screwing me. Jack knew bloody well that sooner or later I was going to take what was mine and get out. I was a fool to get involved with those men in the first place. They sat there like pigs taking everything for themselves while I did all the work and took all the risk. They thought because I'm a woman I wouldn't dare defy them. Well, they got what they deserve."

"Does Jack know about this place?"

"Arthur, don't worry about Jack. Jack will never try to hurt me."

"What makes you so sure?"

She sighed. "Believe me, darling, I know. Jack may be cunning and vicious, but he won't come after me. He's very superstitious, and he's terrified of me." She touched his face. "Besides, Jack has other problems."

"You mean Guy Stash?"

"One of them must kill the other. That's the only way it will ever be settled. You know, that was what made up my mind. When I found out Jack knew about Karl and about Guy and Zuluaga, I couldn't believe he'd do that to me. You remember the call, that horrible phone call?"

"When Rickie called you from California."

"Yes. That was the real reason for that call. It was wrong of me to involve Rickie, I know. God how I know. Rickie knew all about Karl. Suzi found out everything. Rickie told Jack when he met him in L.A., and Jack made Rickie phone me. Jack told me just to leave it all alone, that he would take care of it. But I began to see what they were doing, how Saul and Jack were using me and leaving me to take all the heat."

"So you told Gene Machine to kill Karl and take the money."

"I didn't have to tell him. Gene knew what to do. Gene was always loyal to me. I learned that trick from Jack, how to place spies and use them to watch over your allies as well as your enemies."

Grimm gazed at her and said nothing.

"Darling, what else could we do? They were going to get us busted.

Karl and Zuluaga had a plan with Guy Stash. Karl told Gene all about it. So Gene killed him and stuffed him in the trunk of the rental car. He called me at the flat, and I went out and called him back. He told me he'd killed Karl and he was going to leave the body in the car at the airport as a message for Guy and Zuluaga.''

"Then you went to the loft in SoHo and got the money.''

"Yes. I had Gene meet me there. We rented another car, and he took the money out to Saul's. You know, the ironic thing is that all the time the money was right there under Saul's nose. Gene built it into a compartment in the boat. Later, Moon and some friends sailed it to Key West. Then I had them bring it to Grand Caymen. Now all that lovely money is safely lost somewhere in the intricate mysteries of international banking.''

"But why didn't you leave?''

"I didn't want to leave right away, because then they would have known it was me. I was afraid they would try to kill me or go after Rickie, which is what they did anyway, the bastards. I was going to fetch Myrtle and take her and Carmen on a little holiday, but of course, I got busted. I never thought Zuluaga would arrest me if he couldn't find the money, and I didn't dream they would arrest Rickie. And then you came along. You found Karl. I wanted Guy and Zuluaga to find him, then Guy would have had to tell Jack, and Jack would have thought Guy stole the money. You discovered Karl was a rat, and you realized I knew.'' She laughed. "I thought to myself, Goodness, who is this man? He's going to figure out the whole bloody thing.''

"And you were afraid I'd tell Jack.''

"Judy told me you were meeting with him. I didn't know who you were working for.''

"So you told Aaron you wanted me as your lawyer.''

Sonny snuggled up to him again and gave him her innocent little girl look. "Darling, it wasn't as calculated as all that. The truth is, I fell in love with you. I wanted to tell you, but I was—well, I was too scared. Do you still love me? Am I a terrible person?''

Grimm smiled at her. "The answer to the first question is yes.''

"And the second?''

They kissed, their tongues slithering into each other's mouths.

"Grimm,'' she said to him when their lips parted, "you knew all along, didn't you?''

"No," he said.

"I don't believe you. You're as lawless as I am." She kissed him again.

"In any case, let's not talk about that now, all right, my love? Tonight is our special night. Tonight I am going to make love to you better than anyone has ever made love to you before. We can take our time, we can make love all night."

Sonny smiled and sighed at him. "Tonight I have a special surprise for you. Because you've been such a good boy, I'm going to give you the most outrageous blow job you've ever had."

And she did. They indulged themselves in their seclusion. It was like being on a honeymoon. They sat on the bed and slowly undressed each other, prolonging each divestiture as though discovering each other's nakedness for the first time. Then Sonny got to her knees beside the bed. She took hold of him gently and gazed at his phallus. She touched it, she kissed it, she licked and nibbled at it. And then she took him in her mouth.

Grimm lay on the bed and couldn't believe the sensations she evoked in him. He looked at the ceiling, he looked out the sliding glass doors of the bungalow and saw the moonlight on the sea. And then his eyes rolled back in his head as he let her carry him away. He was so far gone he didn't know if he would ever find himself again.

Chapter Twenty-four

They rarely left Innisfree. Sonny remarked that she had traded one prison for another, but it was a trade she could live with. Every few days her parents would drive over from the North Coast with a load of shopping, and they would usually stay one or two nights before returning to their home in Runaway Bay.

Sybil and Edward Byrne-Downes were fine company. They had lived all over the world, the old man was a skillful storyteller, and he was as unconventional in his own way as his daughter. He told fascinating anecdotes about the British in India and Ethiopia, and about Iran under the Shah. He and Grimm would play chess in the evening before dinner. Edward puffed on his pipe, drank brandy and made grunting sounds while he contemplated his moves. In Edward's and Sybil's presence, Grimm was aware of a soothing sense of continuity.

Mr. and Mrs. Byrne-Downes brought along copies of the Kingston newspaper, *The Daily Gleaner*, and an occasional *New York Times* for Sonny. She seemed to be the only one interested in events in the greater world. Grimm would come upon her seated cross-legged in the middle of the bed with a cup of tea and newspapers spread all around.

When they were left alone, they were completely at ease with each other, the three of them living a life of perfect happiness. Only the thought of it having to end was unsettling.

Carmen loved to get up early and make fresh squeezed juice each morning, then bring it to Sonny and Grimm in bed. They rode the horses, swam, sailed and windsurfed together. Grimm's love for

Sonny was rivaled only by his love for Carmen. She welcomed him into her life with a trust and innocence that was immensely gratifying to a man who had never been a father. In the evenings they went for long walks or sat on the patio and played backgammon, chess, or sometimes Clue or Monopoly, which Sonny always seemed to win.

Once, against Grimm's better judgment, they went to Montego Bay and stayed at a hotel for three days while they attended the annual Reggae Sunsplash music festival. That year the event was dedicated to the memory of Bob Marley, the Jamaican superstar who had died of cancer. The last day they were in Montego Bay, as they lounged beside the pool, Sonny handed Grimm the copy of *The New York Times* she'd been reading and pointed to an article.

CRIME FIGURE SLAIN

read the story's headline. Gaetano Stasio's body, Grimm read, had been found dismembered and stuffed in trash bags in a Brooklyn dumpster.

Another time, again at Sonny's insistence, they drove to the North Coast and had dinner at a hotel where a singer Sonny wanted to hear was appearing. The singer, a small man dressed in a zoot suit who went by the name Dr. Dread, performed reggae renditions of rock 'n' roll classics. Sonny was stoned and a little drunk. At one point, she got up and began swaying to the music. Others in the audience followed her lead and soon the whole place broke out in a party. After his set, Dr. Dread came to their table and Grimm quickly grasped there was some sort of financial arrangement between the singer and Sonny. A famous British rock star in the audience, one of The Rolling Stones, also came over to say hello to Sonny. She was the center of attention. For Grimm, it was all a little too high profile. He also found he was jealous.

Twice, Grimm and Sonny drove deep into the mountains of St Anne's parish so Sonny could meet with the Rasta marijuana lord, Brother Norman.

"Don't tell me you're going to start doing scams out of here," Grimm said to her during the first drive to meet Norman. He felt like a scolding parent.

"One must keep one's hand in, darling," was Sonny's reply.

"Why? You don't need the money."

Sonny looked over at him and cocked her eyebrow. "You wouldn't want me to get bored, would you?"

"Are you bored?"

"Not with you here, of course not." She pushed her hair back over her shoulder and looked at him with her strange eye. "But you'll leave. I know you'll never give up doing what you do."

"Sweetheart, that's different. I'm not on the run. What I do is legal."

Sonny laughed her deep, almost masculine chuckle. "Is it really? You could have fooled me."

"Sonny, I'm serious. You could go forever down here without anyone wanting to know who you are. But once you start doing trips, you know what will happen. They'll come looking for you."

"Darling, here it's different. This is Jamaica. The economy of this island would collapse tomorrow if it weren't for the ganja trade. People expect certain things of me, because I have the wherewithal. I can't let them down."

"I'm not talking about the Jamaicans. I'm talking about the Americans. There's DEA down here. They'll send goons after you. They'll kidnap you."

"Fuck the Americans," she said. "Let them kiss my ass. I'm not going to the States with it. They've gone quite mad up there. This is going by commercial freight to Canada and Europe." She turned and winked like a cat.

"Don't worry, my love. It's a lovely setup. I'm working with some of the most powerful people on the island. I couldn't possibly say no."

She told Grimm her job was putting the trips together on the Jamaican end, purchasing the loads and arranging transport. Everything else was taken care of by established smuggling groups. Her exposure was minimal.

While they were out on one of their excursions, Grimm made a prearranged call to the States.

"Hi," said the voice on the other end.

"Hello, Val."

"It's not good," she said. "He's got cancer of the colon. Real bad. The docs say there's nothin' they can do. He'll be history in six months."

In his mind, Grimm had an image of Jack's hand reaching from the edge of the grave to pull Guy Stash to his death.

"He knew," Grimm said. "He as much as told me."

"Sure he knew. He's not even afraid. He makes jokes about it. He said he's literally comin' to a bad end."

"Give him my love," Grimm told her.

"He says he'd like to do somethin' for you. What do you want?"

"Nothing. Just tell him to make sure he takes care of you."

"Oh, don't worry, he has. Listen, one more thing. I saw Cassy. I told her it wasn't you, you know, it was Jack and the Colombians who did that fat guy. I told her you had nothin' to do with it."

"Thanks, kid. That was good of you."

"So when're you gonna be like Stateside?" Val asked.

"I don't know. I'm not sure," Grimm answered.

"Okay, well, be sure 'n' look me up."

Lying in bed one night after making love, Sonny nuzzled up and murmured to him, "Tell me about when you were a little boy."

Grimm was quiet for a moment, thinking of his childhood.

"Do I have to?" he said and Sonny laughed. Another moment and they were both bursting with laughter.

"You sounded so sweet," she said, "the way you said that: 'Do I have to?' "

He awoke to find the bed beside him empty. It was first light, a deep burgundy tinge to the atmosphere. Grimm lay still listening for some sound to tell him where she'd gone.

All he heard was the hushed lapping of the sea on the beach. The curtains billowed with the breeze off the bay. She was not in the bathroom, the door stood open and it was dark. Could she have gone to Carmen's room? He had an irrational fear that she had abandoned him, or somehow been abducted in the night. At almost the same moment, he realized that he had to leave and go back to New York, back to real life. But he was disoriented, with no thought what to do, no sense of where he was. A timeless moment passed.

Then he heard a muted sobbing coming from the terrace. He got out of bed and pulled on his shorts. Sonny was huddled on a chair in her dressing gown. She had her knees pulled up under her chin and she was weeping. Her eyes were open, she was staring out at the sea and crying quietly.

She sensed him come out on the terrace and she turned to look at him. Her face was contorted with grief. Here she really is, he thought, and he understood her pain.

He sat down and put his arms around her. Sonny lay her head on his chest and she cried.

"I can't get him out of my mind," she said after a while. "It just doesn't seem fair. Suzi and the baby. God, how he would have adored that baby. I don't understand it, Arthur. How can I be so happy, and yet feel so guilty?"

There was nothing he could say.

"Just now . . . You know, sometimes I feel so sorry for the love that's gone. I feel his presence so strongly sometimes it's as though he were there in the room with me. Just now I woke from a sound sleep and I was certain Rickie was standing there at the end of the bed looking at me. I could feel him, I could see him. And always it's as though he's asking me why."

"Sonny, don't do this."

She looked at him with anguish in her eyes. "Why, Arthur? Why him when it should have been me?" She clutched at his neck. "If I could die right this moment and give him my life, I swear I would. It's all my fault."

He shook his head. "No—"

"Yes it is. You don't know. You don't understand. He loved me. I was nothing next to him, yet I . . . I had tremendous influence over him, and I knew it, I used it, even though I loved him. If it hadn't been for me, for my selfishness, Rickie never would have been involved."

"You couldn't possibly have known what was going to happen."

She gazed at him, her eyes red and swollen but focused on the thought as though she were seeing into his mind.

"But that's just it," she said after a moment, speaking as though she were in a trance. "I did know. I saw it all before it happened. I knew because . . . because what I was doing was all wrong. What I was doing went against everything I believed in, everything Rickie believed in. Yet I did it anyway."

She seemed to snap to and look at his eyes again. "Do you understand that?"

He did. For that instant he felt he understood exactly what she meant as though he could read the thoughts in her eyes.

But the moment passed. Sonny looked away, out to sea. There was a half-smoked joint on the table and she reached for it while gazing numbly at the dawn.

The surf washed the beach. Grimm looked at Sonny.

"Rickie would tell you to go on living," Grimm said. "He would want you to grow and be stronger for the love you feel for him."

"Mummy." They heard Carmen call. "Shall I make juice?"

Sonny got up, handing the burning joint to Grimm.

Life is a matter of going on, he thought as he watched Sonny move off toward Carmen's room, her intrepid walk full of the grace of motherhood. We keep trying, we keep on. The words sounded in his head as the smoke found him.